DETROIT PUBLIC LIBRARY

P9-AZV-817

CHASE BRANCH LIBRARY
17731 W. SEVEN MILE RD.
DETROIT, MI 48235

AUG -- 2014

THE LONG WAY HOME

LOUISE PENNY

~

THE LONG WAY HOME

MINOTAUR BOOKS
NEW YORK

This is a work of fiction. All of the characters, organizations, and events portrayed in this novel are either products of the author's imagination or are used fictitiously.

THE LONG WAY HOME. Copyright © 2014 by Three Pines Creations, Inc. All rights reserved. Printed in the United States of America. For information, address St. Martin's Press, 175 Fifth Avenue, New York, N.Y. 10010.

www.minotaurbooks.com

Excerpts from "Cressida To Trolius: A Gift" and "Sekhmet, the Lion-Headed Goddess of War" from *Morning in the Burned House: New Poems* by Margaret Atwood. Copyright © 1995. Published by McClelland & Stewart in Canada, and Houghton Mifflin Harcourt Publishing Company in the United States. Used with permission of the author and her publishers (in their respective territories) and the author's agent, Curtis Brown Group Ltd., London, acting on behalf of Margaret Atwood. All rights reserved.

The Library of Congress Cataloging-in-Publication Data is available upon request.

ISBN 978-1-250-02206-6 (hardcover)
ISBN 978-1-250-02207-3 (e-book)

Minotaur books may be purchased for educational, business, or promotional use. For information on bulk purchases, please contact Macmillan Corporate and Premium Sales Department at 1-800-221-7945, extension 5442, or write specialmarkets@macmillan.com.

First Edition: September 2014

10 9 8 7 6 5 4 3 2 1

For Michael
Surprised by Joy

ACKNOWLEDGMENTS

—

While essentially a solitary undertaking, I find that when I write there is a parade of people, of events, of memories keeping me company. And never more so than with *The Long Way Home*.

I won't discuss the themes here, or the reasons I wrote this book in this way, but I do want to mention a few influences, including Joseph Conrad's *Heart of Darkness* and Homer's *Odyssey*. And the remarkable Marilynne Robinson's book *Gilead*. As well as the old spiritual "Balm in Gilead."

And, as always, I have been inspired by the setting, by the history and geography and nature of Québec. And, specifically, by memories of my travels along the glorious St. Lawrence River. By the haunting coastline of the Lower North Shore. And the villages and villagers there. I have traveled a lot in my life, as a journalist and as a private person, but I have never, ever met kindness so profound, and integrity so deep, as I did in kitchens and porches and front rooms along that coast.

Thank you to the people of Mutton Bay, La Tabatière, St. Augustine, Harrington Harbour, and so many other ports. People who asked for so little and gave so much.

I have also been fortunate to spend time in Charlevoix, an area so beautiful it almost defies reason. Now, having said that, I recognize that the Baie-Saint-Paul of this book is not a completely accurate reflection of the actual town. I hope those of you who live there, or visit that lovely area, forgive me some artistic license. Especially the gracious owners of the Auberge La Muse and the Galerie Clarence Gagnon.

This book owes more than I feel I want to admit to my remarkable editor at Minotaur Books/St. Martin's Press in the United States, Hope Dellon. And to Andrew Martin, Sarah Melnyk, Paul Hochman, Cassie Galante, and David Rotstein.

In the UK, I am indebted to the wise counsel of my editor, Lucy Malagoni, and publisher, David Shelley, at Little, Brown.

Many thanks to Jamie Broadhurst and the people at Raincoast Books, for introducing Gamache et al. to so many Canadians.

Many of you found me through my newsletter and website. They're designed and constructed and maintained by the remarkable Linda Lyall. We've been together since before *Still Life* was published. And we've never met. I live in Québec and Linda lives in Scotland. But we've developed as close a bond as any colleagues who share an office.

Thank you to Teresa Chris, who is both my agent and my friend. It feels as though Fate brought us together ten years ago. Actually, the first time we met I almost ran her over with a car. Shhhh. I'm not sure she realizes that.

Thank you to Susan McKenzie, for being a constructive, kind, and thoughtful first reader. And a loving friend.

To my brother Doug, who is also a first reader and tireless champion. Funny, I spent much of my childhood wishing he would go away. And now I cherish his company.

Endless thanks to My Assistant, Lise Desrosiers, who is so much more than an assistant. A sister, a friend, a help-mate, a confidante. *Merci, ma belle.*

And finally, to Michael. Who made all my dreams come true. He is my heart and my home.

It's my turn now, dear Michael.

THE LONG WAY HOME

ONE

——

As Clara Morrow approached, she wondered if he'd repeat the same small gesture he'd done every morning.

It was so tiny, so insignificant. So easy to ignore. The first time.

But why did Armand Gamache keep doing it?

Clara felt silly for even wondering. How could it matter? But for a man not given to secrets, this gesture had begun to look not simply secretive, but furtive. A benign act that seemed to yearn for a shadow to hide in.

And yet here he was in the full light of the new day, sitting on the bench Gilles Sandon had recently made and placed on the brow of the hill. Stretched out before Gamache were the mountains, rolling from Québec to Vermont, covered in thick forests. The Rivière Bella Bella wound between the mountains, a silver thread in the sunlight.

And, so easy to overlook when faced with such grandeur, the modest little village of Three Pines lay in the valley.

Armand was not hiding from view. But neither was he enjoying it. Instead, each morning the large man sat on the wooden bench, his head bent over a book. Reading.

As she got closer, Clara Morrow saw Gamache do it again. He took off his half-moon reading glasses, then closed the book and slipped it into his pocket. There was a bookmark, but he never moved it. It remained where it was like a stone, marking a place near the end. A place he approached, but never reached.

Armand didn't snap the book shut. Instead he let it fall, with gravity,

1

closed. With nothing, Clara noticed, to mark his spot. No old receipt, no used plane or train or bus ticket to guide him back to where he'd left the story. It was as though it didn't really matter. Each morning he began again. Getting closer and closer to the bookmark, but always stopping before he arrived.

And each morning Armand Gamache placed the slim volume into the pocket of his light summer coat before she could see the title.

She'd become slightly obsessed with this book. And his behavior.

She'd even asked him about it, a week or so earlier, when she'd first joined him on the new bench overlooking the old village.

"Good book?"

"*Oui.*"

Armand Gamache had smiled as he said it, softening his blunt answer. Almost.

It was a small shove from a man who rarely pushed people away.

No, thought Clara, as she watched him in profile now. It wasn't that he'd shoved her. Instead, he'd let her be, but had taken a step back himself. Away from her. Away from the question. He'd taken the worn book, and retreated.

The message was clear. And Clara got it. Though that didn't mean she had to heed it.

Armand Gamache looked across to the deep green midsummer forest and the mountains that rolled into eternity. Then his eyes dropped to the village in the valley below them, as though held in the palm of an ancient hand. A stigmata in the Québec countryside. Not a wound, but a wonder.

Every morning he went for a walk with his wife, Reine-Marie, and their German shepherd Henri. Tossing the tennis ball ahead of them, they ended up chasing it down themselves when Henri became distracted by a fluttering leaf, or a black fly, or the voices in his head. The dog would race after the ball, then stop and stare into thin air, moving his gigantic satellite ears this way and that. Honing in on some message. Not tense, but quizzical. It was, Gamache recognized, the way most people listened when they heard on the wind the wisps of a particularly beloved piece of music. Or a familiar voice from far away.

Head tilted, a slightly goofy expression on his face, Henri listened, while Armand and Reine-Marie fetched.

All was right with the world, thought Gamache as he sat quietly in the early August sunshine.

Finally.

Except for Clara, who'd taken to joining him on the bench each morning.

Was it because she'd noticed him alone up here, once Reine-Marie and Henri had left, and thought he might be lonely? Thought he might like company?

But he doubted that. Clara Morrow had become one of their closest friends and she knew him better than that.

No. She was here for her own reasons.

Armand Gamache had grown increasingly curious. He could almost fool himself into believing his curiosity wasn't garden-variety nosiness but his training kicking in.

All his professional life Chief Inspector Gamache had asked questions and hunted answers. And not just answers, but facts. But, much more elusive and dangerous than facts, what he really looked for were feelings. Because they would lead him to the truth.

And while the truth might set some free, it landed the people Gamache sought in prison. For life.

Armand Gamache considered himself more an explorer than a hunter. The goal was to discover. And what he discovered could still surprise him.

How often had he questioned a murderer expecting to find curdled emotions, a soul gone sour? And instead found goodness that had gone astray.

He still arrested them, of course. But he'd come to agree with Sister Prejean that no one was as bad as the worst thing they'd done.

Armand Gamache had seen the worst. But he'd also seen the best. Often in the same person.

He closed his eyes and turned his face to the fresh morning sun.

Those days were behind him now. Now he could rest. In the hollow of the hand. And worry about his own soul.

No need to explore. He'd found what he was looking for here in Three Pines.

Aware of the woman beside him, he opened his eyes but kept them forward, watching the little village below come to life. He saw his friends and new neighbors leave their homes to tend to their perennial gardens or go across the village green to the bistro for breakfast. He watched as Sarah opened the door to her boulangerie. She'd been inside since before dawn, baking baguettes and croissants and *chocolatine*, and now it was time to sell them. She paused, wiping her hands on her apron, and exchanged greetings with Monsieur Béliveau, who was just opening his general store. Each morning for the past few weeks, Armand Gamache had sat on the bench and watched the same people do the same thing. The village had the rhythm, the cadence, of a piece of music. Perhaps that's what Henri heard. The music of Three Pines. It was like a hum, a hymn, a comforting ritual.

His life had never had a rhythm. Each day had been unpredictable and he had seemed to thrive on that. He'd thought that was part of his nature. He'd never known routine. Until now.

Gamache had to admit to a small fear that what was now a comforting routine would crumble into the banal, would become boring. But instead, it had gone in the other direction.

He seemed to thrive on the repetition. The stronger he got, the more he valued the structure. Far from being limiting, imprisoning, he found his daily rituals liberating.

Turmoil shook loose all sorts of unpleasant truths. But it took peace to examine them. Sitting in this quiet place in the bright sunshine, Armand Gamache was finally free to examine all the things that had fallen to the ground. As he had fallen.

He felt the slight weight and bulk of the book in his pocket.

Below them, Ruth Zardo limped from her run-down cottage, followed by Rosa, her duck. The elderly woman looked around, then glanced up the dirt road out of town. Up, up the dusty path, Gamache could see her old steel eyes travel. Until they met his. And locked on.

She lifted her veined hand in greeting. And, like hoisting the village flag, Ruth raised one unwavering finger.

Gamache bowed slightly in acknowledgment.

All was right with the world.

Except—

He turned to the disheveled woman beside him.

Why was Clara here?

Clara looked away. She couldn't bring herself to meet his eyes. Knowing what she was about to do.

She wondered if she should speak to Myrna first. Ask her advice. But she'd decided not to, realizing that would just be shifting responsibility for this decision.

Or, more likely, thought Clara, she was afraid Myrna would stop her. Tell her not to do it. Tell her it was unfair and even cruel.

Because it was. Which was why it had taken Clara this long.

Every day she'd come here, determined to say something to Armand. And every day she'd chickened out. Or, more likely, the better angels of her nature were straining on the reins, yanking her back. Trying to stop her.

And it had worked. So far.

Every day she made small talk with him, then left, determined not to return the next day. Promising herself, and all the saints and all the angels and all the gods and goddesses, that she would not go back up to the bench the next morning.

And next morning, as though by magic, a miracle, a curse, she felt the hard maple beneath her bum. And found herself looking at Armand Gamache. Wondering about that slim volume in his pocket. Looking into his deep brown, thoughtful eyes.

He'd gained weight, which was good. It showed Three Pines was doing its job. He was healing here. He was tall, and a more robust frame suited him. Not fat, but substantial. He limped less from his wounds, and there was more vitality to his step. The gray had left his face, but not his head. His wavy hair was now more gray than brown. By the time he was sixty, in just a few years, he'd be completely gray, Clara suspected.

His face showed his age. It was worn with cares and concerns and worries. With pain. But the deepest crevices were made by laughter. Around his eyes and mouth. Mirth, etched deep.

Chief Inspector Gamache. The former head of homicide for the Sûreté du Québec.

But he was also Armand. Her friend. Who'd come here to retire from that life, and all that death. Not to hide from the sorrow, but to stop collecting more. And in this peaceful place to look at his own burdens. And to begin to let them go.

As they all had.

Clara got up.

She couldn't do it. She could not unburden herself to this man. He had his own to carry. And this was hers.

"Dinner tonight?" she asked. "Reine-Marie asked us over. We might even play some bridge."

It was always the plan, and yet they rarely seemed to get to it, preferring to talk or sit quietly in the Gamaches' back garden as Myrna walked among the plants, explaining which were weeds and which were perennials, coming back year after year. Long lived. And which flowers were annuals. Designed to die after a magnificent, short life.

Gamache rose to his feet, and as he did Clara saw again the writing carved into the back of the bench. It hadn't been there when Gilles Sandon had placed the bench. And Gilles claimed not to have done it. The writing had simply appeared, like graffiti, and no one had owned up to it.

Armand held out his hand. At first Clara thought he wanted to shake it good-bye. A strangely formal and final gesture. Then she realized his palm was up.

He was inviting her to place her hand in his.

She did. And felt his hand close gently. Finally, she looked into his eyes.

"Why are you here, Clara?"

She sat, suddenly, and felt again the hard wood of the bench, not so much supporting her as stopping her fall.

TWO

～

"What do you think they're talking about?" Olivier placed the order of French toast, with fresh-picked berries and maple syrup, in front of Reine-Marie.

"Astrophysics would be my guess," she said, looking up into his handsome face. "Or perhaps Nietzsche."

Olivier followed her gaze out the mullioned window.

"You do know I was talking about Ruth and the duck," he said.

"As was I, *mon beau*."

Olivier laughed as he moved away to serve other patrons of his bistro.

Reine-Marie Gamache sat in her habitual seat. She hadn't meant to make it a habit, it just happened. For the first few weeks after she and Armand had moved to Three Pines, they'd taken different seats at different tables. And each seat and table really was different. Not simply the location in the old bistro, but the style of furniture. All antiques, all for sale, with price tags hanging from them. Some were old Québec pine, some were overstuffed Edwardian armchairs and wing chairs. There was even a smattering of mid-century modern pieces. Sleek and teak and surprisingly comfortable. All collected by Olivier and tolerated by his partner, Gabri. As long as Olivier kept his finds in the bistro and left the running, and decorating, of the bed and breakfast to Gabri.

Olivier was slim, disciplined, aware of his country-casual image. Each piece of his wardrobe was curated to fit the impression he needed to make. Of a relaxed and gracious and subtly affluent host. Everything about Olivier was subtle. Except Gabri.

Oddly, thought Reine-Marie, while Olivier's personal style was restrained, even elegant, his bistro was a mad mix of styles and colors. And yet, far from feeling claustrophobic or cluttered, the bistro felt like visiting the home of a well-traveled and eccentric aunt. Or uncle. Someone who knew the conventions and chose not to follow them.

Huge stone fireplaces anchored either end of the long, beamed room. Laid with logs but unlit now in the midsummer warmth, in winter the flames crackled and danced and defied the darkness and bitter cold. Even today Reine-Marie could catch a hint of wood smoke in the room. Like a ghost or guardian.

Bay windows looked onto the homes of Three Pines, their gardens full of roses and daylilies and clematis and other plants she was just learning about. The homes formed a circle, and in its center was the village green. And in the center of that were the pine trees that soared over the community. Three great spires that inspired the name. Three Pines. These were no ordinary trees. Planted centuries ago, they were a code. A signal to the war-weary.

They were safe. This was sanctuary.

It was hard to tell if the homes were protecting the trees, or the trees guarding the homes.

Reine-Marie Gamache picked up her bowl of *café au lait* and sipped as she watched Ruth and Rosa, apparently muttering together on the bench in the shade of the pines. They spoke the same language, the mad old poet and the goose-stepping duck. And each knew, it seemed to Reine-Marie, only one phrase.

"Fuck, fuck, fuck."

We love life, thought Reine-Marie as she watched Ruth and Rosa sitting side by side, *not because we are used to living, but because we are used to loving.*

Nietzsche. How Armand would kid her if he knew she was quoting Nietzsche, even to herself.

"How often have you teased me for producing some quote?" he'd laugh.

"Never, dear heart. What was it Emily Dickinson said about teasing?"

He'd look at her sternly, then make up some nonsense he'd attribute to Dickinson or Proust or Fred Flintstone.

We are used to loving.

Finally they were together and safe. In the protection of the pines.

Her gaze traveled, inevitably, up the hill to the bench where Armand and Clara sat quietly. Not talking.

"What do you think they're not talking about?" asked Myrna.

The large black woman took the comfortable wing chair across from Reine-Marie and leaned back. She'd brought her own mug of tea from her bookstore next door, and now she ordered Bircher muesli and fresh-squeezed orange juice.

"Armand and Clara? Or Ruth and Rosa?" asked Reine-Marie.

"Well, we know what Ruth and Rosa are talking about," said Myrna.

"Fuck, fuck, fuck," the two women said in unison and laughed.

Reine-Marie took a forkful of French toast and looked again at the bench on the top of the hill.

"She sits with him every morning," said Reine-Marie. "Even Armand's baffled."

"You don't think she's trying to seduce him, do you?" Myrna asked.

Reine-Marie shook her head. "She'd have taken a baguette with her if she was."

"And cheese. A nice ripe Tentation de Laurier. All runny and creamy—"

"Have you tried Monsieur Béliveau's latest cheese?" asked Reine-Marie, her husband all but forgotten. "Le Chèvre des Neiges?"

"Oh, God," moaned Myrna. "It tastes like flowers and brioche. Stop it. Are you trying to seduce me?"

"Me? You started it."

Olivier placed a glass of juice in front of Myrna and some toast for the table.

"Am I going to have to hose you two down again?" he asked.

"*Désolé*, Olivier," said Reine-Marie. "It was my fault. We were talking about cheeses."

"In public? That's disgusting," said Olivier. "I'm pretty sure it was a photo of Brie on a baguette that got Robert Mapplethorpe banned."

"A baguette?" asked Myrna.

"That would explain Gabri's fondness for carbs," said Reine-Marie.

"And mine," said Myrna.

"I'm coming back with the hose," said Olivier as he left. "And no, that's not a euphemism."

Myrna spread a thick piece of toast with melting butter and jam and bit into it while Reine-Marie took a sip of coffee.

"What were we talking about?" Myrna asked.

"Cheeses."

"Before that."

"Them." Reine-Marie Gamache nodded in the direction of her husband and Clara sitting silently on the bench above the village. What were they not talking about, Myrna had asked. And every day Reine-Marie had asked herself the same thing.

The bench had been her idea. A small gift to Three Pines. She'd asked Gilles Sandon, the woodworker, to make it and place it there. A few weeks later an inscription had appeared on it. Etched deeply, finely, carefully.

"Did you do that, *mon coeur*?" she'd asked Armand on their morning walk, as they paused to look at it.

"*Non*," he'd said, perplexed. "I thought you'd asked Gilles to put it on."

They'd asked around. Clara, Myrna, Olivier, Gabri. Billy Williams, Gilles. Even Ruth. No one knew who'd carved the words into the wood.

She passed this small mystery every day on her walks with Armand. They walked past the old schoolhouse, where Armand had almost been killed. They walked through the woods, where Armand had killed. Each of them very aware of the events. Every day they turned around and returned to the quiet village and the bench above it. And the words carved into it by some unknown hand—

Surprised by Joy

Clara Morrow told Armand Gamache why she was there. And what she wanted from him. And when she was finished she saw in those thoughtful eyes what she most feared.

She saw fear.

She'd placed it there. She'd taken her own dread, and given it to him.

Clara longed to take back the words. To remove them.

"I just wanted you to know," she said, feeling her face redden. "I needed to tell someone. That's all—"

She was beginning to blather and that only increased her desperation.

"I don't expect you to do anything. I don't want you to. It's nothing, really. I can handle it on my own. Forget I said anything."

But it was too late. She could not stop now.

"Never mind," she said, her voice firm.

Armand smiled. It reached the deep crevices around his eyes and Clara saw, with relief, that there was no longer any fear there.

"I mind, Clara."

She walked back down the hill, the sun on her face and the slight scent of roses and lavender in the warm air. At the village green she paused and turned. Armand had sat back down. She wondered if he would pull out that book, now that she was gone, but he didn't. He just sat there, legs crossed, one large hand holding the other, self-contained and apparently relaxed. He stared across the valley. To the mountains beyond. To the outside world.

It'll be fine, she thought as she made her way home.

But Clara Morrow knew deep down that she had set something in motion. That she'd seen something in those eyes. Deep down. She hadn't, perhaps, so much placed it there as awakened it.

Armand Gamache had come here to rest. To recover. They'd promised him peace. And Clara knew she'd just broken that promise.

THREE

—

"Annie called," said Reine-Marie, accepting the gin and tonic from her husband. "They're running a little late. Friday night traffic out of Montréal."

"Are they staying the weekend?" Armand asked. He'd started the barbeque and was jostling with Monsieur Béliveau for position. It was a losing battle, since Gamache had no intention of winning but felt he should at least appear to put up a fight. Finally, in a formal gesture of surrender, he handed the tongs over to the grocer.

"As far as I know," said Reine-Marie.

"Good."

Something in the way he said it caught her ear, and then was gone, carried away on a burst of laughter.

"I swear to God," said Gabri, raising a plump hand in an oath, "this is designer."

He turned so that they could appreciate his full splendor. He had on a pair of baggy slacks and a loose lime-green shirt that billowed slightly as he turned.

"I got it from one of the outlets last time we were in Maine."

In his late thirties and slightly over six feet tall, Gabri had passed paunchy a few mille-feuilles back.

"I didn't know Benjamin Moore had a line of clothing," said Ruth.

"Har dee har har," said Gabri. "This happens to be very expensive. Does it look cheap?" he implored Clara.

"It?" asked Ruth.

"Hag," said Gabri.

"Fag," said Ruth. The elderly woman clutched Rosa in one hand and what Reine-Marie recognized as one of their vases filled with Scotch in the other.

Gabri helped Ruth back to her chair. "Can I get you something to eat?" he asked. "A puppy or perhaps a fetus?"

"Oh, that would be nice, dear," said Ruth.

Reine-Marie moved among their friends, who were scattered around the garden, catching bits of conversations in French, in English, most in a mélange of the two languages.

She looked over and saw Armand listening attentively as Vincent Gilbert told a story. It must have been funny, probably self-deprecating, because Armand was smiling. Then he talked, gesturing with his beer as he spoke.

When he finished the Gilberts laughed, as did Armand. Then he caught her eye, and his smile broadened.

The evening was still warm but by the time the lamps in the garden were lit, they'd need the light sweaters and jackets now slung over the backs of chairs.

People wandered in and out of the home as though it was their own, placing food on the long table on the terrace. It had become a sort of tradition, these informal Friday evening barbeques at the Gamache place.

Though few called it the Gamache place. It was still known in the village, and perhaps always would be, as Emilie's place, after the woman who'd lived there and from whose estate the Gamaches had bought the home. While it might be new to Armand and Reine-Marie, it was in fact one of the oldest houses in Three Pines. Made of white clapboard, there was a wide verandah around the front of the house, facing the village green. And in the back there was the terrace and the large neglected garden.

"I left a bag of books for you in the living room," Myrna said to Reine-Marie.

"*Merci.*"

Myrna poured herself a white wine and noticed the bouquet in the center of the table. Tall, effusive, crammed with blooms and foliage.

Myrna wasn't sure if she should tell Reine-Marie they were mostly weeds. She could see all the usual suspects. Purple loosestrife, bishop's weed. Even bindweed that mimicked morning glory.

She'd been through the flower beds with Armand and Reine-Marie many times, helping to bring order to the tangled mess. She thought she'd been clear about the difference between the flowers and the weeds.

Another lesson was in order.

"Beautiful, isn't it?" Reine-Marie said, offering Myrna a morsel of smoked trout on rye.

Myrna smiled. City folk.

Armand strolled away from the Gilberts and was scanning the gathering to make sure everyone had what they needed. His eye fell on an unlikely grouping. Clara had joined Ruth and was now seated with her back to the party, as far from the house as possible.

She hadn't said a word to him since she'd arrived.

That didn't surprise him. What did was her decision to sit with Ruth and her duck, though it often struck Gamache as more accurate to describe the couple as Rosa and her human.

There could be only one reason Clara, or anyone, would seek out Ruth. A profound and morbid desire to be left alone. Ruth was a social stink bomb.

But they weren't completely on their own. Henri had joined them and was staring at the duck.

It was puppy love, in the extreme. A love not shared by Rosa. Gamache heard a growl. From Rosa. Henri quacked.

Gamache took a step back.

That noise, from Henri, was never a good sign.

Clara stood up, to get away. She moved toward Gamache before changing direction.

Ruth wrinkled her nose as rotten egg settled around them. Henri was looking innocently around as though trying to find the source of the foul odor.

Ruth and Rosa were now looking at the shepherd with something close to awe. The old poet took a deep breath, then exhaled, turning the toxic gas into poetry.

"You forced me to give you poisonous gifts," she quoted from her famous work.

> *I can put this no other way.*
> *Everything I gave was to get rid of you*
> *As one gives to a beggar: There. Go away.*

But Henri, the brave and gaseous shepherd, did not go away. Ruth looked at him in disgust, but offered one withered hand to Henri, to lick.

And he did.

Then Armand Gamache went in search of Clara. She'd wandered over to the two Adirondack chairs, side by side on the lawn. Their wide wooden arms were stained with rings from years, decades, of drinks taken in the quiet garden. Emilie's rings had been added to, and overlaid, by the Gamaches' morning mugs and afternoon *apéritifs*. Peaceful lives intertwined.

There were two almost identical chairs in Clara's garden. Turned slightly toward each other, looking over the perennial borders, the river, and into the woods beyond. With rings on the wooden arms.

He watched as Clara grasped the back of a chair and leaned into it, pressing against the wooden slats.

He was close enough to see her shoulders rise and her knuckles whiten.

"Clara?" he asked.

"I'm fine."

But she wasn't. He knew it. And she knew it. She'd thought, hoped, that in finally talking to Armand that morning, the worry would go away. A problem shared . . .

But the problem, while shared, hadn't been halved. It'd doubled. Then doubled again as the day dragged on. In talking about it, Clara had made it real. She'd given form to her fear. And now it was out. And growing.

Everything fed it. The aromas of the barbeque, the blowsy flowers, the chipped and stained old chairs. The rings, the damned rings. Like at home.

All that had been trivial, that had been comforting and familiar and safe, now seemed to be strapped with explosives.

"Dinner's ready, Clara." He spoke the words in his quiet, deep voice. Then she heard his step on the grass moving away from her, and she was alone.

All her friends had gathered on the deck, helping themselves to food. She stood apart, her back to them, looking into the darkening woods.

Then she felt a presence beside her. Gamache handed her a plate.

"Shall we sit?" He motioned to the chairs.

And Clara did. They ate in silence. All that needed to be said had been said.

The other guests helped themselves to steak and chutney laid out on the table. Myrna smiled at the weed centerpiece, still amused. And then she stopped smiling and noticed something. It really was beautiful.

Bowls of salad were passed around and Sarah gave Monsieur Béliveau the largest of the dinner rolls she'd made that afternoon, while he gave her the tenderest piece of steak. They leaned toward each other, not quite touching.

Olivier had left one of the waiters in charge of the bistro and had joined them. The conversation meandered and flowed. The sun set and sweaters and light summer jackets were put on. Tea lights were lit and placed on the table and around the garden, so that it looked like large fireflies had settled in for the evening.

"After Emilie died and the house was closed up, I thought we'd had our last party here," said Gabri. "I'm glad I was finally wrong about something."

Henri swiveled his satellite ears toward the sound of the name. Emilie.

The elderly woman who'd found him at the shelter when he was a puppy. Who'd brought him home. Who'd named him and loved him and raised him, until the day she was no longer there and the Gamaches had come and taken him away. He'd spent months searching for her. Sniffing for her scent. Perking up his ears at the sound of every car arriving. Every door opening. Waiting for Emilie to find him again. To rescue him again, and take him home. Until one day he no longer watched. No longer waited. No longer needed rescuing.

He returned his gaze to Rosa. Who also adored an elderly woman and was terrified her Ruth would one day vanish, as his Emilie had. And she'd be all alone. Henri stared and stared, hoping Rosa might look at him and realize that even if that happened, the wounded heart would heal. The balm, he wanted to tell her, wasn't anger or fear or isolation. He'd tried those. They hadn't worked.

Finally, into that terrible hole Henri had poured the only thing left. What Emilie had given him. As he went for long, long walks with Armand and Reine-Marie, he remembered his love for snowballs, and sticks, and rolling in skunk poop. His love of the different seasons and their different scents. His love of mud and fresh bedding. Of swimming and shaking with abandon while his legs danced beneath him. Of licking himself. Then others.

Until one day the pain and loneliness and sorrow were no longer the biggest thing in his heart.

He still loved Emilie, but now he also loved Armand and Reine-Marie.

And they loved him.

That was home. He'd found it again.

"*Ah, bon. Enfin,*" said Reine-Marie, greeting her daughter Annie and her son-in-law, Jean-Guy, on the front porch.

It was a bit congested as people milled about saying their good-byes.

Jean-Guy Beauvoir said hello and good-bye to the villagers and made a date to go jogging the next morning with Olivier. Gabri offered to look after the bistro instead of joining them, as though jogging was ever an option.

When Beauvoir reached Ruth they eyed each other.

"*Salut*, you drunken old wretch."

"*Bonjour*, numb nuts."

Ruth held Rosa and, leaning into Beauvoir, they kissed on both cheeks. "There's pink lemonade in the fridge for you," she said. "I made it."

He looked at her gnarly hands and knew that opening the can could not have been easy.

"When life gives you lemons . . ." he said.

"It gave you lemons. Thankfully, it gave me Scotch."

Beauvoir laughed. "I'm sure I'll enjoy the lemonade."

"Well, Rosa seemed to like it when she stuck her beak in the pitcher."

Ruth stepped down the wide wooden stairs of the verandah and, ignoring the fieldstone path, cut across the lawn on a trail worn into the grass between the homes.

Jean-Guy waited until Ruth slammed her front door shut, then he took their bags into the house.

It was past ten in the evening and all the guests had left. Gamache fixed a dinner of leftovers for his daughter and son-in-law.

"How's work?" he asked Jean-Guy.

"Not bad, *patron*."

He couldn't yet bring himself to call his new father-in-law Armand. Or Dad. Nor could he call him Chief Inspector, since Gamache had retired, and besides, that sounded too formal now. So Jean-Guy had settled on *patron*. Boss. It was both respectful and informal. And oddly accurate.

Armand Gamache might be Annie's father, but he would always be Beauvoir's *patron*.

They chatted about a particular case Beauvoir was working on. Jean-Guy was alert for signs the Chief was more than just interested. That he was in fact anxious to return to the Sûreté du Québec unit he'd built. But while Gamache was polite, there was no sign it went beyond that.

Jean-Guy poured himself and Annie glasses of pink lemonade, scanning the pulp for downy feathers.

The four of them sat on the back terrace, under the stars, the tea lights flickering in the garden. Then, when dinner and the dishes were finished and they were relaxing over coffee, Gamache turned to Jean-Guy.

"Can I see you for a few minutes?"

"Sure." He followed his father-in-law into the house.

As Reine-Marie watched, the door to the study slowly closed. Then clicked shut.

"Maman, what is it?"

Annie followed her mother's gaze to the closed door, then looked back at the smile frozen on her mother's face.

That was it, thought Reine-Marie. The slight inflection in Armand's voice earlier in the evening when he'd learned Annie and Jean-Guy were coming down. It was more than pleasure at seeing his daughter and her husband.

She'd stared at too many closed doors in her home not to recognize the significance. Herself on one side. Armand and Jean-Guy on the other.

Reine-Marie had always known this moment would come. From the first box they'd unpacked and the first night they'd spent here. From the first morning she'd woken up next to Armand and not been afraid of what the day might bring.

She'd known this day would come. But she'd thought, hoped, prayed they'd have more time.

"Mom?"

FOUR

—

Myrna turned the handle and found Clara's front door locked.

"Clara?" she called, and knocked.

It was rare for any of them to lock their doors, though they knew from some experience that it would be a good idea. But the villagers also knew that what kept them safe in their beds wasn't a lock. And what would wound them wasn't an open door.

But tonight, Clara had bolted herself in. Against what danger? Myrna wondered.

"Clara?" Myrna knocked again.

What was Clara afraid of? What was she trying to keep out?

The door was yanked open, and when Myrna saw her friend's face, she had her answer.

Her. Clara was trying to keep her out.

Well, it hadn't worked. Myrna sailed into the kitchen, as familiar as her own.

She put on the kettle and reached for their usual mugs. Into them she dropped bags of tisane. Chamomile for Clara and mint for herself. Then she turned to the annoyed face.

"What's happened? What the hell's wrong?"

Jean-Guy Beauvoir leaned back in the comfortable armchair and looked at the Chief. The Gamaches had turned one of the main floor bedrooms into a sitting room, and Gilles Sandon had built bookcases on all the walls and even around the windows and door frame so that it looked like a hut made of books.

Behind the Chief, Beauvoir could make out biographies, histories, science books. Fiction and nonfiction. A thick volume on the Franklin Expedition seemed to spring from Gamache's head.

They chatted for a few minutes, not as father-in-law and son-in-law, but as colleagues. As survivors from the same wreck.

"Jean-Guy looks better every time we see him," said Reine-Marie.

She could smell her daughter's peppermint tisane and hear the flapping, tapping, of moth wings against the porch light.

The two women had moved to the front verandah, Annie on the swing and Reine-Marie in one of the chairs. The village of Three Pines was spread before them, amber lights at some of the homes, but most in darkness now.

The women talked not as mother and daughter, but as women who'd shared a life raft and were now, finally, on dry land.

"He's going to his therapist," said Annie. "And to his AA meetings. Never misses. I think he actually looks forward to it now but would never admit it. Dad?"

"He does his physio. We go for long walks. He can go farther every day. He's even talking about taking up yoga."

Annie laughed. She had a face, a body, made not for a Paris runway but for good meals and books by the fire and laughter. She was constructed from, and for, happiness. But it had taken Annie Gamache a long while to find it. To trust it.

And even now, in the still summer night, part of her feared it would be taken away. Again. By a bullet, a needle. A tiny painkilling pill. That caused so much pain.

She shifted her seat and shoved the thought aside. After spending most of her life scanning the horizon for slights and threats, genuine and imagined, she knew the real threat to her happiness came not from the dot in the distance, but from looking for it. Expecting it. Waiting for it. And in some cases, creating it.

Her father had jokingly accused her of living in the wreckage of her future. Until one day she'd looked deep into his eyes and saw he wasn't joking.

He was warning her.

But it was a hard habit to break, especially since she now had so much to lose. And had almost lost it all. To a bullet. A needle. A tiny pill.

As her mother had almost lost it all.

They'd both had the phone call in the middle of the night. *Come quickly. Come now. Before it's too late.*

But it hadn't been too late. Not quite.

And while her father and Jean-Guy might recover, Annie wasn't sure she and her mother ever really would. From the ringing, the ringing in the night.

But for now they were safe. On the porch. Annie saw the rectangle of light through the sitting room window. Where her father and Jean-Guy sat. Also safe.

For now.

No, she warned herself. No. There is no threat.

She wondered when she'd actually believe it. And she wondered if her mother believed it.

"Can you see Dad on the village green doing the sun salutation every morning?"

Reine-Marie laughed. The funny thing was, she could see it. It wouldn't be pretty, but she could imagine Armand doing it.

"Is he really okay?" Annie asked.

Reine-Marie turned in her seat to look at the porch light above the door. What had started as a gentle tapping of moth wings against the bulb had turned into near frantic beating as the moth rammed itself against the hot light on the cool night. It was getting on her nerves.

She turned back to Annie. She knew what her daughter was asking. Annie could see her father's physical improvements—what concerned her now was what was unseen.

"He sees Myrna once a week," said Reine-Marie. "That helps."

"Myrna?" asked Annie. "Myrna?" She gestured toward the "financial district" of Three Pines, which was made up of the general store, the bakery, the bistro, and Myrna's New and Used Bookstore.

Reine-Marie realized her daughter only knew Myrna from the shop.

In fact, she only knew all the villagers from their lives here, not from their lives before. Annie had no idea that the large black woman who sold used books and helped them in the garden was Dr. Landers, a retired psychologist.

Reine-Marie now wondered how newcomers would view her and Armand. The middle-aged couple in the white clapboard house.

Would they be the slightly loopy villagers who made bouquets of weeds? Who sat on their porch with their day-old *La Presse* newspaper? Perhaps they'd only be known as Henri's parents.

Would newcomers to Three Pines ever know that she'd once been a senior librarian at the Bibliothèque nationale du Québec?

Would it matter?

And Armand?

What life would a new villager think he'd left behind? A career in journalism perhaps, writing for the intellectual and almost indecipherable daily *Le Devoir*. Would they think he'd passed his days wearing a pilled cardigan and writing long op-ed pieces on politics?

The more astute might guess that he'd been a professor at the Université de Montréal. The kindly one who was passionate about history and geography and what happened when the two collided.

Would someone new to Three Pines ever suspect that the man tossing the ball to the shepherd, or sipping Scotch in the bistro, had once been the most celebrated cop in Québec? In Canada? Would they guess, could they guess, that the large man doing the sun salutation each morning had once hunted murderers for a living?

Reine-Marie hoped not.

She dared to think that that was behind them. Those lives now lived only in memory. They roamed the mountains that surrounded the village, but had no place here. Had no place now. Chief Inspector Gamache, the head of homicide for the Sûreté du Québec, had done his job. It was someone else's turn.

But her heart tightened as Reine-Marie remembered the door to the sitting room closing. And clicking.

The moth still fluttered around the light, butting and bumping against the bulb. Was it warmth it wanted, Reine-Marie wondered, was it light the moth sought?

Does it hurt? Reine-Marie wondered. The singeing of the wings, the little legs, like threads, landing on the white-hot glass, then pushing away. Does it hurt that the light doesn't give the moth what it so desperately desires?

She got up and turned the porch light off, and after a few moments the beating of the wings stopped and Reine-Marie returned to her peaceful seat.

It was quiet now, and dark. Except for the buttery light from the sitting room window. As the silence grew, Reine-Marie wondered if she'd done the moth a favor. Had she saved its life, but taken away its purpose?

And then the beating started again. Flitting, desperate. Tiny, delicate, insistent. The moth had moved down the porch. Now it was beating against the window of the room where Armand and Jean-Guy sat.

It had found its light. It would never give up. It couldn't.

Reine-Marie got up, watched by her daughter, and turned the porch light back on. It was in the moth's nature to do what it was doing. And Reine-Marie could not stop it, no matter how much she might want to.

"How's Annie?" Gamache asked. "She looks happy."

Armand smiled as he thought of his daughter, and remembered dancing with her on the village green at her wedding to Jean-Guy.

"Are you asking if she's pregnant?"

"Of course not," snapped the Chief. "How could you think such a thing?" He picked up the paperweight on the coffee table, put it down, then picked up a book and fiddled with it as though he'd never held one before. "That's none of my business." He hiked himself up in the chair. "Do you think I think only a pregnancy would make her happy? What sort of man do you think I am? What sort of father?" He glared at the younger man across from him.

Jean-Guy simply stared back, watching the uncharacteristic bluster.

"It's all right to ask."

"Is she?" asked Gamache, leaning forward.

"No. She had a glass of wine at dinner. Didn't you notice? Some detective."

"Not anymore, I'm not." He caught Jean-Guy's eyes and they both smiled. "I really wasn't asking, you know," said Gamache truthfully. "I just want her to be happy. And you too."

"I am, *patron*."

The two men looked at each other, searching for wounds only they could see. Searching for signs of healing only they would know were genuine.

"And you, sir? Are you happy?"

"I am."

Beauvoir didn't need to probe. Having spent his career listening to lies, he recognized the truth when he heard it.

"And how's Isabelle doing?" asked Gamache.

"Acting Chief Inspector Lacoste?" asked Beauvoir with a smile. His protégée had taken over as head of homicide for the Sûreté, a job everyone had once assumed would be his on the Chief's retirement. Though Jean-Guy knew it wasn't accurate to describe what had happened as a retirement. That made it sound predictable. No one could have predicted the events that had caused the head of homicide to quit the Sûreté and buy a home in a village so small and obscure it didn't appear on any map.

"Isabelle's doing fine."

"You mean Ruth Zardo 'fine'?" asked Gamache.

"Pretty much. With a little work she'll get there. She had you as a role model, sir."

Ruth had called her latest slim volume of poetry *I'm FINE*. Only people who read it realized that FINE stood for Fucked up, Insecure, Neurotic, and Egotistical.

Isabelle Lacoste called Gamache at least once a week, and they met for lunch in Montréal a couple times a month. Always away from Sûreté headquarters. He insisted on that, so he wouldn't undermine the new Chief Inspector's authority.

Lacoste had questions only the former Chief could answer. Sometimes procedural issues, but often questions that were more complex and human. About uncertainties, about insecurities. About her fears.

Gamache listened and sometimes talked about his own experiences. Reassuring her that what she felt was natural, and normal, and healthy. He'd felt all those things almost every day of his career. Not that he was a fraud, but that he was afraid. When the phone rang, or there was a knock on the door, he worried there would be a life-and-death issue he could not resolve.

"I have a new trainee, *patron*," Isabelle had told him over their lunch at Le Paris earlier in the week.

"*Ah, oui?*"

"A young agent just out of the academy. Adam Cohen. I think you know him."

The Chief had smiled. "*Merci*, Isabelle."

Young Monsieur Cohen had flunked out on his first try and had taken a job as a guard at a penitentiary. Gamache had met Cohen months ago, when almost everyone else was attacking the Chief. Professionally. Personally. And finally, physically. But Adam Cohen had stood beside him. Hadn't run away, despite having every reason to. Including to save his own skin.

The Chief hadn't forgotten. And when the crisis had passed, Gamache had approached the head of the Sûreté academy and asked that Cohen be given a rare second chance. And then he'd tutored the young man, guided him. Encouraged him. And had stood at the back of the hall, during graduation, and applauded him.

Gamache had asked Isabelle to take Cohen on. To, essentially, take him under her wing. He could not imagine a better mentor for the young man.

"Agent Cohen started this morning," said Lacoste, taking a forkful of quinoa, feta, and pomegranate salad. "I called him into the office and told him that there were four statements that lead to wisdom. I said I was only going to recite them once, and he could do with them as he wished."

Armand Gamache lowered his fork to his plate and listened.

"I don't know. I was wrong. I'm sorry." Lacoste recited them slowly, lifting a finger to count them off.

"I need help," the Chief said, completing the statements. The ones he'd taught young Agent Lacoste many years ago. The ones he'd recited to all his new agents.

And now, sitting at home in Three Pines, he said, "I need your help, Jean-Guy."

Beauvoir grew still, alert, and gave a curt nod.

"Clara came to see me this morning. She has a . . ." Gamache searched for the word. "Puzzle."

Beauvoir leaned forward.

Clara and Myrna sat side by side in the large wooden Adirondack chairs in Clara's back garden. The crickets and frogs were singing and every now and then the women heard rustles in the dark woods.

Below that sound, beyond that sound, the Rivière Belle Bella burbled its way from the mountains, past the village, and out the other side. Heading home, but in no big hurry.

"I've been patient," said Myrna. "Now you need to tell me what's wrong."

Even in the dark, Myrna knew the expression on Clara's face as her friend turned to her.

"Patient?" asked Clara. "It's been an hour since the party broke up."

"Okay, 'patient' might be the wrong word. I've been worried. And it's not just since dinner. Why have you been sitting with Armand every morning? And what happened today between you? You practically ran away from him."

"You noticed?"

"For God's sake, Clara, the bench is on top of the hill out of Three Pines. You might as well have been sitting on a neon sign."

"I wasn't trying to hide."

"Then you succeeded." Myrna softened her voice. "Can you tell me?"

"Can you guess?"

Myrna turned her entire body until she was facing her companion.

Clara still had paint in her wild hair, not the speckles that come from painting a wall or ceiling. These were streaks of ochre and cadmium yellow. And a fingerprint of burnt sienna on her neck, like a bruise.

Clara Morrow painted portraits. And in the process, she often painted herself.

On their way into the garden Myrna had glanced into Clara's studio and seen her latest work on the easel. A ghostly face was just appearing, or disappearing, into the canvas.

Myrna was astonished by her friend's portraits. On the surface they were simple representations of the person. Nice. Recognizable. Conventional. But . . . but if she stood in front of the work long enough, if she let her own conceptions drift away, let her defenses down, let go of all judgment, then another portrait appeared.

Clara Morrow didn't actually paint faces, she painted emotions, feelings, hidden, disguised, locked and guarded behind a pleasant façade.

The works took Myrna's breath away. But this was the first time a portrait had actually frightened her.

"It's Peter," Myrna said as they sat in the cool night air.

She knew that both this conversation, and that eerie portrait, were about Peter Morrow. Clara's husband.

Clara nodded. "He didn't come home."

"So?" said Jean-Guy. "What's the problem? Clara and Peter are separated, aren't they?"

"Yes, a year ago," Gamache agreed. "Clara asked him to leave."

"I remember. Then why would she expect him home?"

"They made a promise to each other. No contact for a year, but on the first anniversary of his leaving, Peter would come back and they'd see where they were."

Beauvoir leaned back in the armchair and crossed his legs, unconsciously mirroring the man facing him.

He thought about what Gamache had just said. "But Peter didn't come back."

"I waited."

Clara held her mug, no longer hot but warm enough to be comforting. The evening was cool and still and she could smell the chamomile rising from her tea. And while Clara couldn't see Myrna beside her, she could sense her. And smell the warm mint.

And Myrna had the sense to be silent.

"The anniversary was actually a few weeks ago," said Clara. "I bought a bottle of wine and two steaks from Monsieur Béliveau, and made that orange, arugula, and goat cheese salad Peter likes. I lit the charcoals in the barbeque. And waited."

She didn't mention that she'd also bought croissants from Sarah's boulangerie, for the next morning. In case.

She felt such a fool, now. She'd imagined him arriving, seeing her and taking her in his arms. Actually, in her more melodramatic moments, she saw him bursting into tears and begging her forgiveness for being such a shit.

She, of course, would be cool and contained. Cordial, but no more.

But the truth was, Clara always felt like a Beatrix Potter creation in Peter's familiar embrace. Mrs. Tiggy-winkle, in her funny little home. She'd found shelter in his arms. That was where she belonged.

But that life had proven a fairy tale, an illusion. Still, in a moment of weakness, delusion, or hope, she'd bought those croissants. In case dinner became breakfast. In case nothing had changed. Or everything had changed. Or Peter had changed, and was no longer such a *merde*.

She'd imagined them sitting in these very chairs, resting their coffee mugs in the rings. Eating the flaky croissants. Talking quietly. As though nothing had happened.

But a lot had happened in that year, to Clara. To the village. To their friends.

But what preoccupied her now was what had happened to Peter. The question occupied her head, then took over her heart, and now it held her completely hostage.

"Why didn't you say something sooner?" asked Myrna. The question, Clara knew, wasn't a criticism. There was no reproach or judgment. Myrna simply wanted to understand.

"At first I thought I might have had the date wrong. Then I got mad and thought, Fuck him. That was good for a couple of weeks. Then . . ."

She lifted her hands, as though in surrender.

Myrna waited, sipping her tea. She knew her friend. Clara might pause, might hesitate, might stumble. But she never surrendered.

"Then I got scared."

"Of what?" Myrna's voice was calm.

"I don't know."

"You know."

There was a long pause. "I was afraid," said Clara at last, "that he was dead."

And still Myrna waited. And waited. And rested her mug in the circles. And waited.

"And," said Clara, "I was afraid he wasn't. That he hadn't come home because he didn't want to."

"*Salut*," said Annie as her husband joined them on the porch. She patted the seat next to her on the swing.

"Can't right now," said Jean-Guy. "But save my place. I'll be back in a few minutes."

"I'll be in bed by then."

Beauvoir was on the verge of saying something, then remembered where they were, and who was with them.

"Are you off?" Reine-Marie asked Armand as she stood and he put his arm around her waist.

"Not for long."

"I'll keep a candle in the window," she said, and saw him smile.

She watched as Armand and their son-in-law strolled across the village green. At first she thought they were going to the bistro for a nightcap, but then they veered to the right. To the light of Clara's cottage.

And Reine-Marie heard them knock on her door. A soft, soft, insistent knocking.

"You told him?"

Clara looked from Gamache to Jean-Guy.

She was livid. Her face was livid, as though she'd fallen face-first onto one of her own palettes. Magenta with a blotch of dioxazine purple seeping up from her neck.

"It was private. What I told you was private."

"You asked for my help, Clara," said Gamache.

"No I didn't. In fact, I told you not to help. That I'd take care of it. This is my life, my problem, not yours. Do you think every damsel is in distress? Did I become just a problem to be solved? A weakling to be saved? Is that it? The great man steps in to take care of things. Are you here to tell me not to worry my pretty little head?"

Even Myrna's eyes widened at this description of Clara's head.

"Wait a minute—" Beauvoir began, his own face turning alizarin crimson, but Gamache placed a large hand on the younger man's arm.

"No, you wait a minute," snapped Clara, rounding on Beauvoir. Beside her, Myrna laid a soft but firm hand on her arm.

"I'm sorry if I misunderstood," said Gamache, and he looked it. "I thought when we talked this morning that you wanted my help. Why else come to me?"

And there it was. The simple truth.

Armand Gamache was her friend. But Reine-Marie was a closer friend. Others in the village were older friends. Myrna was her best friend.

So why had she gone each morning up to the bench, to sit beside this man? And had finally unburdened herself? To him.

"Well, you were wrong," Clara said, the purple spreading into her scalp. "If you're bored here, Chief Inspector, go find someone else's private life to pillage."

Even Beauvoir gaped at that, momentarily so shocked he couldn't find the words. And then he found them.

"Bored? Bored? Do you have any idea what he's offering? What he's giving up? What a selfish—"

"Jean-Guy! Enough."

The four of them stared at each other, shocked into silence.

"I'm sorry," said Gamache, giving Clara a small bow. "I was wrong. Jean-Guy."

Beauvoir hurried to catch up to Gamache's long strides as he left Clara's home and walked toward the bistro. Once there, Gamache ordered a cognac and Beauvoir got a Coke.

Jean-Guy studied the man across from him. And slowly, slowly, it dawned on him that Gamache wasn't angry. He wasn't even hurt that his offer to help Clara had been turned down and he'd been personally insulted.

Beauvoir knew, as he watched the Chief sip his drink and stare ahead, that the only thing Armand Gamache felt at that moment was relief.

FIVE

———

The next morning dawned bright and warm.

Reine-Marie stepped out their front door onto the porch and almost trod on the moth. It had fallen on its back directly beneath the light, face up, its wings spread wide as though in ecstasy.

Armand, Reine-Marie, and Henri strolled up the hill, past the little church, past the old mill, past the Inn and Spa in the old Hadley House. Through the tunnel of trees they walked. They could see their footprints in the dirt from the day before, and the day before that.

And then their footprints stopped. But they walked on. A hundred yards farther. Always a little farther. Until they'd gone far enough and it was time to turn back.

At the bench they paused and sat down.

"It looks like a compass, doesn't it?" said Reine-Marie.

Armand tossed the ball to the eager and tireless Henri, then considered what she'd said.

"You're right," he smiled. "I hadn't seen that before."

The village of Three Pines was built around the village green. The homes formed a circle, and out of that circle ran four roads, like the cardinal directions. Gamache now wondered if they really did head out to true north, south, east, and west.

Was Three Pines a compass? A guide for those blown off course?

"Can you tell me about Clara?" Reine-Marie asked.

"I wish I could, *mon coeur.*"

Gamache looked unhappy. He told his wife almost everything.

Throughout his career he'd told her about the evidence, the suspects, his suspicions. He'd told her because he trusted her and wanted to include her in his life. They'd discussed murder cases he was working on and the books and old documents she was working on in the national archives.

But some things, some things, Gamache kept secret. Those he would tell no one. And he knew Reine-Marie had her secrets too. Confidences she would keep.

"But you told Jean-Guy."

It wasn't an accusation, simply a query.

"That was a mistake. When we went over to Clara's place to discuss it, she made it clear I shouldn't have."

He grimaced slightly and Reine-Marie suspected Clara had been quite clear.

"But she did want your help with something."

Her voice was calm, but her heart pounded. Reine-Marie knew if Clara was asking for help from Armand it wasn't to set a mousetrap or cut some hedges or fix the roof. Clara could do all those things for herself.

If she turned to Armand, it was for something only he could provide.

"I thought she wanted my help." He grinned and shook his head. "It doesn't take long to get rusty, I guess. To miss signals."

"It's not getting rusty, it's getting relaxed," said Reine-Marie.

She looked into his bright eyes and knew that despite what her husband said, not much escaped his notice. And if he thought Clara had been asking for help, she probably was. Once again, Reine-Marie wondered why Clara wanted help, and why she'd changed her mind.

"Would you have given it to her?" she asked.

Gamache opened, then shut, his mouth. He knew what the right answer was. But he also knew the truthful answer. He wasn't sure the two aligned.

"How could I not?" Then realizing how ungracious that sounded, he went on. "Well, it's academic now. She doesn't want anything from me."

"Maybe she just wanted you to listen." Reine-Marie placed her hand on his knee and got up. "Not your body and soul, *mon vieux*. Just an ear."

She bent to kiss him. "I'll see you later."

Armand watched her and Henri walk down the hill. Then he pulled the book from his pocket, put on his half-moon reading glasses and, opening to the bookmark, hesitated, went back to the very beginning, and started again.

"You haven't got very far."

Gamache closed the book and looked up over his glasses. Clara was standing in front of him holding two mugs of *café au lait*. And a bag of croissants.

"A peace offering," she said.

"Like the Paris Conference," he said, accepting it. "If this is about partition, I get Myrna's bookstore and the bistro."

"Leaving me with the bakery and the general store?" Clara considered. "I predict war."

Gamache smiled.

"I'm sorry about last night." She sat down. "I shouldn't have said all that. You were kind to offer to help."

"No, it was presumptuous. No one knows better than me that you can take care of yourself, and then some. You were right—I think I'm so used to being presented with problems that need solving, I just assume that's what people want."

"Must be difficult, being the oracle."

"You have no idea." He laughed and felt lighter. Maybe she did want him to simply listen. Maybe nothing more would be expected of him.

They ate their croissants, the flakes falling to the ground beneath their feet.

"What're you reading?" she asked. It was the first time she'd been so clear in her questioning.

Gamache kept his large hand splayed over the cover of the book, forcing it shut as though trapping the story inside.

Then he lifted his hand and showed it to her, but when she reached out for it, Gamache drew it back. Not far, barely noticeable. But far enough.

"*The Balm in Gilead*," she read the title, and searched her memory. "There's a book called *Gilead*. I read it a few years ago. By Marilynne Robinson. Won the Pulitzer."

"Not the same one," Gamache assured her, and Clara could see that it wasn't. The one that was in his hand, that he was now placing in his pocket, was thin and old. Worn. Read and reread.

"One of Myrna's?" Clara asked.

"*Non*." He examined her. "Do you want to talk about Peter?"

"No."

The Paris Peace Conference had hit a stalemate. He sipped his coffee. The morning mist had almost burned away and the forest spread green as far as he could see. These were old-growth trees, not yet discovered and felled by the lumber industry.

"You never finish the book," she said. "Is it difficult to read?"

"For me, yes."

She was quiet for a moment. "When Peter left, I was sure he'd come back. I was the one who forced the issue, you know. He didn't want to go." She lowered her head and studied her hands. As hard as she scrubbed, she couldn't seem to get the paint out of her cuticles. It was as though the paint was part of her. Had fused there. "And now, he doesn't want to come home."

"Do you want him back?"

"I don't know. I won't know until I see him, I think." She looked at the book just poking out of his pocket. "Why's it so difficult for you to read? It's in English, but I know you read English as well as French."

"*C'est vrai*. The words I understand, it's the emotions in the book that I struggle with. Where it takes me. I find I need to tread carefully."

Clara looked at him full on. "Are you all right?"

He smiled. "Are you?"

Clara pushed her large hands through her hair, leaving croissant flakes behind. "May I see it?"

Gamache hesitated, then tugged the book out of his pocket and gave it to her, watching closely, his body suddenly taut as though he'd handed her a loaded gun.

It was a slender hardback, the cover worn. She turned it over.

"*There is a balm in Gilead,*" she read from the back, "*to make the wounded whole—*"

"*There's power enough in Heaven / To cure a sin-sick soul.*" Armand Gamache finished the phrase. "It's from an old spiritual."

Clara stared at the back cover. "Do you believe it, Armand?"

"Yes." He took the book from her and grasped it so tightly in one hand she half expected words to squeeze out.

"Then what are you struggling with?"

When he didn't answer, she had her answer.

The problem wasn't with the words, it was with the wounds. Old wounds. And maybe a sin-sick soul.

"Where's Peter?" she asked. "What's happened to him?"

"I don't know."

"But you know him. Is he the sort to just disappear?"

Gamache knew the answer to that, had known since the day before when Clara had brought her problem to him.

"No."

"So what happened to him?" she pleaded, searching his face. "What do you think?"

What could he say? What should he say? That Peter Morrow would have come home if he could? That for all his faults, Peter was a man of his word, and if he couldn't for some reason show up in person he'd have called, or emailed, or written a letter.

But nothing had come. Not a word.

"I need to know, Armand."

He looked away from her, across the forest that went on and on forever. He'd come here to heal and, perhaps, to hide. Certainly to rest.

To garden, and walk, and read. To spend time with Reine-Marie and their friends. To enjoy Annie and Jean-Guy's weekend visits. The only problem he wanted to solve was how to hook up the garden hose. The only puzzle was whether to have the cedar plank salmon or the Brie and basil pasta for dinner at the bistro.

"Do you want my help?" he asked at last, not daring to look at her in case his face betrayed his offer.

He saw Clara's shadow on the ground. It nodded.

He lifted his eyes to hers. And nodded. "We'll find him."

His voice was reassuring, confident.

Clara knew she was hearing the same voice, seeing the same face, so many others had. As the large, calm man had stood before them. And handed them their worst fears. And assured them he'd find the monster who had done it.

"You can't know that. I'm sorry, Armand, I don't mean to be ungrateful, but you don't know for sure."

"*C'est vrai*," Gamache conceded. "But I'll do my best. How's that?"

He didn't ask if she was prepared for the answer to her question. He knew that while Clara wanted Peter, she also wanted peace. She was as prepared as she could be.

"You don't mind?" she asked.

"I don't mind at all."

She studied him. "I think you're lying." Then she touched his large hand. "Thank you for that." She got up, and he rose with her. "A brave man in a brave country."

He was unsure what to say to that.

"It's a prayer, from the other *Gilead*," Clara explained. "It's a dying father's prayer for his young son." She thought for a moment, remembering. Then she recited, "*I'll pray that you grow up a brave man in a brave country. I will pray you find a way to be useful.*"

Clara smiled.

"I hope I'm useful," he said.

"You already have been."

"Who do you want to know about this?"

"Might as well tell everyone now," she said. "What do we do first?"

"First? Let me think about that. We can probably find out a lot and not even leave home." He hoped his relief at that wasn't too obvious. He watched her closely. "You can stop it at any time, you know."

"*Merci*, Armand. But if I'm ever going to get on with my life, I need to know why he didn't come home. I'm not expecting to like the answer," she assured him. She left and walked down the hill.

He sat back down and thought about a dying father's prayer for a young son. Had his own father thought of him, at the moment of impact? At the moment he knew he was dying? Did he think of his young son, at home, waiting for headlights that would never, ever arrive?

Was he still waiting?

Armand Gamache did not want to have to be brave. Not anymore. Now all he wanted was to be at peace.

But, like Clara, he knew he could not have one without the other.

SIX

⁓

"The first thing we need to know is why Peter left."

Gamache and Beauvoir sat on one side of the pine table in Clara's kitchen, and Clara and Myrna were across from them. Gamache's large hands were folded together on the table. Beside him, Jean-Guy had his notepad out and a pen at the ready. They'd unconsciously slipped right back into their old roles and habits, from more than a decade investigating together.

Beauvoir had also brought his laptop and connected to the Internet over the phone line, in case they needed to look anything up. The laborious musical tones for each number it dialed filled the kitchen. And then the shriek, as though the Internet was a creature and connecting to it hurt.

Beauvoir shot Gamache a cautionary glance. *Don't, for God's sake, not again.*

Gamache grinned. Each time they used dial-up in Three Pines—the only way to connect since no other signal reached this hidden village—the Chief would remind Jean-Guy that once even dial-up had seemed a miracle. Not a nuisance.

"I remember . . ." the Chief began, and Beauvoir's eyes widened. Then Gamache caught the younger man's eyes and smiled.

But when the Chief turned to Clara, his face was serious.

She took a deep breath, and took the plunge.

It had begun. The search for Peter had started.

"You know why," Clara said. "I kicked him out."

43

"*Oui*," agreed Gamache. "But why did you do that?"

"Things hadn't been good between us for a while. As you know, Peter's career sort of plateaued, while mine . . ."

". . . took off," said Myrna.

Clara nodded. "I knew Peter was struggling with that. I'd thought he'd get over his jealousy eventually and be happy for me, like I'd been happy for his success. And he tried to be. He pretended to be. But I could tell he wasn't. Instead of getting better it was getting worse."

Gamache listened. Peter Morrow had long been the more prominent artist in the family. Indeed, one of the most prominent artists in Québec. In Canada. His income was modest, but it was enough for them to live on. He supported the family.

He painted very slowly in excruciating detail, while Clara seemed to slap together a work daily. Whether or not it was art was open for debate.

Where Peter's creations were beautiful studies in composition, there was nothing studied about what his wife produced in her studio.

Clara's works were exuberant. Vital, alive, often funny, often just plain baffling. Her *Warrior Uteruses*, her series of rubber boots, her whore televisions.

Even Gamache, who loved art, had difficulty fathoming much of it. But he recognized joy when he saw it, and Clara's creations were filled with it. The pure joy of creation. Of striving. Of striding forward. Searching. Exploring. Pushing.

And then, the breakthrough. *The Three Graces.*

One day Clara had decided to try something different, yet again. A painting this time, and her subject would be three elderly neighbors. Friends.

Beatrice, Kaye, and Emilie. Emilie, who had saved Henri. Emilie who had owned the Gamaches' home.

The Three Graces. Clara had invited them into her home to paint them.

"May I?" Gamache asked, and gestured toward her studio.

Clara got up. "Of course."

They all walked across the kitchen and into her studio. It smelled of overripe bananas and paint and the strangely evocative and attractive scent of turpentine.

Clara turned the lights on and the room came alive with faces. People looked at them from the walls and easels. One of the canvases was draped in a sheet, like a child's idea of a ghost. She'd covered her latest work.

Gamache made his way past it and straight across the studio, trying not to be distracted by the other works that seemed to be watching him.

He stopped at the large canvas on the far wall.

"Everything changed with this, didn't it?" he said.

Clara nodded, also staring at it. "For better, and for worse. It was Peter's idea, you know. Not the subject matter, but he kept at me to stop doing installations and to try painting. Like him. So I did."

The four of them stared at the three elderly women on the wall.

"I decided to paint them," said Clara.

"*Oui*," said Gamache. That much was obvious.

"No," Clara said, smiling. "My plan was to actually paint them. Put paint right on them. They'd be nude. Beatrice was going to be green. The heart chakra. Kaye was going to be blue. The throat chakra. She talked a lot."

"A blue streak," confirmed Myrna.

"And Emilie would be violet," said Clara. "The crown chakra. One-ness with God."

Beauvoir made a slight squeal, as though he'd just connected to the Internet. Gamache ignored him, though he could sense the rolling eyes.

Clara turned to Beauvoir. "I know. Nuts. But they were willing to try it."

"And did you paint them?" Beauvoir asked.

"Well, I would have, but I realized I didn't have enough violet, and I couldn't really leave Emilie half finished. I was going to send them home, when Emilie suggested just doing their portrait. I wasn't very enthusiastic. I'd never done portraits."

"Why not?" Gamache asked.

Clara thought about that. "I guess because it seemed so old-fashioned. Not avant-garde. Not creative."

"So you'd paint the person, but not their portrait?" asked Beauvoir.

"Exactly. Pretty creative, no?"

"That's one word for it," he said, and then mumbled something that sounded like "*merde.*"

Gamache turned back to the canvas. He'd met all three women, but Clara's painting of them always stunned him. They were old. Worn. Lined. Creviced. Their clothes were comfortable, sensible. Taken in parts there was nothing remotely remarkable about them in this painting.

But the whole? What Clara had captured? It was breathtaking.

Emilie, Beatrice, and Kaye reached out to each other. Not grasping. These women weren't drowning. They weren't clinging to each other.

All three were laughing, with open-faced pleasure in each other's company.

In her first portrait Clara had captured intimacy.

"It had been a mistake, then?" asked Beauvoir, pointing to the painting.

"Well, that's one word for it," said Clara.

"And what did Peter say when he saw it?" asked Gamache.

"He said it was very good, but that I might have to work on perspective."

Gamache felt a spike of anger. This was a form of murder. Peter Morrow had tried to kill not his wife, but her creation. He'd clearly recognized a work of genius and had tried to ruin it.

"Do you think he knew then what was going to happen?" Beauvoir asked.

"I don't think anyone could have known what would happen," said Clara. "I sure didn't."

"But I think he suspected," said Myrna. "I think he looked at *The Three Graces* and saw the Visigoths on the seventh hill. He knew his world was about to change."

"Why wasn't he happy for Clara?" Gamache asked Myrna.

"Have you ever been jealous?"

Gamache thought about that. He'd been passed over for promotions. In his youth girls he'd had crushes on had turned him down, only to date one of his friends. Which somehow made it worse for his young heart. But the closest he'd come to consuming, corroding jealousy was seeing other kids with their parents.

He'd hated them for that. And, God help him, he'd hated his parents. For not being there. For leaving him behind.

"It's like drinking acid," said Myrna, "and expecting the other person to die."

Gamache nodded.

Is that how Peter had felt, looking at this painting? Had Peter taken his first gulp of acid? Had he felt his insides curdle when he saw *The Three Graces*?

Gamache knew Peter Morrow well and had no doubt even now that he loved Clara with all his heart. And that must have made it worse. To love the woman but hate and fear what she'd created. Peter didn't want Clara to die, but he'd almost certainly wanted her paintings to die. And he'd do what he could to kill them. With a quiet word, an insinuation, a suggestion.

"May I?" Gamache pointed out the door of the studio to the closed door across the hall.

"Yes." Clara led the way.

Peter's studio was tidy, organized, calm. It felt serene, to Clara's disorder. It smelled of paint, with a slight undertone of lemon. Pledge, thought Gamache. Or lemon meringue pie.

The walls were covered with studies for Peter's careful, brilliantly executed creations. Early on in his career, Peter had discovered if he took a simple object and magnified it, it looked abstract.

And that's what he painted. He loved the fact that something banal, often natural, like a twig or a leaf, could look abstract and unnatural when examined closely.

At first it had been exciting. Fresh and new, his paintings had taken the art world by storm. But after ten, twenty years of essentially the same thing, over and over . . .

Gamache looked at Peter's works. They were spectacular. At first glance. And then they faded. They were, finally, examples of great draftsmanship. There was no mistaking a work by Peter Morrow, you could spot one a mile away. Admire it for a minute, then move on. There was a center, maybe even a message, but no soul.

Though the studio walls were covered with his works, the space felt cold and empty.

Gamache considered the canvas in front of him, and found himself still consumed by Clara's painting. The actual image of *The Three Graces* might fade a little in memory, but how the work made him feel would not.

And that wasn't even Clara's best painting. Her works since had only grown in their power and depth. In all they evoked.

But these? Peter's canvases made him feel nothing.

Peter's career would have languished all by itself, eventually, independent of what happened to Clara. But her unexpected and spectacular ascent made his decline seem all the sharper.

What did flourish, though, what grew and grew, was his jealousy.

As Gamache followed Clara from the studio, he found his anger toward Peter had been replaced by a sort of pity. The poor sod hadn't stood a chance.

"When did you know it was over?" he asked.

"The marriage?" Clara considered. "Probably a while before I actually faced it. It sorta grows in the gut. But I wasn't sure. It seemed impossible that what I was feeling from Peter was real. And it was a confusing time, so much was happening. And Peter had always been so supportive."

"When you were failing," said Myrna quietly.

They were standing in the kitchen now. There were no paintings on the walls, but the windows acted as works of art, framing the view of Three Pines out the front, and the garden out the back.

Clara looked like she was going to take exception to what Myrna said, but then didn't. Instead she nodded.

"Funny, I'm so used to defending Peter, I do it even now. But you're right. He never understood my art. He tolerated it. What he couldn't tolerate was my success."

"That must've hurt," said Beauvoir.

"It was shattering, inconceivable."

"No, I meant it must have hurt him," said Beauvoir.

Clara looked at him. "I guess."

She looked at Beauvoir and knew he knew how that felt. To turn against people you'd loved. To see allies as threats and friends as enemies. To be eaten alive. From within.

"Did you talk to him about it?" asked Gamache.

"I tried, but he always denied it. Told me I was insecure, too sensitive. And I believed him." She shook her head. "But then it became so obvious even I couldn't deny it."

"And when was that?" Gamache asked.

"I think you know. You were there. It was last year, when I had the solo show at the Musée d'art contemporain in Montréal."

The pinnacle of her career. What every artist dreamed of happening. And on the surface, Peter had been pleased for his wife, accompanying her to the *vernissage*. A smile on his handsome face. And a stone in his heart.

That's what the end so often looked like, Gamache knew. Not the smile, not even the stone, but the crevice in between.

"Let's get some fresh air," said Myrna, opening the back door into the garden. She joined them a few minutes later with a platter of sandwiches and a pitcher of iced tea.

They sat in the shade of a grove of maples, their four Adirondack chairs like the points of a compass, Gamache realized.

The Chief leaned forward and chose a sandwich, then slid back in his chair.

"You asked Peter to leave shortly after your solo show opened last year," he said, chasing the bite with a sip of iced tea.

"After an argument that lasted all day and night," Clara said. "I was exhausted and finally fell asleep at about three in the morning. When I woke up Peter wasn't in bed anymore."

"He'd left?" asked Beauvoir. He'd already finished most of his baguette, filled with paté and chutney. The iced tea perspired on the arm of his chair.

"No. He was against the wall of our bedroom, his knees up to his chin. Staring. I thought he'd had a breakdown."

"Had he?" asked Myrna.

"I guess, of sorts. Maybe more a breakthrough. He said it came to him in the middle of the night that he'd never been jealous of my art."

Myrna snorted into her glass, sending tea onto her nose.

"I know," said Clara. "I didn't believe him either. And then we fought some more." She sounded weary to the bone as she described it.

Gamache had been listening closely. "If he wasn't jealous of your art, then what did he say was the problem?"

"Me, I was the problem," said Clara. "He was jealous of me. Not that I painted friendship and love and hope, but that I felt them."

"And he didn't," said Myrna. Clara nodded.

"He realized in the night that he'd been pretending all his life and that deep down there was nothing. Just a hole. Which was why his paintings had no substance."

"Because he had no substance," said Gamache.

Their little circle fell silent. Bees buzzed in and out of the roses and tall foxglove. Flies tried to drag crispy baguette shards off the empty plates. The Rivière Bella Bella bubbled by.

And they considered a man who had a hole where his core should have been.

"Is that why he left?" asked Myrna, finally.

"He left because I told him to. But . . ."

They waited.

Clara looked across the garden so that they could only see her in profile.

"I expected him back." She smiled suddenly and looked at them. "I thought he'd miss me. I thought he'd be lonely and lost without me. And he'd realize what he had, with me. I thought he'd come home."

"What did you say to him exactly?" asked Beauvoir. "The morning he left?"

His notebook had replaced the empty plate on the arm of the chair.

"I told him he had to go, but that he should come back in a year and we could see where we were each at."

"Did you say a year exactly?"

Clara nodded.

"I'm sorry to keep going over this," said Beauvoir, "but this is crucial. Did you set a date? You did say a year exactly?"

"Exactly."

"And when was he supposed to come back?"

She told him and Beauvoir did a quick calculation.

"In your opinion, did Peter take that in?" Gamache asked. "His world was collapsing around him. Is it possible he was nodding and appearing to understand, but he was really in shock?"

Clara thought about that. "I suppose it's possible, but we talked about having dinner together. We actually planned it. It wasn't a passing comment."

She fell silent. Remembering sitting in that very chair. The steaks ready. The salad made. The wine chilled.

The croissants in the paper bag on the kitchen counter.

Waiting.

"Where was he headed that day he left?" asked Gamache. "To Montréal? To his family?"

"I think that's unlikely, don't you?" said Clara, and Gamache, who'd met Peter's family, had to agree. If Peter Morrow had a hole where his soul should be, his family had put it there.

"When he didn't show up, did you get in touch with them?" asked Gamache.

"Not yet," said Clara. "I've been saving that little treat."

"Do you have any idea what Peter would've been doing in the past year?" Beauvoir asked.

"Painting probably. What else?"

Gamache nodded. What else? Without Clara, there was only one thing left in Peter Morrow's life, and that was art.

"Where would he have gone?" Gamache asked.

"I wish I knew."

"Was there some place Peter always dreamed of visiting?" he asked.

"Because of the kind of paintings he did, the location wasn't important," said Clara. "He could do them anywhere." She paused for a moment, thinking. "*I'll pray that you grow up a brave man in a brave country.*"

She turned to Gamache. "When I said that this morning, I wasn't thinking of you, you know. I know you're a brave man. I was thinking of Peter. I've prayed every day that he grows up. And becomes a brave man."

Armand Gamache leaned back in his chair, the wooden slats warm against his shirt, and thought about that. And wondered where Peter had gone. And what he'd found.

And whether he'd had to be brave.

SEVEN

—

The ugliest man alive opened the door and gave Gamache a grotesque smile.

"Armand." He held out his hand and Gamache took it.

"Monsieur Finney," said the Chief.

Bowed by arthritis, the elderly man's body was twisted and humped.

With effort, Gamache held Finney's eyes, or at least one of them. And even that was no mean feat. Finney's protruding eyes rolled in all directions, as though in perpetual disapproval. The only thing stopping them from rolling together was his bulbous purple nose, a venous Maginot Line, with vast trenches on either side from which a war on life was being waged and lost.

"*Comment allez-vous?*" asked Gamache, losing his hold on the wild eye.

"I'm doing well, *merci*. You?" Monsieur Finney asked. His eyes spun swiftly over the large man who towered over him. Scanning him. "You're looking well."

But before Gamache could answer, a pleasant singsong voice came down the hallway.

"Bert, who is it?"

"It's Peter's friend. Armand Gamache." Monsieur Finney stepped back to allow Armand into the Montréal home belonging to Peter Morrow's mother and stepfather.

"Oh, how nice."

Bert Finney turned to their guest. "Irene will be happy to see you."

He smiled, the sort of grin that wide-eyed children imagined beneath their beds at night.

But the real nightmare was yet to come.

When Gamache had been so gravely injured, he'd received among thousands of cards a beautiful one signed by Irene and Bert Finney. Grateful for the card, the Chief Inspector nevertheless understood that courtesy should not be mistaken for genuine kindness. One was nurture, a polite upbringing. The other was nature.

One of these two was courteous. The other kind. And Gamache had a pretty good idea which was which.

He followed Finney down the hall and into a light-filled living room. The furniture was a mix of British antiques and fine Québec pine. The Chief, a great admirer of both the early Québécois and the furniture they made, tried not to stare.

A comfortable sofa was slipcovered in a cheerful but muted pattern, and on the walls he saw works by some of the most prominent Canadian artists. Jean Paul Lemieux, A. Y. Jackson, Clarence Gagnon.

But not a single Peter Morrow. Nor was there a work by Clara.

"*Bonjour.*"

The Chief walked across the room to the chair by the window and the elderly woman who sat there. Irene Finney. Peter's mother.

Her silken white hair was done in a loose bun, so that it framed her face. Her eyes were of the clearest blue. Her skin was pink and tender and scored with wrinkles. She wore a loose dress on her plump body and a kindly expression on her face.

"Monsieur Gamache." Her voice was welcoming. She held up one hand and he took it, bowing slightly over it.

"Fully recovered, I see," she said. "You've gained weight."

"Good food and exercise," said Gamache.

"Well, good food anyway," she said.

Gamache smiled. "We're living in Three Pines now."

"Ahh, well, that explains it."

The Chief stopped himself from asking what it explained. That was the first step into the cave. And he had no desire to enter this woman's lair any further than he already had.

"What can I get you?" asked Monsieur Finney. "A coffee? A lemonade perhaps?"

"Nothing, thank you. I'm afraid this isn't a social call. I've come . . ."

He paused. He could hardly say "on business" since this was no longer his business, nor was it really his personal affair. The elderly couple looked at him. Or Madame Finney looked while her husband pointed his nose in Gamache's direction.

The Chief could see the beginning of concern on Monsieur Finney's face, so he plunged ahead.

"I've come to ask you a couple of questions."

The relief on Finney's misshapen face was obvious, while Madame Finney remained placid, polite.

"So there's no bad news?" Finney asked.

Armand Gamache had become used to this reaction after decades with the Sûreté du Québec. He was the knock on the door at midnight, he was the wobbly old man on the bicycle, the grim-faced doctor. He was a good man with bad news. When the head of homicide came calling, it was almost never a happy occasion. And it seemed this specter had followed him into retirement.

"I'm just wondering if you've heard from Peter lately."

"Why are you asking us?" asked Peter's mother. "You're his neighbor."

The voice remained warm, pleasant. But the eyes sharpened. He could almost hear the scrape against the stone.

Gamache considered what she'd just said. She obviously didn't know that Peter hadn't been in Three Pines for more than a year. Nor did they know that Peter and Clara were separated. Neither Clara nor Peter would thank him for spilling their private life all over his family.

"He's away on a trip, probably painting," said Gamache. That much might be true. "But he didn't say where he was going. I just need to get in touch with him."

"Why don't you ask Claire?" asked Madame Finney.

"Clara," her husband corrected. "And she probably went with him."

"But he didn't say they went away," she pointed out. "He said, 'he.'"

Irene Finney turned her soft face to Gamache. And she smiled.

No fact escaped this woman, and the truth interested her not at all.

She'd have made, Gamache thought, a great inquisitor. Except that she wasn't at all inquisitive. She had no curiosity, simply a sharp mind and an instinct for the soft spot.

And despite Gamache's care, she'd found it. And now she drilled down.

"He's finally left her, hasn't he? Now she wants Peter back and you're the hound who's supposed to find him and take him back to that village."

She made Three Pines sound like a peasant slum and the act of returning Peter a crime against humanity. And she'd called Gamache a dog. Fortunately, Armand Gamache had a great deal of time for hounds, and had been called worse.

He held those gentle eyes and met her smile. He neither flinched nor looked away.

"Does Peter have a favorite place to paint? Or someplace he spoke of when he was growing up that he always wanted to visit?"

"You don't really think I'm going to help you find him, just to take him back there?" she asked. Her tone remained personable. A slight note of disapproval, but that was all. "Peter could have been one of the great painters of his generation, you know. Had he lived in New York or Paris or even here in Montréal. Where he could grow as an artist, get to know other painters, network with gallery owners and patrons. An artist needs stimulation, support. She knew that, and she took him as far from culture as she could. She buried him and his talent."

All this Madame Finney patiently explained to Gamache. Simply stating facts that should have been obvious, had the large man in front of her not been slightly dim, and dull, and also buried in Three Pines.

"If Peter's finally escaped," she said, "I won't help you find him."

Gamache nodded and broke eye contact to look at her walls. There he found immediate comfort in the images of rural Québec. The craggy, sinuous, rugged landscapes he knew so well.

"A remarkable collection," he congratulated her. And his admiration was sincere. Madame Finney had an eye for art.

"Thank you." She inclined her head slightly, acknowledging the compliment and the truth. "Peter used to sit in front of them for hours as a child."

"But you've put up none of his own works."

"No. He hasn't yet earned the right to be hung beside them." She tilted her head toward the wall. "One day perhaps."

"And what would he have to do to earn a spot?" Gamache asked.

"Ah, the age-old question, Chief Inspector? Where does genius come from?"

"Was that what I was asking?"

"Of course you were. I don't surround myself with mediocrity. When Peter paints a masterpiece I'll hang it. With the others."

The works on the wall had taken on a different complexion. A. Y. Jackson, Emily Carr, Tom Thomson. They seemed imprisoned. Hung until dead. As a reminder to a disappointing son. Peter had sat in front of them as a boy, and dreamed of one day joining them. Gamache could almost see the boy, in proper shorts and immaculate hair, sitting cross-legged on the carpet. Staring up at these works of genius. And longing to create a painting so fine it would warrant space in his mother's home.

And failing.

The walls, the works, now seemed to close in on Gamache and he wanted to leave. But couldn't. Not yet.

Madame Finney glared at him. How many had looked into those eyes, Gamache wondered. Within sight of the guillotine, the smoldering stake, the noose.

"All the works on your walls are landscapes," Gamache pointed out, his eyes not leaving hers. "Most painted in Québec villages. These artists found inspiration there, were able to create their best works there. Are you suggesting that muses are confined to large cities? That creation isn't possible in the countryside?"

"Don't try to make a fool of me," she snapped, the veneer cracking. "Every artist is different. I'm his mother. I know Peter. Some might thrive in the middle of nowhere, but Peter needs stimulation. She knew that, and she deliberately isolated him. Crippled him, instead of supporting and encouraging him and his art."

"As you do?" Gamache asked.

Monsieur Finney's pilgrim eyes came to an abrupt halt and he stared at the Chief. There was silence.

"I believe I've been more supportive of my son than your own parents were of you," Madame Finney said.

"My parents didn't have the chance, madame, as you know. They died when I was a child."

Her eyes never left his face. "I can't help but wonder how they'd have felt about your choice of career. A police officer." She shook her head in disappointment. "And one whose own colleagues tried to murder him. That can't be considered a success. In fact, weren't you actually shot by one of your own inspectors? That is what happened, isn't it?"

"Irene," said Monsieur Finney, a warning in the normally docile voice.

"To be fair, madame, I also shot one of my colleagues. Perhaps it was karma."

"Killed him, as I remember." She glared at Gamache. "In the woods, outside that village. I'm surprised it doesn't haunt you every time you walk by. Unless, of course, you're proud of what you did."

How did this happen? Gamache wondered. He was in the cave after all. Dragged there by a smiling, twinkling creature. And eviscerated.

And she wasn't finished with him yet.

"I wonder how your mother and father would have felt about your decision to quit. To run away and hide in that village. Peter's off painting, you say? At least he's still trying."

"You're quite right," he said. "I'll never know how my parents would have felt about my life."

He held out his hand. She took it and he bent down so that his face was next to her ear. He could feel her silken hair on his cheek and smell her scent of Chanel No. 5 and baby powder.

"But I know my parents loved me," he whispered, then pulled back so that his eyes locked on to hers. "Does Peter?"

Gamache straightened up, nodded to Monsieur Finney, and walked back down the dark corridor to the front door.

"Wait."

The Chief paused at the door and turned to see Finney hobbling toward him.

"You're worried about Peter, aren't you?" the older man said.

Gamache studied him, then nodded. "Was there a place he went to

58

as a child? A place that might have been special? A favorite place?" He thought for a moment. "A safe place?"

"You mean a real place?"

"Well, yes. When people are in turmoil they sometimes go back to a place where they were once happy."

"And Peter's in turmoil, you think?"

"I do."

Finney thought, then shook his head. "I'm sorry but nothing comes to mind."

"*Merci*," Gamache said. He shook hands with Finney, then left, trying to keep his pace measured. Trying not to speed up. Speed up. Speed away from this house. He could almost hear Emily Carr and A. Y. Jackson and Clarence Gagnon calling him back. Begging to be taken with him. Begging to be appreciated, and not valued simply for their appreciation.

Once in his car, Gamache took a deep breath, then pulled out his phone and found a message from Beauvoir. Jean-Guy had come into Montréal with him, and Gamache had dropped him at SQ headquarters.

Lunch? the text asked.

Mai Xiang Yuan, Chinatown, Gamache wrote back.

Within moments his device trilled. Jean-Guy would meet him there.

A short while later, over dumplings, they compared notes.

EIGHT

~

Jean-Guy Beauvoir tore a small hole in the top of a dumpling and dripped in tamari sauce. Then, using a spoon, he put the whole thing in his mouth.

"Mmmmmm."

Gamache watched, pleased to see Jean-Guy's appetite so strong.

Then he picked up a round shrimp and cilantro dumpling with his chopsticks and ate it.

Beauvoir watched and noted that the Chief's hand didn't tremble. Not much. Not anymore.

The hole-in-the-wall restaurant in Chinatown was filling with customers.

"Some din," said Jean-Guy, raising his voice over the lunch noise.

Gamache laughed.

Beauvoir wiped his chin with a thin paper napkin and looked over at his notebook, splayed open on the laminate table beside his bowl.

"Okay, here's the thing," he said. "I did a quick search on Peter's credit cards and his bank card. When he left Clara, he stayed in a hotel in Montréal for a week or so. A suite at the Crystal."

"A suite?" asked Gamache.

"Not the largest one, though."

"So he packed his hair shirt after all," said Gamache.

"Well, yes. Is cashmere considered hair?"

Gamache smiled. By Morrow standards the elegant Hotel Le Crystal was probably the equivalent of the rack. It wasn't the Ritz.

61

"And then?" asked Gamache.

"Air Canada to Paris. A geographical?" asked Beauvoir.

The Chief thought about that. "Perhaps."

The investigators knew that people who took off were running from unhappiness. Loneliness. Failure. They ran, thinking the problem was one of location. They thought they could start fresh somewhere else.

It rarely worked. The problem was not geographical.

"Where did he stay in Paris?"

"The Hotel Auriane. In the 15th arrondissement."

"*Vraiment?*" asked Gamache, a little surprised. He knew Paris well. Their son Daniel, his wife, Roslyn, and their grandchildren lived in Paris, in the 6th arrondissement in an apartment the size of a pie plate.

"Not what you expected, *patron*?" asked Jean-Guy, who, at dinner parties, pretended to know Paris, but didn't. He also pretended not to know east-end Montréal. But did.

With Gamache he'd long since given up the pretense.

"Well, the 15th is nice," said Gamache, thinking about it. "Residential. Lots of families."

"Not exactly the artistic hub."

"No," said Gamache. "How long did he stay?"

Beauvoir consulted his notes. "At the hotel? A few days. Then he rented a furnished apartment, for four months. He left just before his lease was up."

"And from there?"

"His credit card shows a TGV ticket, one way, to Florence. Then, after a couple of weeks, on to Venice," said Beauvoir. "He was covering a lot of territory."

Yes, thought Gamache. The hounds were nipping at Peter Morrow's heels. Gamache caught a whiff of desperation in this flight across Europe. There didn't seem to be a plan.

And yet it couldn't be a complete coincidence that the cities Peter chose were famous for inspiring artists.

"All I have so far are the credit card and bank records," said Beauvoir. "We know that he flew from Venice to Scotland—"

"Scotland?"

Beauvoir shrugged. "Scotland. From there he came back to Canada. Toronto."

"Is that where he is now?"

"No. Guess where he went from Toronto."

Gamache gave Beauvoir a stern look. After his visit with Peter's mother and stepfather, he wasn't in the mood for guessing games.

"Quebec City."

"When was that?" Gamache asked.

"April."

Gamache did a quick calculation. Four months ago. Gamache put down his cup of green tea and stared at Beauvoir.

"In Quebec City he took three thousand dollars from his bank account."

Beauvoir looked up from his notebook and slowly closed it.

"And then, no more. He disappeared."

Clara and Myrna sat in the Gamaches' living room. The fireplace was lit and Gamache was pouring drinks. A cold front had rolled in and brought with it chilly temperatures and a soft drizzle.

The fire wasn't really necessary. It was more for cheer than heat.

Annie had arranged to have dinner with her friend Dominique at the bistro, leaving her parents and her husband to talk with Clara.

"Here you go," said Gamache, handing Myrna and Clara glasses of Scotch.

"I think you should leave the bottle," said Clara.

She had the look of a frightened flier staring at the flight attendants during takeoff. Trying to read their expressions.

Are we safe? Are we going down? What's that smell?

Gamache sat next to Reine-Marie while Beauvoir dragged the wing chair over from the corner. Closing their small circle.

"This is what we found out," said Gamache. "It isn't much yet, and it's far from conclusive."

Clara didn't like the sound of that. The attempt to pacify, to reassure. It meant that reassurance was necessary. It meant something was wrong.

It meant that smell was smoke and the sound was an engine failing.

Armand and Jean-Guy told them about their day. On hearing about the visit to Peter's mother, Clara took a deep, deep breath.

Across from her, Myrna listened, absorbing the information, in case Clara missed some vital pieces.

"When Peter left here he went to Montréal for a few days, then flew to Paris," said Jean-Guy. "Then he moved on to Florence, then Venice."

Clara nodded to show she was following him. So far, so good.

"From Venice, Peter flew to Scotland," said Beauvoir.

Clara stopped nodding. "Scotland?"

"Why would Peter go to Scotland?" Myrna asked.

"We hoped you could tell us," Gamache said to Clara.

"Scotland," Clara repeated softly to herself and stared into the fire. Then she shook her head. "Where in Scotland?"

"It's easier to see on a map. Let me show you." Gamache rocked out of the deep sofa and returned a minute later with an atlas. He splayed it open on the coffee table and found the page.

"He flew into Glasgow."

Armand pointed.

They leaned in.

"From there Peter took a bus." He traced a line from Glasgow south. South. Along a winding road. Past towns named Bellshill, Lesmahagow, Moffat.

And then he stopped.

Clara leaned closer to the map.

"Dumfries?" she asked.

Her brows were drawn together, trying to either read the word or make sense of it, or both. Finally she sat back and looked at Gamache, who was watching her.

"Are you sure?" asked Clara.

"Pretty sure," said Beauvoir.

There was a pause.

"Is it possible it wasn't Peter? That someone stole his credit card?" Clara asked. "And his passport?"

She met Armand's eyes. Not looking away from what that question implied. No living man would lose his documents, or have them stolen, without reporting it. If they were taken, it was from a dead man.

"It's possible," Gamache admitted. "But unlikely. They'd have to have his codes and look exactly like him. Security and Customs agents look closely at passport photos now."

"But it's still a possibility?" Clara asked.

"Remote. We have agents looking into it," Beauvoir admitted. "We're going on the most likely scenario that it was actually Peter."

"But how likely is it that Peter left Venice for Dumfries?" asked Myrna.

"I agree," conceded Gamache. "It's odd. Unless Peter had a particular interest in Scotland."

"Not that he ever mentioned," said Clara. "Though he does like Scotch."

Myrna smiled. "Maybe it's that simple. Paris for great wine, Florence for Campari, and Venice for . . ."

She paused, stumped.

"The Bellini," said Reine-Marie. "We had one in Harry's Bar, where it was invented. Remember, Armand?"

"We sat at the bar at quaiside watching the vaporetti go by," he said. "It was named after the color of a robe in a Bellini painting. Pink."

"Pink?" Jean-Guy mouthed to Gamache.

"Are you suggesting Peter's drinking his way across Europe?" asked Clara. "The Ruth Zardo Grand Tour."

"Don't look at me," said Gamache. "It's not my theory."

"Then what is your theory?" Clara asked.

His smile faded, and he took a deep breath. "I don't have one. It's too early. But I do know one thing, Clara. As strange as all this seems, there's a reason Peter went to these places. We just have to work it out."

Clara leaned forward again, staring at the dot on the map. "Is he still there?"

Beauvoir shook his head. "He went to Toronto—"

"He's in Toronto?" Clara interrupted. "Why didn't you tell me this to begin with?" But on seeing their expressions, she stopped. "What is it?"

"He didn't stay there," said Gamache. "Peter flew from Toronto to Quebec City in April."

"Even better," said Clara. "He's on his way home."

"Quebec City," Gamache repeated. "Not Montréal. If he was coming back here he'd have gone to Montréal, *non?*"

Clara glared, hating him for a moment. For not allowing her her delusions, even briefly.

"Maybe he just wanted to see Quebec City," she said. "Maybe he wanted to paint it, while he waited." Her words, rapid-fire and insistent, faltered. "While he waited," she repeated, "to come home."

But he hadn't.

"He took three thousand dollars out of his bank account," Jean-Guy said, forging ahead. Then he stopped and looked at Gamache.

"That's the last we found of him," said Armand. "That was April."

Clara grew very still. Myrna put her large hand over Clara's, and it felt icy.

"He might still be there," said Clara.

"*Oui,*" said Gamache. "Absolutely."

"Where was he staying?"

"We don't know. But it's early days yet. You're right, he might still be in Quebec City, or he might have taken that money and gone elsewhere. Isabelle Lacoste is using the resources of the Sûreté to find him. Jean-Guy is looking. I'm looking. But it might take time."

Reine-Marie threw a log into the fire, sending embers and sparks up the chimney. Then she went into the kitchen.

They could smell salmon, and a slight scent of tarragon and lemon.

Clara stood. "I'm going to Quebec City."

"And do what?" Myrna also got up. "I know you want to do something, but that won't help."

"How do you know?" asked Clara.

Gamache rose. "There is something you could do. I'm not sure anything'll come of it but it might help."

"What?" asked Clara.

"Peter has family in Toronto—"

"His older brother Thomas," said Clara. "And his sister Marianna."

66

"I was going to call them tomorrow and ask if Peter was in touch, maybe stayed with one of them."

"You want me to call?"

He hesitated. "I was actually thinking you might go there."

"Why?" asked Myrna. "Can't she just call? You were going to."

"True, but face-to-face is always better. And even better if you know the people." Gamache looked at Clara. "I think you'll know if they're lying to you."

"I will."

"But what does it matter?" Myrna asked. They were walking toward the kitchen to join Reine-Marie. "He's not there anymore."

"But he was there for a few months," said Gamache. "He might have told his brother or sister where he was going next, and why. He might have told them why he was in Dumfries."

Gamache stopped and looked at Clara. "We have no leads in Quebec City but we have a few in Toronto. It might not help. But it might."

"I'll go," said Clara. "Of course I'll go. First thing in the morning."

She looked relieved to finally have something to do besides worry.

"Then I'll go with you," said Myrna.

"What about the shop?" Clara asked.

"I think the hordes desperate for secondhand books can wait a couple of days," said Myrna, putting out knives and forks. "I might ask Ruth to look after the store. She spends most of her time asleep in the chair by the window anyway."

"That's Ruth?" asked Reine-Marie. "I thought it was a mannequin."

Clara sat down and pushed the salmon around on her plate. While the others talked she listened to the drum of rain against the window.

She was anxious to get going.

NINE

⌒

Clara and Myrna caught the morning train out of Montréal's Central Station.

Clara listened to the sound of the wheels and felt the comforting, familiar movement. She leaned back, her head lolling on the rest, and stared out the window at the forests and fields and isolated farms.

This was a journey she'd made many times. First on her own, to art college in Toronto. A great adventure. Then with Peter to art shows in Toronto. Always his, never hers. Prestigious juried shows his work had been selected for. She'd sat beside him, holding his hand. Excited for him.

Today the train felt both familiar and foreign. Peter wasn't there.

In the reflection of the window she noticed Myrna staring at her. Clara turned to face her friend.

"What is it?"

"Do you want Peter back?"

It was the question Myrna had been wanting to ask for a while, but the time had never seemed right. But now it did.

"I don't know."

It wasn't that Clara couldn't answer that question, but that she had too many answers.

Waking up alone in bed, she wanted him back.

In her studio, painting, she didn't.

With her friends in the bistro, or over dinner with them, she didn't miss him at all.

But eating alone, at the pine table? In bed at night? She still sometimes spoke to him. Told him about her day and pretended he was there. Pretended he cared.

And then she turned out the light, and rolled over. And missed him even more.

Did she want him back?

"I don't know," she repeated. "I asked him to leave because he stopped caring for me, stopped supporting me. Not because I'd stopped caring for him."

Myrna nodded. She knew this. They'd talked about it through the past year. Their close friendship had grown closer and more intimate as Clara opened up.

All the stuff stuffed down, all the stuff that women were not supposed to feel, and never, ever show, Clara had showed Myrna.

The neediness, the fear, the rage. The terrible, aching loneliness.

"Suppose I'm never kissed on the lips again?" Clara had asked one afternoon in midwinter, as they ate lunch in front of the fire.

Myrna knew that fear too. She knew all of Clara's fears because she shared them. And admitted them to Clara.

And over the course of the year, as the days grew longer, their friendship deepened. As the night receded, the fear had also receded. And the loneliness of both women had ebbed away.

Do you want Peter back?

Myrna had asked Clara the question she was afraid to ask herself.

In the window, imposed over the endless forest, Myrna could see her ghostly self.

"Suppose something's happened to him?" Clara spoke to the back of the seat in front of her. "It would be my fault."

"No," said Myrna. "You asked him to leave. What he did after that was his choice."

"But if he stayed in Three Pines he'd be fine."

"Unless he had an appointment in Samarra."

"Samarra?" Clara turned to look at her friend. "What're you talking about?"

"Somerset Maugham," said Myrna.

"Are you having a stroke?" Clara asked.

"Maugham used the old fable in a story," Myrna explained. "I spend my days reading, remember. I know all these obscure things. I'm lucky I don't work in Sarah's bakery."

Clara laughed. "I just want to find him, to know he's all right. And then I can get on with my life."

"With or without him?"

"I think I'll know when I see him."

Myrna tapped Clara's hand lightly. "We'll find him."

Once in Toronto they checked into the Royal York hotel. Myrna had a shower and when she came out she found Clara on her laptop.

"I've marked the major art galleries on the map," said Clara over her shoulder, nodding to the map open on the bed. "We can do them tomorrow."

Myrna rubbed her wet hair and sat on the bed, studying the map with its Xs and circles.

"I thought we should start with Peter's brother and sister," said Clara. "Thomas's office is just up Yonge Street. We have an appointment at four. Marianna is meeting us for a drink in the hotel bar at five thirty."

"You've been busy," said Myrna. She got up to look at the page Clara was reading on her laptop. "What's so interesting?"

And then she stopped.

At the top of the page were the words "W. Somerset Maugham."

"A servant goes into the marketplace in Baghdad," Clara read off the screen, her back to her friend. *"There he bumps into an old woman. When she turns around, he recognizes her as Death."*

"Clara," said Myrna. "I didn't—"

"Death glares at him and the servant, frightened, runs away. He goes straight to his master and explains that he met Death in the market and that he needs to get away, to save himself. The master gives him a horse and the servant takes off, riding as fast as he can for Samarra, where he knows Death won't find him."

"I don't know why I mentioned—"

Clara made a subtle movement with her hand, and Myrna fell silent.

"Later that day the master is in the marketplace and he too meets Death," Clara continued reading. *"He asks her why she frightened his*

71

servant and Death explains that she hadn't meant to scare him. She was just surprised."

Clara turned around and stared at Myrna. "You finish the story. You know it."

"I should never have said—"

"Please," said Clara.

Finally Myrna, in a soft voice, spoke.

"Death said, I was simply surprised to see him in the market. Because I have an appointment with him tonight. In Samarra."

"Did you get Peter's photograph?" Gamache asked Lacoste.

"*Oui.* And I've sent it to Quebec City," she said. "They're looking into it. I've also sent it out across the Sûreté du Québec network and to police in Paris, Florence, and Venice. I've asked them to track his movements. It's been almost a year, so I'm not expecting much, but I have to try."

Gamache smiled. Many had thought him mad, or hopped up on painkillers, when he'd appointed an inspector in her early thirties as his successor to lead the famed homicide division. But he'd prevailed. And had never, ever doubted his choice of Isabelle Lacoste.

"Good."

He was about to ring off when he remembered, "Oh, and Dumfries. Could you check that out too, please?"

"Right. I forgot."

He hung up and tapped the phone a few times with his finger. Then he went over to his computer and dialed into the Internet.

Once connected, he went to Google and typed in "Dumfries."

"Well, that wasn't very helpful," said Myrna. "Is he always like that?"

They'd descended the TD Bank Tower and were standing in the lobby. Myrna was taking a moment to admire the Mies van der Rohe design. The light and height. A contrast to the closed-off, closed-in, squalid little scene they'd left on the 52nd floor.

Thomas Morrow was elegant, tall, gracious. He appeared, in many ways, an animated version of the building itself. Except there was nothing open and bright about him.

The office tower was more than it initially appeared. Thomas Morrow was less.

"Worse," said Clara. "I think you being there made him nicer than he normally is."

"You're joking," said Myrna. Their shoes rapped on the marble floor. The clock above the long marble security desk said four thirty-five. Thomas Morrow had made his sister-in-law wait twenty minutes and then had given them ten minutes of his time before moving on to more pressing issues than a missing brother.

"I'm sure Peter's fine," Morrow had said, a smile on his face that only managed to look condescending. "You know him. He's gone off to paint and lost track of the time."

Myrna said nothing, she simply observed Thomas Morrow. He was in his early sixties, she guessed. He sat with his legs splayed open, inviting the women to stare at his crotch. His suit was beautifully cut and his tie was silk. His back was to the view, which meant his visitors saw him against the backdrop of the huge black towers around him and the glittering great lake beyond.

He was like a monarch, surrounding himself with the symbols of power, hoping to disguise his own weakness.

Clara kept her temper. "I'm sure you're right, but I'm really just interested in knowing if you saw him when he was here."

Thomas shook his head. "But I wouldn't expect him to get in touch. No art on my walls."

He pointed with some pride to the bank of photographs. Not of family or friends, but of business triumphs. Golfing trophies. Famous people he'd met.

Strangers.

"He was probably going to shows and checking out galleries," said Thomas Morrow. "Have you asked the galleries?"

"That's a good idea," said Clara with a tight smile. "Thank you."

Morrow got up and walked to the door. "I'm glad I could help."

And that was that.

"We could've done that over the phone," said Myrna as they walked out into the blast furnace of the Toronto summer. The heat shimmered off the buildings and bounced off concrete and drilled into the pavement, which gave off the scent of melting asphalt in the heavy, humid air.

Myrna found it strangely calming. Her mother's and grandmother's comfort smells were cut grass and fresh baking and the subtle scent of line-dried sheets. For Myrna's generation the smells that calmed were manufactured. Melting asphalt meant summer. VapoRub meant winter, and being cared for. There were Tang and gas fumes and long-gone photocopy ink.

All comforted her, for reasons that beggared understanding, because they had nothing to do with understanding.

After years in Three Pines, her comfort scents were evolving. She still loved the smell of VapoRub, but now she also appreciated the delicate scent of worms after a rain.

"I wanted to be able to watch him," said Clara as they waited at a corner with a crowd of other perspiring people for the light to turn. "To see if he was lying, or holding something back."

"And was he? Do you think he saw Peter, or spoke to him?"

"I don't think so."

Myrna thought about it. "Why did he say that about his walls?"

She could see the imposing façade of the Royal York up ahead. A massive anachronism at the foot of the modern city. And she could almost taste the beer she'd soon be drinking.

"Who knows why the Morrows say anything," said Clara, pausing just outside the door of the old hotel. The doorman, perspiring in his uniform, had one hand on the handle, ready to yank it open.

"I guess it was a swipe at Peter," said Myrna. "Saying he was more interested in art than in his brother."

"And he'd have been right," said Clara.

"Let's get a beer," said Myrna, and headed straight for the bar.

TEN

—

Reine-Marie tucked the heavy book under her arm and stepped into the glare of the day.

"Inside or out, *ma belle*?" Olivier asked.

She looked around and decided a table on the *terrasse*, under one of the large Campari umbrellas, would be perfect.

Olivier returned a few minutes later with a tall ginger beer, already beading in the heat, and a bowl of assorted nuts.

"*Parfait*," said Reine-Marie. "*Merci.*"

She took a sip and opened the book, only looking up twenty minutes later when a head dropped into her lap.

Henri.

She kneaded his extravagant ears, and felt a kiss on the top of her head.

"I hope that's you, Sergio."

"Sorry, only me," said Armand with a laugh.

He pulled up a chair and nodded to Olivier, who disappeared inside.

"*The History of Scotland*," Gamache read the cover of Reine-Marie's book. "A sudden passion?"

"Why Dumfries, Armand?" Reine-Marie asked.

"I've been trying to figure that out as well. Went on the Internet to look it up."

"Did you find anything?"

"Not really," he admitted. "I printed out some of what I found." He put the sheets on the table. "You?"

"I've just started reading."

"Where'd you get it?" he asked. "Ruth?"

He looked over at Myrna's New and Used Bookstore.

"Rosa. Ruth was asleep in the philosophy section."

"Asleep or passed out or . . ."

"Dead?" asked Reine-Marie. "No, I checked."

"No farmhouse on top of her?" Olivier asked, placing Gamache's ginger beer on the table.

"*Merci, patron*," Armand said.

They sipped their drinks, absentmindedly ate the nuts, and read about a town in Scotland.

"Oh, my God," said Myrna, looking around.

She was stopped dead in the doorway of the Royal York bar, causing a bit of a jam behind her.

"How many?" the young woman asked.

"Three," said Clara, looking around the stationary bulk of Myrna.

"Follow me."

The two perspiring women followed the cool, slender maitre d'." Myrna felt like a giant. All big and galumping, disheveled, and fictional. Not really there at all. Invisible behind the siren showing them to their table.

"*Merci*," said Clara out of force of habit, forgetting she was in English Ontario and not French Québec.

"Oh, my God," Myrna whispered again as she dropped into the plush wing chair, upholstered in rose-colored crushed velvet.

The bar was, in fact, a library. A place Dickens would have been comfortable in. Where Conan Doyle might have found a useful volume. Where Jane Austen could sit and read. And get drunk, if she wanted.

"A beer, thank you," said Myrna.

"Two," said Clara.

It felt like they'd stepped out of the glare and throbbing heat of twenty-first-century Toronto into a cool nineteenth-century country house.

They might be giants, but this was their natural habitat.

"Do you think Peter had an appointment in Samarra?" asked Clara.

Her voice was flat, in a way Myrna recognized from years of listening to people trying to rein in their emotions. To squash them down, flatten them, and with them their words and their voices. Desperately trying to make the horrific sound mundane.

But Clara's eyes betrayed her. Begging Myrna for reassurance.

Peter was alive. Painting. He'd simply lost track of time.

There was nothing to worry about. He was nowhere near Samarra.

"I'm sorry I said that," said Myrna, smiling at the waiter who brought their drinks. Everyone else in the bar seemed to be having some sort of smart cocktail.

"But did you mean it?" Clara asked.

Myrna considered for a moment, looking at her friend. "I think the story isn't so much about death as fate. We all have an appointment in Samarra."

She put down her beer and leaned across the mahogany table, lowering her voice so that Clara had to lean forward to hear her.

"What I do know for sure is that Peter's life is his. Stay in the marketplace. Go to Samarra. His fate. Not yours. Would you take credit for anything wonderful Peter's done in this past year?"

Clara shook her head.

"And yet you think it's your fault if something bad happens."

"Do you think something bad has happened?"

Myrna was about to say, slightly exasperated, that that wasn't her point. But looking at Clara she knew it wouldn't matter. Clara needed only one thing, and it wasn't logic.

"No." Myrna took her hand. "I'm sure he's fine."

Clara took a deep breath, squeezed Myrna's hand, then leaned back in the wing chair.

"Really?" She searched Myrna's eyes, but not too deeply and not long.

"Really."

They both knew Myrna had just lied.

"Is that her?" Myrna asked, and Clara turned in her chair to see Marianna Morrow approaching.

Clara had first met Marianna when Peter's sister was living a bohemian life in Cabbagetown, an artist enclave in Toronto. She was pretending to be a poet and trying to catch the attention of her disinterested parents. Her weapon of choice was worry.

The young woman of equal parts abandon and desperation had so imprinted herself on Clara's brain that she still expected to see that Marianna. It took a few moments to realize there was gray in Marianna's hair, and while she still looked like a poet, she was in fact a successful designer. With a child. And the only one of Peter's family Clara could stomach. And that only barely.

"Marianna." Clara rose, and after introducing Myrna, all three sat. Marianna ordered a martini, then looked from one to the other.

"So," she said. "Where's Peter?"

"Why Dumfries?" asked Gamache, looking up from his sheaf of papers. "It seems an attractive enough place, but why would Peter leave Venice to go there?"

Reine-Marie lowered her heavy book. "There's nothing obvious here. A nice Scottish town. Druid at one time, then the Romans appeared, then the Scots took it back."

"Any prominent artists?"

"No prominent citizens at all, from what I can see."

Gamache leaned back and sipped his ginger beer, watching the children on the village green. Watching his friends and neighbors go about their business this warm day in August. Watching the cars drive slowly into and out of Three Pines.

Then he leaned forward.

"Dumfries might not have been where Peter was actually going." He pulled her book toward him. "Maybe it's on the way to somewhere else."

"What do you mean?" asked Clara.

"You and Peter are always together," said Marianna Morrow. "I just assumed he'd be joining us for drinks."

Clara's heart sank. "I came to ask you the same question."

Marianna turned in her chair to look squarely at Clara. "You wanted to ask me where Peter is? You don't know?"

Myrna tried to read the expression, the inflection. There was, on the surface at least, concern. But there was also something else swirling around under that.

Excitement. Myrna leaned slightly away from Marianna Morrow.

At least Thomas, with his splayed legs and knowing smile, didn't really try to hide his contempt. This one did. Though what she hid wasn't contempt, Myrna felt, so much as a sort of hunger.

Peter's sister looked as though Clara was an all-you-can-eat buffet, and Marianna was starving. Ravenous for the bad news Clara was offering.

"He's missing," said Clara.

And Myrna watched Marianna's eyes grow even brighter.

"That's terrible."

"When did you last see him?" Clara asked.

Marianna thought. "He had dinner with us this past winter, but I can't remember when exactly."

"You invited him over?"

"He invited himself."

"Why?" asked Clara.

"Why?" Marianna repeated. "Because I'm his sister. And he wanted to see me."

She appeared to be insulted, but they all knew she wasn't.

"No, really," said Clara. "Why?"

"I have no idea," Marianna Morrow admitted. "Maybe he wanted to see Bean."

"Bean?" asked Myrna.

"Marianna's . . ." Clara hesitated, and hoped the woman across from her would jump in with an answer. But Marianna Morrow just watched. And smiled.

"Marianna's child," said Clara at last.

"Ahhh," said Myrna, though the hesitation puzzled her.

Marianna examined Clara. "When was the last time you saw him?"

To Myrna's surprise, Clara didn't hesitate to tell her. "We've been separated for more than a year. I haven't seen or heard from him since last summer. It was supposed to be a trial separation. He was supposed to come back a year after leaving."

Myrna was watching Clara closely. There was little hint of the load those words carried. Of the weight, as Clara lugged them around, all day. All night.

"But he didn't." Marianna still clung to the shreds of concern, but her satisfaction was all too obvious now.

Myrna wondered why Clara didn't just shut up.

"But please don't tell anyone."

"I won't," said Marianna. "I know he visited the art college while he was here. He told us that when he came for dinner."

"Where we went to school," Clara told Myrna.

"I think he also visited some galleries."

Now Marianna Morrow was voluble and Myrna understood why Clara had told her so much. She was feeding Marianna, stuffing her. And Marianna ate it up, a glutton at a bad news banquet. Overstuffed, sleepy, her guard down. Drooling information.

"I have an idea. Why don't you two come over for dinner tonight?"

Myrna saw Clara smile for a moment, and then it was gone. And Myrna looked at her friend with renewed awe.

"Find anything?" Armand looked up from the book on Scotland.

Reine-Marie shook her head and put down the printouts.

They'd exchanged material, in hopes the other would find something they'd missed.

"You?" she asked.

He took off his reading glasses and rubbed his eyes. "Nothing. But there's something else that puzzles me about Peter's travels." Gamache sat forward at their table outside the bistro. "He went almost directly from here to Paris."

Reine-Marie nodded. "*Oui*."

"And found a place in the 15th arrondissement."

Now Reine-Marie understood why Armand was perplexed. "Not exactly a haunt of artists."

"We need a detailed map of Paris," he said, getting up. "There's one at home, but I bet the bookstore has one."

He returned a few minutes later with an old map, an old guidebook, and an old poet.

Ruth sat in Gamache's chair, grabbing his ginger beer with one hand and the last of the nuts with the other.

"Peter was last heard from in Quebec City," she said. "So what does Clouseau here come looking for? A map of Paris. Christ. How many people did you have to poison to become Chief Inspector?"

"So many that one more wouldn't matter," he said, and Ruth snorted.

She shoved his drink back to him with a wince and flagged down Olivier.

"Pills," she ordered. "Alcohol."

Reine-Marie told her about Peter's choice of neighborhood, and Ruth shook her head. "Crazy. But then, anyone who'd leave Clara must be. Don't tell her I said that."

The three of them went over the map and guidebook, scouring the 15th arrondissement for anything that would explain why Peter would stay there.

"Planning a trip?" asked Gabri. He put a small platter of pickles, cold cuts, and olives on their table, then joined them. "Can I come?"

When told what they were doing, he made a face. "The 15th? What was he thinking?"

Twenty minutes later they stared at each other. None the wiser.

What had Peter Morrow been thinking?

"And this is Bean," said Marianna.

Standing in front of Clara and Myrna was a child of twelve or thirteen. In jeans and a bulky shirt, with shoulder-length hair.

"Hello," said Myrna.

"Hi."

"Bean, you remember Aunt Clara."

"Sure. How's Uncle Peter?"

"Well, he's off painting," said Clara, and felt the sharp eyes of Bean watching her.

There was a lot that was obvious about Bean. The child was polite, quiet, clever. Observant.

What was not clear was whether Bean was a boy or a girl.

Marianna Morrow, finding she couldn't worry her parents into noticing her, had taken another route. She'd produced, out of wedlock, a child. She'd named that child Bean. And in a coup de grâce, had not told her family if Bean was a boy or a girl. Marianna had produced both a child and a biological weapon.

Clara had assumed Bean's sex would become obvious after a while. Marianna would either tire of the charade, or Bean her/himself would give it away. Or it would be clear as Bean matured.

None of those things had happened. Bean remained androgynous and the Morrows remained in the dark.

They ate dinner in near silence, Marianna apparently regretting her invitation almost as soon as it was issued. After dinner, Bean took them upstairs to show them the color wheel Uncle Peter had taught Bean how to make.

"Are you interested in art?" Myrna asked, following the child up the stairs.

"Not really."

The door to Bean's bedroom opened and Myrna's eyebrows rose. "Good thing," she whispered to Clara.

Bean's walls, instead of being covered with posters of the latest pop idol or sports star, were covered with paintings, tacked up. It looked, and felt, like a neolithic cave in downtown Toronto.

"Nice paintings," Aunt Clara said. Myrna shot her a warning look.

"What?" Clara whispered. "I'm trying to be encouraging."

"You really want to encourage that?" Myrna jabbed a thick finger at the walls.

"They're crap," said Bean, sitting on the bed and looking around. "But I like them."

Clara tried to suppress a smile. It was pretty much how she'd felt about all her early works. She knew they were crap. But she liked them. Though no one else did.

She looked around at the bedroom walls again, this time with an open mind. Determined to find something good in what Bean had done.

She moved from painting to painting. To painting. To painting.

She stood back. She stood close. She tipped her head from side to side.

No matter how she looked at them, they were awful.

"That's okay, you don't have to like them," said Bean. "I don't care."

It was also what the young Clara had said, when watching the all-too-familiar sight of people struggling to say something nice about her early works. People whose opinions she valued. Whose approval she longed for. I don't care, she'd said.

But she did. And she suspected Bean did too.

"Do you have a favorite?" Aunt Clara asked, side-stepping her own feelings.

"That one."

Bean pointed to the open door. Aunt Clara closed the door to reveal a painting there. It was, if such a thing was possible, more horrible than the rest. If the others were neolithic, this one was a large evolutionary step backward. Whoever painted this almost certainly had a tail, and knuckles that dragged on the ground. And through the paint.

If Peter had taught Bean the color wheel, he was a very, very bad teacher. This painting flaunted all the rules of art and most of the rules of common courtesy. It was a bad smell tacked to the wall.

"What do you like about it?" Myrna asked, her voice strained from keeping some strong emotion, or her dinner, inside.

"Those."

From the bed, Bean waved a finger toward the painting. Clara realized that with the door closed Bean would see this painting last thing at night and first thing in the morning.

What was so special about it?

She looked over at Myrna and saw her friend examining it. And smiling. Just a grin at first, that grew.

"Do you see it?" Myrna asked.

Clara looked more closely. And then something clicked. Those funny red squiggles were smiles. The painting was filled with them. Lips.

It didn't make the painting good. But it made it fun.

Clara looked back at Bean and saw a large smile on the earnest face.

"Clearly the artistic gene hasn't been passed to Bean," said Myrna as they sat in the cab back to the hotel.

"I'd give a lot of money for Peter to see what his lesson has produced," Clara said, and heard Myrna grunt with laughter beside her.

"What did you two get up to today?" Reine-Marie asked Annie and Jean-Guy as they ate dinner on the terrace in their back garden.

"Dominique and I took the horses through the woods," said Annie, helping herself to watermelon, mint, and feta salad.

"And you?" Armand asked Jean-Guy. "I know for sure you didn't go horseback riding."

"Horse?" said Beauvoir. "Horse? Dominique says they're horses but we all know there's at least one moose in there."

Reine-Marie laughed. None of Dominique's horses could be considered show-worthy. Abused and neglected and finally sent to the slaughter-house, Dominique had saved them.

They had that look in their eyes, as though they knew. How close they'd come.

As Henri sometimes looked, in his quiet moments. As Rosa looked. The same expression she sometimes caught in Jean-Guy's eyes.

And Armand's.

They knew. That they'd almost died. But they also knew that they'd been saved.

"Marc and I did some yard work," said Jean-Guy. "What did you get up to?"

Gamache and Reine-Marie described their afternoon, trying to figure out why Peter went to Dumfries.

"And why the 15th arrondissement in Paris," said Reine-Marie.

"Dad, what is it?" Annie asked.

Armand had gotten up and, excusing himself, he went into the house, returning a minute later with the map of Paris.

"Sorry," he said. "I just need to check something."

He spread the map out on the table.

"What're you looking for?" Jean-Guy joined him.

Gamache put on his reading glasses and hunched over the map before finally straightening up.

"When you went riding, did you stop in to see Marc's father?" Armand asked his daughter.

"Briefly, yes," said Annie. "We took him some groceries. Why?"

"He still doesn't have a phone, does he?"

"No, why?"

"Just wondering. He lived in Paris for a while," said Gamache.

"He spent quite a bit of time there, after Marc's mother kicked him out," said Annie.

"I need to speak to him." Armand turned to Jean-Guy. "Ready to saddle up?"

Beauvoir looked horrified. "Now? Tonight? On horses or whatever those are?"

"It's too dark now," Gamache said. "But first thing in the morning."

"Why?" asked Annie. "What can Vincent Gilbert possibly know about Peter's disappearance?"

"Maybe nothing, but I remember talking to him about his time in Paris. He showed me where he stayed."

Gamache placed his finger on the map.

The 15th arrondissement.

ELEVEN

—

The Toronto galleries were a bust. None remembered seeing Peter Morrow and all tried to convince Clara she should show at their space. The very same galleries that had rejected and mocked her work just a few years earlier were now trying to seduce her.

Clara didn't carry a grudge. They were far too heavy and she had too far to go. But she did notice, and she noticed something else. Her own ego, showing some ankle. Eating up the fawning words, the come-hither smiles of these late-to-the-party suitors.

"Has he been here?" Clara asked the owner at the last gallery on their list.

"Not that I remember," she said, and the receptionist confirmed there'd been no appointment with a Peter Morrow in the past twelve months.

"But he might've just dropped in," Clara persisted, and showed the owner an image of Peter's striking work.

"Oh, I know him," she said.

"He was here?" Clara asked.

"No, I mean I know his work. Now, let's talk about your paintings . . ."

And that was that. Clara was polite, but fled as quickly as she could, before she was seduced. But she took the owner's card. You never knew.

Their last stop before getting on the afternoon train was the art college, where Peter and Clara had met almost thirty years ago.

"The OCCA—" the secretary said.

"Obsessive-compulsive . . ." said Myrna.

"Ontario College of Canadian Arts," said the secretary.

He gave them a pamphlet and signed Clara Morrow up to the alumni list. He did not recognize her name, which Clara found both a relief and annoying.

"Peter Morrow?" That name he recognized. "He was here a few months back."

"So he spoke to you?" said Clara. "What did he want?"

She'd actually wanted to ask, "How did he look?" but stopped herself.

"Oh, just to get caught up. He wanted to know if any of the staff was still around from when he was here."

"Are they?"

"Well, one. Paul Massey."

"Professor Massey? You're kidding. He must be—"

"Eighty-three. Still teaching, still painting. Mr. Morrow was eager to see him."

"Professor Massey taught conceptual drawing," Clara explained to Myrna.

"Still does," said the secretary. " 'Translating the visual world onto canvas,' " he quoted by heart from the brochure.

"He was one of our favorite professors," said Clara. "Is he in now?"

"Might be. It's summer break, but the professor often comes in to his studio when it's quiet."

"Professor Massey was wonderful," Clara said as she hurried along the corridor. "A mentor for lots of the younger artists, including Peter."

"And you?"

"Oh, no. I was a lost cause," said Clara, laughing. "They didn't really know what to do with me."

They arrived at the studio and Myrna opened the door. The familiar scent of linseed, oil paints, and turpentine met them. As did the sight of an elderly man on a stool. His white hair was thinning and his face was pink. Despite his age he looked robust. A grain-fed, free-range artist. Not yet put out to pasture.

"Yes?" he said, getting off his chair.

"Professor Massey?"

His expression was quizzical but not alarmed or annoyed. He looked, Myrna thought, the sort of teacher who actually liked students.

"Yes?"

"I'm Clara Morrow. I understand my husband came by to see you—"

"Peter," said the professor, smiling and coming toward her, his hand extended. "Yes. How are you? I've been following your success. Very exciting."

He seemed to mean it, thought Myrna. He looked genuinely happy for Clara, and happy to see her.

"Did Peter tell you about it?" Clara asked.

"I read about it in the papers. You're our greatest success. The student has outstripped the master." Professor Massey studied the woman in front of him. "Probably because we were never really your masters, were we, Clara? Perhaps that was the key. You didn't follow us. You didn't follow anyone." He turned to Myrna and confided, "Not easy to have a pupil who was genuinely creative. Hard to grade, harder still to corral. To our shame, we tried."

He spoke with such humility, such awareness of his own limitations, that Myrna found herself drawn to him.

"I'm afraid I can't remember any of your works," he said.

"I'm not surprised," said Clara with a smile. "Though they were heavily featured in the college's Salon des Refusés."

"You were part of that?" Professor Massey shook his head sadly. "A terrible thing to do to vulnerable young people. Humiliating. I am sorry. We took care that that never happened again, you know. Peter and I talked about it too."

"Well, I survived," said Clara.

"And flourished. Come in, sit down." He walked across the studio without waiting for their answer and pointed toward a group of shabby chairs and a sofa whose middle sagged to the concrete floor. "Can I get you a drink?" He stepped toward an old refrigerator.

"You used to stock it with beer," said Clara, following him. "We'd have parties in your studio after class on Fridays."

"Yes. Can't do that anymore. New administration. New rules. Lemonade?"

He offered them a beer.

Clara laughed and accepted.

"Actually, I'd prefer a lemonade if you have one," said Myrna, who was parched after a morning trudging from gallery to gallery in sizzling Toronto.

Professor Massey handed her one, then turned back to Clara.

"What can I do for you?"

"Oh, much the same as for Peter," she said, sitting on the sofa. Her knees immediately sprang up to her shoulders and a whitecap of beer landed on her lap.

She should have been prepared for that, she realized. It was the same sofa they'd sat on as students, all those years ago.

Professor Massey offered Myrna a chair, but she preferred to wander the studio, looking at the works. She wondered if they were all painted by the professor. They seemed good, but then Myrna had bought one of Clara's *Warrior Uteruses*, so she was hardly a judge of art.

"Well," said the professor, taking a chair across from Clara, "Peter and I talked mostly about the other students and faculty. He asked about some of his favorite teachers. Many of them gone now. Dead. A few demented, like poor Professor Norman, though I can't say he was anyone's favorite teacher. I like to think it was the paint fumes, but I think we all know he came in demented, and working here might not have helped. I myself have escaped detection by having a mediocre career and always agreeing with the administration."

He laughed, then fell silent. There was a quality about the silence that made Myrna turn from the blank canvas on the easel to look at them.

"Why are you really here?" Professor Massey finally asked.

It was said softly, gently.

His blue eyes watched Clara and seemed to place a bubble around her. A shield. Where no harm would come to her. And Myrna understood why Professor Massey was a favorite teacher. And why he would be remembered for things far more important than "translating the visual world onto canvas."

"Peter's missing," said Clara.

—

Their progress through the woods reminded Jean-Guy of something. Some old image.

Gamache was ahead of him, on what they all suspected was not really a horse. For the past fifteen minutes, Beauvoir had ducked branches as they snapped back into his face, at about the same time Gamache called, "Watch out."

And when he wasn't being bitch-slapped by nature, all Beauvoir could see was Bullwinkle's ass swaying in front of him.

He was not yet having fun. Fortunately for Beauvoir, he hadn't expected to.

"Can you see it?" he called ahead for the tenth time in as many minutes.

"Just enjoy the scenery and relax," came the patient response. "We'll get there eventually."

"All I see is your horse's ass," said Jean-Guy, and when Gamache turned around with mock censure, he added, "sir."

Beauvoir rocked back and forth on his own horse and couldn't quite bring himself to admit he was beginning to enjoy himself. Though "enjoy" might be overstating it. He was finding the soft, rhythmic steps of the careful animal reassuring, calming. It reminded him of the rocking of monks as they prayed. Or a mother soothing a distressed child.

The forest was quiet, save for the clopping of the hooves and the birds as they got out of the way. The deeper they went, the more peaceful it became, the greener it became.

The heart chakra. A villager who ran a nearby yoga center once told him that.

"Green's the color of the heart chakra," she'd said, as though it was a fact.

He'd dismissed it then. And, for the record, for public consumption, he'd dismiss it now. But privately, in the deep green peace, he began to wonder.

Ahead he could see Gamache, swaying on his creature. A map of Paris sticking out of the saddlebag.

"Are we at the Louvre yet?" Jean-Guy asked.

"Be quiet, you silly man," said Gamache, no longer bothering to turn around. "You know damn well we passed it a while back. We're looking for la Tour Eiffel and beyond that, the 15th arrondissement."

"*Oui, oui, zut alors,*" said Beauvoir, giving an exaggerated French nasal laugh. Hor, hor.

Ahead of him he heard the Chief grunting in laughter.

"There it is." The Chief pointed, and in that moment Beauvoir knew exactly what this reminded him of. A drawing of Don Quixote he'd seen in a book.

Gamache was pointing toward a rude cabin in the woods, with a ruder man inside. Or it might have been a giant.

"Should we tilt at it?" Beauvoir asked, and heard the soft rumble of unmistakable laughter from the Chief.

"Come, Sancho," he said. "The world needs our immediate presence."

And Jean-Guy Beauvoir followed.

Professor Massey listened, not interrupting, not reacting. Simply nodding now and then as Clara told him about Peter. About his career, his art, their life together.

And finally there was nothing left to say.

The professor inhaled, a breath that seemed to go on forever. He held it for a moment, his eyes never leaving the woman in front of him. And then he exhaled.

"Peter's a lucky man," he said. "Except in one respect. He doesn't seem to know how lucky he is."

Myrna sat down then, on the stool by his easel. He was right. It was what she'd long known about Peter Morrow. In a life filled with great good fortune, of health, of creativity, of friends. Living in safety and privilege. With a loving partner. There was just one bit of misfortune in his life, and that was that Peter Morrow seemed to have no idea how very fortunate he was.

Professor Massey reached out and Clara put her large hands in his larger ones.

"I'm hopeful," he said. "You know why?"

Clara shook her head. Myrna shook her head. Mesmerized by the soft, sure voice.

"He married you. He could have chosen any of the bright, attractive, successful students here." Professor Massey turned to Myrna. "Peter was clearly a star. A deeply talented student. Art college isn't just about art, as it turns out. It's also about attitude. The place is full of scowling kids in black. Including Peter. The only exception was . . ."

He jerked his head dramatically toward Clara, who was blotting beer off her jeans.

"As I remember it, Peter did his share of dating," said Massey. "But in the end he was attracted not to the talented girls with attitude, but to the apparently talentless, marginal girl."

"I feel there's an insult in there," said Clara with a laugh. She also turned to Myrna. "You didn't know him then. He was spectacular. Tall with all this long, curly hair. Like a Greek sculpture come alive."

"So how'd you win him over?" Myrna asked. "Your feminine wiles?"

Clara laughed and fluffed her imaginary bouffant. "Yes, I was quite the vixen. He didn't stand a chance."

"No, really," said Myrna, getting up from the stool and wandering over. "How did you two get together?"

"I honestly have no idea," said Clara.

"I do," said Professor Massey. "Attitude is tiring after a while. And boring. Predictable. You were fresh, different."

"Happy," said Myrna.

She'd walked past the sitting area, and into the back of the studio, examining the canvases on the walls.

"Yours?" she asked, and Massey nodded.

They were good. Very good. And one, near the back, was exceptional. Professor Massey followed her with his eyes. No matter the age, thought Myrna, an artist is always slightly insecure.

"So we know what Peter found attractive in you," said Myrna. "What did you like about him? Beyond the physical. Or was that it?"

"At first, for sure," said Clara, thinking. "I remember now." She laughed. "It sounds so small, but it was huge back then. When my work was displayed in the Salon des Refusés, instead of treating me like a leper, Peter actually came and stood beside me." She ran her hands through her hair, so that it stood almost straight out from her head. "I was an outcast, a joke. The weird kid who did all these crazy installations. And not crazy in a Van Gogh, artistic, cool way. My stuff was considered superficial. Silly. And so was I."

"It must've been upsetting," said Myrna.

"It was, a little. But you know, I was still happy. I was at the OCCA, doing art. In Toronto. It was exciting."

"But you were upset about the Salon des Refusés," said Professor Massey.

Clara nodded. "That was a professor doing it. It was humiliating. I remember staring at my work, front and center in the gallery reserved for failures. Where Professor Norman had put it. Peter came over, and he stood beside me. He didn't say anything, he just stood there. For all to see."

She smiled at the memory.

"Things changed after that. I wasn't exactly accepted, but neither was I mocked. Not so much, anyway."

Myrna had no idea Peter had done that. He'd always seemed slightly superficial to her. Handsome, physically strong. And he knew the right things to say, to appear thoughtful. But there was a weakness about the man.

"Can I give you some advice?" Professor Massey asked.

Clara nodded.

"Go home. Not to wait for him, but go home and get on with your life and your art. And trust that he'll meet you there, when he's found what he's looking for."

"But what's he looking for? Did he tell you?" Clara asked.

Professor Massey shook his head. "I'm sorry."

"Why Dumfries?" asked Myrna.

The two artists turned to her.

"I can understand Paris and the other places," she continued. "But why a small town in Scotland? He'd just returned from there when he came to see you. Did he tell you about his trip?"

Again the professor shook his head.

"We talked about his time here, at the college," he said.

"Is there anything that connects all those places he visited?" Clara asked.

"Not that I know of," said the professor, looking perplexed. "As you say, Paris and Florence and Venice make sense for an artist. But then a small town in Scotland? Did he have family there?"

"No," said Clara. "Then from here he went to Quebec City. Do you know why?"

"I'm sorry," said the professor, and looked terribly sad. Myrna began to feel they were harassing the elderly man, haranguing him for answers he so clearly didn't have.

She walked over. "I think we should be going. We have to catch the train back to Montréal."

At the door, Professor Massey shook Myrna's hand.

"We should all have a friend like you."

Then he turned to Clara. "This should be the happiest time of your life. A time of celebration. Makes it all the more painful. It reminds me of Francis Bacon and his triptych."

Then he brightened. "I'm an idiot. I just heard that one of our professors had to drop out because of illness. He taught painting and composition to first-year students. You'd be perfect for it. I know you should be teaching a much more advanced class"—he held up his hand as though to ward off Clara's objections—"but believe me, by the time they get to third year they're insufferable. But the new students? That's exciting. And they'd adore you. Interested?"

Clara had a sudden image of standing in a large studio, like this. Her own studio at the college. Her own sofa, her own fridge stocked with contraband beer. Guiding eager young men and women. Emerging artists.

She'd make sure that what was done to her wasn't done to them. She'd encourage them. Defend them. No Salon des Refusés for them. No mocking, no marginalizing. No pretending to encourage creativity, when all the college really wanted was conformity.

They'd come to her studio on Fridays and drink beer and talk nonsense. They'd throw around ideas, philosophies, predictions, bold and half-baked plans. It would be her own salon. A Salon des Acceptés.

And she would be the gleaming center. The world-renowned artist, nurturing them.

She would have arrived.

"Think about it," Professor Massey said.

"I will," said Clara. "Thank you."

Dr. Vincent Gilbert lived in the heart of the forest. Away from human conflict, but also away from human contact. It was a compromise he was more than happy to make. As was the rest of humanity.

Gamache and Gilbert had met many times over the years and, against all odds, isolation and a life dedicated just to himself had not improved Dr. Gilbert's people skills.

"What do you want?" Gilbert asked, looking out from under a straw hat he might have stolen from Beauvoir's horse on an earlier visit.

He was in the vegetable garden and looked, to Gamache, more and more like a biblical prophet, or a madman. Gilbert wore a once white, now gray, nightshirt down to mid-calf, and plastic sandals he could hose off. Which was a good thing, because he was up to his ankles in compost.

"Can't a neighbor come to visit?" asked Gamache, after securing his mount to a tree.

"What do you want?" Dr. Gilbert repeated, straightening up and walking toward them.

"Drop the act, Vincent," said Gamache with a laugh. "I know you're happy to see me."

"Did you bring me anything?"

Gamache gestured toward Beauvoir, whose eyes widened.

"You know I'm a vegetarian," said Gilbert. "Anything else?"

Gamache reached into his saddlebags and pulled out a brown paper bag and the map.

"Welcome, stranger," said Gilbert. He grabbed the paper bag, opened it, and inhaled the aroma of the croissants.

Tossing one precious pastry into the woods, without explanation, he took the rest into his log cabin, followed by Gamache and Beauvoir.

The train lurched forward but was soon traveling swiftly and smoothly toward Montréal.

"What was that about Francis Bacon?" Myrna asked. The steward had taken their lunch order. "I'm presuming he meant the twentieth-century painter and not the sixteenth-century philosopher."

Clara nodded but said nothing.

"What did Professor Massey mean?" Myrna pressed. It had clearly meant something.

Clara looked out the window, at the rear end of Toronto. For a moment Myrna wondered if she'd heard the question. But then Clara spoke. To the overflowing garbage bins. To the washing on the line. To the graffiti. Not actual art, but the artist's name over and over. Declaring himself. Spray-painted in huge, bold, black letters. Over and over.

"Bacon often painted in threes." Clara's words created a fine fog on the window. "Triptychs. I think the one Professor Massey had in mind was George Dyer."

That meant nothing to Myrna, but it clearly meant a great deal to Clara.

"Go on."

"I think Professor Massey was trying to warn me." Clara turned away from the window and looked at her friend.

"Tell me," said Myrna, though it was clear Clara would have rather done just about anything else than put these thoughts into words.

"George Dyer and Bacon were lovers," said Clara. "They went to Paris for a huge show of Bacon's paintings. It was the first great triumph of his career. While Bacon was being celebrated—"

Clara stopped, and Myrna felt the blood rush from her own face.

"Tell me," she repeated softly.

"Dyer killed himself in their hotel room."

The words were barely audible. But Myrna heard them. And Clara heard them. Put out into the world.

The women stared at each other.

"It's what you were trying to warn me about," Clara said, her voice still barely above a whisper. "When you told me about Samarra."

Myrna couldn't answer. She couldn't bear to add to the dread in Clara's face. In her whole body.

"You think Peter has done the same thing," said Clara.

But still Clara's eyes pleaded with Myrna. To tell her she was wrong.

To reassure her that Peter was just off painting. He'd lost track of the time. The date.

Myrna said nothing. It might have been kindness. Or cowardice. But Myrna remained silent, and allowed Clara her delusion.

That Peter would come home. Might even be waiting for them, when they got back. With beer. A couple of steaks. An explanation. And profuse apologies.

Myrna looked out the window. The tenements were still whizzing by, apparently endless. But the graffiti artist's name had disappeared.

A fine hotel room in Paris, she thought. Samarra. Or some corner of Québec. However he got there, Myrna was afraid Peter Morrow had reached the end of the road. And there he'd met Death.

And she knew that Clara feared the same thing.

Vincent Gilbert's log cabin hadn't changed much since the last time Beauvoir had visited. It was still a single room, with a large bed at one end, and a kitchen at the other. The rough pine floor was strewn with fine Oriental carpets, and on either side of the fieldstone fireplace were shelves crammed with books. Two comfortable armchairs with footstools sat facing each other across the hearth.

Before Vincent Gilbert had moved in, this rustic cabin had been the scene of a terrible crime. A murder so unnatural it had shocked the nation. Some places held on to such malevolence, as though the pain and shock and horror had fused to the structure.

But this little home had always felt strangely innocent. And very peaceful.

Dr. Gilbert poured them glasses of spring water and made sandwiches with tomatoes still warm from his garden.

Gamache spread the map of Paris on the table, smoothing it with his large hand.

"So, what do you want, Armand?" Dr. Gilbert asked for the third time.

"When you went to Paris, after you left your wife, where did you go?"

"I've told you that before. Weren't you paying attention?"

"I was, *mon ami*," said Gamache soothingly. "But I'd like to see again."

Gilbert's eyes filled with suspicion. "Don't waste my time, Armand. I have better things to do than repeat myself. There's manure to spread."

Some considered Vincent Gilbert a saint. Some, like Beauvoir, considered him an asshole. The residents of Three Pines had compromised and called him the "asshole saint."

"But that doesn't mean he isn't still a saint," Gamache had said. "Most saints were assholes. In fact, if he wasn't one that would disqualify him completely."

The Chief had walked away with a smile, knowing he'd completely messed with Beauvoir's mind.

"Asshole," Beauvoir had hissed.

"I heard that," said Gamache, not turning back.

And now Jean-Guy looked at the two men. Gilbert elderly, imperious, thin and weathered, with sharp eyes and a temperament quick to take offense. And Gamache, twenty years younger, larger, calmer.

Jean-Guy Beauvoir had seen great kindness in Gilbert, and ruthlessness in Gamache. Neither man, Beauvoir was pretty sure, was a saint.

"Show me on the map exactly where you stayed in Paris," said Gamache, paying absolutely no attention to Gilbert's little tantrum.

"Fine," the doctor huffed. "It was here." His fingernail, black-rimmed with earth, fell on the map.

They bent over to examine the spot, like scientists over a litmus test. Then Gamache straightened up.

"Did you ever talk about your time in Paris with Peter Morrow?" he asked.

"Not specifically, no," said Gilbert. "But he might've heard me talking about it. Why?"

"Because he's missing."

"I thought Clara sent him away."

"She did, but they made a date to meet up exactly a year later. That was a few weeks ago. He never showed."

Vincent Gilbert was obviously surprised.

"He loved Clara. I miss a lot in life," said Gilbert. "But I have a nose for love."

"Like a truffle pig," said Beauvoir, then regretted it when he saw the asshole saint's reaction.

Then, unexpectedly, Gilbert smiled. "Exactly. I can smell it. Love has an aroma all its own, you know."

Beauvoir looked at Gilbert, amazed by what he'd just heard.

Maybe, he thought, *this man was—*

"Smells like compost," said Gilbert.

—an asshole after all.

TWELVE

Armand Gamache swayed on his horse/moose and thought about their visit to Vincent Gilbert. And Paris.

His Paris. Gilbert's Paris. Peter's Paris. And as he thought, the cool forest receded and the gnarled old tree trunks metamorphosed. They shifted and reformed until they were no longer impenetrable woods but a grand Parisian boulevard. Gamache was riding down the middle of a wide street, lined with magnificent buildings. Some Haussmann, some art nouveau, some beaux arts. He rode past parks and small cafés and great monuments.

He turned his horse/moose down boulevard du Montparnasse. Past the red awnings, past Parisians reading at round marble-topped tables. Past La Coupole, La Rotonde, Le Select—cafés where Hemingway and Man Ray lived and drank. Where centuries of writers and artists debated and inspired each other. And some never left. Off to his left Gamache could just see the Cimetière du Montparnasse, where Baudelaire lay and Sartre and Simone de Beauvoir would spend eternity under a single slab, in the company of *The Kiss*, the glorious sculpture by Brancusi.

And in the near distance, beyond the cemetery, the hideous Tour Montparnasse rose as a kind of warning against the modern belief that it was possible to improve on perfection.

Gamache and Beauvoir clopped past the past. Beyond the long-dead artists and writers. Beyond Montparnasse. To the neighborhood Peter Morrow had chosen to stay. So close to such an explosion of creativity.

But a world away.

They turned onto rue de Vaugirard. And the charm slowly, slowly dissipated. The City of Light faded and became just another city. At times lovely. Lively. But not the Paris of Manet and Picasso and Rodin.

Finally they arrived at their destination.

Gamache pulled softly on the reins and felt a slight shudder as Beauvoir's horse head-butted his mount.

Both Beauvoir and his horse had fallen into a stupor. But now they woke up.

"Why did we stop?" Beauvoir and his horse looked around.

Gamache was staring at a tree as though expecting the trunk to swing open and admit them.

Oomph. Clara landed in one of the Adirondack chairs in her garden and slid to the back, until she hit the pillow. On one wide armrest was the gin and tonic she'd been dreaming of since getting in Myrna's sweltering car for the drive home from Montréal. On the other armrest was a bowl of chips.

She was happy to be home.

"You first," she said, feeling her body relax into the pillow.

Reine-Marie, Armand, Jean-Guy, and Myrna were in her back garden, exchanging information.

"I think I know where Peter went when he left here," said Gamache.

"We already know," said Clara. She gestured toward the map Gamache was spreading on the table. "Paris."

"Yes. Paris, Florence, Venice," said the Chief, looking at Clara over his reading glasses. "It all seemed to make sense, except for one obvious question."

"Dumfries," said Reine-Marie.

Her husband nodded. "Why go to Dumfries? I got distracted by that big question, by the forest, and failed to look more closely at one very odd tree. A detail."

"Why go all the way to Paris and stay in the 15th arrondissement?" asked Clara, sitting up in her chair again.

"*Oui*. Exactly." His deep brown eyes glowed. It was unmistakable.

Not that he was enjoying this, but that he was good at it. He was like a miner, carrying a torch. Illuminating dark passages. Digging deep, often dangerously deep. To get at what was buried there.

Reine-Marie recognized that gleam. And heard, again, the beating of the moth's wings.

It was all she could do not to stand up. To look at her watch. To suggest to Armand that they had to go. Had to leave. Had to get back to their cheerful home. Where they belonged. Where they could garden, and read, sip lemonade and play bridge. And if they died, it would be in bed.

Reine-Marie shifted in her seat and cleared her throat.

Armand looked at her.

"Go on," she said. He held her gaze and when she smiled, he nodded and turned back to Clara.

"Why the 15th?" he said. "This afternoon Vincent Gilbert gave us the answer."

"You visited the asshole saint?" asked Myrna. It was said without rancor or judgment. They'd gotten so used to calling him that they'd almost forgotten his real name and occupation. Even Vincent Gilbert answered to that name, though he occasionally corrected them by saying, "It's Dr. Asshole Saint to you."

He'd begun as a successful and celebrated physician. He'd ended up a recluse in a one-room log cabin. A lot had happened in between, but it all began with a visit to Paris's 15th arrondissement.

"I think Gilbert and Peter were drawn to the same place," said Gamache. "Here."

He pointed to the dirty fingerprint on the map. It sat over the spot like a cloud.

They all leaned in, except Jean-Guy.

He knew what Gamache was pointing at.

LaPorte. The Door.

As the others moved toward the map, Jean-Guy sat in the garden and closed his eyes and breathed in the fresh evening air. And missed Annie. She'd returned to her job in Montréal that morning. He'd been prepared to return with her, but as they lay in bed, Annie had suggested he stay.

"Find Peter," she'd said. "You want to, and Dad needs your help."

"I don't think he does."

She'd smiled, and traced his arm, from shoulder to elbow, with her finger.

For most of his adult life, Jean-Guy Beauvoir had dated bodies. He'd married Enid for her breasts, her legs, her delicate face. Her ability to make his friends weak at the knees.

But when his own body had been battered and bruised and the life almost taken from it, only then did Jean-Guy discover how very attractive a heart and mind could be.

A coy smile could capture him, but it was finally a hearty laugh that had freed him.

No knees would buckle for Annie Gamache. No eyes would follow her substantial body. No wolf calls for her pretty plain face. But she was by far the most attractive woman in any room.

Late into his thirties, with a broken body and a shattered spirit, Jean-Guy Beauvoir had been seduced by happiness.

"I want to go back with you," he said, and meant.

"And I want you to," she said, and meant. "But someone needs to find Peter Morrow, and you owe Clara. Dad owes her. You need to help."

That was why she was happy. He now knew that happiness and kindness went together. There was not one without the other. For Jean-Guy it was a struggle. For Annie it seemed natural.

They curled toward each other and he held her fingers, intertwined in his, in the space between their naked bodies.

"You're on partial leave," said Annie. "Will Isabelle agree?"

Beauvoir was still unused to asking a Sûreté agent who was once his subordinate for permission. But he called Chief Inspector Lacoste first thing in the morning and she'd agreed. He could stay and help find Peter Morrow.

Isabelle Lacoste also owed Clara.

Annie had left. And now, at the edge of the day, Jean-Guy Beauvoir sat in the garden listening to the conversation and allowed himself a moment to drift from his head to his heart. He unconsciously held out his right hand, palm up, as though waiting for Annie's hand.

"LaPorte?" asked Clara, straightening up after bending close to the map. "The Door? The place Frère Albert created?"

"*Oui*," said Gamache. "I might be wrong, but that's what I think."

Like most people who admitted the possibility of being wrong, they knew he knew he probably wasn't. But Clara was far from convinced. And Myrna didn't seem any closer.

"Why would Peter go to LaPorte?" Myrna asked, sitting back down. She was disappointed. It was hardly a breakthrough.

"Why did Vincent Gilbert?" asked Jean-Guy, joining the conversation.

Myrna thought about that. "He'd had a successful career," she said, remembering her conversations with the asshole saint. "But then his marriage fell apart."

Gamache nodded. "Go on."

Myrna thought some more.

"It wasn't just the end of his marriage that did it," she said, thinking out loud. "Lots of people get separated or divorced without having to hare off to a commune in France."

Myrna lapsed into silence and thought about the missing piece. What would prompt a successful middle-aged man to give up his career and live in a community created by a humble priest, to serve children and adults with Down's syndrome?

That was LaPorte's vocation. It was to open a door for these people, after so many doors had been shut in their unusual faces. Frère Albert's LaPorte offered not simply, though crucially, a place to live, but mostly it offered dignity. Equality. Belonging.

Frère Albert's brilliance was in knowing that a community created to help others would never thrive. But one created for equal benefit would. He knew he too was flawed. Perhaps not in ways as obvious as someone with Down's syndrome. But in ways more subtle, yet equally challenging.

The great genius of LaPorte was the absolute knowledge that everyone there had something to learn from, something to give to, the other. There was no distinction between the Down's syndrome member and anyone else.

"Dr. Gilbert went there to volunteer as the community's medical director," said Myrna. "Not because he could heal them, but because he needed to be healed."

"Exactly," said Gamache. "We all need to be healed at some time in our lives. We've all been deeply hurt. His hurt was, I think, the same as Peter's. Not physical, but spiritual. They both had a hole. A tear."

This was met with silence.

Everyone around that table knew how that felt. The horror of realizing all the toys, all the success, all the powerful boards and new cars and accolades hadn't filled the hole. They'd actually made it bigger. Deeper.

There was nothing wrong with success, but it had to have meaning.

"Vincent Gilbert knocked on LaPorte hoping to find himself," said Gamache.

"And you think Peter did too?" asked Clara.

"Do you?" he asked her.

"*I'll pray that you grow up a brave man in a brave country,*" Clara said.

"*I will pray you find a way to be useful,*" Gamache completed the quote.

Reine-Marie dropped her eyes to her hands and saw the paper napkin twisted and shredded there.

Clara nodded slowly. "I think you might be right. Peter went to Paris not to find a new artistic voice. It was simpler than that. He wanted to find a way to be useful."

The sun was going down and the birds and crickets and scrambling creatures grew quiet. The scent of roses and sweet peas drifted toward them on the heavy evening air.

"Then why didn't he stay?" Clara asked.

"Maybe the hole was too big," said Myrna.

"Maybe his courage failed," said Reine-Marie.

"Maybe while LaPorte was Dr. Gilbert's answer, it wasn't Peter's," said Jean-Guy. "His was somewhere else."

Gamache nodded. He had a call in to the Sûreté in Paris, asking them to visit LaPorte with Peter Morrow's picture and the dates. To confirm what they suspected. Peter had been there.

And Peter had left there.

THIRTEEN

―――

"Anyone else hungry?" Myrna asked. "Who has the time?"

She couldn't read her watch in the dark. The sun had set as they'd listened to Armand. So absorbed were they that they hadn't noticed the darkness. Or their hunger. But now they did.

"Almost ten," said Beauvoir, whose watch illuminated. "Will Olivier and Gabri still be serving?"

By now they were making their way out of Clara's back garden, toward the bistro. It was a pleasant evening and they could see late diners lingering over dessert and coffee on the *terrasse*.

"Quid pro quo," said Clara. "We'll feed them information and they'll feed us food."

Quid pro quo was a specialty of Olivier's Bistro.

They took a table inside, tucked into a corner. Far from the other diners. Gabri and Olivier were able to join them, happy to be off their feet.

Ruth joined them, limping in with Rosa from the bookstore.

"Can I close it now?" she demanded.

Myrna turned her head and whispered to Clara, "Jesus, I'd forgotten about her."

"Who knew she'd even open the bookstore," said Clara under her breath, "never mind not burn it down."

"We just got back," Myrna looked Ruth in the eye and lied. "Thank you for looking after the store."

"Rosa did most of the business."

" 'The' business or 'her' business?" Gabri asked.

Myrna and Clara exchanged worried glances. It was a good question and an important distinction.

"A few people came in," said Ruth, ignoring the question. "Bought books and guides to Paris. I quadrupled the price. What's for dinner?"

She picked up Jean-Guy's drink out of habit, then realizing it was just a Coke she quickly snatched up Myrna's Scotch just before Myrna got to it.

"It's good to have you back," Ruth said.

"Are you talking to me or the drink?" Myrna asked, and once again Ruth looked at her as though for the first time.

"The drink, of course."

They ordered dinner, then Gamache looked at Clara.

"Your turn."

And so, as they shared an assortment of starters, Clara told them about their meeting with Thomas Morrow and dinner with Marianna and Bean.

"Is Bean a boy or a girl?" Jean-Guy asked. "It must be obvious by now."

He'd met the Morrow family a few years earlier and had been struck, once again, by how crazy the English had become. Insular and inbred, he suspected. He decided he should count their fingers from now on. He looked at Ruth and wondered how many toes she had. Then he wondered if cloven hooves even had toes.

"Still can't tell," admitted Clara. "But Bean seems happy, though clearly the artistic gene didn't pass to him. Or her."

"Why d'you say that?" Gabri asked, dipping char-grilled calamari into a delicate garlic aioli.

"Peter taught Bean the color wheel. Bean did a few paintings and put them up on the bedroom walls. They were pretty awful."

"Most masterpieces are, at first," said Ruth. "Yours look like a dog's breakfast. That's a compliment."

Clara laughed. Ruth was right, on both counts. It was a compliment. And her paintings started off a real mess. The worse her paintings looked at first, the better they seemed to turn out.

"You too?" she asked Ruth. "How do your poems start out?"

"They start as a lump in the throat," she said.

"Isn't that normally just a cocktail olive lodged there?" Olivier asked.

"Once," Ruth admitted. "Wrote quite a good poem before I coughed it up."

"A poem begins as a lump in the throat?" Gamache asked Ruth. The elderly woman held his eyes for a moment before dropping them to her drink.

Clara was quiet, thinking. She finally nodded.

"For me too. The first go-round is all emotion just shot onto the canvas. Like a cannon."

"Peter's paintings look perfect right from the start," said Olivier. "They never have to be rescued."

"Rescued?" Gamache asked. "What do you mean by that?"

"It's something Peter told me," said Olivier. "He was proud that he never had to rescue a canvas because he'd screwed it up."

"And 'rescuing' a painting means fixing it?" Gamache asked.

"It's an artist's expression," said Clara. "Kinda technical. If you put too many layers of paint on a canvas, the pores get all clogged and the paint doesn't hold. It gets all gloppy, the paint starts to slip off. The painting's ruined. Mostly happens when you overwork it. Like cooking something too long. You can't then uncook it."

"So it's not the subject of the painting that's wrong," said Myrna. "It's just a physical thing. The canvas gets saturated."

"Right, though the two mostly go together. You almost never over-work a canvas you're happy with. It happens when you're in trouble. Trying to save it. Going over and over it, trying to capture something that's really difficult. Turning a dog's breakfast into something mean-ingful. That's when the canvas can get clogged."

"But it's sometimes possible to rescue it?" asked Reine-Marie.

"Sometimes. I've had to do it. Most of the time they're too far gone. It's really awful, because the canvas gives up just as I'm really close. Al-most got it. Sometimes when I've just gotten it, put the last dab on. Then suddenly the paint shifts, starts to slip. Won't hold and everything's lost. Heartbreaking. It's like you're writing a book and you edit and edit, and you finally get it, and just as you write 'The End' all the words disappear."

"Oh shit," said Myrna and Ruth together, while on Jean-Guy's lap Rosa muttered, "Fuck, fuck, fuck."

"But sometimes you can pull the painting back?" asked Reine-Marie. "You can save it?"

Clara looked over at Ruth, who was picking a piece of asparagus out of her teeth.

"I had to save her," she said.

"You're kidding," said Gabri. "You had a choice, and you saved her?"

"I mean the painting," said Clara. "The one I did of Ruth."

"The little one?" asked Reine-Marie. "The one that got all that attention?"

Clara nodded. If the huge painting *The Three Graces* was a shout, then the tiny one of Ruth was a quiet beckon. Easily missed and easily dismissed.

Most people walked right past the small canvas. Many who paused were repulsed by the expression on the old woman's face. Rage radiated from the frame where the old woman glared, bitter, seething at a world that was ignoring her. All the gabbing, chatting, laughing people in the gallery walked right past, leaving her alone on the wall.

Her thin, veined hand clutched at the ragged blue shawl at her neck. She despised them.

But for the very few who did linger, they saw more than rage. They saw an ache. A plea. For someone to stop. To keep her company, if only for a few moments.

And those who heeded that plea were rewarded. They saw this wasn't just some embittered old woman.

Clara had painted the poet as Mary. The mother of God. Elderly. Alone. All miracles faded and forgotten.

And those who stood before her a very long time, who kept her company, were rewarded further. The final offering. The last miracle.

Only they saw what Clara had really painted.

Only they saw the rescue.

There, in her eyes, was a dot. A gleam. The elderly woman was just beginning to see something. There, in the distance. Beyond the giddy cocktail crowd.

Hope.

Clara had captured, with a single dot, the moment despair turned to hope.

It was luminous.

"You saved it?" asked Reine-Marie.

"I think it was mutual," said Clara, and looked at Ruth, who was now taking a bit of bread from Jean-Guy's plate and feeding it to Rosa. "That painting made my career."

No one said it, but all were thinking that had Clara painted Peter in that instant she might have captured the moment hope turned to despair.

Clara told them about their visits just that morning to the prominent art galleries in Toronto. No one had remembered seeing Peter.

Armand Gamache watched her closely as she spoke. Taking everything in. Her words, her tone, her subtle movements.

Just as Clara put together the elements of a painting, as Ruth the elements of a poem, Gamache pieced together the elements of a case.

And like a painting or a poem, at the heart of his cases there was a strong emotion.

"So no luck?" asked Olivier. "No trace of Peter?"

"Actually, we did finally manage to find someone who not only saw him, but spent time with him," said Clara. And she told them about their visit to the art college.

"Why would he go back to your old college?" asked Gabri. "Has he done it before?"

"No, neither Peter nor I ever went back," said Clara.

"Then why do you think he went back this past winter?" asked Gamache, ignoring his grilled shrimp with mango salsa. "What did he want?"

"I don't really know what Peter wanted. Do you?" she asked Myrna.

"I think he wanted to recapture the feelings he had when he was there as a student," said Myrna slowly. "Professor Massey said they talked a lot about Peter's time there. The students, the professors. I suspect he wanted to be reminded of when he was young, vigorous, admired. When the world was his."

"Nostalgia," said Gabri.

Myrna nodded. "And maybe something slightly more than that. He might have wanted to recapture some magic."

Clara smiled. "I don't think Peter was into magic."

"No, he wouldn't have called it that," Myrna agreed. "But it would come to the same thing. Art college was a magical time for him, so in his distress he was drawn back to the place where good things happened. In case he could find it again."

"He wanted to be rescued," said Ruth.

She'd moved Gamache's dinner in front of her and was finishing off the last grilled shrimp.

"Too many layers of life," she continued. "His world was slipping away. He wanted to be rescued."

"And he went to the college for that?" asked Olivier.

"He went to Professor Massey for that," said Myrna, nodding. Only slightly annoyed that demented Ruth should see what had eluded her. "To be reassured he was still vigorous, talented. A star."

Reine-Marie looked around the quiet bistro. Out the mullioned windows to the now-empty tables on the *terrasse*. To the ring of homes, with soft light in the darkness.

Rescued.

She caught Armand's eye and saw again that look. Of someone saved.

For his part, Gamache took a piece of baguette and chewed it as he thought.

What did Peter want? He surely wanted something, and was quite desperate for it, to travel so far and so fast. Paris, Florence, Venice, Scotland. Toronto. Quebec City.

His journey had the smell of desperation, of both the hunt and the hunted. A one-man game of hide and seek.

"Your professor mentioned a Salon des Refusés," he said. "What was that?"

"Actually, I mentioned it," said Clara. "I don't think Professor Massey was all that happy to be reminded of it."

"Why not?" asked Jean-Guy.

"Not the college's finest moment," said Clara with a laugh. "There is an annual end-of-year show. It's juried, judged by the professors and prominent art dealers in Toronto. Only the best get in. One of the professors thought this was unfair, so he set up a parallel show."

"The Salon des Refusés," said Olivier.

Clara nodded. "A show for the rejected. It was modeled on a famous exhibition in Paris back in 1863, when a Manet painting was refused entry in the official Paris Salon. A Salon des Refusés was set up, and the rejected artists showed there. And not just Manet, but Whistler's *Symphony in White* ended up in the Salon des Refusés." She shook her head. "One of the great works of art."

"You know a lot about it, *ma belle*," said Gabri.

"I should. My works were front and center in the college's Salon des Refusés. First I knew that they'd been rejected by the jury. There they were, in the parallel exhibition."

"And Peter's?" asked Gamache.

"Front and center in the legitimate show," said Clara. "He'd done some spectacular paintings. My works were not exactly spectacular, I guess. I was experimenting."

"Not yet rescued?" said Gabri.

"Beyond saving."

"Avant-garde," said Ruth. "Isn't that the term? Ahead of your time. The rest just needed to catch up. You didn't need rescuing. You weren't lost. You were exploring. There's a difference."

Clara looked at Ruth's rheumy, tired eyes. "Thank you. But still, it was humiliating. They fired the professor who set it up. He had strange ideas about art. Didn't fit in. An odd duck." She turned to Rosa. "Sorry."

"What'd she say?" asked Ruth.

"She said you're an old fuck," said Gabri loudly.

Ruth gave a low, rumbling laugh. "She isn't wrong there." She turned to Clara and Clara leaned away from her. "But you're wrong about the Salon. That's where real artists want to be. With the rejects. You shouldn't have been upset."

"Tell that to my twenty-year-old self."

"What would you rather be?" Ruth asked. "Successful in your twenties and forgotten in your fifties? Or the other way around?"

Like Peter, everyone thought. Including Clara.

"As we were leaving, Professor Massey mentioned Francis Bacon," said Clara.

"The writer?" asked Reine-Marie.

"The painter," Clara clarified. She explained the reference.

"Seems a cruel thing to say," said Olivier.

"I don't think he meant it that way," said Clara. "Do you?"

Myrna shook her head. "He seems to care about Peter. I think he just wanted to prepare Clara . . ."

"For what, that Peter killed himself?" Ruth asked with a guffaw, then she looked around. "You don't all think that, do you? That's ridiculous. He has too high an opinion of himself. Loves himself too much. No, Peter might kill someone else, but never himself. In fact, I take that back. He's much more likely to be the victim than the killer."

"Ruth!" said Olivier.

"What? You all think it too. Who here hasn't wanted to kill him, at least once? And we're his friends."

They protested perhaps a shade too passionately. Each outraged defense fueled by the memory of how good it would have felt to hit Peter with a frying pan. He could be so smug, so self-satisfied, so entitled, and yet so oblivious.

But he could also be loyal, and funny, and generous. And kind.

Which made his absence and silence so disconcerting.

"Look," said Ruth. "It's natural. I want to kill most of you most of the time."

"You want to kill us?" asked Gabri, barely able to breathe for the unfairness of it. "You? Us?"

"Do you think he's alive?" asked Clara, not able to word the question the other way.

Ruth stared at her, and they held their breaths.

"I think if I can win the Governor General's award for poetry, and you can become a world-famous painter, and these two bumbling idiots can make a success of a bistro, and you"—her gesture took in Reine-Marie—"can love this lump of a man"—she turned to Gamache—"then miracles can happen."

"But you think it would be a miracle?" asked Clara.

"I think you should leave well enough alone, child," said Ruth quietly. "I've given you the best answer I can."

They all knew the worst answer. And they all knew the most likely answer. That perhaps Three Pines had had more than its share of miracles.

Armand Gamache looked down at his plate. Empty. All the wonderful food gone. He was sure it must have been delicious, but he couldn't remember eating a single bite.

After a dessert of raspberry and chocolate mousse they went home. Myrna up to her loft above the bookstore. Clara to her cottage. Gabri and Olivier checked that all was in order in the kitchen, then headed to their B and B. Beauvoir walked Ruth and Rosa home and then returned to the Gamaches' house. They'd left the porch light on for him, and a light in the living room. But the rest of the home was dark and silent and peaceful.

After calling Annie, Jean-Guy lay in the darkness and thought about being rescued. While upstairs, Reine-Marie lay in the dark and thought about their peaceful life slipping away.

FOURTEEN

—

Clara took her morning toast and coffee into Peter's studio. Crumbs fell to the concrete floor as she ate her breakfast while sitting on the stool in front of his unfinished painting.

She knew Peter would have howled, as though the crumbs were acid and the floor his skin.

Clara was perhaps not as careful as she should have been. As she could have been. Perhaps it was a mostly unconscious desire to wound Peter in his most private of parts. To hurt him, as he was hurting her. This was the only private part she still had access to. Peter should really have considered himself lucky.

Or maybe her messiness meant nothing. Though, as a blob of strawberry jam hit the floor, she doubted it.

Outside it was cloudy, muggy. Rain threatened, and would likely pour down before lunch. Even with its windows looking onto the Rivière Bella Bella, the studio was close and gloomy.

But she sat there, taking in the canvas on the easel. It was very Peter. Very detailed, precise, controlled. Technically brilliant. It made the best of all the rules.

This was no dog's breakfast.

Unlike Bean's creations. With a smile Clara remembered the wild splashes of conflicting, of contrasting, of clashing colors. Vivid colors from a vivid, unrestrained imagination.

The last bite of toast stopped partway to her mouth. Another glob of jam slid closer and closer to the crumbly edge and the great leap down-ward.

But Clara didn't notice. She was staring, openmouthed, at Peter's painting.

And then the jam dropped.

Myrna Landers stood at the window of her loft, looking between the panes. The glass was so old it had imperfections, distortions, but she'd gotten used to seeing the world that way, and made allowances.

This morning she stood in her pajamas with a mug of coffee and watched the village wake up. It was a common sight. Unremarkable. Except to someone coming from a certain chaos and turmoil. Then it was remarkable.

She watched her neighbors walk their dogs on the village green. She watched them chatting, exchanging pleasantries.

Then her gaze traveled up the dirt road out of Three Pines and stopped at the boundary, at the bench overlooking the village. There she saw Armand sitting, as he did every morning, holding the book in his hands. Even from this distance, she could see it was a very small book. Every morning he sat there with it, and read. Then closed it, and just stared.

Myrna Landers wondered what he was reading. She wondered what he was thinking.

He came to her once a week for therapy, but had never once men-tioned this book. And she hadn't asked, preferring him to offer. And he would. When the time was right.

Still, there was plenty to talk about. The injuries of the past. The ones seen and unseen. The bruises on his mind and body and soul. They were healing, slowly. But the wounds that seemed to hurt him the most weren't even his own.

"Jean-Guy's life isn't your responsibility, Armand," she'd said. Over and over. And he'd leave, nodding and thanking her. And under-standing.

And then the next session, Armand would admit the fear was back.

"Suppose he drinks again? Or uses?" he'd ask.

"Suppose he does?" she'd ask back and hold those worried eyes. "He and Annie have to work it out themselves. He's in rehab and has his own therapist. He's doing what he has to do. Let it go. Concentrate on your own side of the street."

And she could see that it made sense to Gamache. But she also knew they'd have this same conversation again. Over and over. Because his fears weren't about sense. They didn't live in his head.

But she could see progress. One day he'd get there. And once there, he'd find peace.

And this was the place to do it, Myrna knew, as she watched the large man on the edge of the village open the little book, put on his reading glasses, and begin again.

They'd all come here to begin again.

Armand Gamache looked down at the book and read. Not long, not much. But he found even these few words every day comforting. Then, as he did each morning, he closed the book, removed his reading glasses, and looked at the village. Then he lifted his eyes to the misty forest and mountains beyond.

There was a world out there. A world filled with beauty and love and goodness. And cruelty and killers, and vile acts contemplated and being committed at this very moment.

Peter had left and been gobbled up by that world.

And it was coming closer. Coming here. Nibbling at the edges of the village.

He felt his skin tingle, and the sudden, overwhelming need to get up. To go. To do something. To stop it. It was like an out-of-body experience, so powerful was the urge to act.

He gripped the edge of the bench, closed his eyes, and did as Myrna had taught him.

Deep breath. In. And out.

"And don't just breathe," he heard her calm, melodic voice. "Inhale. Take in the smells. Listen to the sounds. The real world. Not the one you're conjuring."

He breathed in, and smelled the pine forest, smelled the damp earth.

Felt the cool, fresh morning air on his cheeks. He heard, far off, the excited yapping of a puppy. And he followed that back. The puppy led him through the howls and shrieks and alarms in his head.

He held on to the sound. To the scents. As Myrna had taught him.

"Follow anything you can," she'd advised. "Back to reality. Back from the edge."

And he did.

Deep breath in. The cut grass, the sweet hay by the side of the road. Deep breath out.

And finally, when the alarms were dulled and his heart stopped pounding, pounding, he thought he could hear the forest itself. The leaves not rustling, but murmuring to him. Telling him he'd made it. Home. He was safe.

Gamache let go of the hard edge of the wooden bench and slid back, until he felt himself come to rest, against the wood. Against the words.

Deep breath in. Deep breath out.

He opened his eyes, and the village lay before him.

And once again he was saved. He was surprised by joy.

But what would happen if he left? And went back into that world he, better than most, knew was not just his imagination?

Myrna Landers turned slowly from the window.

Each morning she saw Armand read. And then she watched him put down the mysterious book and stare into space.

And each morning she saw the demons approach, and swarm and surround him until they found their way in. Through his head, through his thoughts. And from there they gripped his heart. She saw the terror possess him. And she saw him fight it off.

Each morning she got up, made a coffee, and stood looking through the pane. Only turning away when he was safely through his own.

Clara put down her coffee before she dropped it. She put the last bite of toast in her mouth, before she dropped it too.

And she stared at Peter's painting. Letting her mind leap from image

120

to image. From thought to thought. Until it came to the same conclusion her instincts had hit a few minutes earlier.

It wasn't possible. She must have taken a leap in the wrong direction. Connected things that should not be put together. She sat back down on the stool and stared at the easel.

Had Peter been trying to tell them something?

Myrna spread a thick layer of brilliant gold marmalade on her English muffin. Then she dipped her knife into the raspberry jam and added it to the mix. Her own invention. Marmberry. It looked grotesque, but then great food so often did. Never mind what the chefs tell you, she thought, as she took a bite. All the best comfort food looked like someone had dropped the plate.

She smiled down at her own failed "color wheel," and thought of Bean, and the paintings. That was what her English muffin looked like. The palette Bean had used to create those brilliant, and not in a good way, pictures.

What had Ruth called Clara's first efforts? A dog's breakfast.

"The dog's breakfast." Myrna raised the muffin in salute, and took a bite.

But her chewing slowed, slowed until it stopped. She stared into space.

Her thoughts, tentative at first, sped up. Finally racing along, racing toward a completely unexpected conclusion.

But it wasn't possible. Was it?

She swallowed.

Perhaps the only good thing about the torment he experienced, thought Gamache, taking a deep breath of the sweet morning air, was that once it was gone he emerged into this.

He smiled at the sight of the stone and clapboard and brick cottages, radiating in circles from the village green.

And when the hell stopped, when he finally banished his demons, would heaven stop too?

Would he love this place less because he needed it less?

Again he looked at Three Pines, the little village lost in the valley, and felt the familiar lifting of his heart. But would it lift if there was no load?

Was the final fear that, in losing his fears, he would also lose his joy?

He'd been so worried about Jean-Guy and his addictions, what about his own? He wasn't addicted to pain, to panic, but he might be addicted to the bliss of having them stop.

The mind, he knew, really was its own place. *Can make a Heaven of Hell, a Hell of Heaven.*

Gamache was pretty sure that's what Peter Morrow had done. He'd turned heaven into hell. And as a result, he'd been kicked out. Paradise Lost.

But Peter Morrow wasn't Lucifer, the fallen angel. He was just a troubled man who lived in his head, not realizing that Paradise was only ever found in the heart. Unfortunately for Peter, feelings lived there too. And they were almost always messy. Peter Morrow did not like messes.

Armand laughed as he remembered the conversation from the night before.

It was how Clara had described her first attempt at a painting. No, not a mess, it was something else. A dog's breakfast. Ruth had called it that and Clara had agreed. Ruth tried to capture feelings in her poetry. Clara tried with color and subject to give form to feelings.

It was messy. Unruly. Risky. Scary. So much could go wrong. Failure was always close at hand. But so was brilliance.

Peter Morrow took no risks. He neither failed nor succeeded. There were no valleys, but neither were there mountains. Peter's landscape was flat. An endless, predictable desert.

How shattering it must have been, then, to have played it safe all his life and been expelled anyway. From home. From his career.

What would a person do when the tried-and-true was no longer true?

Gamache's eyes narrowed as he looked at the landscape before him. And listened. Not to the dogs this time. Not the birds or even the oaks and maples and murmuring pines. Now he listened to snippets of conversation, floating up from his memory. Remembering in more detail the conversation from the night before. Putting together a sentence here, a gesture there. A dab, a dot, a brush stroke of words. Until a picture formed.

He stood up, still staring into the distance. Waiting for the final elements. And then he had it.

As he stuffed the book back into his pocket and started down the hill, he saw Myrna leave her bookstore, still in her dressing gown, and practically run across the village green.

They were headed, he knew, for the same place.

Clara's home.

"Where are you?" Myrna called.

"In here."

Clara got off the stool and went to the studio door and saw Myrna standing like an Easter Island monument, if they'd been carved out of flannel. Myrna often dropped by, but rarely this early and normally she got dressed. Rarely did Myrna bother announcing herself. And Clara had rarely heard this tone in her voice.

Panic? No, not panic.

"Clara?"

Another voice, but the same tone, had arrived.

It was Armand and the tone was excitement.

"I think I know what Peter's been doing," he said.

"So do I," said Myrna.

"So do I," said Clara. "But I have to make a call."

"*Oui,*" said Gamache as he and Myrna followed Clara to the telephone in the living room.

A few minutes later she hung up and, turning to them, she nodded.

They were right. A huge piece of the puzzle had appeared, or at least soon would.

FIFTEEN

⁓

"It came to me just now when I looked at his latest work," said Clara.

They'd moved into Peter's studio, drawn there by the canvas on the easel.

"How'd you figure it out?" she asked Myrna.

"The color wheel." Myrna described her vivid English muffin. Gamache, who hadn't yet had breakfast, thought the marmberry sounded genius.

"You?" Myrna asked him.

"I was thinking of the dog's breakfast," he said, and described his different route to the same conclusion. "And how very difficult it must be to paint a feeling. A real mess at first."

In front of them was the painting Peter had left behind. It was all in shades of white. Beautifully nuanced. It was almost impossible to distinguish the canvas from the paint. The medium from the method.

Someone would probably pay a lot of money for that. And one day, Gamache thought, it might be worth a lot of money. Like finding an artifact from a lost civilization. Or, more accurately, a dinosaur bone. Bleached and fossilized. Valuable only because it was extinct. The last of its kind.

Such a contrast to Myrna's and Clara's descriptions of Bean's exuberant paintings.

They were a mess. A riot of clashing colors. Without technique. Having heard the rules, Bean had understood them, then ignored them. Choosing instead to move away from the conventions.

"When you looked at the paintings on Bean's wall," he asked his companions, "what did you feel?"

Clara smiled broadly, remembering. "Honestly? I thought they were awful."

"You thought that," Gamache persisted, "but what did you feel?"

"Amusement," said Myrna.

"Were you laughing at them?" he asked, and Myrna considered.

"No," she said slowly. "I think they made me happy."

"Me too," said Clara. "They were weird and fun and unexpected. I felt sorta buoyed up, you know?"

Myrna nodded.

"And this?" Gamache gestured toward the easel.

All three looked again at the bleached, tasteful canvas. It would go perfectly in someone's penthouse, in the dining room. No danger of ruining the appetite.

Both women shook their heads. Nothing. It was like looking into a void.

"So Bean is the better painter after all," said Gamache. "If only Bean had painted them."

And that was the giant piece of the puzzle they'd all found at the same time.

Bean hadn't painted those silly pictures. Peter had.

They were a mess, because they were the beginning. Peter's first chaotic steps toward brilliance.

"You need to describe the paintings for me, in more detail," said Gamache.

They'd moved with their coffees into Clara's garden, feeling the need for fresh air and color after the tasteful oppression of Peter's studio.

Rain was still threatening but hadn't yet arrived.

"What struck me first were the purples and pinks and oranges all squashed in together in that one over Bean's desk," said Myrna.

"And the one by the window?" asked Clara. "It was like someone had thrown buckets of paint at a wall, and the drips had somehow taken shape."

"And those mountains in the one behind the door," said Myrna. "The smiles."

Clara smiled. "Amazing."

Taking a *pain au chocolat*, she ripped a section off so that the gooey dark chocolate core was exposed and flakes of pastry fell to the table.

"I don't want you to think they were great," Clara said to Gamache, who'd put strawberry jam on a croissant and was reaching for the marmalade. "It's not like we're turning them into masterpieces in our minds now that we know a kid hadn't painted them."

"They're still crap," agreed Myrna. "But happy *merde*."

"Peter did them." Clara shook her head. It was unbelievable. But true.

She'd called Peter's sister, Marianna, and caught Bean in. She asked Bean who'd painted the pictures and Bean's answer came immediately, and with surprise. Surely Aunt Clara knew.

"Uncle Peter."

"He gave them to you?"

"Yes. And some he mailed. We got a pipe thing with more a few months ago."

It was at that point Clara spoke to Marianna again and arranged for all the paintings to be couriered to her in Three Pines.

"I'll get them out this morning. I'm sorry, I thought you knew he'd painted them. Not very good, are they?" Marianna said with barely disguised pleasure. "He showed some to me when he came over. Seemed to want me to say something about them. I didn't know what to say, so I said nothing."

Poor Peter, Clara thought as she sat in the garden. So used to applause for everything he did. So used to getting it right the first time. How strange it must be to suddenly not be very good at something he was once celebrated for. Like a great golfer changing his swing, to become greater. But making it worse in the short term.

Sometimes the only way up is down. Sometimes the only way forward is to back up. It seemed that was what Peter had done. Thrown out all he knew and started again. In his mid-fifties.

A brave man, thought Clara.

"I received a message from the Sûreté in Paris this morning," said Gamache. "They visited LaPorte and spoke with their Chef des bénévoles. He confirmed that Peter had volunteered there last year, but had left after a couple of months."

"Why go all the way to Paris, to volunteer at LaPorte, then leave so soon?" asked Clara.

"Peter went to LaPorte because it had worked for Vincent Gilbert," said Myrna. "Vincent arrived at LaPorte a selfish, callow, vile asshole. And he emerged an asshole saint."

"Progress," said Gamache. "Of a kind. I think it was like Oz and Peter was the Tin Man, looking for a heart. He thought he could find it there, doing a good deed for the less fortunate. And that would in turn make him a better painter."

"No heart, no art," said Myrna. "He must've thought that if it worked for such a ridiculous creature as Vincent Gilbert, surely it would work for him. But Peter's reasons were selfish, and more than a little condescending. That might've changed, had he toughed it out, but he took off. Looking for another quick fix."

"Sometimes the magic works," said Clara, and looked at them expectantly. "You don't know where that comes from?"

Gamache and Myrna shook their heads.

"It's from my favorite scene in a movie," she said. "*Little Big Man*. Chief Dan George is old and frail and he decides his time has come. He and Dustin Hoffman build a bed on stilts and Chief Dan George climbs up, lies down, and folds his arms over his chest."

Clara mimicked the action, closing her eyes and turning her face to the cloudy skies.

"Dustin Hoffman is devastated," she said. "He loves the Chief. He keeps vigil all night and in the morning, just as the sun rises, he goes over to the deathbed and Chief Dan George's face is still and quiet. He's at peace."

Clara opened her eyes and looked at her audience, still and quiet.

"And then Chief Dan George opens his eyes and sits up. He looks at Dustin Hoffman and says, 'Sometimes the magic works. Sometimes it doesn't.'"

After a stunned silence, Myrna and Armand started laughing.

"That's what Peter's travels remind me of," said Clara.

"Keeps coming up, doesn't it? This idea of magic," said Myrna. "We wondered last night if Peter might've gone back to the college hoping to recapture the magic of his youth. And now we're talking about it again, at LaPorte."

"I think we're talking about it because we believe in it, not because Peter does."

"And yet something happened to him," said Gamache, getting up. "Judging by your description of his new paintings. Something changed him. Not in Paris perhaps, but somewhere, something happened to change his painting so completely."

"Where're you going?"

"To call Scotland."

He left them in the back garden and walked slowly home, thinking about Peter and Paris. And Peter's flight across Europe. Because that's how it appeared to Gamache. After pursuing many people over many decades, he recognized the difference between fleeing and seeking.

This seemed like flight to Gamache. Paris to Florence to Venice to Scotland.

That was a lot of travel for a stationary man.

Why did people flee? Gamache asked himself as he nodded to neighbors and raised his hand to return a wave. They fled because they were in danger.

Had Peter left LaPorte so quickly for reasons that had more to do with saving his body than his soul?

As he walked home across the village green, Gamache worried that Peter hadn't run fast enough or far enough. Or maybe he'd run smack into Samarra.

SIXTEEN

———

"Eh?"

"I asked if there were any artist colonies in your area, sir."

"Wur yur, colonnades air?"

"Eh?"

Gamache stood in his study, phone gripped to his ear, as though pressing it harder to his head might make the conversation easier to understand.

It did not.

He'd bypassed the Chief Constable of Police Scotland. He'd bypassed the assistants and the directors. He knew from experience that as well informed and well meaning as those senior officers might be, the people who really knew the community were the ones who protected it every day.

So he'd called through to the Dumfries detachment directly and introduced himself. That had taken a few minutes, until the person at the other end was satisfied he was neither a victim of crime, nor a criminal.

It seemed when speaking English, his accent, combined with the Scottish ear, was producing a sort of white noise of nonsense.

In Dumfries, Constable Stuart tried to be patient. He looked out the window of the police station, at the whitewashed buildings. At the gray stone buildings. At the redbrick Victorian buildings. At the tall clock tower at the far end of the market square. At the people rushing by, the cold rain driving them toward the pubs and shops.

And he tried to be patient.

He tried to figure out what this man was going on about. A colonnade? Why call the police to ask about that? Then he thought he heard something about artists, but that was equally ridiculous. Again, why call the police to discuss art?

He wondered if this man might be off his head, but he sounded calm and rational and even a bit exasperated himself.

Constable Stuart became more alert when he made out the word "homicide," but when he asked if this man was calling to report one, he got the only clear answer so far.

No.

"Then what, may I ask, are you wanting?"

He heard a long, long sigh down the phone line.

"*Mon dieu*," he also heard.

"Did you say '*Mon dieu*'?" he asked. "Do you speak French?"

"*Oui*," said Gamache. "Do you?" He asked that in French and was rewarded with a laugh.

"Oh, aye. *Je parle français*."

And finally the two men could communicate. In French. Thanks to Constable Stuart's affair with a Frenchwoman who was now his wife. She'd eventually learned English and he'd learned French.

Gamache explained that he was the former Chief Inspector of homicide for the Sûreté du Québec, in Canada, and he needed Constable Stuart's help. But not with a murder case. This was a private enquiry. Trying to find a missing friend. An artist. He'd been traced to the Dumfries area in the early winter. Gamache gave Constable Stuart the dates when Peter was there. But Gamache didn't know where he went, what he did, or why Peter was even there. He wondered if there was an artist colony, or something that might draw a painter to the area.

"Well, now, this is a very beautiful part of the world, you know."

Gamache envied Constable Stuart his accent. In French it became soft and charming, the rolling Scottish burr melding perfectly with the French language.

Who knew?

"So there are famous artists?"

"Not exactly famous." There was a pause. "No, I cannot say they're famous. But very good. And any artist would be inspired by the setting." Constable Stuart looked out the window at the cold, gray day. At the sheets of rain pouring down.

It was beautiful.

"Now, we do have a number of very pretty gardens. Some remarkable, apparently. Would a gardener do?"

"I'm afraid not. I think it needs to be an artist. No idea why my friend might have gone to Dumfries?"

"Beyond the fact I think everyone should? No, sir."

Gamache looked out the sitting room window. A heavy mist had descended and he could barely see the three pines on the village green. The bistro was just a ghostly outline with a slight glow of light in the window.

It was beautiful.

"We know by his bank withdrawals that he was in your area, but there's no record of where he stayed."

"Now, that's not unusual. There're a lot of B and Bs in the town and surrounding area. They prefer cash."

"I'd like to send you a photograph and description of my friend."

"Perfect. I'll circulate it."

He sounded cheerful, helpful. Hopeful. But the charming accent could not disguise the fact there was little to be hopeful about. The chances of Constable Stuart finding any trace of Peter Morrow's activity from months ago were tiny. Still, he was willing to try and Gamache was grateful.

Peter had gone all the way to Dumfries for a reason. But that reason remained obscure. What they did know was that Peter wasn't there now. He'd eventually left and popped up in Toronto.

The two men said their good-byes and Gamache sat in the easy chair. The window was open and he could hear the rain pelting down. Striking the leaves, hitting the porch and drumming against the window. The weather, and the Chief, had settled in for the day.

He leaned back, wove his fingers together and stared into space, considering. Thinking about Peter, and Dumfries, and his conversation with Constable Stuart. The Scots and the Québécois had a lot in common. They'd both been conquered by the English. Both had managed to keep their language and culture alive, against great odds. Both had nationalistic aspirations.

But Gamache knew Peter Morrow hadn't gone to Scotland to study self-determination. Not on a national level anyway. His was a more personal quest for self.

Somewhere along the line something had happened and Peter Morrow had painted those extraordinary pictures.

Gamache was anxious to see them for himself.

They arrived at Clara's home first thing the next morning. The cheerful UPS driver, in his brown truck and brown shorts, handed Clara what looked like the love child of a baseball bat and a baguette.

Clara signed for the long brown tube and waved it toward Gamache and Reine-Marie, who were breakfasting on the terrace of the bistro with Jean-Guy and Ruth.

The rain had stopped in the night and the day had dawned clear and warm, the sun gleaming off the moisture beaded on the leaves and flower petals, the roofs and grass. As it evaporated, vaporized by the sun, it filled the air with the scent of rose and lavender and asphalt shingles.

By noon the village would be sizzling, but for now it was gleaming and fragrant. But all that was lost on Clara. She only had eyes for the UPS tube. Taking it inside, she called Myrna.

Then she waited. Clutching the tube. Staring at the tube. Picking at the brown paper wrapping. Fortunately, she didn't have long to wait. Within minutes everyone had arrived and Clara tore the wrapping off.

"Let's see, let's see," said Ruth.

"You know that's not a giant joint, right?" said Jean-Guy.

"I know, numb nuts." Still, much of Ruth's enthusiasm waned. Then she took a closer look at the tube and perked up.

"There's no bottle of Scotch inside either," said Jean-Guy, reading her thoughts. It was a source of some concern that he could.

"Then what's all the excitement?"

"Peter's paintings are inside," said Reine-Marie, staring at the tube, anxious to see them.

It was as though Peter had mailed himself. Not his physical self. She hoped. Peter had posted his thoughts, his feelings. Inside that tube was a diary of where he'd gone, creatively, since he'd left Three Pines.

They crowded around as Clara removed the brown paper. A note, scribbled by Marianna, came loose and drifted to the floor. Jean-Guy scooped it up and read.

"Here're the paintings. Three on canvas are the most recent. Peter sent them to Bean in May. Don't know where they were mailed from. The other three are on paper. He gave them to Bean when he visited in the winter. Glad to send them."

That sounded to Jean-Guy like "Glad to get rid of them."

"Let's see," said Gabri.

He'd just arrived and he and Ruth were elbowing each other for position.

Jean-Guy took one of the canvases and Reine-Marie took another. They unfurled them, but the sides kept curling back up.

"I can't see," snapped Ruth. "Hold them open."

"This is too awkward," said Myrna.

They looked around the kitchen and finally decided to place the three canvases on the floor, like area rugs.

They smoothed out the canvases, placing a large book at each corner, then stepped back. Rosa waddled toward the pictures.

"Don't let her step on them," Clara warned.

"Step on them?" asked Ruth. "You'll be lucky if she shits on them. Could only improve 'em."

No one disagreed.

Gamache looked at them. Tilting his head this way and that.

Clara was right. They were a mess. And he realized he hadn't quite believed they would be.

He'd hoped that the paintings would at least show promise. But he'd actually expected they'd be better than that. Unconventional, yes. Unexpected. Even slightly difficult to fathom. Like a Jackson Pollock. All wild color. Blobs and drips and lines of what looked like spilled paint. Accidents on canvas.

But those coalesced into a form, a feeling.

Gamache leaned slightly to the left. To the right. To the center.

No.

These were just messes.

Sitting on the floor like that, Peter's paintings literally looked like a dog's breakfast. If the dog had no sense of taste. And then had thrown up.

Whatever Rosa might drop on the paintings wouldn't do any damage, thought Gamache.

Clara was across the kitchen and had taken the elastics off the smaller paintings and placed them on the table, anchoring each corner with salt and pepper shakers and mugs.

"So," she said as the others joined her, "according to Marianna, these are Peter's earlier works."

They stared.

These works were no better. In fact, they were, if such a thing was possible, even worse than what lay on the floor.

"Are we sure Peter did them?" Gamache asked. It was extremely difficult to believe the same artist who'd painted the bland, tasteful, precise works in the studio was responsible for these.

Clara was looking doubtful herself. Leaning in, she examined the lower right corner.

"There's no signature." She was gnawing the side of her mouth. "He normally signs his works."

"Yeah, well, he normally takes six months to do a painting," said Ruth. "He normally doesn't show any of his works until they're perfect. He normally uses shades of cream and gray."

Clara looked at Ruth in astonishment. Perhaps her head wasn't quite as far up her ass as Clara had assumed.

"Do you think they're Peter's?" she asked Ruth.

"They're his," said Ruth decisively. "Not because they look like his but because no one in their right mind would take credit for these if they hadn't painted them."

"Why didn't he sign them?" Jean-Guy asked.

"Would you?" Ruth asked.

They went back to studying the three paintings on the table.

Now and then one of them, as though repelled by these three, broke away and went over to the paintings on the floor.

Then, as though repelled again, they returned to the table.

"Well," said Gabri, after consideration. "I have to say, they stink."

The paintings were garish, splashes and clashes of color. Reds and purples, yellows and oranges. Fighting with each other. Dashed on the paper and canvas. It was as though Peter had taken a club to every rule he'd learned. Hacking away at them. Breaking them like a piñata. And out of those shattered certainties paint had poured. Gobs and gobs of brilliant paint. All the colors he'd sniffed at, sneered at, mocked with his clever artist friends. All the colors he'd withheld and Clara had used. They poured out. Like blood. Like guts.

They hit the paper and this was the result.

"What does this say about Peter?" Gamache asked.

"Do we really need to look in that cave?" Myrna whispered to him.

"Perhaps not," he admitted. "But is there any difference between these"—he pointed to the ones on the table—"and those?" He gestured toward the floor. "Do you see an improvement? An evolution?"

Clara shook her head. "They look like an exercise in art school. You see here?"

She pointed to a checkerboard pattern in one of the paintings on the table. They leaned in and nodded.

"Every high school art student does something like that, to learn about perspective."

Gamache's brows came together in consideration. Why would one of the most successful artists in Canada paint these? And include an exercise kids are taught in school?

"Is this even art?" Jean-Guy asked.

It was another good question.

When Beauvoir had first met these people, and this village, he knew little about art and what he knew was more than he found useful. But after many years of exposure to the art world, he'd become interested. Sort of.

What mostly interested him wasn't the art, but the environment. The infighting. The casual cruelty. The hypocrisy. The ugly business of selling beautiful creations.

And how that ugliness sometimes grew into crime. And how the crime sometimes festered into murder. Sometimes.

Jean-Guy liked Peter Morrow. A part of him understood Peter Morrow. The part Beauvoir admitted to very few.

The fearful part. The empty part. The selfish part. The insecure part.

The cowardly part of Jean-Guy Beauvoir understood Peter Morrow.

But while Beauvoir had fought hard to face that part of himself, Peter had simply run from it. Increasing the chasm, the tear.

Fear didn't make the hole bigger, Beauvoir had learned. But cowardice did.

Still, Jean-Guy Beauvoir liked Peter Morrow, and was worried that something horrible had happened to the man. But at least no one would kill for these pictures. Except perhaps Peter. He might kill to suppress them.

But he hadn't, had he? In fact, far from suppressing them, he'd actually taken pains to make sure they were safe.

"Why did he keep these?" Jean-Guy asked. "And why give them to Bean?"

Instead of answering any questions, the paintings had created even more.

Ruth left. Bored and more than a little revolted.

"They're revolting," she'd said, in case anyone had missed how she felt. "I'm off to clean out Rosa's litter box. Anyone want to help?"

It was tempting, and shortly after Ruth left, Gabri made his excuses.

"I think I should dig the hair out of the bathroom drains," he said as he made for the door.

Peter's works seemed to remind people of disgusting chores. If he'd set out into the world to find a way to be useful, this probably wasn't what he had in mind.

Armand, Reine-Marie, Clara, Myrna, and Jean-Guy were left standing uncertainly around the paintings.

"Okay," said Gamache, walking over to the canvases on the floor. "These are the more recent works. Mailed by Peter in late spring. They're on canvas, while the earlier works"—he took three long strides over to the pine table—"given to Bean in the winter, are on paper."

They looked like some living thing had fallen from a great height. And hit the table.

They could not be considered a triumph. Or a success. Or a good end.

But these, Gamache knew, weren't anywhere close to an end. These were the beginning. They were signposts. Markers.

The Inuit used to erect stone men as a navigation tool, to mark their path. To point out where they were going and where they'd been. The way forward and the way home. *Inuksuit*, they were called. Literally, a substitute for a man. When found by Europeans they were initially destroyed. Then they were loathed as heathen. Now they're recognized as not only markers, but works of art.

That's what Peter had done. These might be works of art, but more than that, they were markers, signposts. Pointing out where he'd been and where he was going. The route he was traveling, artistically, emotionally, creatively. These odd paintings were his *inuksuit*, recording not so much his location, but the progress of his thoughts and feelings.

These paintings were a substitute for the man. Peter's insides, out.

With that insight, Gamache looked more closely at the six paintings. What did they tell him about Peter?

They at first appeared to be simply splashes of color. The most recent ones, on canvas, seemed to clash even more violently than the early ones.

"Why paint some on paper and the rest on canvas?" Reine-Marie asked.

Clara had been wondering that herself. She stared at the groupings. Frankly, they all seemed equally crappy to her. It wasn't like the three on canvas were clearly better and worth preserving and the paper ones were disposable.

"I guess there might be a couple of reasons," she said. "He either didn't have any canvases when he painted the first three, or he knew they'd be experiments. Not meant to last."

"But these were?" Jean-Guy pointed to the works on the floor.

"Sometimes the magic works . . ." said Clara, and Gamache gave a small laugh.

"Peter's a smart man," said Reine-Marie. "A successful artist. He must have realized these aren't great. They're not even good."

Jean-Guy nodded. "Exactly. Why keep them? And not just keep them, but give them to someone else, let someone else see them?"

"What do you do with the works you don't like?" Reine-Marie asked Clara.

"Oh, I keep most."

"Even the ones you couldn't save?" asked Reine-Marie.

"Even those."

"Why?"

"Well, you just never know. On a slow day, or when I'm stuck for inspiration, I'll pull them out and look again. Sometimes I even put them on their sides, or upside down. That can give me a different perspective. Jog something loose that I hadn't seen before. Some small thing that's worth pursuing. A color combination, a series of strokes, that sort of thing."

Beauvoir looked at the paintings on the floor. Only a series of strokes would explain them.

"You keep the ones that don't work out," said Myrna. "But you don't show them off."

"True," admitted Clara.

"Jean-Guy's right. There's a reason Peter kept these," said Gamache. "And a reason he sent them to Bean."

He walked over to the smaller images on the worn pine table.

"Where's the one you said was a smile?" Gamache asked Myrna. "The lips? I can't see them."

"Oh, that. I'd forgotten," she said. "It's over in this group." She walked him back to the floor show. "You find it."

"Dreary woman," he said, but didn't protest. After a minute or so Myrna opened her mouth, but the Chief stopped her. "Now, don't tell me. I'll get it."

"Well, I'm going outside," said Clara.

They poured lemonades and went into the garden, but Beauvoir stayed behind with the Chief.

Gamache bent over each painting, then straightened up and held his hands behind his back. He rocked slightly back and forth, heel to toe. Heel to toe.

Beauvoir took a few steps back. Then a few more. Then he dragged one of the chairs over from the pine table and got up on it.

"Nothing from up here."

"What're you doing?" Gamache demanded, striding over to Jean-Guy. "Get off that chair right now."

"It's sturdy. It'll hold my weight." But he jumped down anyway.

He didn't like the tone in the Chief's voice.

"You don't know that," said Gamache.

"And you don't know it won't," said Beauvoir.

The two stared at each other until a sound made Gamache turn around. Myrna stood at the door, the empty lemonade jug in her hand.

"Am I interrupting?"

"Not at all," the Chief said, and forced a smile. Then he took a deep breath, expelled the air, and turned back to Beauvoir, who was still glaring.

"I'm sorry, Jean-Guy. Get back up if you want to."

"No, I've seen what I need to see."

Gamache had the feeling he was talking about more than the paintings.

"There it is," said Jean-Guy.

Gamache joined him.

Jean-Guy had found the smile. The smiles.

And Gamache realized his mistake. He'd been looking for one big set of lips. A valley that formed a mountain. But Peter had painted a whole bunch of them, tiny smiles, small valleys of mirth that marched across and deep into the painting.

Gamache grinned.

It didn't make the painting good, but it was the first of Peter's works that had produced any feeling at all in him.

He turned to look at the table. Even those paintings had created a feeling, though he didn't think nausea was considered an emotion. But it was at least something. In the gut. Not in the head.

If this was the start, Armand Gamache was even more anxious to know where the smiles led.

SEVENTEEN

⌒

Reine-Marie was smiling.

Gamache had shown her the parade of tiny lips. It had taken her a moment to actually recognize what they were, but he knew the moment it clicked.

Her own lips curled into a grin. Then into a full-blown smile.

"How could I have missed it, Armand?" She turned to him, then back to the painting.

"I missed it too. It was Jean-Guy who found them."

"*Merci*," she said to her son-in-law, who bowed slightly in acknowledgment. She wondered if he realized that was one of Armand's mannerisms.

While Reine-Marie turned back to the painting, Gamache turned his attention to the other two canvases on the floor. Clara was staring down at them.

"Anything?" he asked.

She shook her head, then leaned closer to the paintings. Then stepped back.

Was there something in those pictures like the lips? An image, an emotion Peter had embedded there, waiting to be discovered, like a country or planet or strange new species.

If there was, neither Gamache nor Clara could see it.

Gamache sensed eyes on him and assumed they were Beauvoir's, but the younger man was busy making sandwiches in the kitchen.

Reine-Marie was still smiling down at the lip painting. Clara was examining the other two canvases.

And Myrna was examining him.

She led him away from the others.

"Is this too much, Armand?"

"What do you mean?"

She gave him a shrewd look and he grinned.

"You noticed the little exchange with Beauvoir."

"I did." She studied him for a moment. "Clara would understand if you told her you needed to stop."

"Stop?" He looked at her with astonishment. "Why would I do that?"

"Why did you snap at Beauvoir just now?"

"He was standing on a chair. An old pine chair. It could've broken."

"'It' could've broken?"

"Oh, come on." Gamache laughed. "Don't you think you're reading more into this than it deserves? I was momentarily angry with Jean-Guy and showed it. *Point final*. No big deal. Drop it."

His voice, on the last two words, had hardened. And his eyes contained a warning. *Do not cross this line.*

"Life is made up of 'no big deals,'" said Myrna, crossing the line. "You know that. Isn't that what you say about murders? They're rarely provoked by one huge event, but by a series of tiny, almost invisible, events. No big deals, that combine to create a catastrophe."

"What's your point?" His eyes hadn't wavered.

"You know my point. I'd be a fool to ignore what just happened. And so would you. It was, on the surface, a small thing. He got up on a chair, you chastised him. He got off. And if I didn't know you, didn't know what had happened, I would've thought nothing of it. But I do know you. And I know Jean-Guy. And I know that 'broken' means more to you, and him, than to most people."

They stared at each other, Gamache not relenting. Not accepting that Myrna could be right.

"It's just a chair," he said, his voice low but not soft.

Myrna nodded. "But it's not just a man. It's Jean-Guy."

"If the chair had broken he wouldn't have been hurt," said Gamache. "He was a foot and a half off the ground."

"I know that. You know that," said Myrna. "But it's no longer a matter of knowing, is it? If life was purely rational there'd be fewer wars, or poverty, or crime. Or murders. Fewer things would be broken. Your reaction wasn't rational, Armand."

Gamache was silent.

She looked at him closely. "Is this too much?"

"Too much? Do you have any idea what I've seen? And done?"

"I have an idea," she said.

"I don't think you have." He stared at her and a wave of images washed over Myrna. Of mangled bodies. Of glassy eyes. Of harrowing scenes. Of the very worst one person can do to another.

And it had been his job to follow the bloody trail. Into the cave. To face whatever was in there.

And then to do it again. And again.

The miracle wasn't that the killer was caught, but that the man before her had kept his own humanity throughout it all. Even after he himself had been dragged into the cave. And so deeply hurt.

And now he was offering to get up and help once again.

And she was offering to give him a pass. But he wasn't taking it.

"I'm not that fragile, you know," said Gamache. "Besides, this is simply a missing person, not a murder. Easy."

He tried to sound relaxed and managed to sound simply weary.

"Are you so sure?" she asked.

"That it's not a murder?" he asked. "Or that it's easy?"

"Both."

"No," he admitted. "And you're right about one thing. I'd rather stay here in Three Pines. Sleep in, enjoy a lemonade at the bistro, or garden—"

He held up his hand to stop her from commenting on his so-called gardening.

"I'd love to only do what Reine-Marie and I want."

As he spoke, Myrna could feel the depth of his longing.

"Sometimes there's no choice," he said softly.

"There is a choice, Armand. There's always a choice."

"Are you so sure?"

"Are you saying that you can't refuse to help Clara?"

"I'm saying that sometimes refusing does more damage."

He let that sit there between them.

"Why did you help me, months ago?" he asked. "You knew the danger. You knew to help could bring terrible consequences to you, to the village. In fact, it almost certainly would. But still you did it."

"You know why."

"Why?"

"Because my life and this village would lose all meaning, if we turned our backs."

He smiled. "*C'est ça*. The same for me now. What's the use of healing, if the life that's saved is callow and selfish and ruled by fear? There's a difference between being in sanctuary and being in hiding."

"So you have to leave sanctuary in order to have it?" she asked.

"You did," he said.

She watched him walk back across the kitchen. The limp barely noticeable anymore. The tremble in his right hand all but gone.

Gamache joined Clara and Reine-Marie.

"Anything?"

But he could tell by their expressions they'd found nothing else in the paintings.

"Doesn't mean there isn't something there . . ." Clara's voice trailed off.

The odd thing was, Gamache realized as he stared at the other two canvases on the floor, that while there was no overt image that evoked a feeling, he actually did feel something as he looked at them.

They were, as far as he could tell, simply tangles of clashing paint.

Why had Peter sent these as well as the joyous lip painting? What did Peter see in them that escaped Gamache? And escaped Clara? Escaped them all?

What was escaping from these paintings, undetected?

"Jean-Guy?" Gamache called, and the younger man put down the bread knife and joined him.

"*Oui?*"

"Can you help me?"

Gamache picked one of the canvases off the floor.

"Clara, can we put this up on the wall?"

Jean-Guy held one corner, Gamache the other, while Clara nailed it into place. Then they nailed the others. Three crimes against art, nailed to the wall.

Once again, they all stepped back to better consider the paintings.

Then they stepped back again. Considered. Stepped. Considered. Like a very, very slow retreat. Or a dirge.

They stopped when their backs hit the far wall. Distance and perspective had not improved the paintings.

"Well, I'm hungry."

Beauvoir walked over to the kitchen island and picked up the platter of sandwiches he'd made. Myrna got the pitcher of lemonade she'd refilled, and together they made for the garden door, drawing the others to them. Away from the paintings and into the warm summer day.

Flies rested on Clara's ham sandwich. She didn't bat them away. They could have it.

She wasn't hungry. Her stomach was upset. Not nauseous exactly. Nothing she'd eaten. More like something she'd seen.

Those paintings were upsetting her. As her friends ate and talked, she thought about the pictures.

When she'd first seen them, in Bean's bedroom, she'd been amused. Especially by the lips. But seeing them in her own home had made her queasy. It was a sort of seasickness. The horizon was no longer steady. Some shift, some upheaval, had occurred.

Was she jealous? Was that possible? Was she worried that these paintings by Peter really did signal an important departure for him as an artist? While laughable right now, might they actually lead to genius? And at the pointy end of that thought, another thought perched. A genius greater than hers?

After feeling quietly smug about Peter and his petty jealousy, was she no better? Worse, in fact? Jealous and hypocritical and judgmental. Oh, my.

But there was more. Somewhere else her thoughts were leading. Something else was running for cover.

Her friends were in an animated discussion about the paintings and why Peter had mailed them to Bean.

"I asked that an hour ago," Jean-Guy protested. "And no one listened. Myrna asks it now and suddenly it's a brilliant question?"

"The cruel fate of the avant-garde, *mon beau*," said Reine-Marie, then turned back to Myrna.

"So what do you think?"

As they discussed it, Clara held her lemonade, the glass slippery with condensation, and examined her feelings.

"Clara?"

"Huh?"

She looked at Myrna, who was smiling at her in obvious amusement.

"Where'd you go?" Myrna asked.

"Oh, just enjoying the garden. Wondering if I should put up more sweet pea on that trellis."

Myrna now looked at Clara with less amusement. Like most people, Myrna Landers did not like being lied to. But unlike most people, she was willing to call them on it.

"What were you really thinking?"

Clara took a deep, deep breath. "I was thinking about Peter's paintings and how they made me feel."

"And how was that?" Reine-Marie asked.

Clara looked at the faces watching her.

"Unsettled," she said. "I think the paintings frightened me a little."

"Why?" asked Gamache.

"Because I think I know why he mailed them to Bean."

They leaned toward her.

"Why?" Beauvoir asked.

"What makes Bean different from most other people?" Clara asked.

"Well, we don't know if he's a girl—" said Reine-Marie.

"—or she's a boy," said Gamache.

"Bean's a child," said Beauvoir.

"True," said Clara. "All true. But there's something else that distinguishes Bean."

"Bean's different," said Myrna. "In the Morrow family where everyone's expected to conform, Bean doesn't. Peter probably identifies with that. Might even want to reward that."

"And sending those awful paintings is a reward?" asked Beauvoir.

"Of sorts," said Myrna. "The act is often more important than the actual object."

"Tell that to a kid who gets socks for Christmas," said Beauvoir.

"Ask a child who gets a gold star in their workbook," said Myrna. "The sticker is useless, but the act is priceless. Symbols are powerful, especially for kids. Why do you think they want trophies and badges? Not because they can play with them, or buy things with them, but because of what they mean."

"Approval," agreed Reine-Marie.

"Right," said Myrna. "And Uncle Peter sending Bean the paintings made Bean feel special. I think Peter identifies with Bean, sympathizes with the child, and wanted to let Bean know it's okay to be different."

Myrna looked at Clara, waiting for her approval. Waiting for the gold star.

"That could be the reason," said Clara. "But I actually think it's far simpler than that."

"Like what?" asked Beauvoir.

"I think Peter knew that Bean could keep a secret."

Bean had kept the secret of his or her own sex. The pressure to tell must have been enormous, but Bean had told no one. Not family. Not schoolmates. Not teachers. No one.

"Peter knew the paintings would be safe with Bean," said Reine-Marie.

"But if they're secret, why didn't he keep them himself?" Jean-Guy asked. "Wouldn't they be safest with him?"

"Maybe he believed he wasn't safe," said Gamache. "That's what you're thinking, isn't it?"

Clara nodded. That was the feeling in the pit of her stomach. Peter needed to keep these paintings secret.

She looked toward her house.

But what was hidden in those odd paintings? What did they reveal?

149

EIGHTEEN

~

"A poem begins as a lump in the throat," said Armand Gamache as he took a seat on one of Ruth's white preformed chairs.

"You make it sound like a fur ball," said Ruth. She slopped Scotch into a glass, not offering him any. "Something horked up. My poems are finely honed, each fucking word carefully chosen."

Rosa was asleep in her nest of blankets beside Ruth's chair, though Gamache thought he noticed the duck's eyes open a slit. Watching him.

It would have been unnerving if he didn't keep reminding himself it was just a duck. Just a duck. An unnerving duck.

"Well, you're the one who said it." Gamache tore his eyes from the watch duck.

"Did I?"

"You did."

Ruth's kitchen was filled with found objects, including the plastic chairs and table. Including the Scotch bottle, found in Gabri's liquor cabinet. Including Rosa. Found as an egg, Gamache knew. Ruth had spotted the nest by the pond on the village green one Easter morning and had touched the two eggs inside. The touch had tainted them, and the eggs had been abandoned by their mother. So Ruth took them home. Everyone had naturally assumed she'd meant to make an omelet. But instead the old poet had done something unnatural, for her. She'd made a tiny incubator out of flannel, and warmed the eggs in the oven. She'd turned them, watched them, stayed up late into the night in case they started to hatch and needed her. Ruth paid her Hydro-Québec bill, to make sure her power wasn't cut off. She paid it with money she'd found at Clara's.

She prayed.

Rosa had hatched on her own but her sister, Flora, had fought to get out. So Ruth had helped. Peeling back the shell. Cracking it further.

And there, inside, was Flora. Looking up into those weary, wary old eyes.

Flora and Rosa had bonded with Ruth. And Ruth had bonded with them.

They followed her everywhere. But while Rosa thrived, Flora grew frail.

Because of Ruth.

Flora was meant to fight her way out of her shell. The struggle would make her strong. Ruth's helping hand had weakened her. Until, late one night, Flora had died in that same helping hand.

It had confirmed all Ruth's fears. Kindness killed. No good could come of helping others.

And so Ruth made it a policy to turn her back. Not for herself, but to protect those she loved.

"What do you want?" she asked.

"*A poem begins as a lump in the throat. A sense of wrong,*" Gamache continued the quote. "*A homesickness, a lovesickness.*"

Ruth glared at him over the rim of her cut glass tumbler, one she'd found in the Gamaches' home.

"You know the quote," she said, cupping the glass between two scrawny hands. "Not one of mine, as you know."

"Not even a poem," said Gamache. "It's from a letter Robert Frost wrote to a friend describing how he wrote."

"Your point?"

"Is the same true for any work of art?" he asked. "A poem, a song, a book."

"A painting?" she asked, her rheumy eyes sharp, as though a barracuda was staring at him from the bottom of a cold lake.

"Does a painting begin with a lump in the throat? A sense of wrong?

A homesickness, a lovesickness?" he asked. In his peripheral vision he saw that Rosa was awake and watching her mother. Closely.

"How the hell should I know?"

But finally, under Gamache's patient gaze, she gave one curt nod.

"The best ones do, yes. We express ourselves differently. Some choose words, some notes, some paint, but it all comes from the same place. But there's something you need to know."

"*Oui?*"

"Any real act of creation is first an act of destruction. Picasso said it, and it's true. We don't build on the old, we tear it down. And start fresh."

"You tear down all that's familiar, comfortable," said Gamache. "It must be scary." When the old poet was quiet he asked, "Is that the lump in the throat?"

"Can I ask you a question?" Clara asked.

Olivier was busy setting the bistro tables for dinner. One of the servers had called in sick and they were shorthanded.

"Can you fold napkins?" Without waiting for a response, he handed her a pile of white linen.

"Suppose," said Clara uncertainly.

Olivier searched through his tray of antique silver knives and forks and spoons for sets that matched. And then he separated them. First he matched, then he mismatched.

"Do you know where Peter went?" Clara asked.

Olivier paused, a spoon in his hand, like a microphone. "Why would you ask me that?"

"Because you were good friends."

"We all were. Are."

"But I think you and he were especially close. I think if he was going to tell anyone, it'd be you," said Clara.

"He'd have told you, Clara," said Olivier, going back to setting the table. "What's this about?"

"So he didn't tell you?"

"I haven't heard from him since he left." Olivier stopped what he was doing to look at her directly. "I'd have said something earlier, when he didn't show up. I'd never have let you stew."

He gathered up more silverware and Clara folded the napkins. They moved around one table, then over to the next.

"When you left Three Pines—" she began, but Olivier interrupted.

"When I was taken away," he corrected.

"Did you miss Gabri?"

"Every day. All day. I couldn't wait to come back. It's all I dreamed of."

"But you told me that the night you returned you stood out there"— she fluttered a napkin toward the bay window of the bistro—"afraid to come inside."

Olivier continued to set the places, his expert hands making sure the old silver was properly mismatched and properly placed.

"What were you afraid of?" Clara asked.

"I already told you."

They'd moved on to another table, and were circling it, setting it.

"But I need to hear it again. It's important."

She watched his blond and balding head bowed over the chairs, as though the empty places were sacred.

Olivier straightened up so abruptly it gave Clara a start.

"I was afraid I no longer belonged. I stood out there and watched you all in here, laughing, having fun. You seemed so happy. Without me. Gabri seemed so happy."

"Oh, Olivier." She handed him a napkin and he covered his face in the white linen. He rubbed his eyes and blew his nose and for a moment after he lowered the napkin he looked just fine. But then another drop made its way down his cheek. Then another. He seemed unaware it was happening.

And perhaps, thought Clara, he was. Maybe this was now normal for Olivier. Maybe every now and then he simply wept. Not in pain or sadness. The tears were just overwhelming memories, rendered into water, seeping out. Clara could almost see the images inside the tears. It was winter. A bitterly cold night. And Olivier stood outside the bistro. Through the frosted panes he saw the logs in the hearth. He saw the drinks and festive food. He saw his friends, he saw Gabri. Not just moving on, but apparently happy. Without him.

It no longer really hurt, but neither could it be forgotten.

"You know he missed you so much it almost killed him," said Clara. "I've never seen anyone so sad."

"I know that now," said Olivier. "And I knew it then. But seeing—"

Words failed. He fluttered the napkin and Clara knew what he meant, and how he'd felt. And in his tears she saw all Olivier's fears and insecurities and doubts.

She saw all he had, and all he stood to lose.

"I know," she said.

Olivier looked at her with annoyance, as though she was laying claim to his territory. But his irritation disappeared when he saw her expression.

"What's happened?" he asked.

"Peter sent some paintings to Bean in Toronto."

"*Oui*," he said. "Gabri told me."

"Did he tell you what they looked like?"

"A little." Olivier grimaced. "On the bright side, since looking at them he's cleaned out the drains in the B and B and is now scraping guck off the oven." Olivier jerked his head toward the swinging doors into the bistro kitchen. "I'm thinking of hanging some of Peter's paintings at home."

Despite herself, Clara grinned. "Ten dollars and they're yours."

"You'll have to pay him more than that, I'm afraid," said Gabri.

He'd come out of the kitchen wearing bright yellow rubber gloves, holding them up as though emerging from surgery.

"They're not that bad," said Clara.

Gabri stared at her in disbelief. The patient was clearly beyond help.

"Okay, they're not great," Clara admitted. "But when was the last time Peter's painting made you feel anything, never mind drove you to actually do something?"

"I don't think running away is what most artists want," said Gabri, peeling off the gloves.

"Actually, some do. They want to provoke. Push and shove your preconceptions. Challenge."

"Peter?" asked Olivier, and Clara had to remember he hadn't yet seen the latest paintings.

"What did you feel, when you looked at them?" Clara asked Gabri.

"Revolted."

But Clara waited, and she could see Gabri considering.

"They were awful," he said finally, "but they were also kind of fun. So ridiculously inept they were sort of silly. Almost endearing."

"Peter?" asked Olivier again.

"I think what upset me were all those colors mashed together—"

"Peter?" Olivier demanded. "Colors? Come on."

"And you didn't even see the lips," said Clara.

"What lips?" they asked together.

"Peter put smiles in one of his paintings. It was sort of genius."

As she said it, she felt light-headed, off balance. Gabri was yacking away about the likelihood of what he saw being anything other than soft and smelly. But Olivier was watching her.

"What's happened?" he asked again, quietly.

Clara knew then that those paintings, and especially the one with the lips, were her mullioned windows. Frames through which she could see into Peter's life. Like Olivier watching Gabri on that cold winter night.

And like Olivier, what she clearly saw was that Peter was happy. That was the message of the paintings. He was experimenting, he was searching. He'd left all that was artistically safe behind. He'd broken the ropes, the rules, and sailed off, leaving the known world behind. Exploring. And he was having the time of his life.

The works were messy. But emotions were.

Clara had looked through the window of those works and seen that Peter was happy.

Finally.

Without her.

Olivier looked around the bistro for a napkin to give Clara. Only then did he notice that she'd twisted the linen into all sorts of shapes. Intentionally or not, the napkins looked like creatures of the deep. Washed ashore in Three Pines. Landing on the bistro tables.

Olivier offered a napkin to Clara, who took it with surprise. She didn't realize she'd made them. And she didn't realize she'd been crying. She dabbed a sea creature to her cheeks and wondered what Olivier saw in her tears.

Gamache tossed the ball and watched Henri bound after it, through the deep grass and wildflowers.

He and Henri had walked up the hill and out of the village to the meadow behind the old mill. He needed to be alone with his thoughts.

Gamache knew that what Ruth had said about the creative process was significant. Important. And he felt on the verge of the answer. Almost there.

Toss, retrieve. Toss, retrieve.

A sense of wrong. A homesickness. A lovesickness. The words of Robert Frost surrounded him.

A lump in the throat. Every act of creation came from the same place, Ruth had said. And every act of creation was first an act of destruction.

Peter was dismantling his life. Picking it apart. And replacing it with something new. Rebuilding.

Toss, retrieve.

And the paintings were snapshots of the process.

That's why he wanted to keep them. As a testament. A travelogue. A diary.

Gamache's arm stopped. Henri, tail wagging his entire backside, stared as the hand and the ball slowly lowered.

Then Gamache threw, and both the ball and the dog sailed into the meadow.

Peter had left his home, physically, emotionally, and creatively. He was turning his back on everything familiar, everything safe.

Where once Peter used muted colors, now he used bright, clashing colors.

Where once Peter's images were tightly controlled, now they were chaotic, unruly. Slapdash.

Where once his paintings were almost painfully self-satisfied and even pretentious, now they were silly, playful.

Where once Peter stuck to the rules, now he broke them. His first act of destruction. Experimenting with color, perspective, with distance and space. He wasn't very good, yet. But if Peter kept trying, he'd get to where he wanted to be.

This new Peter was willing to try. Willing to fail.

Gamache stepped forward, approaching the answer. Seeing it just ahead of him. Henri had lost the ball in the thick growth and was rooting around, his bottom high and his nose down.

Every now and then he looked over at Gamache, for guidance, but Armand had his own search.

Where once Peter's paintings were abstract, now . . . now.

Henri lifted his head in triumph. The ball in his mouth, along with a good chunk of wildflowers and grass.

Henri stared at Gamache. And Gamache stared at him. Both had what they were looking for.

"Well done," Armand said to Henri. He took the slobbery tennis ball and clipped the shepherd on to the leash. "Well done."

They hurried back to Three Pines, Gamache's thoughts racing ahead.

Though he'd lived in the countryside, Peter had kept nature at arm's length, eschewing it as the territory of amateurs. Still lifes, landscapes. All too figurative, too obvious. Unworthy of a great artist. Like himself. Who saw the world as more complex. As abstract.

Gamache had assumed the splashes of paint on Peter's latest works were exercises but still abstracts. They were the first attempts of a tidy mind to be messy.

But if Peter had left everything else behind, why not his style as well?

Suppose they weren't abstract?

Suppose Peter was painting what he saw?

Gamache knocked on Clara's door, then opened it.

"Clara?"

There was no answer.

He scanned the village green, then looked over to the bistro.

"To hell with it," he said, and walked into Clara's home. He and Henri found the paintings where they'd been left, nailed to the kitchen wall.

He stared at them, then walked over to the pictures still on the kitchen table, their corners kept from curling by salt and pepper shakers and chipped coffee mugs.

Pulling out his device, he took photos, then left.

He drove to Cowansville, where he could connect to high speed and email the photos. He looked at his watch.

Four thirty-five. Nine thirty-five in the evening in Scotland. Late, too late to expect a response. But still, for twenty minutes Gamache sat in his car and stared at his device. Willing an answer to appear.

It did not.

As he drove back to Three Pines, he thought about the Robert Frost quote. He'd come across it years ago and remembered it because, while a poem might begin as a lump in the throat, so did a murder investigation.

So did a murder.

NINETEEN

⁓

"Anything?" Reine-Marie asked when her husband crawled back into bed.

"Nothing," he whispered.

It was just after 3 a.m. and he'd gotten up to check his emails. Henri had lifted his head, but even the dog was too tired to take this seriously.

Gamache had connected to the dial-up, wincing as the beeping and screaming filled the quiet night. Finally the messages downloaded.

Russian brides.

Lottery winnings.

Some emails from a prince in Nigeria, but nothing from Scotland.

It was 8 a.m. there. He'd hoped Constable Stuart might have an early shift. He also hoped Constable Stuart would care enough about the message to act on it.

This was, truth be told, the third time that night Gamache had gotten up to check his emails. The first two without real hope, but this time there'd been a chance.

He returned to bed and fell back into a restless sleep.

An hour later he got up again. As he crept down the stairs he saw a rectangle of light coming from the study. He didn't think he'd left a lamp on and smiled as he stood in the door frame.

"Anything?"

"*Tabarnac!*" Beauvoir started. "You scared the shit out of me. Sir."

"I hope not." Gamache went in and looked over Jean-Guy's shoulder. "Porn?"

"Not unless waiting ages for the damned dial-up to connect turns you on."

"I remember when—" Gamache started and was rewarded with a surly look from Jean-Guy.

Finally the emails started downloading.

"*Rien*," said Beauvoir, pushing away from the desk. "Nothing."

The two men walked into the living room.

"You think that constable will recognize something from the paintings?" Beauvoir asked, sitting on the arm of the sofa. Gamache dropped into an armchair, crossed his legs and adjusted his dressing gown.

"Frankly, I'm hoping he doesn't just delete my messages."

"You really think those paintings are landscapes?" Beauvoir seemed less than convinced.

"I think it's a possibility."

Maybe, thought Gamache, Peter's paintings really were markers, recording where he was. His *inuksuit*.

"If those're landscapes, Scotland must be a pretty weird place."

Gamache laughed. "I didn't say he was good at it."

"No kidding."

"It might be like the Impressionists. They painted nature, but it was like they painted with their feelings."

"Then he couldn't have liked Scotland much." Beauvoir slid off the arm of the sofa and landed on the seat. "But if he was so interested in experimenting with landscapes, couldn't he have done it in Paris or Venice? Why Scotland?"

"And why Dumfries?" said Gamache. He hauled himself up. "Back to bed."

But at that moment there was a *ping*.

They looked at each other. An email had arrived.

Reine-Marie felt the bed beside her. It was cool. She sat up and looked out the window. The sun wasn't yet up. But Armand was.

Putting on her dressing gown, she went downstairs. This time Henri followed, his toenails clicking on the wood floors.

"Armand?"

The living room was in darkness but a light was on in the study.

"In here," came the familiar voice.

"Anything?" she asked.

"Something," said Jean-Guy, stepping out of the way so that his mother-in-law could get a good view. "I think."

Gamache offered her his chair.

Reine-Marie sat down and looked at the screen.

"*It's cosmic*," she read, then looked up at her husband. "I don't understand. Do you think he means 'comic'?"

Armand and Jean-Guy were staring at the curt message with as much puzzlement as she felt.

Constable Stuart had replied to Gamache's email with two short words.

It's cosmic.

Robert Stuart had been in the pub the night before when his iPhone buzzed. He had it programmed so that it made different sounds depending on who was trying to reach him.

This was clearly a work email, and normally it would never occur to him to check it, except that the man on the next barstool had been prattling on and on about how he'd been screwed on some tax bill.

Stuart lifted his iPhone and gave his companion an apologetic shrug, which the man ignored, and continued to babble. Stuart took his iPhone and his pint and found a seat in a quiet corner.

The message was from that man in Canada. The French guy with the weird accent. It couldn't be important.

Constable Stuart put the device down. The email had served its purpose in allowing him to escape. The actual message could wait until the morning.

He sipped his beer and looked around, but his eyes kept falling back to the worn wooden table. Finally he picked up the device and opened the message. His eyes widened a bit in interest, then he opened the attachments.

Scrolling through the pictures quickly, he shook his head and felt vaguely disappointed. He didn't know much about art, but he knew shit when he saw it. He was glad Apple hadn't yet figured out how to send smells.

And yet. And yet. There was something about one of the images in particular. The Canadian man, a retired homicide investigator he said, hadn't asked him to judge the art. Just to tell him if any of the places looked familiar.

They did not. Truth be told, they didn't look like "places." Just splotches of bright paint.

Except for one. One had bright paint, but it had something else.

"Hey, Doug." He waved a fellow over. "Look at this, will ya?"

Doug took the device and appeared to be having trouble focusing.

"What the fook is that?"

"Does it look familiar?"

"It looks like a migraine."

He tossed the device back to Stuart.

"Look again, you great scrotum," said Stuart. "I think I know this place."

"It's a place?" Doug took it and looked again. "On earth? Poor ones."

"Not just on earth, down the road."

"You're pissed," Doug said, but continued to study the picture. Then his eyes widened and he looked at Stuart.

"Speculation, lad."

"Aye," said Stuart. "I thought so too. It's cosmic."

Next morning, Constable Stuart got up early and drove six miles north. The sun was just coming up and burning off the mist when he parked the car and got out.

He changed into rubber boots and took his cell phone with him. Studying the photos Gamache had sent, Constable Stuart set off across the grass.

Once away from the road, the land dipped and he found himself in a gully where the mist and fog pooled. He wore a sweater, but suddenly wished it was thicker, heavier. And he suddenly wished he wasn't alone.

Constable Stuart was not given to flights of imagination. Not more than any other Celt. But standing there, all color drained from the

164

world, most color drained from him, the ghouls of his maternal grandmother's tales came back. The warnings of his paternal grandfather came back.

The ancient ghosts, the restless souls, the malevolent spirits came back. They took all the colors from the world, and in the drained mist they settled around him.

"Pull yourself together," he told himself. "Do this quickly, then get back in time for a coffee and a bacon butty."

The very idea of the bacon sandwich cheered him as he walked carefully through the fog, his feet testing the ground in front of him.

He kept the image of the bacon butty in the forefront of his mind, like a talisman. A charm. A replacement for the crucifix his grandmother once wore.

Pulling out his device, he paused to send the Québec fellow a message.

"It's cosmic" he typed, and got no further.

His foot slipped on the grass, wet with dew. His arms pinwheeled, trying to move backward in time. To before the misstep. To before he arrived. To before he'd decided to come to this God-forsaken place.

His right leg slipped out from under him. Then his left. His hand opened and his iPhone flew away. It went sailing through the air, to be grabbed by the ghouls in the mist. For an instant, Constable Robert Stuart was suspended in midair. Flying.

And then he fell, hitting the ground hard, knocking the wind out of him. Everything became a confusion of images and sensations as he skidded and tumbled and somersaulted down the slope, disoriented and grabbing, grappling for purchase. And finding none in the dew-slick grass.

He hurtled and skidded downward. Where would it end? With a tree? A cliff?

And then, as suddenly as it started, it was over. It took him a moment to realize he was no longer moving. His head swam, his eyes unfocused, his body and brain in two separate places.

Constable Stuart lay still. It was over.

And then the panic. It wasn't over.

His eyes widened. His mouth widened.

He couldn't move and he couldn't breathe. He was paralyzed. The blades of grass, so close to his eyes, were huge. He knew they were the last things he'd see. Trees of grass.

He was about to die. His neck broken. Internal bleeding. He'd die in the gully. Where no one would find him for days. Weeks. And when they did he'd be unrecognizable. He'd seen enough bodies like that, and thought them grotesque. He was about to become grotesque.

They'd hold a state funeral for him, of course. His coffin draped in the Scottish flag. They'd sing "Flower of Scotland," his grieving widow, his friends and colleagues. Inconsolable, his—

A whoop of air was sucked into his lungs. Expanding them. And then he exhaled. A long, painful moan.

He breathed in. He breathed out. He closed his hands, clutching the grass. The soft, sweet grass. He could move. He could breathe.

Stop the music. Put the funeral on hold. His life wasn't over yet.

Robert Stuart lay there for a long time, breathing in. Breathing out. Staring up as the ghostly mist burned off into blue sky.

He sat up slowly. Then stood up on shaky new legs. And looked around.

He'd never been here before. This place rumored to exist by its own rules. In its own reality, its own space and time. With the power of life and death. Or death then life. This place that first killed and then resurrected.

Stuart stared at the world he'd tumbled into. A netherworld. An underworld.

A few yards up the hill he spotted his iPhone. Grasping it, he began taking photographs. Trying to capture what he saw. Only in reviewing them later did he realize no photo could really do that.

But those paintings had. Or at least they'd come close. Suddenly those paintings seemed a lot less odd.

TWENTY

—

"Well, I'll be damned," said Gamache, staring at the computer screen.

After the cryptic first message from Constable Stuart, *It's cosmic*, there'd been nothing. Until now.

A strange photograph had just appeared.

"I think it's taken eighty years to download," said Jean-Guy.

It certainly looked like the picture had been snapped long ago. It was black and white and shades of gray, and seemed frayed at the edges.

"What is it?" Reine-Marie asked.

Stare as she might, Reine-Marie couldn't quite make out what she was seeing. And she sure couldn't see a connection between the information they'd asked for from the officer in Dumfries and this.

Armand had sent pictures of Peter's paintings to Scotland, suspecting they were indeed landscapes. In hopes the constable would recognize where they were painted.

And in response, Constable Stuart had sent this.

Had he misunderstood the request? Reine-Marie wondered.

Then a finger, Jean-Guy's finger, lightly touched the screen. There, along the contours of a small hill, snaking in and out of the mist, was a vague checkerboard pattern. It wove along the shape of the ground as though the fabric of the earth had torn, to reveal the black and white checks in the wound.

Reine-Marie felt herself drawn into the image. It looked like a place not quite of this world, and not quite of the next.

She looked away, into Armand's eyes, and in them she saw a reflection of the otherworldly image on the screen. Then she looked over to Jean-Guy. Both men were staring, transfixed.

"Well, I'll be damned," Jean-Guy whispered.

"One of Peter's paintings has this checkerboard pattern," said Gamache. "We thought he was just fooling around with an old art school exercise. But he wasn't."

"He was painting what he saw," said Reine-Marie.

"But what is it?" Jean-Guy asked.

"And where is it?" Gamache added. "May I?"

Reine-Marie stood up and Armand sat in front of the computer. He tapped out an email to Constable Stuart, asking for more specifics.

"May I?" Jean-Guy replaced Gamache in front of the computer and brought up a search engine. He put in key words. *Dumfries. Checkerboard.*

But nothing useful appeared.

"Try Dumfries, Scotland, checkerboard," Gamache suggested.

Still nothing.

"May I?" Reine-Marie replaced Beauvoir and added one word to his search. Then hit enter.

And up flashed the answer as though it had been waiting for the magic word.

Cosmic.

"Well, I'll be damned," whispered Reine-Marie.

"The Garden of Cosmic Speculation?" Clara asked. "Are you kidding me?"

But their faces told her this was probably not a joke.

Her phone had rung ten minutes earlier and she'd bolted upright, answering on the first ring and looking at the clock. Not yet 6 a.m.

It was Armand. They wanted to come over.

"Now?"

"Now."

Now four people in dressing gowns, and a dog, stood in Clara's kitchen. Jean-Guy placed the laptop on the pine table next to Peter's early paintings.

"Well, I'll be damned," said Clara.

She looked at Peter's paintings. Then back to the laptop.

Then back to the paintings. One in particular.

"That's not an exercise in perspective," she said, staring at the black and white checkerboard pattern that snaked across Peter's painting. "It's this."

She turned back to the photograph, where a black and white pattern wound in and out of the mist. Like a cobra.

"Whoever took this must've been almost exactly where Peter stood when he did the painting," she said. She spoke as though to herself.

Clara felt her heart race, pound. Not in excitement—this was no happy dance in her breast.

There was something eerie about the photograph. It showed a world where anything could come out of the mist. Where anything might crawl out of that rent in the ground, formed by the black and white pattern.

That feeling now transmitted itself to Peter's painting. While the photo showed a gray world, Peter's normal world, his actual painting was a wild confusion of color.

But both images had one thing in common. They coalesced around the simple, clear checkerboard snake. In the garden.

She felt her skin crawl and tingle as the blood crept away from the surface. Away from the painting and the photograph. To hide in her core.

"Here," she said, pointing to the painting. "This is where it happened."

"What happened?" asked Reine-Marie.

"Where Peter started to change. I was wondering why he didn't save any of his other works. He probably did some in Paris, he probably did some in Florence and Venice. But he didn't save them, didn't give them to Bean to keep safe. Why not?"

"I was wondering the same thing," said Armand. "Why didn't he?"

"Because they weren't worth saving?" Jean-Guy suggested, and was rewarded with a beam from Clara.

"Exactly. Exactly. But he saved these. He must've heard about this garden in his travels and decided to go there—"

"But why?" asked Beauvoir.

"I don't know. Maybe because it's so strange. Venice and Florence and Paris are beautiful, but conventional. Every artist goes there for inspiration. Peter wanted something different."

"Well, he found it," said Jean-Guy, looking at the paintings.

They were still *merde*. It was as though Peter had fallen into a pile of shit. Then painted it.

"I don't know what happened," said Clara. "But something in that garden changed Peter. Or began the change."

"Like a ship," said Gamache. "Changing course. It might take a while to get to port, but at least it was going in the right direction."

Peter was no longer lost. He'd finally found his North Star, thought Gamache.

If so, why had he then flown to Toronto? Was it to deliver the paintings to Bean? But they could have been mailed, like the others.

Was it to visit his old professor? Was he looking for approval, for a mentor? Or maybe it was simpler, more human. More Peter.

Maybe he was running away again, frightened by what he'd seen in the garden. Unwilling to go further down that path. Maybe he went to Toronto to hide.

And once again the Samarra story came to mind. There was no hiding. Not from fate. Peter's destiny would find him.

Toronto, then, was another step closer to his destination.

As though they'd all had the same thought at the same time, they turned as one to look at the far wall. And the canvases tacked up there. Peter's latest works. Perhaps his last works. Certainly his last signposts.

"Gimme a bacon butty," said Constable Stuart. He said it as a Wild West sheriff might've ordered a shot of whiskey.

He took off his jacket and smoothed his wet hair.

"What happened to you, boy?" the waiter at the breakfast bar asked, as he wiped crumbs off the melamine surface.

"What do you know about that garden down the road?"

The circular motion of the damp rag slowed. To a stop. The elderly man considered the constable.

"It's just a garden. Like any other."

Stuart got up off the round stool. "I'll let you think about that answer. When I get back I'd like a better one. And that butty. And a black coffee."

In the men's room Stuart used the toilet, then washed his hands and scrubbed his face, trying to get off the dirt and grass ground into his skin. Some of the dirt turned out to be bruises and he stopped scrubbing.

He gripped the porcelain sink and leaned toward the mirror, staring into his wide eyes. He knew that lawyers were taught never to ask a question unless they were prepared for the answer. They did not like surprises.

But cops were the opposite. They were almost always surprised. And rarely in a good way.

Robert Stuart wondered if he was prepared for the answer that awaited him.

Clara sat at the laptop Jean-Guy had brought over when they'd arrived.

Coffee had been made and poured, and now she brought the computer out of sleep mode.

There on the screen was a home page.

"What is it?" Clara asked. "It can't be just a normal garden. Not with a name like that."

"We didn't have a chance to read much about it," said Reine-Marie, bringing a chair over to sit beside Clara. "We wanted to get here as quickly as possible. All we know is that it's not far from Dumfries."

The men also brought over chairs and sipped coffee and read about a garden of cosmic speculation.

Constable Stuart swung his leg over the stool. A bacon butty and black coffee awaited him, but there was no sign of the elderly waiter. Or anyone else. But he did hear voices from behind the swinging door.

He took a huge bite of the grilled sandwich. It was warm and the smoked bacon crackled and tasted of his settled childhood. Reluctantly he put the butty down and looked around to see if anyone was watching. But he was alone in the diner. He walked swiftly and softly over to the door.

"What're you going to tell 'im?" a woman's voice, elderly and difficult, was asking.

"The truth."

Stuart recognized the waiter.

"You ridiculous old man, you don't know the truth any more than I do. There is no 'truth.'"

"There is. Look, at least I've been there. You haven't."

"You went there to shoot hares. Nothing cosmic about it."

"I didn't say there was." Now the old man sounded petulant.

"You've bored enough people with your drunken tale. Now get out there before he steals the condiments," said the cook. "I know the type. Sneaky."

Constable Stuart stood up straight, miffed, then sneaked quickly back to his breakfast.

Clara scrolled through image after image of the garden on the website. In one, several huge DNA double helixes rose from the ground as though expelled. In another part of the garden, bold sculptures representing various scientific theories mixed with tall trees to form a forest. Man-made, nature-made. Almost indistinguishable.

And then there were the checkerboard patterns that swooped up and down and in and out, bursting through from another dimension.

The photographs on the website had been taken in daylight, in sunshine. But still there was something disturbing about them. This was no temporary sculpture garden. This one felt old, enduring.

It felt like Stonehenge or the haunting hilltop shards of Bryn Cader Faner in Wales. Their meaning obscured, but their power unmistakable.

Why? Clara asked herself. Why had someone created this garden? And why had Peter gone there?

"Never met the owner," said the elderly man, whose name turned out, unexpectedly, to be Alphonse.

"Should I call you Al?" Constable Stuart asked.

"No."

"Did he create the garden?" Stuart asked.

"With his late wife, aye. Nice people from what I hear. Did it just for themselves, but when word got out, they decided to open it to the public."

Stuart nodded. He knew that much. And he also knew it was open for only one day a year.

"Not a day," Alphonse corrected. "Five hours. Once a year. The first Sunday in May."

"Is that when you saw it?" Stuart asked, knowing the answer.

"Not exactly. I went there in the evening."

"Why?"

This was clearly not the line of questioning Alphonse had expected. Should he say he'd gone there to poach hares? Not for food, they had plenty of that. But for fun. As he'd done since he was a boy. Shooting squirrels and rabbits. Moles and voles.

Should he tell this policeman about the last time he'd gone shooting in the garden? It had been dusk. He'd seen movement and had raised his rifle.

He had the hare in the crosshairs. It was sitting on one of the strange sculptures, a bone-white stairway that cascaded down a hill, cut into the grass from a great height.

It was a magnificent hare. Huge. Old. Gray. As Alphonse watched through the sight of his rifle, the hare stood up slowly on its hind legs. Tall. Alert. Sensing something.

Alphonse stared at him down the barrel of his gun. And pulled the trigger.

But nothing happened. The gun had jammed.

Swearing, Alphonse had broken open the chamber, replaced the shell and snapped it shut, expecting the hare to be long gone.

But it remained where it was. Like a sculpture. Like a part of the garden. An old gray stone. Both alive and inanimate.

Alphonse raised his gun, knowing he had the power to decide which one the hare would be.

"The first Sunday in May?" Reine-Marie read out loud from the website. "But Peter had come back to Canada by then. He must've done the painting sometime in the early winter."

"That means he must've trespassed," said Clara. She tried to make it sound nonchalant. A simple statement of fact. But it was much more than that. For her.

The man she knew followed rules. He followed recipes, for God's sake. He read instructions, paid his bills on time and had his teeth cleaned twice a year. He did as he was told and taught. It was not in his nature to trespass.

But Peter had changed. He was no longer the man she knew.

She'd sent him away, hoping he'd change. But now faced with more evidence that he had, she found herself suddenly afraid. That he'd not only changed, but changed course. Away from her.

To hide her upset, she went back to studying the website. At first she just stared, hoping no one would notice her distress, but after a few moments the images sunk in. They were like nothing she'd ever seen before.

The creators of the garden wanted to explore the laws of nature, the mysteries of the universe, and what happened when the two intersected.

Collided.

Was it like a nuclear bomb, wiping out all life? Or was it like the double helix. Creating life?

There were no answers in the garden, only questions. Speculation.

The Peter Clara knew was about certainties. But he'd gone halfway around the world to a place where questions were planted. And grew. Where uncertainty flourished.

And Clara began to feel a small seed of relief. It was the sort of place she would love to visit. The old Peter would have scoffed. He might have accompanied her, but grudgingly, and with snide asides.

But this Peter had gone to the Garden of Cosmic Speculation on his own.

Perhaps, perhaps, he was changing course, but not away from her. He was moving closer. If not physically, then in every other way.

"Huh," Reine-Marie grunted, reading. "It's a garden but not in the conventional sense. It's a mix of physics and nature," she said, looking up from the screen. "A sort of crossroads."

Peter had placed his easel at that crossroads, and created.

Clara longed to speak to him. To find out what he found. To hear how he felt. He'd finally turned the corner. Moved toward her. And then fallen off the face of the earth.

"It's become quite a draw," said Alphonse. "People come from all over to see it. Some call it mystical."

He said it with a snort, but Constable Stuart was unconvinced. He'd heard what the cook had said. The warning. Not to tell his drunken tale again.

"What happened to you in the garden, Alphonse?"

Clara went back to Peter's paintings. Not the one with the checkerboard snake, but the other two.

She didn't know for sure, but she suspected they'd also been painted in the Garden of Cosmic Speculation. The palette was the same, the urgency the same.

Like the first one, these were explosions of color. Clashing, almost frantic. Unlikely, unattractive combinations of color. Peter seemed to have painted them with abandon, desperate to grab hold of something fleeting, to capture it.

"It looks as though his brain exploded onto the page," said Jean-Guy, standing beside Gamache.

What had Peter seen, Clara wondered, in the Garden of Cosmic Speculation? What had he felt?

Alphonse looked behind him, toward the swinging door into the kitchen, then leaning his elbows on the counter, he lowered his voice.

"This is to go no further, understand?"

Constable Stuart lied, and nodded.

"It was sometime last fall. I went there in the early evening to shoot rabbits."

And out came the story.

He paused after describing the first, failed attempt to kill the hare.

"I'd done it many times before, mind. Since I was a boy."

"Had you been to the garden before?" Stuart asked.

Alphonse nodded. "Killed lots of rabbits there. But never seen one quite like this."

"How was it different?"

Alphonse studied the constable. He no longer seemed like a waiter in a roadside diner. He was inches from Constable Stuart's face, and he looked ancient. But not frail. He looked like a seaman who'd turned his face into the wind all his life. Navigating. Searching.

Until he'd found what he sought. Dry land.

"Shall I tell you?" he asked.

And Constable Stuart wondered, yet again, if he really wanted the answer.

He nodded.

"I watched as he stood on his hind legs, this hare. Straight up. Huge. Gray. He didn't move. Even when I raised my rifle again. He just stood there. I could see his chest. I could see him breathing. I could see his heart beating. And then I noticed something behind him."

"A movement? The owner?"

"No. Not a man. But another hare. Almost as big. Just standing there too. I'd been so taken with the one I hadn't noticed the others."

"Others?"

"Must've been twenty. All standing on their hind legs. Straight upright. In a perfect circle. Not moving."

Constable Stuart felt himself grow very quiet. Very still. The old man's eyes were on him, like searchlights.

"The wife says I was drunk, and I'd had a few. But not more than usual. She says I was seeing double. Triple. She says I was seeing things."

He dropped his eyes and his head and spoke into the hacked and stained old counter.

"And she was right. I saw something."

"What?"

"What's that?" Clara asked, leaning closer to the vile colors.

"What?" asked Reine-Marie, getting to within inches of the painting.

"There, by that zigzag."

"They're stairs, I think," said Armand.

"No, I don't mean the zigzag, I mean beside it." Clara spoke urgently, as though it would disappear at any moment.

"It's a stone," said Jean-Guy.

Clara peered closer.

"The hares were made of stone."

The two men stared into each other's eyes.

"It's a sculpture garden," said Constable Stuart. "They probably were stone."

"No."

Alphonse spoke softly, almost regretfully. And Constable Stuart understood then that this man hadn't been searching for dry land. He'd been searching for company. One person. Who'd believe him.

"I saw the old one move. I saw his heart beat. And I saw him turn to stone."

"It's a circle of stones," said Armand, also leaning in.

Their eyes were adjusting to Peter's wild colors, until what had appeared to be chaos became a design.

"But the website doesn't show a stone circle, by the stairs," said Clara.

"And then they turned back into rabbits," said Alphonse. "They came alive again."

His eyes shone, not with fear, but with wonderment. The astonishment of an elderly man, closer to death than life.

"Did you ever go back?" Stuart asked.

"Every night. I go back every night. But I don't take my rifle anymore."

Alphonse smiled. Constable Stuart smiled.

When the others left to get dressed, Gamache stayed behind.

"Do you mind?" he asked Clara, and she shook her head.

"Make some more coffee," she waved toward the old electric perk. "I'll be down in a few minutes."

While the coffee perked, Gamache carried a chair over, to face the wall of paintings. He sat and stared.

"Oh, God," came the familiar voice. "Am I walking in on something I shouldn't know about?"

Gamache stood up. Myrna was in the doorway holding a loaf of what he could smell was fresh banana bread.

"What do you mean?" he asked.

She waved her hand up and down to indicate both his attire and his very presence.

He looked down and realized he was still in his dressing gown and slippers. He pulled the gown more securely around him.

"Did you and Clara have a slumber party?" Myrna asked, putting the warm loaf on the kitchen counter.

"This is Clara's house?" he asked, apparently bewildered. "Damn. Not again."

Myrna laughed and, walking to the counter, she cut and buttered thick slices of the loaf while Gamache poured coffees.

"What's up?" Myrna asked.

He brought her up to speed on the Garden of Cosmic Speculation.

She peppered him with questions, all of which started with why and none of which he could answer.

"That's better," said Clara, returning to the kitchen and pouring herself a coffee. All three took their seats and stared at the latest paintings as though waiting for the show to begin.

If the works Peter painted in the Garden of Cosmic Speculation looked like his head had exploded onto the paper, these later ones looked like his guts had exploded.

"Something happened to Peter in the Garden of Cosmic Speculation," said Gamache. He found he liked saying the name and pledged to say it every morning while in his own garden, speculating. "He left and came back to Canada. And painted these."

"How do we know these weren't painted in the garden too?" asked Myrna, indicating with her banana bread the three canvases nailed to the wall.

"Because Peter gave those three"—Gamache pointed with his slice to the paintings on the table—"to Bean in the winter. When he'd returned from Dumfries. He only mailed these bigger ones later."

"Ergo, he painted them on his return to Canada," said Clara.

"Ergo?" asked Myrna.

"Don't tell me you've never wanted to use it," said Clara.

"Not now that I hear how it really sounds."

They fell silent, staring at the works.

"Do you think they're landscapes too?" Myrna finally asked.

"I do," said Armand, though he sounded not completely convinced. It didn't look like any landscape he'd ever seen. Besides the flying lips, nothing really even looked like anything.

"Clara," said Gamache slowly, elongating her name. Buying time to sort his thoughts. "What did you say you do with your failed paintings?"

"I keep them and bring them out when I'm between projects."

Gamache nodded slowly. "And what do you do with them?"

"I told you before," said Clara, confused by the question. "I look at them."

Gamache said nothing and Clara wondered what he was getting at, and then her eyes widened. She'd remembered what she did with her old paintings.

She got to her feet and, pulling the nails out of the wall, she took down Peter's lip painting.

"The only reason we put these paintings up this way around," she said as Myrna and Armand went to help, "is because it's how Bean had them on the bedroom wall. But suppose Bean was wrong? There's no signature to tell which way is up."

She nailed it back into place. Upside down. And all three stepped back. To examine it.

Not upside down at all, but finally the right way around.

"Well, I'll be damned," said Myrna.

The slashes of vivid color had become a wide and turbulent river. The bold red lips had become waves. What had appeared to be trees now became cliff faces.

The three of them stood in front of what Peter had really created. The smiles weren't smiles at all. There was nothing giddy, nothing joyous about this picture. Peter had painted a vast and endless river of sorrow.

"I know this place," said Gamache.

TWENTY-ONE

—

"Armand." Reine-Marie appeared in Clara's kitchen with a sheet of paper. "Constable Stuart wrote back."

She looked perplexed and handed him the email she'd printed out.

He took it and in turn pointed her to the wall of paintings. She walked over as he read, his brows drawing together as he got further and further into the message.

He handed the paper to Clara and joined Reine-Marie at the wall of paintings.

"All right?" he asked, noticing her pale face.

"*Oui.* Peter finally figures out how to paint emotions, and he paints this." She paused. "Poor one."

"Come with me," he said.

They left the sad painting on the wall and returned to the Garden of Cosmic Speculation on the pine table.

Clara finished reading and passed the page on to Myrna.

"You don't believe it, do you?" asked Reine-Marie, looking from Clara to Armand and nodding toward the letter now in Myrna's hands.

"One impossible thing before breakfast?" Armand asked.

He placed his hand, splayed, in the center of one of the paintings on the table. And turned it.

Only then did they see what Peter had done.

He hadn't created something with these paintings. He'd captured something. A moment in a garden at dusk.

What had looked like a circle of stones in the painting when it was the other way around was indeed a circle of stones. Tall, solid, gray.

But now they saw something else. Long, strong slashes of color off the top of the stones.

Rabbit ears.

"Peter would never have believed such a thing," said Clara. But in her heart she knew she had to stop saying that. If they had a hope of finding out what had happened to him, she had to accept that the man she'd known was indeed gone.

Down the rabbit hole. Where impossible things happened.

Where hares turned to rune stones.

Where giddy smiles turned into vast sorrow. And back again. Depending on your perspective.

When she'd started the search there'd been an element of guilt. Of responsibility. She'd wanted to find him, she wanted him to be safe. But she hadn't been sure she wanted him back.

But the more they discovered about Peter now, the more desperate she was to meet this man. To get to know him. And have him meet her, for the first time.

Clara realized she was falling in love. She'd always loved Peter, but this was something else. Some deeper vein.

"It doesn't matter what we believe," said Myrna, joining them to stare at the picture. "What matters is what Peter believed he saw."

They looked from the table over to the paintings on the wall.

One was now quite clear. The waves of red lips. Frowning. Moaning. Sighing.

They'd turned the other two paintings around as well, but those had yet to give up their secrets.

"Should we go to Dumfries?" Clara asked. "See for ourselves? Talk to this Alphonse?"

"*Non*," said Armand. "Whatever happened there is in the past. Both Peter and time have moved on. We're going there."

He pointed to the river of sighs.

To a place Gamache knew well. It was in Québec but not of Québec. This area was unique in the world, having been created hundreds of millions of years earlier, by a catastrophe. A cosmic catastrophe.

Gamache, Jean-Guy, and Reine-Marie stood at the large map of Québec tacked up on their sitting room wall.

How often, Beauvoir wondered, had they stood in front of this very map when it had been in the Gamaches' Montréal home, plotting the best way to get to a crime scene? A body. A murder.

He hoped that wasn't what they'd find at the end of this journey too.

But the silence from Peter was ominous, and the sooner they could get there the better. And at least now they knew where "there" was.

The Chief's finger traced a line from Three Pines, near the Vermont border, up to Autoroute 20. Along to Quebec City, then over the bridge, skirting the city, and up again.

Up, up along the north shore of the St. Lawrence River. Traveling northeast.

To their destination in the Charlevoix region.

"Is that the best route?"

As the men discussed various options, Reine-Marie stared at the dot on the map. How often had she stood in front of this very map, staring at a dot? Imagining Armand inside it. Willing him safe, willing him home.

The dot had a name. Baie-Saint-Paul.

Saint Paul. Another one who'd seen something unlikely on the road. And whose life had changed.

"We're on the road to Damascus," said Armand with a smile. "Or Charlevoix anyway."

It was an area so beautiful, so unique, it had attracted visitors for centuries. At least one American president had had a summer home there. But what Charlevoix mostly attracted were artists, Québec artists, Canadian artists. Artists from around the world.

And now it had attracted Peter Morrow.

"How long will you be gone?" Reine-Marie asked a few minutes later, as she helped Armand pack a suitcase.

He paused, his hand full of socks. "Hard to say. It'll take the better part of the day to drive there, and then we need to find out where he's staying."

"If he's still there," she said, placing shirts in the suitcase. After considering, she added one more.

Through the sitting room window, Gamache could see Jean-Guy loading two suitcases into the Volvo. Perplexed, Gamache slipped the small book into the pocket of his satchel and they went outside.

As he walked down the path, Gamache saw Clara and Myrna standing by the car. Clara had Peter's rolled-up canvases in her hand, and Myrna had a map.

"You're here to see us off?" asked Gamache, but he already knew that wasn't true. Clara shook her head and looked toward their suitcases, already in the Volvo.

"You're coming with us?" Gamache asked.

"No," said Clara. "You're coming with us."

It was said with a smile, but the distinction was clear.

"I see," said Armand.

"Good." Clara watched him closely. "I'm not kidding, Armand. I'm going to find Peter. You can come if you'd like, but if you do, you have to agree that I make the final decisions. I don't want this to turn into a power struggle."

"Believe me, Clara, I have no wish for power." He paused and became so still that Clara also stilled. "I'm not bringing any art supplies."

"What's that supposed to mean?"

"I'm not an artist."

"And I'm not an investigator," she said, grasping his meaning.

"You don't know what you'll find," he said.

"No, I don't. But I need to be the one looking."

"And what will you do when we get there?" he asked.

"I'll find out where Peter's staying."

"And suppose he isn't still there?"

"Are you treating me like a child, Armand?"

"No. I'm treating you like a responsible adult, but one who's trying to do something she's unprepared for. Not trained for. I can't paint a very good picture. You can't conduct a very good investigation. This is your life, yes. But it's what we've done for a living." He paused and leaned so close to her no one else could hear. "I'm very good at it. I will find Peter."

And she replied, so close that he felt the warm words in his ear, "You might know how to investigate, but I know Peter."

"You knew Peter." Gamache saw the words slap her. "You think he's the same man, and he's not. If you don't accept that, you'll go off course. Fast."

She stepped back. "I know he's not the same man." She stared at him. "Peter's changed. He's following his heart now. That's my territory. I can find him, Armand. I'll know."

Gamache and Jean-Guy simply stared at her and she felt herself getting angry. Angry at them for not understanding, and angry at herself for not being able to explain it. And angry at the fact that it sounded so fucking lame.

"You like Peter," she finally said. "But I love him. Laugh if you want, but it makes a difference. I'll be able to find him."

"If love was compass enough," said Armand quietly, "there would be no missing children."

Clara felt the breath leave her body. There was nothing she could say to that. It was so monumentally true. And yet, and yet, Clara knew she needed to go. And not follow Gamache, but be in the lead.

She could find Peter.

"I would never laugh at you," Armand was saying, though he seemed so remote. "And I would never, ever mock the power of love. But it can also distort. Slip over into desperation and delusion."

"Which is why you need to come with us," said Clara. "Please. But I need to be in charge. I can find him."

Gamache nodded.

"You're in charge. We're here to support you."

"You're kidding, right?" Jean-Guy whispered to Gamache as the two men walked around the car. "If things start going bad, you'll take over."

"They won't go bad."

"But if they do?"

"If they do, Clara's in charge."

"Following what? Her heart? Love droppings?" asked Beauvoir.

The Chief turned to him and lowered his voice. "And if Annie was missing? Would you let someone else look for her?"

Jean-Guy paled at the very thought. "Never."

"Clara's right, Jean-Guy. She has a better chance than anyone of knowing what Peter would do and where he'd go. If she follows her heart and we follow our heads, we might find him."

"I guess that leaves me with the stomach," said Myrna, who'd overheard their conversation. She held up a paper bag filled with sandwiches from Sarah's boulangerie. "Who wants to follow me?"

She put the sandwiches and a cooler in the car while the others loaded up the men's suitcases. They were about to get in themselves when Clara held out her hand.

Jean-Guy looked at Gamache, who nodded. Beauvoir dropped the keys into Clara's palm, walked around the car and was about to get into the passenger side when Myrna stepped in front of him. Once again Jean-Guy looked at Gamache, and once again the Chief nodded.

The men got into the backseat.

Clara was in the driver's seat.

"Are you sure this is such a good idea?" Beauvoir whispered to Gamache.

"Clara's an excellent driver. We'll be fine."

"I don't mean that, and you know it."

"Clara will be fine," said the Chief.

"Yeah. Fine."

Jean-Guy leaned forward just as the car started to move.

"Are we there yet?" he asked.

"Are you sure this is such a good idea?" Myrna asked Clara.

"He'll be fine." She pressed the gas and turned the car toward the road out of the village. The north road.

"I'm hungry," said Jean-Guy. "I have to pee."

As they passed the bench at the top of the hill, inscribed with *Surprised by Joy*, Gamache turned in his seat. And looked back.

And there he saw Reine-Marie standing in the middle of the road.

He turned away, concentrating on the road ahead and trying to ignore the lump in his throat.

TWENTY-TWO

⌒

"Now what?" asked Jean-Guy.

He'd naturally turned to Gamache, but the Chief deflected the question over to Clara.

They'd gone around to all the B and Bs in Baie-Saint-Paul. All the country auberges. All the hotels, both shabby and high-end.

No Peter.

To make matters worse, Baie-Saint-Paul was enjoying the height of the summer tourist crush, and it became clear that while they were having trouble finding Peter, they would also have trouble finding a place to stay that night.

Clara looked this way and that, up and down the crowded main street. It was hot and she was frustrated. She'd thought they'd drive into Baie-Saint-Paul and find Peter standing on a street corner. Waiting.

"Can I make a suggestion?" Myrna said, and Clara nodded, grateful for the help. "I think we need to regroup. We have to find someplace to sit down and think."

She looked around at the crowded *terrasses* and the happy tourists eating and drinking and laughing. It was all very annoying.

"We've thought enough," said Clara. "That's all we did for days and days in Three Pines. Now we need to act."

"Thinking is an action," said Gamache from a few paces away. "Running around might feel good, but it accomplishes nothing. And at this stage, wasting time is doing damage."

"He's right," Myrna said, and received a filthy look from Clara.

"I have to use the toilet."

"You said that all the way here," snapped Clara.

"Well, this time it's true."

They turned to look at Jean-Guy, who was shifting from one foot to the other.

Clara surrendered. "Oh, Christ. Okay. Let's regroup."

"This way." Jean-Guy pointed and led them down a slight hill, along a narrow side street, taking them further and further away from the tourist hubbub.

These streets, not much more than alleyways, were lined with row homes and old-fashioned, unfashionable businesses. Hardware stores, family-run drugstores, *dépanneurs* selling cigarettes and lottery tickets and soft, white POM bakery bread. Every now and then they caught a glimpse of grayish blue between the bright clapboard and fieldstone buildings. The river. So vast, so wide it looked like the ocean. Jean-Guy Beauvoir led them away from the tourist crush, into an area only locals knew.

"Over here."

They followed Beauvoir to a shabby inn.

"But we've already asked here," said Clara. "Haven't we?"

She turned around. Beauvoir's serpentine route had disoriented her.

"*Oui*," he said. "But we came in the front way. This is the back."

"And you expect a different answer depending on which door we go through?" asked Myrna. "I suspect Peter still isn't here, even if we climb in through the window."

Which, she thought, they might have to do if they didn't find a place for the night soon.

"We're asking a different question." Beauvoir now looked like his hair was on fire. "Through here."

He led them through a small archway, and suddenly they were confronted with the thing only hinted at through the cracks between buildings. Like catching glimpses of a huge creature, but just its tail, or nose, or teeth.

But here it was before them, exploding into view as they walked through the archway.

The St. Lawrence River. Magnificent, wild, eternal. Fought over, painted, turned into poetry and music. It stretched into infinity before them.

"Where're the toilets?" Beauvoir asked a server who came out onto the hidden terrace. Not waiting for an answer, Jean-Guy disappeared inside.

Only one other table was occupied in this small fieldstone courtyard. Two locals drank beer, smoked pungent Gitanes and played backgammon. They looked at the newcomers with vague interest, then went back to their game.

Clara chose a table right up against the wooden railing. On the other side was a sheer drop. And uninterrupted views of the *baie* of Baie-Saint-Paul.

They ordered iced teas and nachos.

Clara looked down at the place mat in front of her. As in many restaurants and brasseries across Québec, the place mat had a schematic of the village, not to scale, showing its history, as well as spots of interest and businesses. Inns, restaurants, galleries, and boutiques that had paid to be placed on the tourist map.

Peter had been here. Perhaps not to this very *terrasse*, but to this area.

"I'd forgotten that Cirque du Soleil started in Baie-Saint-Paul," said Myrna, reading her place mat. "Some places are like that."

"Like what?" asked Jean-Guy, returning from the toilet.

"Hot spots," said Myrna. "Of creativity. Of creation. Three Pines is one. Charlevoix is obviously another."

"I see there was a syphilis epidemic in the late seventeen hundreds," said Jean-Guy, reading the place mat. "Called the Evil of Baie-Saint-Paul. Quite a little hot spot."

He helped himself to nachos.

"How'd you know this *terrasse* was here?" Clara asked.

"It's my superpower."

"Jean-Guy Beauvoir," said Gamache. "Boy Wonder."

"They think we're the sidekicks," Beauvoir whispered to Myrna.

"Oh, how I'd love to get you on my couch," she replied.

"Get in line, sister."

Myrna laughed.

"I have an uncanny ability to find bathrooms," he said.

"Seems a limited sort of superpower," said Myrna.

"Yeah, well, if you really had to go, which power would you rather have? Flight? Invisibility? Or the ability to find a toilet?"

"Invisibility might be useful, but point taken, Kato."

"I told you, I'm not the sidekick." He gestured surreptitiously toward Gamache.

"Have you been here before?" Clara asked. "Is that how you knew?"

"*Non.*" He looked out across the ravine and seemed momentarily caught by the view. Then he returned his eyes to Clara. And in them she saw trees on the shoreline desperate for root. And an endless river.

"It's not magic, if that's what you're thinking," he said. "I could tell there was a drop-off, and when we first came here I suspected no innkeeper would have access to this view and not take advantage of it."

"You guessed?" asked Myrna.

"Yes."

But both women knew it wasn't really a guess. Jean-Guy Beauvoir might behave like a boy wonder, a sidekick. But they of all people knew that was just the façade. He too had an archway, and a secret courtyard. And views he kept hidden.

They sipped their drinks and caught their breath.

"Now what?" Myrna asked.

"We've been to the inns and B and Bs," said Clara, ticking off the hotels on the place mat. "We've shown Peter's picture around. Now we need to take around his paintings."

She pointed to the rolled-up canvases on the table.

"To innkeepers?" asked Jean-Guy.

"No. The galleries. Baie-Saint-Paul is thick with them." Again she gestured toward the place mat. "If Peter is here, he probably visited one or more."

"That's a good idea," said Jean-Guy, not bothering to disguise his surprise.

"You two go to the ones on this side of Baie-Saint-Paul." She drew a circle on the place mat. "And we'll take the other." She looked at her watch. It was nearing five. Nearing closing time. "We need to hurry."

She got up and they all took their place mats.

"Where should we meet?" Myrna asked.

"Here."

Clara's finger fell onto a brasserie in the center of town.

La Muse.

Myrna and Clara took two of Peter's paintings, including the one with the lips. Jean-Guy picked up the one that was left and examined it, not at all sure which way was up.

He looked, briefly, from the painting to the view, and back to the painting.

And shook his head.

How does that become this? he wondered. Perhaps, he thought, as he rolled up the canvas and followed the others back through the archway, he was the boy wonder after all.

There was, in Beauvoir's opinion, a great deal to wonder about.

Gamache and Jean-Guy were the first to make it back to La Muse.

Two of the five galleries in their area were already closed by the time they got there, including the Galerie Gagnon.

Gamache adored the works of Clarence Gagnon and was pleased that Clara had given them the territory that included the gallery dedicated to the Québécois artist. But Gamache could only peer through the front window, the paintings tantalizingly close.

Jean-Guy had gone to the back door and pounded, hoping the curator or someone else would still be there, but it was locked up tight.

Now, sitting on the verandah of La Muse, Gamache realized why he felt so relaxed here.

He was, essentially, sitting in a Clarence Gagnon painting, not unlike the one he'd seen on the wall of Peter's mother's home. Lucky man, Peter, to have been raised with a Gagnon. Though he'd also been raised with a gorgon. Not so lucky.

Gamache squinted slightly. If he took away the people, it would look almost exactly like the works the old master had painted of Baie-Saint-Paul more than seventy years ago. The brightly colored homes lining the village street. The sweep and swoop of the mansard roofs. The pointy dormers. The tall spires of the churches in the background. It was quaint and comforting and very Québécois.

All that was missing was a workhorse pulling a cart in the background, or kids playing. Or snow. So many of Gagnon's works featured snow. And yet the images were far from frigid.

He called Reine-Marie and brought her up to speed on the search.

"And the other three galleries?" she'd asked.

"Two were really more framing places, but we asked anyway and they didn't know Peter and showed no interest in the painting. The other carried works by contemporary local artists. Some really wonderful pieces."

"But no Peter Morrow?"

"No. The owner hadn't even heard of him."

"Did you show him Peter's canvas?" Reine-Marie asked.

"Yes. He was . . ." Gamache searched for the word.

"Repulsed?"

Armand laughed. "Polite. He was polite."

He heard Reine-Marie groan.

"It is worse, isn't it?" he said.

"Have you found a place to stay yet?"

"No. Jean-Guy's gone off to see if there've been any cancellations. I'll let you know."

"And do you have a plan B?" she asked.

"As a matter of fact, I do. There's a very nice park bench across the way," he said.

"Vagrancy. My mother said it would come to this. I'm sitting on our porch with a gin and tonic and some old cheese."

"And me," came a familiar voice.

"You're the 'some old cheese,'" said Reine-Marie, and Gamache heard Ruth's grinding laugh. "She's been telling me all about her misspent youth. Did you know she was—"

And they got cut off.

Gamache stared at his phone and smiled. He suspected Reine-Marie had hung up on purpose, to tease him. A minute later he received an email saying she loved him and to hurry home.

"Nothing, *patron*," said Beauvoir, taking his seat beside the Chief.

Nothing. Their search of Baie-Saint-Paul had yielded no Peter, no sign of Peter and no bed for the night. This might not, Gamache thought, have been his very best idea.

Jean-Guy nudged him and pointed down the winding street. Clara and Myrna were walking quickly toward them. Clara was waving the rolled-up canvases and both men could see both women were pleased.

Something. Finally something. Beauvoir was so relieved he forgot to be annoyed that Clara and Myrna were the ones who'd found something.

They joined the men on the *terrasse* of La Muse and Clara wasted no time. She unrolled one of Peter's paintings, while Myrna unfolded a map of Charlevoix.

"There." Clara's finger, like a bolt of lightning, hit the map. "This is where Peter painted that."

They looked from the map to the lip painting, then back again.

"One of the galleries told you?" Gamache asked.

As he looked up from the map, he noticed a man across the *terrasse* staring at them. The man quickly looked away as soon as Gamache met his eyes.

The former Chief Inspector was used to that, after all the times he'd been on the news. Still, Gamache had the impression the man wasn't so much staring at him as past him, to Clara.

"No, the galleries were mostly closed," Clara was saying. "Myrna and I were on our way here when I suddenly thought about someone else to ask."

"Who?" asked Beauvoir.

Gamache listened, but kept the man in his peripheral vision. He was again staring in their direction.

"Those two old guys playing backgammon," said Myrna. "They looked like they'd been here forever—"

"And they have been." Clara picked up the story. "Their families have been here for generations. As far back as anyone can remember. They even knew Clarence Gagnon. Split his wood for him when they were kids." She was silent for a moment. "Imagine meeting Gagnon? He painted villages and landscapes, but unlike anything that was being done at the time. It was like Gagnon stripped the skin off the world and painted the muscle and sinew and veins of a place. I make it sound grotesque, but you know what I mean."

"I know."

But it wasn't one of her companions who'd spoken. It was the man across the *terrasse*.

As Clara was talking, Gamache had noticed the man get up, drop some money on his table and then walk in their direction.

Gamache could see that Jean-Guy had also noticed. And was watching. Wary. Ready.

"*Excusez-moi.*" The man was now standing beside their table. "I'm sorry to disturb you."

He was casually dressed, but Gamache recognized the good cut of his shirt and trousers. Fifty years old, Gamache guessed, perhaps slightly younger.

The man looked at each of them, politely. His eyes paused on Gamache and there was a flicker of interest. But then his gaze came to rest on Clara.

"I heard you speak of Clarence Gagnon and wanted to introduce myself. I too am a fan of Gagnon's works. May I join you?"

He was slightly shorter than Gamache, and slender. He wore glasses and behind those glasses were intelligent blue eyes.

Clara got up and smiled at him.

"I'm afraid we have to leave."

"If there's anything I can do during your stay in Baie-Saint-Paul, please let me know."

He handed her a card.

"It would be a pleasure to talk. To compare thoughts on art," he said, and with unexpected dignity, he bowed slightly and said, "*Au revoir.*"

Gamache watched him leave. And he watched Clara place his card in her pocket.

"Coming?" Myrna grabbed the paintings and the map from the table.

Within minutes they were driving out of Baie-Saint-Paul, heading east. But not along the well-traveled highway 138. Instead, Clara turned the car slightly south. Toward the river. And then along a much narrower, less-traveled road.

Highway 362 hugged the cliffs and followed the St. Lawrence. And just before the village of Les Éboulements, she pulled over.

She knew it was obscenely stupid, but she half expected to see Peter silhouetted against the early evening sky. Standing at his easel. Painting.

And waiting. For her. As she'd waited for him weeks ago in their garden.

There was no Peter, but there was something else.

They got out of the car and Myrna reached over for Peter's canvases, then stopped. She, Clara, Armand, and Jean-Guy took a few steps forward.

There was no need to consult the paintings. They were here. This was where Peter had stood.

The St. Lawrence stretched before them, even more magnificent than in the village. Here the grandeur, the wild splendor of the place was both obvious and impossible.

The four friends stood side by side on the bluff.

It was here, on this very spot, that a meteor had hurtled to earth. Had hit the earth. Three hundred million years ago. It had struck with such force it killed everything beneath it, and for miles and miles around. It struck with such violence that even now the impact site could be seen from space.

Earth, thrown up in waves, had petrified there, forming smooth mountains and a deep crater.

Nothing lived. All life was extinguished. The earth laid to waste. For thousands of years. Hundreds of thousands of years. Millions of years.

Barren. Empty. Nothing.

And then. And then. First water, then plants, then fish. Then trees started to grow, in the rich soil. Bugs, flies, bats, birds, bear, moose, deer.

What had been a wasteland became a cauldron, a crucible of life. So rich, so diverse, it created an ecosystem unique in the world.

Porpoises, seals, blue whales.

Men. Women. Children.

All drawn here. All made their home here. In the crater.

This was Charlevoix.

This was where the four friends stood, in search of a fifth. Below them the river wound into and over and past the wound in the earth. Where all life ended. And began, again.

A terrible impact had created one of the most magical, most remarkable places on earth.

That's what Peter had tried to capture. This catastrophe. This miracle.

Armand Gamache turned, slowly, full circle. Like Clara, he half expected to see Peter Morrow watching them.

Peter had traveled from Scotland to here. From cosmic speculation to cosmic fact. A purely rational man was chasing the magical. Had tried to paint it.

As Gamache looked over the cliff to the St. Lawrence, the setting sun caught the waves of the great river, turning their foaming crests bright red. Turning them into frowns, then smiles. Then frowns. That morphed again into brilliant, giddy red smiles. A river of eternal emotion.

Gamache stood, captivated. He sensed more than saw Clara and Myrna and Jean-Guy beside him, also staring. Astonished.

They watched until the sun had set and all that was left was a dark river and a pink glow in the sky.

Peter had been here. He'd committed this sight to canvas, as best he could. Trying to record wonder. Awe. Not just beauty, but glory.

And he'd mailed it off. Away from here. Why?

And where was he now? Had he moved on, heading deeper into his own wound? Still searching?

Or— Gamache stared into the crater. Had Peter never left? Was he with them now, lying in the woods at the bottom of the cliff? Becoming part of the landscape? His silence profound because it was now unending?

Beside him, Clara stared at the river Peter had painted, and let the emotions roll over her. Her own, and his. She felt Peter very keenly.

Not his presence but his absence.

TWENTY-THREE

—

"Where're we going to stay?" Jean-Guy whispered.

They were heading back to the village of Baie-Saint-Paul, and reality. Leaving behind the cosmic in favor of down-to-earth concerns. Like food and shelter.

"I don't know," Gamache whispered back.

"Aren't you worried?" Beauvoir asked.

"We can sleep in the car if we have to," said Armand. "Not for the first time."

"Sure, we can. But do we want to? We can't do nothing, *patron*. We have to plan our next move. Clara's a nice person, but this's beyond her."

"I wonder," murmured Gamache, and turned to look out the window. And through it he saw stars. And the lights of Baie-Saint-Paul.

It was not possible to tell which was which. Which lights were celestial, which were of this earth.

"Where're we going to stay?" Myrna whispered to Clara.

"I don't know."

Myrna nodded, and stared out the windshield at the starry, starry night.

She missed her loft. She missed her bed. She missed her tisane and chocolate chip cookies.

But she knew that Clara missed all those things too. And she also missed Peter. Peter, who'd suddenly felt both very, very close while they'd stood on that cliff, and very, very far away.

Myrna looked over at Clara. She was staring straight ahead, concentrating on the windy road. Trying to keep them on track.

Trying not to go over the edge.

Myrna leaned back in her seat and took a deep breath. And calmed herself by looking at the stars. Or at the lights of the village. She couldn't quite tell which was which. And it didn't matter. Both were calming.

As they got closer, the lights of Baie-Saint-Paul grew brighter and the stars dimmed. Then they were back at La Muse bistro. It was now nine in the evening and they were starving. They ordered dinner, and while Myrna stayed at their table, the other three walked up and down the streets, checking at the auberges and B and Bs to see if there were any cancellations.

There were not.

They returned just as their dinners arrived.

Steak frites all around, the steaks char-grilled and thick. The fries thin and seasoned.

Beauvoir, while no fan of sleeping in cars, wasn't really worried. This was the great benefit of seeing worse. Fewer things worried him now.

"What next?" he asked as he took a forkful of tender steak and melting garlic butter.

"We know for sure Peter was here," said Clara. "Now we need to know if he's still here, and if not, where he went."

By "what next" Jean-Guy had meant "what's for dessert," but he was happy to talk about the case. For case this was, in his mind. And, he could see, in the Chief's as well.

There'd been no mistaking the look in Gamache's eye as he'd surveyed the cliff. Once their awe had passed, the Chief's brain had kicked in.

Scanning. Assessing.

Where could a body be? If a person fell? If a person was pushed?

Where would he end up?

When the meal was over and their coffees had arrived, Gamache turned to Clara.

"Would you like to hear what I think?"

She studied him for a moment. "Probably not, judging by your face."

Gamache gave a curt nod of agreement. "I think we should speak to the local police. Get them involved."

"In finding out where Peter might be staying?"

"In finding out where Peter might be," said Gamache, his voice low, but firm. His eyes not leaving Clara.

Her face paled as his meaning sunk in.

"You think he's dead?"

"I think he came here and painted those pictures. I think he mailed them to Bean. And then disappeared. That was months ago."

Gamache was quiet for a moment. He looked down at his espresso, the crème caramel brown on top. Then he met her eyes once again.

"The woods are thick here," he said.

Clara grew very, very still. "You don't think we'll ever find him."

"It was months ago, Clara," he repeated. "I hope I'm wrong. I hope we find him in a cabin somewhere. His beard bushy and his clothes covered in paint. Surrounded by canvases." He held her eyes. "I hope."

Clara looked over to Jean-Guy, who was also watching her. His face both boyish and grim.

Then to Myrna. Optimistic, hopeful, buoyant Myrna. She looked sad.

"You agree," said Clara. She could see it in Myrna's face.

"You must've known it was a possibility, Clara. You admitted you might not like what you find."

"I thought I might find Peter happy on his own," she said. "I thought I might even find him with another woman." She looked around the table, at their faces. "But I always thought I'd find him. Alive."

She was challenging them now. Daring them to argue with her.

When none did, she got up. "And I still do."

Clara walked out of La Muse.

"Should we go after her?" Jean-Guy asked.

"No, give her time," said Myrna.

Beauvoir watched as Clara walked up the road, her head down, like a torpedo. Tourists stepped out of her way just in time. And then she disappeared from view.

Beauvoir got up and wandered around the brasserie. There were paintings on the walls, with price tags slightly askew. From years of dusting.

They were pretty landscapes, but in Charlevoix a painting needed to be more than that to sell.

If he hadn't looked into the windows of the Galerie Gagnon, Jean-Guy might have thought these were quite good. But he had looked. And now he knew the difference. Part of him regretted that. He might now like better things, but he also liked fewer.

"Look who I found."

Beauvoir heard Clara's voice across the brasserie, heard the triumph, and turned quickly.

The man who'd spoken to them earlier at La Muse was standing beside her.

Beauvoir felt his heart, which had taken a great leap, simmer down. And he realized he'd actually thought she meant she'd found Peter.

"Madame Morrow called and told me of your plight," the man said. And then he introduced himself. "Marcel Chartrand." He shook their hands. "I run the Galerie Gagnon. I've come to take you home."

By the time they got settled in Chartrand's apartment above the Galerie Gagnon, it was approaching midnight.

He proved to be a gracious and accommodating host. Not everyone, Gamache knew, would welcome a call at eleven at night from a stranger asking for a place to stay. For herself and three friends.

But Marcel Chartrand had opened his home to them and was now pouring nightcaps as they relaxed in the living room.

He was either a saint, thought Gamache as he watched Chartrand chatting with Clara, or a man with his own agenda. Gamache had not forgotten the predatory look on Chartrand's face when he'd first spotted them in La Muse.

First spotted Clara.

"This isn't my main house," said Chartrand. He'd brought out a plate of cookies, and after pouring cognacs for Clara and Myrna he offered a glass to Jean-Guy. When the younger man waved him aside, Chartrand moved on to Gamache. "I have a *maison* a few minutes away, toward Les Éboulements."

"Overlooking the St. Lawrence?" Gamache asked, also declining the drink.

"*Oui, Chef*," said Chartrand, and poured himself a finger in the bottom of a bulbous glass.

It was not lost on either Gamache or Beauvoir that their host had just let slip that he knew precisely who his guests were. Or, at least, one of them.

"We were just there," said Gamache. "Astonishing view of the river."

"Yes. Breathtaking."

Marcel Chartrand subsided into an armchair and crossed his legs. In repose he retained a bit of a smile. Not, Gamache thought, a smirk. While some faces relaxed into a slight look of censure, this man looked content.

His face, from a distance, was handsome, urbane. But close up his skin was scored with small lines. A weathered face. From time spent in the elements. Skiing or snowshoeing or chopping wood. Or standing on a precipice, looking at the great river. It was an honest face.

But was he an honest man? Gamache reserved judgment.

It was possible Chartrand was older than he first appeared. And yet there was an unmistakable vitality about the man.

Gamache wandered the room. The walls were thick fieldstone. Cool in summer and warm in winter. The windows were small and recessed and original to this old Québécois home. Chartrand clearly respected the past and the *habitant* who'd built this place by hand hundreds of years ago. It was made in a hurry, but with great care, to protect himself and his family from the elements. From the approaching winter. From the monster who marched down the great river, picking up ice and snow and bitter cold. Gaining in strength and power. So few early settlers survived. But whoever had built this home had. And the home was still offering shelter to those in need.

Behind him, Chartrand was offering Clara and Myrna another glass of cognac. Myrna declined, but Clara took a half shot.

"Perhaps to take to bed, with a cookie," said Clara.

"There's that pioneering spirit," said Myrna.

The floors were original. Wide pine planks, made of trees that stood tall on this very site, and that now lay down. They were darkened by generations of smoky fires. Two sofas faced each other across the fireplace and an armchair faced the fire, a footstool in front of it, with books piled on a side table. Lamps softly lit the room.

But it was the walls that intrigued Gamache. He walked around them. Sometimes leaning closer, drawn into the original Krieghoff. The Lemieux. The Gagnon. And there, between two windows, was a tiny oil painting on wood.

"Beautiful, isn't it?"

Chartrand had come up behind Gamache. The Chief had sensed him there, but hadn't taken his eyes off the painting. It was of a forest and a spit of rocks jutting into a lake. And a single tree clinging to the rocky outcropping, its branches sculpted by the relentless wind.

It was stunning in both its beauty and its desolation.

"Is this a Thomson?" Gamache asked.

"It is."

"From Algonquin Park?"

The rugged landscape was unmistakable.

"*Oui.*"

"*Mon dieu,*" said Gamache on an exhale, aware that he was breathing on the same painting as the man who'd created it.

The two men stared at the tiny rectangle.

"When was it done?" Gamache asked.

"1917. The year he died," said Chartrand.

"In the war?" asked Jean-Guy, who'd wandered over to join them.

"No," said the gallery owner. "In an accident."

Now Gamache straightened up and looked at Chartrand. "Do you believe that?"

"I want to. It would be horrible to think otherwise."

Jean-Guy looked from Chartrand to Gamache. "There's a question?"

"A small one," said Gamache, walking back to the sofa, as though not wanting the painting to overhear their conversation.

"What question?"

"Tom Thomson painted mostly landscapes," Chartrand explained. "His favorite subject was Algonquin Park, in Ontario. He seemed to like his solitude. He'd canoe and camp by himself, then trek out with the most wonderful paintings."

He gestured toward the small one on his wall.

"Was he famous?" asked Beauvoir.

"No," said Chartrand. "Not at the time. Not many knew him. Other painters, but not the public. Not yet."

"It took his death for him to come to their attention," said Gamache.

"Lucky for whoever had his paintings," said Beauvoir.

"Lucky for his gallery owner," Chartrand agreed.

"So what's the mystery? How'd he die?"

"The official cause was drowning," said Gamache. "But there was some question. Rumors persist even now that he was either murdered or killed himself."

"Why would he do that?" Beauvoir asked.

They were sitting down, Gamache and Beauvoir on a sofa, Chartrand on his chair facing the empty fireplace.

"The theory is that Thomson was despondent because he wasn't getting any recognition for his work," said Chartrand.

"And the murder theory?" asked Beauvoir.

"Perhaps another artist, jealous of his talents," said Chartrand.

"Or someone who owned a lot of his works," said Gamache, looking directly at their host.

"Like his gallery owner?" Chartrand smiled in what appeared to be genuine amusement. "We are greedy, feral people. We love to screw both the artist and our clients. We'd do anything to acquire what we want. But perhaps not murder."

Though Beauvoir and Gamache knew that was not true.

"Who're you talking about?"

Clara and Myrna had been across the room admiring a Jean Paul Lemieux, but now Clara sat on the sofa opposite Gamache.

"Tom Thomson." Chartrand waved toward the small painting, like a window on the wall that looked into another time, another world. But one not so unlike Charlevoix.

"*Désolé*," said Gamache quietly, not taking his eyes off Clara. "That was insensitive."

"*Désolé?*" asked Chartrand. He looked from one to the other, perplexed by the sudden intensity of emotion. "Why would it be upsetting?"

"My own husband is missing. That's why we're here." Clara turned to Gamache. "Didn't you ask him about Peter when you went to the gallery?"

"It was closed," said Gamache. "I thought you discussed it when you called him up."

"Why would I? I thought you'd already asked him and he didn't know Peter."

"Peter?" asked Chartrand, looking from one to the other.

"My husband. Peter Morrow."

"Your husband's Peter Morrow?" said Chartrand.

"You knew him?" Gamache asked.

"*Bien sûr,*" said Chartrand.

"Him or his art?" asked Myrna.

"Him, the man. He spent many hours in the gallery."

Clara was stunned into silence, momentarily. And then questions jumbled together in her brain, and created a logjam. None able to escape. But finally, one popped out.

"When was this?"

Chartrand thought. "In April, I guess. Maybe a little later."

"Did he stay with you?" asked Clara.

"*Non.* He rented a cabin down the road."

"Is he still there?" She stood up as though about to leave.

Chartrand shook his head. "No. He left. I haven't seen him in months. I'm sorry."

"Where did he go?" Clara asked.

Chartrand faced her. "I don't know."

"When was the last time you saw him?" Gamache asked.

Chartrand thought about that. "It's now early August. He left before the summer. In late spring, I think."

"Are you sure he left?" Jean-Guy asked. "Did he tell you he was leaving?"

Chartrand looked like a punch-drunk boxer, staggering from questioner to questioner. "I'm sorry, I can't remember."

"Why can't you remember?" asked Clara, her voice rising.

Chartrand appeared flustered, confused. "It didn't seem important," he tried to explain. "He wasn't a close friend or anything. He was here one day, and not here the next."

He looked from Clara to Gamache and back again.

"Is that why you invited us here?" Jean-Guy asked. "Because Peter had told you about her?"

He gestured toward Clara.

"I told you, I didn't know he was her husband. I invited you here because it was late, the hotels are full and you needed a place to stay."

"And because you recognized us," said Gamache, not letting Chartrand get away with it. He might be a very, very good man. But he was also a not completely honest one.

"True. I know of you, Chief Inspector. We all do. From the news. And I knew Clara, from articles about her in the art magazines. I approached you in La Muse because . . ."

"Yes?"

"Because I thought you might make interesting conversation. That's all."

Gamache took in, yet again, the single, solitary chair. Which now seemed to envelop, consume, Marcel Chartrand. And Gamache wondered if it was that simple.

Did this man just want company? Someone he could talk to, and listen to?

Was it the art of conversation Marcel Chartrand finally yearned for? Would he trade these silent masterpieces for a single good friend?

Chartrand turned back to Clara.

"Peter never mentioned he had a wife. He lived the life of a *religieux* here. A monk." Chartrand smiled reassuringly. "He'd visit me, but more for the company of my paintings than me. He'd take a meal at one of the diners in town. Rarely anything as fancy as La Muse. He spoke to almost no one. And then he'd go back to his cabin."

"To paint," said Clara.

"Perhaps."

"Did he show you what he was working on?" Gamache asked.

Chartrand shook his head. "And I never asked to see it. I'm approached often enough, I don't need to seek it out. Except on rare occasions."

He turned back to Clara. "What you said at La Muse earlier today, about Gagnon stripping the skin off the land and painting the muscle, the veins, was exactly right. Far from being ugly or gruesome, what he painted was the wonder of the place. The heart and soul of the place. He painted what so few really see. He must've had a very powerful muse to let him get so deep."

"Who was Gagnon's muse?" Gamache asked.

"Oh, I didn't mean a person."

"Then what did you mean?"

"Nature. I think like Tom Thomson, Clarence Gagnon's muse was Nature herself. Doesn't get more powerful than that." He turned back to Clara. "What Gagnon did for landscapes, you do for people. Their face, their skin, their veneer is there for the outside world. But you also paint their interiors. It's a rare gift, madame. I hope I haven't embarrassed you."

It was clear he had.

"I'm sorry," he said. "I promised myself I wouldn't mention your work. You must get it all the time. Forgive me. And you have more pressing concerns. How can I help?"

He turned from Clara to Gamache.

"Did you know Peter's earlier works?" Gamache asked.

"I knew he was an artist and a successful one. I can't say I remember seeing any particular painting."

Chartrand's voice had changed. Still gracious, there was now a distance. He was talking business.

"Did you talk to him about his work?" Clara asked.

"No. He never asked for my opinion and I never volunteered."

But they had only his word for that, thought Gamache. And the Chief already knew Chartrand was not always completely honest.

TWENTY-FOUR

———

Gamache woke up early in the unfamiliar bed, to unfamiliar sounds outside the open window.

The lace curtain puffed out slightly, as though taking a breath, then subsided. The air that was inhaled into the room smelled fresh, with the unmistakable tang that came from a large body of water nearby.

He looked at his watch on the bedside table.

Not yet six but the sun was already up.

Beauvoir, however, was not. He was fast asleep in the next bed, his face squished into the pillow, his mouth slightly open. It was a sight Gamache had seen many times and knew that Annie saw every day.

It must be love, he decided as he quietly got up and prepared for the day, pausing to pull back the lace at the window and look out. It had been well past midnight when they'd finally gotten to sleep under the comforters. Gamache had no idea what he'd see outside the window, and was surprised and delighted that this bedroom looked out over the metal roofs of the old Charlevoix village. And to the St. Lawrence beyond.

Once showered and dressed, he crept downstairs and outside.

It was a pastel time of day. Everything soft blues and pinks in the early sun. The tourists were asleep in their inns and B and Bs. Few residents were up, and Gamache had the village to himself. Far from feeling abandoned, the place felt expectant. About to give birth to another vibrant day.

But not just yet. For now all was peaceful. Anything was possible.

He found a bench not far away, sat down, reached into his pocket and brought out the book. His constant companion.

He started reading. After a few pages he closed the book and held his large hand over the cover so that the title was slightly obscured. Like the river between the old homes. Hinted at. There, but not completely seen.

The Balm in Gilead.

He pressed it closed and thought, as he did each morning since his retirement, of the last hands that had shut the book.

. . . to cure a sin-sick soul.

Was there a cure for what he'd done in those woods outside Three Pines, eight months ago? It wasn't so much the act of killing. The taking of a life. It was how he'd felt about it. And the fact he'd intended to do it, even hoped to do it, when he'd arrived.

Mens rea. The difference between manslaughter and murder. Intent. *Mens rea.* A guilty mind. A sin-sick soul.

He looked at the book beneath his hand.

How would the previous owner of this book have felt about what he'd done?

Armand Gamache was pretty sure he knew the answer to that.

He turned his back on the river, on the rugged shoreline, on the container ships and the whales gliding beneath the surface. Huge and unseen.

Gamache walked back to the home of Marcel Chartrand.

"I thought I heard someone leave," said Chartrand from the porch as Gamache approached. "How'd you sleep?"

"Perfectly."

"You must be used to strange beds," said their host, handing Gamache a mug of coffee that steamed in the fresh morning air.

"I am," the Chief admitted. "But few as comfortable as yours. *Merci.*" He lifted the mug toward Chartrand in appreciation.

"*Un plaisir.* Would you like to see the gallery?"

Gamache smiled. "Very much."

He felt like a child given a private pass to Disneyland.

Chartrand unlocked the door and turned on the lights. Gamache walked to the center of the room and stood there. He realized, with some alarm, that he felt like weeping.

Here, around him, was his heritage. His country. His history. But it was more than that. Here on the walls, were his insides. Out.

The brightly painted homes. Red and mustard yellow. The smoke tugged from the chimneys. The church spires. The winter scenes, the snow on the pine boughs. The horses and sleighs. The soft light through the windows at night.

The man with the oil lamp. Walking a path worn through the deep snow. Toward home in the distance.

Gamache turned. He was surrounded. Immersed. Not drowning, but buoyed. Baptized.

He sighed. And looked at Marcel Chartrand, who was beside him. He also looked as though he might weep. Did the man feel like this each day?

Was this his bench above the village? Was he also surprised by joy each day?

"Peter Morrow came here often," said Chartrand. "Just to sit. And stare at the paintings."

Sit and stare.

God knew Gamache did enough of that himself, but the combination of words, and the inflection, triggered a memory. Not an old one. It sat near the top. And then Gamache had it.

Someone else had described Peter sitting and staring. As a child.

Madame Finney, Peter's mother. She'd told Gamache that young Peter would just stare, for hours on end. At the walls. At the paintings. Trying to get closer to the pictures. Trying to join the genius that saw the world like that, and painted how he felt about it.

All flowing strokes, lines that joined each other, so that solid homes became land, became trees, became people, became sky and clouds. That touched the solid homes.

And all in bright, joyous colors. Not made-up hues, but ones Gamache actually saw now through the windows of the gallery. No need to embellish. To fictionalize. To romanticize.

Clarence Gagnon saw the truth. And didn't so much capture it as free it.

Young Peter longed to be set free too. And the paintings on the walls of that grim home were his way out. Since he couldn't actually escape into them, he'd done the next best thing.

He became an artist. Despite his family. Though his family had accomplished one thing. They drained the color and creativity from him, leaving him and his art attractive but predictable. Safe. Bleached.

Gamache stared at the walls of the Galerie Gagnon. At the vivid colors. At the swirls and flowing brush strokes. At the landscapes that were as much internal as external.

Peter had stared at these same walls. And then disappeared.

And for a moment Armand Gamache wondered if Peter had achieved the magic he seemed so desperate to find, and had actually entered one of the paintings.

He leaned closer, examining the man with the lantern. Was it Peter? Plodding toward home?

Then he grinned. Of course not. This was Baie-Saint-Paul, not the Twilight Zone.

"Is this why Peter came to Baie-Saint-Paul?" Gamache indicated the paintings lining the gallery.

Chartrand shook his head. "I think it was a perk, but not the reason."

"What was the reason?"

"He seemed to be looking for someone."

"Someone?"

"Someone or something, or both. I don't know," said Chartrand.

"Why didn't you tell us this last night?"

"I hadn't really thought about it. Peter was an acquaintance, nothing more. Just another artist who came to Charlevoix hoping for inspiration. Hoping that what inspired these"—he gestured toward the Gagnons on the walls—"would also inspire him."

"That Gagnon's muse would find him and come out to play again," said Gamache.

Chartrand considered for a moment. "Do you think he's dead?"

"I think it's very difficult for people to just disappear. Much harder than we realize," said Gamache. "Until we try."

"Then how's it done?"

"There's only one way. We need to stop living in this world."

"You mean die?"

"Well, that would do it too, but I mean remove yourself from society completely. Go to an island. Go deep into the woods. Live off the land."

Chartrand looked uncomfortable. "Join a commune?"

"Well, most communes these days are pretty sophisticated." He studied his host. "What do you mean?"

"When Peter first visited the gallery, he asked after a man named Norman. I had no idea who he meant, but I said I'd ask around."

"Norman?" Gamache repeated. The name sounded familiar. "What did you find out?"

"Nothing useful."

"But you did find something?" Gamache pushed.

"There was a guy who'd set up an artist colony in the woods, but his name wasn't Norman. It was No Man."

"Noman?"

"No Man."

They stared at each other. Repeating the same thing, almost.

Finally Chartrand wrote it down and Gamache nodded. He understood, though his puzzlement increased.

No Man?

Clara and Myrna came down a few minutes later, followed by Jean-Guy.

"No Man?" asked Myrna.

They'd left the gallery and were walking down a narrow street toward a local café, for breakfast.

"No Man," Chartrand confirmed.

"How odd," said Clara.

Beauvoir didn't know why she was surprised. Most artists he'd met shot way past odd. Odd for them was conservative. Clara, with her wild food-infested hair and *Warrior Uteruses*, was one of the more sane artists.

Peter Morrow, with his button-down shirts and calm personality, was almost certainly the craziest of them all.

"Peter wasn't looking for No Man. He was trying to find a guy named Norman," said Chartrand.

"And did he?" asked Clara.

"Not that I know of."

They'd arrived at the small restaurant and sat at a table inside. At Gamache's request, Chartrand had taken them to the local diner where Peter sometimes ate.

"*Oui*, I knew him," said their server when shown the photograph of Peter. "Eggs on brown toast. No bacon. Black coffee."

She seemed to approve of this spartan breakfast.

"Did he ever eat with other people?" Clara asked.

"No, always alone," she said. "What do you want?"

Jean-Guy ordered the Voyageur Special. Two eggs and every meat they could find and fry.

Chartrand ordered scrambled eggs.

The rest had blueberry crêpes and bacon.

When the server came back with their food, Gamache asked if she knew of a Norman.

"First or last name?" she asked, pouring more coffee.

"We don't know."

"*Non*," she said, and left.

"Did Peter say where he knew this Norman from?" Jean-Guy asked.

Chartrand shook his head. "I didn't ask."

"Can you think of a Norman in Peter's life?" Gamache asked Clara. "A friend maybe? An artist he admired?"

"I've been trying to think," she said. "But the name means nothing."

"Where does No Man come in?" Jean-Guy asked.

"He doesn't really," Chartrand admitted. "Just some guy who set up an artist colony around here. It failed, and he moved on. Happens a lot. Artists need to make money and they think teaching or doing retreats will help make ends meet. It almost never does." He smiled at Clara. "The retreat was abandoned long before Peter came here. Besides, Peter didn't seem the joining sort."

"*He travels the fastest who travels alone*," said Gamache.

"I've always wondered if that's true," said Myrna. "We might go faster, but it's not as much fun. And when we arrive, what do we find? No one."

No man, thought Gamache.

"Clara? You're quiet," said Myrna.

Clara was leaning back in her chair, apparently admiring the view. But her eyes had a glazed, faraway look.

"Norman," she repeated. "There was someone." She looked at Myrna. "A professor named Norman at art college."

Myrna nodded. "That's right. Professor Massey mentioned him."

"He was the one who set up the Salon des Refusés," Clara said.

"Do you think it could be the same person?" Gamache asked.

Clara's brows drew together. "I don't see how. Peter took his course and thought it was bullshit. It couldn't be the same person, could it?"

"Might be," said Myrna. "Is he the one Professor Massey said was nuts?"

"Yes. I can't believe Peter would want to track him down."

"*Excuse-moi.*" Gamache had been listening to this and now he got up and took his phone to a quiet corner. As he spoke he turned and looked out the window. To the west. He talked for a couple of minutes, then returned to their table.

"Who'd you call?" Clara asked.

But Jean-Guy knew, even before the Chief answered the question. He knew by Gamache's body language. His stance, his face, and where he'd gazed as he spoke.

To the west. To a village in a valley.

Beauvoir knew because that's where he turned, when speaking with Annie.

Toward home.

"Reine-Marie. I asked her to go to Toronto. To talk to your old professor, see the records if possible. Find out what she can about this Professor Norman."

"But we could call from here," said Myrna. "It'd be faster and easier."

"Yes, but this is delicate and we have no right to the files. I think Reine-Marie will get further than a phone call. She's very good at getting information."

Gamache smiled as he said it. His wife had spent decades working in the national archives of Québec. Collecting information. But the truth was, she was far better at guarding it than giving it out.

Still, if anyone could wheedle classified information out of an institution, she could.

He glanced again to the west, and there he met Beauvoir's gaze.

TWENTY-FIVE

⁓

The plane gathered speed and bumped down the runway at Montréal's Trudeau International Airport.

Reine-Marie had booked on the airline that flew into the small Island Airport in downtown Toronto, rather than the huge international airport outside the city. It was far more convenient.

But it meant a prop plane and not everyone on board was comfortable with that. Including the woman sitting beside her.

She gripped the armrest and had a grimace on her face like a death mask.

"It'll be all right," said Reine-Marie. "I promise."

"How can you know, turnip head?" the woman snapped. And Reine-Marie smiled.

Ruth couldn't be that frightened if she remembered to insult her.

The plane popped into the air. If a jet took off like a bullet, the small turboprop took off like a gull. Airborne, but subject to wind currents. It bobbed and wobbled and Ruth started praying under her breath.

"Oh, Lord, shit, shit, shit. Oh, Jesus."

"We're up now," said Reine-Marie in a soothing voice. "So you can relax, you old crone."

Ruth turned piercing eyes on her. And laughed. As they broke through the cloud, Ruth's talon-grip released.

"People weren't meant to fly," said Ruth, over the roar of the engines.

"But planes are, and as luck would have it, we're in one. Now, we have an hour before landing, tell me more about your time in that Turkish prison. I take it you were a guard, not an inmate."

Ruth laughed again, and color returned to her face. So afraid to fly, Ruth had come with Reine-Marie anyway. To keep her company. And, Reine-Marie suspected, to help find Peter.

Ruth gabbed away, nervous nonsense, while Reine-Marie placed her hand over Ruth's, and kept it there for the entire flight of lunacy.

"Have you shown Chartrand those paintings?"

Gamache gestured toward the rolled-up canvases Clara carried with her all the time now, like a divining rod.

"No. I thought about it, but Peter could've shown them to him and chose not to. If he didn't, then I don't think I should." She looked at Gamache closely. "Why? Do you think I should?"

Gamache thought about it. "I don't know. I can't honestly see how it could matter. I suppose I'm just curious."

"About what?"

"About what Chartrand would make of them," he admitted. "Aren't you?"

"Curious isn't the word," said Clara with a grin. "More like afraid."

"You think they're that bad?"

"I think they're strange."

"And is that so bad?" he asked.

She thought about his question, bouncing the canvases in her hand. "I'm afraid people will see these and think Peter's nuts."

Gamache opened his mouth, then closed it again.

"Go on," she said. "Say what's on your mind. Peter is nuts."

"No," he said. "No. I wasn't going to say that."

"Then what were you going to say?"

Far from feeling defensive, Clara found she really did want to know.

"*Warrior Uteruses*," he said.

Clara stared at him. She could have spent the rest of her life guessing what Armand would say, and she'd never have come up with those two words.

"*Warrior Uteruses*?" she repeated. "What's that got to do with it?"

"You did a series of sculptures a few years ago," he reminded her. "They were uteruses, all different sizes. You decorated them with feathers and leather and fancy soaps and sticks and leaves and lace and all sorts of things. And you put them into an art show."

"Yes," Clara laughed. "Oddly enough I still have them all. I considered giving one to Peter's mother as a Christmas present, but chickened out." She laughed. "I guess while I can sculpt them, I don't actually have one. A warrior uterus, I mean."

"That series wasn't all that long ago," Gamache reminded her.

"True."

"Do you regret it?"

"Not at all. It was such fun. And strangely powerful. Everyone thought it was a joke, but it wasn't."

"What was it?" Gamache asked.

"A step along the way."

He nodded and got up. But before leaving, he bent down and whispered, "And I bet everyone thought you were nuts."

"He wasn't just crazy," said Professor Massey. "He was insane."

He looked from one woman to the next. They were seated in his classroom studio. He'd given Ruth what was clearly his favorite chair. The one that looked across the open space filled with drop sheets and easels, old gummed-up palettes. Blank canvases were stacked in a corner and Massey's own paintings, unframed, were here and there on the walls, as though stuck up casually. They were very good, enlivening and warming the space.

"And not the fun sort of insanity," Professor Massey warned. "Not eccentric. This was the dangerous kind."

"Dangerous? Like violent?" Reine-Marie asked.

Try as she might to catch and hold his eye, the elderly professor's attention never stayed on her for long. His eyes kept drifting back.

To Ruth.

Ruth, for her part, seemed to have lost her mind. But found, Reine-Marie thought, her heart.

The old poet had actually giggled when Professor Massey had taken her hand in greeting.

They'd arrived half an hour earlier, unannounced, though Reine-Marie had called ahead to make sure that Professor Massey would be there.

He was.

He always was, it seemed. And now Reine-Marie started noticing other things. A pillow with blankets folded neatly on top of it, beside the worn sofa.

A microwave oven on the counter by the paint-encrusted sink. A hotplate. A small fridge.

She looked around the classroom and realized it felt less a classroom and more a studio. And less like a studio and more like a loft space. A living space.

Reine-Marie's gaze returned to the elderly man. Perfectly turned out in pressed corduroy slacks, a crisp cotton shirt, a light sweater vest. Neat. Clean.

How did it happen, she wondered? Did he once have a wife and children? A home in the Annex?

Did the children move away? Did the wife pass away?

Did he just stop going home? Until this became home? In the company of familiar and comforting scents. And blank canvases. Where students dropped by at all hours. To ask questions. To have a drink and a sandwich and to talk pretentious nonsense.

She looked at the canvas on the easel.

How long, she wondered, had it sat there. Empty.

"Not violent," he said. "Not physically anyway. Not yet. We couldn't take the chance. Sébastien Norman was the messianic sort. The kind who held strong and inflexible views. We didn't know that when we hired him, of course. He was to teach art theory. A fairly benign course, you'd have thought." Massey smiled. "I suppose we weren't clear that it was art theory he was to teach, not his own personal one. We began to realize fairly early on that we had a problem."

"How so?" Reine-Marie asked.

"Rumbles in the corridors. I started overhearing what his students were saying. Most mocking him, laughing. My instincts are always to defend a fellow professor, so I asked them what was so funny. And they told me."

"Go on."

"Well, it sounds so silly now." Professor Massey looked embarrassed, and glanced at Ruth. Reine-Marie simply waited, and finally he seemed to overcome his reluctance.

"Apparently Professor Norman believed in the tenth muse."

He grimaced as though to apologize for the stupidity of what he'd just said.

Now Ruth spoke. "But there were only nine."

"Yes, exactly. Nine daughters of Zeus. They personified knowledge and the arts. Music, literature, science," he said.

"But not painting," said Reine-Marie. "I remember now. There was no muse for art itself."

Now Professor Massey turned his full attention to her. And what attention it was. Reine-Marie felt the force of his personality. Not violent, but overwhelming. Enveloping.

She felt his intelligence and his calm. And for the first time in her life she wished she'd been an artist, if only to have studied with this professor.

"Strange, isn't it?" he said. "Nine Muses. That's quite a gang. But not a single one for painting or sculpture. God knows the Greeks liked their murals and sculptures. And yet, they didn't assign them a muse."

"Why not?" asked Reine-Marie.

Massey shrugged and raised his white brows. "No one knows. There're theories, of course."

"Which brings us back to Professor Norman," said Reine-Marie. "What was his theory?"

"I never spoke to him about it directly," said Massey. "What I know was cobbled together from speaking to his students. I'm not even sure I'll get it right now. It's been so long. All I know is that he believed there had in fact been a tenth muse. And that to be a great artist you had to find her."

"Did he believe this tenth muse lived in an actual place?" Reine-Marie asked. "That you could knock on the door, and there she'd be?"

"I'm sorry, I don't know what Professor Norman really believed. It was a long time ago. I should have known. It's my fault. I actually encouraged the college to hire him."

"Why?"

"Well, I'd seen a few of his works and thought they showed promise. He was new to Toronto, didn't have much money or many connections. This seemed perfect. He could teach part-time, make some money, meet some people."

His voice faded away. All that energy, all that force of personality, seemed spent and the quite magnificent man deflated. The very thought of Professor Norman seemed to sap him of life.

"It was a mistake," the professor said. He was quiet for a moment, casting his mind back to that time. "Norman wasn't fired for his crazy beliefs, you know. We were a very liberal institution then. Though his theories weren't approved of, and the students had no respect for him. His appearance didn't help."

"He looked crazy?" asked Reine-Marie, and, unexpectedly, Professor Massey laughed.

"We all looked like lunatics. He looked like a banker. A prosperous banker. Everyone else was sorta seedy, or at least tried to be. It was the uniform of the time. Now we all try to look successful, respectable."

He gazed down at his clothing, then over at seedy Ruth.

And Reine-Marie wondered if that canvas on the easel would have been so blank had Professor Massey not been so respectable.

"Why was he fired if not for this tenth muse theory?"

"I was on the Board of Governors and we agonized over it. Norman wasn't violent, at least not yet. That's the problem, isn't it, with these things? Hard to fire someone on suspicion they might do something."

"But what made you think he'd become violent?" asked Reine-Marie.

"We just didn't know. He had outbursts, verbal. He shook with rage. I tried talking to him, but he denied there was anything wrong. He said that real artists are passionate, and that was all it was. Passion."

"You didn't believe it?"

"He might've been right. Maybe real artists are passionate. Lots are nuts. But the issue wasn't whether he was a real artist, but if he was a good teacher."

"What made him angry? What would set him off?"

"Anyone who disagreed with his tenth muse theory. And anything he judged to be mediocre. The two went together in his mind. Unfortunately, as the year went on he became more and more unbalanced. We didn't know when he'd go over the edge, and who he might take with him. We had to protect the students. But we didn't act in time."

"There was an incident?" asked Reine-Marie.

Beside her, Ruth was no help at all. Reine-Marie wasn't even sure she was listening. There was a goofy smile on her face as she watched Professor Massey.

"Not violence," said the professor. "Not physical anyway. Without telling anyone, or getting the college's permission, Sébastien Norman created the Salon des Refusés."

"Clara Morrow told us about that. But what was it?"

"It was a show that ran parallel to the real exhibition. It featured the rejected works."

"And why was that so bad?"

Reine-Marie could immediately feel his censure. It radiated from him, waves of disapproval, of disappointment. In her. And she found herself regretting asking the question. Intellectually she knew that was silly. It was a legitimate question. But in her gut she felt she'd let this man down in not knowing the answer.

Even Ruth deserted her now. She drifted off and started examining the paintings on the walls. Pausing before each one. Paying more attention to them than she ever had, as far as Reine-Marie knew, to Clara's or Peter's.

"Are you a teacher?" Professor Massey asked.

Reine-Marie shook her head. "A librarian."

"But you have children?"

"Two. Both grown up now. And two grandchildren."

"And when they go to school and get an assignment wrong, would you like the teacher to hold it up in front of the class? In front of the school? For ridicule?"

"No, of course not."

"Well, that's what Professor Norman did. Ask your friend Clara how it felt. How it still feels. These are young people, Madame Gamache. They're gifted, and many are fragile, having been marginalized most of their lives for being creative. We live in a society that doesn't value being different. When they come here, to art college, it's probably the first time in their lives they feel they belong. Safe. Not just valued, but precious."

He held her eyes, his voice deep and calm, almost mesmerizing. And Reine-Marie felt again the pull of this man, even in his old age. How powerful he must have been in his prime.

And how comforting his message to the young, lost, wounded men and women who straggled into the college with their screw-you attitudes and piercings and broken hearts.

Here they were safe. To experiment, to explore. To fail and try again. Without fear of ridicule.

She looked at the worn sofa and could almost see the generations of young, excited artists lounging about in animated debate. Finally free.

Until Professor Norman got ahold of them. And then it was no longer safe.

The Salon des Refusés.

Reine-Marie was beginning to see just how vile that was.

"Would the college have Professor Norman's address in their files?"

"They might. He was from Québec. I know that. He had a funny sort of accent."

"Do you know where in Québec?" Reine-Marie asked, and he shook his head.

"Did Peter ask these questions, when he visited you?"

"About Professor Norman?" Massey was clearly both surprised and amused. "No. We talked about him briefly, but I think I was the one who brought him up."

"Is it possible Peter's looking for Professor Norman?" Reine-Marie asked.

"I doubt it," said Massey. "He said nothing about that when he left. Why?"

"Clara and my husband and some others are trying to find Peter," she said. "And it seems Peter was trying to find someone named Norman."

"I'd be shocked if it was the same man," said Massey. And he looked shocked. "I hope that's not true."

"Why?"

"If Sébastien Norman was insane thirty years ago, I hate to think what he is now." Massey took a breath and shook his head. "When she left, I advised Clara to just go home. To get on with her life. And that Peter would come back, when he was ready."

"Do you think he planned to return to her?" Reine-Marie asked.

"He didn't mention it," Massey admitted. "But that doesn't mean he wasn't going to do it."

"Like looking for Norman, perhaps."

"Perhaps."

The professor's gaze left Reine-Marie and found Ruth. She was down at the far end of his studio looking at another painting.

"I don't suppose you have a picture of Professor Norman?"

"In my wallet?" Professor Massey smiled. "Actually, I might be able to find you one. In our yearbook."

While Massey examined the bookcase, Reine-Marie walked over to Ruth.

"Is this the painting Myrna said was so good?" asked Reine-Marie. She looked at it and saw what Myrna meant. The rest were good. This was great. Mesmerizing.

She rallied herself and turned to Ruth. "Are you ready to leave or are you measuring the windows for curtains?"

"And would that be so laughable?" Ruth asked.

Reine-Marie was shocked into silence. Stunned not by what Ruth said, but by her own behavior. Belittling, even ridiculing, Ruth's feelings for the professor.

"I'm so sorry," said Reine-Marie. "That was stupid of me."

Ruth looked over at the elderly man, pulling out yearbooks, examining them, then returning them.

The old poet drew herself up and said, "*Noli timere*."

Reine-Marie sensed the words were not for her ears, just as the look on Ruth's face was not for her eyes.

"Here it is."

Professor Massey walked toward them holding up a yearbook in triumph. "I was afraid it'd gotten lost in the renovations. Or sealed up in the walls. You'd be surprised what they found when they took them down."

"What?" asked Ruth, while Reine-Marie took the yearbook.

"Well, asbestos for one, but they expected to find that. That's why they did the renovations. It was the other stuff that was a surprise."

The yearbook was dusty and Reine-Marie turned to the professor. "Asbestos?"

"Yes." He looked at her, then understood why she'd asked. He laughed. "Don't worry. That's just two decades of dust. No asbestos on it."

He took the book back, wiped it off with his sleeve, and handed it back. He led them to the sofa.

Ruth and Paul Massey sat, while Reine-Marie stood and flipped through the yearbook.

"What did they find in the walls?" asked Ruth. Her voice was almost unrecognizable to Reine-Marie.

"Old newspapers mostly. Turns out the building, or its foundations, were much older than anyone thought. Some Italian workers had left parts of sandwiches, and biologists were able to grow some tomato plants from the old seeds they found. Plants that had become all but extinct. They also found a couple of canvases."

"Was that one?" Ruth pointed to the painting they'd been looking at, at the back of the studio.

Professor Massey laughed. "You think that's garbage?"

He didn't seem insulted, simply amused. Pleased even.

"Professor Massey painted that," said Reine-Marie, jumping in to smooth over a potentially embarrassing moment, though she seemed the only one uncomfortable over what Ruth had said.

"You can see the paintings they found in a display case near the front door," said Massey. "Nothing remarkable, I'm afraid. No Emily Carr or Tom Thomson stuffed in for insulation."

As they talked, Reine-Marie studied page after page of photographs of young men and women. Most of the students were white. Most with long greasy hair. And tight turtlenecks, and tighter jeans. And petulant, disinterested expressions.

Too cool for school. Too cool to care.

Reine-Marie stopped and turned back a page.

There, unmistakably, was Clara, with hair that looked like Einstein's. Wearing a shapeless smock and a huge, happy grin on her face.

And beside her on the sofa, the same sofa Reine-Marie had just been on, various students slouched. Professor Massey, younger and even more vigorous, was standing behind them, speaking to a young man.

They were locked in earnest conversation. A cigarette hung from the young man's mouth, a puff of smoke obscuring his face. Except for one eye. Sharp, assessing. Aware.

It was Peter.

Reine-Marie smiled at the photograph, then returned to searching for Sébastien Norman. But when she found the section on the professors it was a disappointment.

"I'd forgotten," said Massey, when shown the section. "That was the year the editors decided not to use our actual photographs. Maybe in response to the Salon des Refusés, they published pictures of our art instead. I think they deliberately chose the most embarrassing examples."

He took the book back and turned a few pages, and grimaced. "That's mine. The worst thing I think I've done."

There were columns of bright paint, with slashes through it. It seemed to Reine-Marie quite dynamic. Not bad at all.

But then, artists probably weren't the best judges of their own work.

"May I take this?" she asked, indicating the yearbook.

"Yes, as long as you bring it back."

He spoke, not surprisingly, to Ruth. He said it so tenderly that Reine-Marie was tempted to answer for her.

"I'll be waiting," he said to the old poet. "*I just sit where I'm put, composed of stone and wishful thinking.*"

Reine-Marie recognized the quote from one of Ruth's poems. She wanted to warn this man to stop. She wanted to tell him that while he might think he was wooing Ruth with her own words, he had no idea what he was poking.

Ruth turned to Professor Massey and spoke, her voice strong and clear.

"*That the deity who kills for pleasure will also heal.*"

She'd completed the couplet.

As they left for home, Reine-Marie mulled over what she'd heard.

About Professor Norman. His passion, and his folly. The tenth muse. The missing muse.

That the deity who kills for pleasure will also heal.

Was the tenth muse that deity? Like the other muses, did it inspire? Did it heal?

But did this one also kill, for pleasure?

TWENTY-SIX

Marcel Chartrand placed the rolled-up canvases on the wooden table.

They were in his office at the back of the gallery, away from prying eyes.

The gallery itself was open, and tourists and artists and enthusiasts had streamed in all day. Not to buy, but to pay homage.

It was easy to spot those from away, and those from Québec. The tourists from other provinces or countries stood before the Clarence Gagnon oil paintings and smiled, appreciating the works of art.

Those from Québec looked about to burst into tears. An unsuspected yearning uncovered, discovered. For a simpler time and a simpler life. Before Internet, and climate change, and terrorism. When neighbors worked together, and separation was not a topic or an issue or wise.

Yet the Gagnon paintings weren't idealized images of country life. They showed hardship. But they also showed such beauty, such peace, that the paintings, and the people looking at them, ached.

Gamache stood at the door between the office and the gallery and watched the patrons react to the paintings.

"Armand?"

Clara called him back in. He closed the door behind him and joined the others at the table.

Over lunch they'd discussed what to do next. They'd spent the morning driving to the cabin Peter had rented. Far from being a charming little Québécois chalet, this was a nondescript, cheap one-room hovel, one step up from a slum.

The landlady remembered Peter.

"Tall. Anglo. Paid cash," she said, and looked around with distaste at the room, under no illusions about its quality. "Rents by the month. You interested?"

She eyed Clara, the most likely prospect.

"Did he have any visitors?" Clara asked.

The landlady looked at her as though it was a ridiculous question, which it was, but one that had to be asked. As was the next—

"Did he ask you about a man named Norman?"

Same response.

"Do you know a man named Norman?"

"Look, you want the place or not?"

Not.

The landlady locked up.

"Did he say why he was here?" Clara tried one more time as they stood outside the door.

"Oh, sure, we had long discussions over fondue and white wine."

She looked at Clara with distaste. "I don't know why he was here. I don't care. He paid cash."

"Did he tell you where he was going, when he left?" Clara persevered in the face of obvious defeat.

"I didn't ask, he didn't tell."

And that was that.

Then they went back to the brasserie, to cleanse their palates with burgers.

"What next?" Clara asked.

"Reine-Marie should be at your college in Toronto," Gamache said, looking at his watch. "She'll let us know what she finds out."

"And until then?" Myrna asked.

"There is one thing we can do, I suppose," said Clara, shooting a glance at Gamache. "We could show Peter's paintings to Marcel."

Clara turned to Myrna and laid a hand on the rolled-up canvas.

"What do they tell you?"

Myrna noticed the protective action. "I take it you don't want my opinion as an art critic."

"Since you happen to think I'm a genius, I think your expertise in that area is unquestioned. But no, it's the other I want."

Myrna studied her friend for a moment. "They tell me that Peter was deeply troubled."

"Do you think he'd lost his mind?" Clara asked.

"I think," said Myrna slowly, "that Peter could afford to lose some of his mind. It wouldn't necessarily be a bad thing."

Myrna smiled then. Just a little.

"Right," said Clara, getting up and grabbing the scrolled paintings. "Let's go."

She marched away like a Crimean war general leading a futile charge.

She headed up the hill to the Galerie Gagnon, leaving the others, and the bill, behind.

"She has flair, I'll give her that," said Jean-Guy, hurriedly taking a last huge bite of his hamburger. Gamache, paying, knew that "flair" was not one of Beauvoir's compliments.

And now they stood over the table as Marcel Chartrand unrolled the canvases.

The one on top was of the lips.

Gamache studied the curator as Chartrand studied the painting. But study, Gamache realized, was the wrong word. Chartrand was absorbing it. Trying not to think about the painting, but to experience it. In fact, the other man's eyes were almost closed.

Chartrand tilted his head a little this way. Then that.

And then a slight smile formed. His trained eye had seen the painted lips.

For the painting was smile-up. It was the giddy, laughing perspective.

"It's a bit of a mess," Chartrand said. "Here and here." He waved his hands over the canvas. "It looks like Peter was just filling in gaps, not sure what to do. There's no cohesion. But there is, I have to admit, a certain"—he searched for the word—"buoyancy."

Clara reached out and slowly turned Peter's painting. Like the rotation of the earth. Around. Slowly around. Until day became night. Smiles became frowns. Laughter became sorrow. Sky became water.

"Oh."

That was all Chartrand said, and needed to say. His expression said the rest. His body, in its sudden tension, spoke.

Gamache felt his phone vibrate in his pocket. Excusing himself, he stepped out the back door.

"*Bonjour?* Reine-Marie?"

"*Oui.* We're in the airport lounge, catching the next flight back to Montréal. I wanted to give you a quick call."

"How'd it go?"

"I'm not really sure."

She filled him in on their visit to the art college and Professor Massey. And Professor Norman.

"So he was from Québec," said Armand. "But they don't know where?"

"The office is looking," she said. "The registrar is a bit overwhelmed right now. Getting ready for her own vacation, but I think I convinced her to look for Professor Norman's dossier. The old files aren't on computer, so she'll have to go through them manually."

"And she's willing to do it?"

"Fortunately you only really need that one kidney, right, Armand?"

He grimaced. "As long as that's the only body part you offered her."

Reine-Marie's laughter came down the line and he smiled as he turned in her direction. In the background he heard them calling her flight.

"Armand, what do you know about the Muses?"

"The Muses?" He wasn't sure he heard her over the general boarding announcement. And then there was another, clearer voice.

"Get off the phone, for chrissake."

"Is that Ruth?"

"She came with me. I think she has a crush on Professor Massey."

"Ruth?"

"I know. You should've seen her. All giggly and blushing. They even recited part of her poetry together. *I just sit where I'm put* . . . That one."

"Ruth?"

"Hurry up," came the snarly voice. "If we get on now we might down a Scotch before the fucking thing takes off."

Ruth.

"I have to go," said Reine-Marie. "I'll tell you more once we're home. Professor Massey gave me a yearbook. I'll study it on the flight."

"*Merci*," he called down the line. "*Merci*."

But she was gone.

He returned to the office to find the four of them bent over one of the other canvases.

"Anything?" he asked.

"Nothing." Chartrand shook his head and straightened up as though repulsed by the canvas. "Poor Peter."

Clara met Gamache's eye, her fears realized. It felt like Peter's dirty underwear was spread out on the desk.

"You?" Jean-Guy asked, pointing to the phone still in the Chief's hand.

"Reine-Marie. She and Ruth are just getting on the flight back to Montréal."

"Ruth?" asked Clara.

"Yes, she went with Reine-Marie. Seems Professor Massey took a shine to her."

"He seemed so sane," said Myrna, shaking her head. "Did he survive?"

"Oh, he survived," said Gamache. "Ruth even giggled."

"No 'numb nuts'?" asked Jean-Guy. "No 'shithead'? Must be love. Or hate."

"Did Reine-Marie find out anything?" Clara asked.

"Only that Professor Norman was considered unbalanced. He taught art theory. He's from Québec. She's waiting to find out where."

"I'd forgotten about that," said Clara. "Had a strange accent, though. Hard to place."

"Just as their flight was called, she asked if I knew anything about the Muses," said Gamache. "Does that make sense?"

"The brasserie?" asked Myrna.

"No, I think she meant the actual Greek goddesses."

Clara snorted. "God, I'd forgotten about that too. Professor Norman was obsessed by the Muses. Peter used to laugh about that."

"But what's so funny?" Myrna asked. "Don't most artists have a muse?"

"Absolutely, but Norman turned it into a sort of mania. A prerequisite."

"A muse is supposed to inspire an artist, right?" said Jean-Guy.

"*Oui*," said Chartrand. "There was Manet's Victorine and Whistler's Joanna Hiffernan—" He paused. "How odd."

"How so?" asked Gamache.

"Both those women inspired works that ended up in the first Salon des Refusés."

"So much for muses," said Jean-Guy.

"But there're lots of other examples," said Chartrand. "And even those two paintings were eventually considered works of genius."

"Because of the muses?" asked Jean-Guy. "Don't you think the artists' talent might've had something to do with it?"

"*Absolument*," said Chartrand. "But something magical happens when a great artist meets his or her muse."

There's that word again, thought Gamache. *Magic.*

Clara listened but couldn't bear to look at Beauvoir as Chartrand tried to explain the inexplicable. Jean-Guy was so like Peter, in so many ways.

Peter hadn't believed in muses. He believed in technique and discipline. He believed in the color wheel and rules of perspective. He believed in hard work. Not in some mythical, magical being who would make him a better artist. It was absurd.

Clara had secretly hoped that, despite what Peter believed, she was his muse. His inspiration. But she'd had to eventually surrender that thought.

"Who's your muse?" Jean-Guy asked.

"Mine?" asked Clara.

"Yeah. If a muse is so important, who's yours?"

She wanted to say Peter. Would have said Peter a while ago, if only out of loyalty. It was the easy and obvious answer.

But not the truthful one.

Myrna spared her from having to answer.

"It's Ruth."

Clara smiled at her friend, and nodded.

Demented, drunken, delusional Ruth inspired Clara.

Ruth, with the lump in her throat.

"Only successful artists have muses?" Beauvoir asked.

"Oh no," said Chartrand. "Many artists have one, or a series of them. A muse might inspire them, but it doesn't make them great artists or guarantee success."

"Sometimes the magic works?" Jean-Guy looked at Clara, and smiled. Leading her to wonder if he knew more, or understood more, than he let on.

"If the muse is a person," said Beauvoir, thinking out loud, "what happens to the artist if their muse dies?"

Clara, Myrna, Chartrand, and Gamache looked at each other. What did happen if a muse died? A muse was a very powerful person in an artist's life.

Take that away, and what do you have?

Beauvoir could see his question had stumped them. But far from feeling he'd scored a point, he felt a growing disquiet.

He thought about what he'd heard and what he knew about the art world. And artists. Most would sell their soul for a solo show. And they'd kill for recognition.

In Beauvoir's experience, the only thing worse for an artist than not being celebrated was if someone they knew was.

It could be enough to drive an already unbalanced artist over the edge. Drive them to drink. To drugs. To kill.

Themselves. Or the other artist. Or, maybe, the muse.

TWENTY-SEVEN

⌒

Reine-Marie finished the email to Armand while waiting for Ruth at the airport in Montréal. Their flight had landed twenty minutes earlier, and Ruth had limped right over to the public washroom.

The old poet had refused to use the facilities on the plane, fearing if it crashed she'd be found dead in there.

"Are you really afraid of what people would think?" Reine-Marie had asked.

"Of course not. But where would I haunt? I have my afterlife mapped out. I die in my home in Three Pines and then haunt the village. If I die in a plane toilet, where would I go?"

"Good thinking," said Reine-Marie.

And so Ruth had headed off to the facilities at Trudeau Airport, which apparently was worth the risk of eternity. Reine-Marie reread her email, detailing their visit to Professor Massey. She would call Armand when they got back to Three Pines, but she wanted him to have some of the details in writing.

She almost hit send, but then remembered something she'd left off the message. An attachment. She'd already attached one photo, but now she added another.

Reine-Marie opened the yearbook, found the section on the professors, and took a photo. Then she closed the book quickly, squashing the image inside like a bug.

No need to spend more time looking at it than necessary. She felt almost guilty sending it off to Armand. She hoped he read her email before opening the attachment. It would come as a shock otherwise.

She hit send just as Ruth reappeared.

"So, tell me about the tenth muse," Reine-Marie said as they walked slowly through the airport to their car.

"It's bullshit," said Ruth. "The tenth muse doesn't exist."

"But the other nine do?"

Ruth grunted in laughter. "*Touché.*" She gathered her thoughts before speaking. "The Nine Muses were created by the Greeks. They're goddesses of knowledge and inspiration. They represented poetry, history, science, drama." Ruth searched her memory as they walked. "Dance." She thought some more. "And a bunch of others. They're the daughters of Zeus and Mnemosyne. Memory."

"Ironic," said Reine-Marie. "But none for art? Why not?"

"How the hell should I know? There's at least one muse for poetry, that's all I care about."

"Do you have a muse?"

"Do I look like a lunatic?"

"Well, you have a duck. It seemed possible you also have a muse."

Ruth smiled. "Fair play. But no, I have no muse."

"Why not?"

"Too much power. Suppose it left? Where would I be then? No, I prefer to rely on my own meager talents."

They walked in silence for a few paces, until Ruth gave a long, low guttural prompt.

"But, Ruth, your talent is legendary. Mammoth," said Reine-Marie. "The only thing that's meager is your ego."

"You mean that?" said Ruth, with a smile.

"Can we get back to the Muses?" asked Reine-Marie. They were at the car, and after getting Ruth settled, she sat in the driver's seat, thinking. "Nine Muses. So where does this tenth one come in?" Reine-Marie asked.

"There's a theory that there were actually ten sisters," said Ruth. "But somewhere along the line, one was dropped. Erased."

"The one for art?"

Ruth shrugged.

Reine-Marie started up the car and left the parking lot, heading back to Three Pines.

"Muses work all day long," said Ruth. *"And then at night get together and dance."*

Reine-Marie tried to keep her eyes on the road, but she shot Ruth a glance.

"You say that like you've seen them."

The old woman laughed. "It's a quote from Degas. But sometimes, on moonlit nights on the village green . . ."

Reine-Marie looked again at Ruth, who had a crooked smile on her crooked face.

"Was the moon lit, or were you?" asked Reine-Marie, and Ruth laughed.

Still, as Reine-Marie drove off the island of Montréal toward the Eastern Townships, she could imagine them. Not on the village green, but deep in the woods. In a copse. Nine young women, sisters, in a circle, dancing. Holding hands, vigorous, healthy, joyous.

"A beautiful image, isn't it?" asked Ruth, as though she shared Reine-Marie's vision. "Now, imagine someone else, standing just off to the side. Watching."

Reine-Marie saw the circle of happy, robust young goddesses. And in the background another young woman was watching. Waiting. To be invited in.

Waiting. Forever.

"The tenth muse," Reine-Marie said. "But if she existed, if she was one of the sisters, why was she left out?"

"Not just excluded, but erased," said Ruth. "Her very existence denied."

"Why?" asked Reine-Marie.

"How the fuck should I know?" And the old woman turned to look at the woods rushing by.

Armand Gamache read the email from Reine-Marie about their meeting with Professor Massey. She explained that Professor Massey had given her a yearbook. She'd attached an old photo of Clara and Peter in

Massey's studio. She'd hoped to find a picture of Professor Norman too, but the editors had decided not to have photos of the professors that year—instead they'd reproduced one of their pieces of art.

Gamache sighed, disappointed. A photo, even an old one, would have been helpful.

He clicked on one of the attachments. And smiled. There was Clara. Unmistakable. Beaming. Her gladness all the more evident for the apparent world-weariness of those around her on the sofa. And standing behind the sofa was a very young Peter, one keen eye looking out through a haze of smoke that Gamache chose to believe was cigarette.

And then he opened the second attachment.

And inhaled. Not a gasp, exactly. Not that dramatic. But a sharp breath.

A face had appeared. A portrait. Distorted. Not abstract, like a Picasso, but distended as though bloated with emotion. And what this man felt was obvious. There was nothing subtle about the painting.

He was howling with rage. Not at the gods. Not toward Heaven and Fate. His focus was closer, more personal. It was just over the shoulder of the observer.

Gamache felt the urge to turn around. To see if there was indeed someone or something back there.

But this ghastly portrait wasn't screaming a warning, it wasn't some horror movie heroine. This was outrage.

Gamache felt a pit in his stomach. An ache. Not the ill-formed nausea he'd felt when first looking at Peter's gaudy works. This was focused and formed and unmistakable.

Madness spilled from the portrait. Uncontrollable, unharnessed. Something chained had broken free.

It was in the mouth. It was in the eyes. It was in every brush stroke.

Gamache looked at the lower right corner.

Norman. It was a self-portrait. By Professor Norman.

And then he looked closer.

His phone rang. It was Reine-Marie.

"Armand, I think there's something I forgot to put in my message," she began. "Not really forgot, but I wasn't precise."

"I was just about to call you," he said. "Do you see it?"

"See what?"

She was sitting in their garden, in one of the Adirondack chairs, Henri stretched out on the grass beside her. She'd just fed and walked him, then poured herself a gin and tonic. The glass sat in one of the rings on the wide arm.

"The portrait you sent," he said. "Do you have the yearbook?"

"Yes, it's on the table here. Pretty awful. I mean, I think the painting's probably brilliant, but what it says about the man? It's a self-portrait, isn't it?"

"*Oui*," said Gamache. "Can you find it again, please, and look at the signature?"

"You mean it's not by Professor Norman?" she said.

"Just tell me what you see."

He heard vague sounds as she put the phone down and did as he'd asked. Then she was back.

"Norman," she read.

"Look closer."

"I'm sorry, Armand. It still says Norman. Just a moment."

He heard more sounds, then silence. Then footsteps and a crackle as the phone was picked up.

"I got my device. Hold on, I'm bringing up the camera and the photographs. I can zoom in."

He waited.

"Oh." Was all he heard. And all he needed to hear.

"What did you want to tell me?" he asked.

It took Reine-Marie a moment to tear her eyes, and her mind, away from what she'd just seen.

She lowered the device, dropping the madman to her lap.

"Professor Norman taught art theory at the college," she said. "But according to Professor Massey, he didn't teach the traditional theories about perspective and aesthetics and the nature of art. He taught his own theories."

"Yes," said Gamache. "About the place of a muse in an artist's life."

"But Professor Norman wasn't advising the students to get a muse," she said. "He was teaching them about the tenth muse."

Armand drew his brows together, trying to remember.

"The tenth muse? I thought there were just the nine sisters."

"There's a theory that a tenth muse existed," said Reine-Marie. "That's the theory Professor Norman was teaching. Armand, none of the original muses represented painting or sculpture."

"But they must have," he said.

She shook her head, even though he couldn't see her. "No. Poetry, dance, history even. The word 'museum' comes from 'muse.' 'Music' and even 'amuse' come from the word 'muse.' But there was no muse for art itself."

"Hardly seems possible," he said, though he believed her.

"Professor Massey admitted he couldn't remember the details, if he ever knew them, but he did know that Professor Norman's theory was that there was in fact a muse for art. The tenth muse. And to be a successful artist you needed to find her."

"Are you saying that Norman believed this tenth muse actually exists? Is living somewhere?"

"I'm not saying it. Professor Massey wasn't even saying it. But Sébastien Norman was apparently teaching it to his students. But there's something else. Something Ruth said."

"I'm ready," he said, and sounded so stoic Reine-Marie smiled.

"She quoted Degas saying the muses work all day and get together to dance all night."

"Nice image."

"Ruth wondered what it would be like to be standing in the forest, watching. Eternally excluded."

Another image sprang to mind. Of a shadowy figure. Among the trees. Longing to belong.

Instead she was rejected.

And eventually that pain turned to bitterness, and the bitterness turned to anger, and the anger became rage.

Until that rage became madness.

And the madness became a portrait.

Gamache dropped his eyes to the image on his device. Now, because of the angle, the face appeared to be shrieking at Gamache's chest. His breast pocket.

Where the small book sat. The book about the balm. Of Gilead.

That made the wounded whole.

Had the tenth muse, and the pursuit of her, driven Professor Norman mad? Or was he already mad, and she was his salvation? His balm.

Would she make him whole?

Gamache stared at that distorted face.

If ever there was a sin-sick soul, this was it.

TWENTY-EIGHT

⁓

"That was Reine-Marie," Gamache said when he got back to the group in Chartrand's office. Peter's canvases were now rolled up and sitting civilly on the desk.

"What is it?" asked Clara, seeing his face.

"She sent this." Gamache handed her the device. "From your year-book."

"Am I going to want to see it?" Clara made a face. "I wasn't always the elegant woman I am today."

She clicked the device while the others gathered round.

"You're not kidding," said Jean-Guy.

"That's not me, dickhead," said Clara, and for the first time Beauvoir saw evidence of Ruth as Clara's muse.

The madman glared out at them. Disfigured with wrath.

"Poor man." Myrna was the first to react. She, alone among them, was familiar with madness. If not immune to it.

Her "poor man" reminded Gamache of something Marcel Chartrand had said when looking at Peter's paintings.

Poor Peter, he'd said.

While Peter's lip painting hadn't achieved the horror of this portrait, there was a similarity. Like looking at a younger self. And seeing where it was heading.

"Professor Norman?" Myrna asked, and Gamache nodded.

"A self-portrait," he said. "Look at the signature."

They did.

"Enlarge it," he said.

They did.

And then they looked at him, confused.

"But it doesn't say Norman," said Clara.

And it didn't. Only in enlarging it was the signature clear.

No Man.

"I need some fresh air," said Clara. She looked as though someone had just put a pillowcase over her head. Disoriented, she put down the device, picked it up again, then gave it to Myrna.

She turned full-circle, looking around for the door, and finding it, she left.

The others followed her.

She walked quickly and they had to rush to catch up, until they were strung out behind her like a tail.

Far from slowing down, Clara gathered speed. She sped down the alleyways, down the back streets, the cobbled streets, the side streets, where tourists never ventured. She headed past the faded Québécois homes, chased by that bloated face, until she'd left the town behind.

Until she reached the edge. Until there was no more there there. Only air. And the river beyond.

Only then did she stop.

Jean-Guy was the first to reach her. Then Gamache and Chartrand and finally, huffing and puffing but undeterred, Myrna arrived.

Clara stared ahead, clear-eyed, her chest heaving.

"What does it mean?" She spoke as though the vast river might know. Then she turned and looked at them. "What does it mean?"

"It suggests that Professor Norman and this No Man are the same person," said Gamache.

"Suggests?" said Clara. "Is there any other interpretation?"

"Not really."

"And if Norman and No Man are the same person?" Clara demanded. "What does that mean?"

"For us?" asked Gamache. "You know what it means."

"It means Professor Norman came here when he was fired," said Clara. "He was probably from around here. He came back, but not as Sébastien Norman. He decided to become No Man."

"But why change his name?" Beauvoir asked.

"Shame, maybe," said Myrna. "He'd been fired."

"Or maybe it was the opposite of shame," said Gamache. "He wasn't exactly in hiding. You said he started an artist colony."

Chartrand nodded and looked troubled. "He did, but I don't think he meant to."

"What do you mean?"

"He built a place for himself not far from here. In the woods. But then people started joining him. Other artists. Uninvited. It just sort of happened."

"Peter came here looking for him," said Clara. "He wanted to find Professor Norman for reasons I can't begin to understand. But did he find No Man instead?"

"*Non*," said Chartrand. "*C'est impossible*. No Man was long gone by then. His colony collapsed years ago. Long before Peter arrived."

"Why did Peter come all this way looking for Professor Norman?" Clara asked. "What did he want from him?"

There was no answer to that, and so they remained silent.

"Where is he?" Clara asked. "Where's Peter?"

"Where's No Man?" Beauvoir asked.

Gamache hadn't taken his eyes off Chartrand. "Well?"

"Well, what?"

"Where's No Man?"

"I don't know," said the gallery owner. "I've already told you that."

"If you don't know where he is, you at least know where he was," said Gamache. And Chartrand nodded. And pointed.

Away from the river and into the woods.

Ten minutes later they were walking along an overgrown path through the woods.

And then, as though they'd crossed some barrier, the woods stopped and they emerged into sunshine. Before them was a clearing overgrown with grasses and bushes. They had to force their way through the bracken until they were in the middle of a large circular field.

It was pocked with bumps and lumps. Gamache assumed they were tree stumps, but then realized they formed shapes. Squares. Rectangles.

Foundations.

What was now a tangle of wildflowers and burrs and weeds had once been homes.

Not just abandoned, but dismantled. Taken apart. Until just the bare bones remained as evidence that anyone had once lived here.

Gamache heard a noise beside him. A sort of exhale, a moan.

He looked over at Clara, who was standing very still and staring ahead of her. He followed her eyes, but saw nothing unusual.

"Clara?" Myrna asked. She'd also noticed the sudden stillness, the focus, in her friend.

Now Clara moved. Rapidly. She unrolled Peter's paintings and, dumping the other two on the ground, grabbed one and started walking, this way and that. The painting held open at arm's length, like a map. She searched the field, a dowser desperate to find the wellspring.

She stumbled over the rocks and stones and foundations.

And then she stopped.

"Here. Peter was here when he painted this."

They joined her. And exchanged glances. There was no correlation between the wild colors and fierce strokes of the painting and this bucolic scene. A desperate wife had seen something not there.

But the longer they looked, the more it fell into place.

If the clearing wasn't seen literally, if the true colors weren't looked for on the canvas, then slowly it revealed itself.

What Clara held was a strange marriage, a sort of alchemy, between reality and perception. Between what they saw and what Peter felt.

"He was here," Myrna agreed. "And the other?"

Myrna retrieved the other painting and, with Beauvoir beside her, held it up and walked through the field. Until they stopped.

"Here."

And then they all looked at Marcel Chartrand.

"You knew, didn't you?" said Gamache.

"Not at first," he said. "Not when I saw the paintings in my office. It's impossible to connect them with here."

Reluctantly, Gamache had to agree. But he still stared at Chartrand.

"When did you know that Peter had been here?"

"After we realized Professor Norman and No Man are the same person. You have to understand, I hadn't given this fellow No Man a thought in years. Artist colonies pop up around here all the time. There was one a few years back where the members only painted in shades of green. Another where they only spoke Latin. Some of the communities survive for a while, most don't. That's just the way it is."

"But you didn't tell us Peter came here," said Beauvoir. He and Myrna had rejoined them.

"I still wasn't sure until we got here." Chartrand looked at Clara.

"How'd he know how to find it?" Gamache asked. "It's not exactly on the tourist place mat. Did you tell him? Did you bring him here?"

"I told you, no. But it wasn't a secret. Everyone knew about the colony. As I said, it was just one of many. There're probably former members still living in the area. Maybe one of them told Peter about it."

"But you knew where it was. You've been here before," Gamache said.
"Once."

"Were you a member?" He watched Chartrand closely.

"Me?" The gallery owner seemed genuinely surprised at the suggestion. "No. I'm not an artist."

"Was this place really about art?" Myrna asked. "Or about the tenth muse?"

"Art, as far as I know."

"Why did you come here if not for the art?" Gamache asked.

"No Man asked me to talk about Clarence Gagnon. He was interested in him. All the members were."

"Why?" Gamache asked.

"You know why," said Chartrand. "I can see it when you look at his paintings. The man wasn't just a genius, he was courageous, bold. Willing to break with convention. He painted traditional images, but with such—" Chartrand searched for the word, and in the silence they could hear the buzz of flies and bees. "Grace. He painted with grace."

And Gamache knew the truth in that.

"Do you think Clarence Gagnon had found the tenth muse?"

The question came from Jean-Guy Beauvoir, without a hint of sarcasm.

Marcel Chartrand took a deep breath and thought about that.

"I think if there was a muse for art, then Clarence Gagnon had found her. Here, in Baie-Saint-Paul. There're lots of beautiful places in Québec, but this one is like a magnet for artists. I think No Man suspected Clarence Gagnon had found the tenth muse here. And that's why he came. To find her."

They looked around the empty, abandoned field. At the lumps and bumps that had once been homes and now looked like burial mounds. And Armand Gamache wondered what he'd see if he returned at night. Probably no human. No Man. But would he see the muses, dancing?

Nine of them?

Or just one. Twirling like a dervish. Alone, powerful. Expelled. As No Man had been.

Driven mad. Driven here.

TWENTY-NINE

⁓

It was getting late by the time they returned to Baie-Saint-Paul.

Chartrand parked at the gallery, and Beauvoir, after a glance at Gamache, excused himself and walked down the cobblestone street.

"Where's he going?" Myrna asked.

"To get an iced tea," said Gamache.

"I wouldn't mind one myself," she said. But by the time she turned around, Beauvoir had disappeared. She turned back to Gamache. "What're you up to, Armand?"

He smiled. "If you were a member of No Man's colony, and the place fell apart, what would you do?"

"Go home."

"Suppose this was home?"

"I'd—" She thought about it. "Find work, I guess."

"Or maybe start your own business," said Gamache.

"I might. An art gallery, for instance?" She studied him, then dropped her voice. "You don't believe Chartrand, do you?"

"I don't believe anyone. Not even you."

She laughed. "Nor should you. I lied just now. I'm not interested in an iced tea, I just wanted to know where Jean-Guy raced off to."

"Can you guess?" asked Gamache.

Myrna thought about it, then a smile spread across her face. "You sneak. He's gone to the brasserie. La Muse."

Armand smiled. "Worth a try."

"And you think she'll be there? This tenth muse?" Myrna asked.

"Do you?"

Jean-Guy grabbed a table inside. All the ones on the *terrasse* were already taken, but he wanted to be inside anyway. Where he could watch the servers.

He picked up the menu and looked at the image laminated on the cover. It was a simple line drawing of a woman. Dancing.

"What can I get you?" the server asked. Her voice was crisp, business-like, but her eyes had scanned him. Taking in the lean body, the dark hair and eyes. His ease.

Beauvoir was used to this, and used to returning the look. But now he found, while he absorbed the fact of her presence, it meant nothing to him. Far from feeling he'd lost something, he once again was reminded of all he'd found. In Annie.

"A ginger beer, *s'il te plaît*. Nonalcoholic."

She brought him the drink.

"How long have you worked here?" He gave her a five-dollar bill, telling her to keep the change.

"Couple of years."

"You an artist?"

"No. I'm studying architecture. I work here in the summers."

"Is the owner around?"

"Why? Is something wrong?" She looked concerned.

"No, I just wanted to meet him." Beauvoir held up the menu. "Interesting design."

"He did it himself. He's an artist."

Beauvoir tried not to show his interest. "And is he here? I'd like to compliment him."

She looked like she neither believed him, nor cared. "He's away."

"Oh. When will he be back?"

"A week, maybe two."

"Do you know how I can find him?"

She shook her head. "He goes off somewhere down the coast painting every year."

"In the busy season here?" Beauvoir asked. "Can't he do it in winter?"

"Would you?"

She had a point.

They strolled through the cobblestone streets of Baie-Saint-Paul, Clara and Chartrand ahead, Myrna and Gamache a few paces behind.

"They're quite friendly," said Gamache, gesturing toward the two ahead.

"Yes," said Myrna. She watched as Chartrand lowered his head so that he could better hear Clara. Clara was gesturing with Peter's rolled-up paintings.

Talking about art, Myrna thought. And she realized it had been a long time since she'd seen Peter bend down, to better hear Clara. And since she'd heard them talk about art, or anything, in the intimate way Clara and Chartrand were now talking.

"I like him," said Myrna.

Beside her, Gamache put his hands behind his back, and held them there, rocking slightly as he walked.

"Do you think the tenth muse exists?" he asked.

Now it was Myrna's turn to walk in silence. Considering.

"I think muses exist," she said. "I think something happens when an artist or writer or musician meets someone who inspires them."

"That's not the same thing, and you know it," said Gamache. "I'm not talking about a person who inspires an artist. I'm asking you about the tenth muse. You didn't answer my question."

"You noticed that, did you?" she smiled, and began to also rock slightly as she walked, in a rhythmic motion mirroring his. "I've never given the actual Muses any thought," she said at last. "But now that I am, I have to say if I can believe in nine, I can stretch it to ten."

Beside her, Gamache gave a low laugh. "And can you believe in nine? Or ten?"

Myrna was quiet for another few paces, watching Clara now look up at Chartrand as he spoke. Watching him gesture in ways Peter never did.

Myrna stopped, and Gamache stopped with her. The other two, not seeing this, continued on.

"Hundreds of millions of people believe in a God of some sort. They believe in karma, in angels, in spirits and ghosts. In reincarnation and heaven. And the soul. They pray and light candles and chant and carry good-luck charms and interpret events as omens. And I'm not talking about marginal people. This is the mainstream."

Between the old homes they could see the river.

"Why not Muses?" she asked. "Besides, how else do you explain Ruth's poetry? You can't tell me that drunken old woman writes them without some supernatural help."

Gamache laughed. "A ghost writer?"

"It really doesn't matter if the Muses exist," said Myrna. "What matters is that No Man believed it. He believed it so strongly he risked ridicule and even his job. That's powerful, Armand, but it's something else. That kind of passion, that kind of certainty, is very attractive. Especially to people who are directionless."

"Are you coming?" Clara called.

She and Chartrand had stopped to wait for them.

Myrna and Gamache joined them and together they walked until they reached the archway that led to the hidden courtyard. It was where they'd first regrouped twenty-four hours ago. It seemed so long ago now, so much had happened.

While the others had been keen to join Jean-Guy at La Muse, Gamache had convinced them that Beauvoir might not do his best work with the four of them looking on.

So they found themselves in the now-familiar courtyard. The *terrasse*, which should have been crammed with tourists admiring the view, was all but empty.

This place seemed to exist only for them, and two lone backgammon players. Still there. Perhaps always there. Shabby guardians at a forgotten gate.

Beauvoir scanned the other servers, and his eyes fell on a middle-aged man who'd just appeared out of a door by the bar. Jean-Guy picked up his drink and moved to one of the stools. It made him feel slightly uncomfortable. Or, worse, he felt too comfortable. Too familiar.

He stood up.

"*Salut*," he said to the older man, who was now behind the bar looking at order forms.

The man looked up and gave Beauvoir a quick, professional smile. "*Salut.*"

Then returned to what he was doing.

"Nice place," said Beauvoir. "Interesting name. La Muse. Where does it come from?"

He had the man's attention, though it was clear he considered Beauvoir feeble, or drunk, or lonely, or just a pain in the ass.

But the professional smile flashed again. "Been called that for as long as I've worked here."

"And how long's that?"

Beauvoir knew he was making a fool of himself. How useful flashing his Sûreté ID would be right about now. Such a difference between an inspector of homicide asking questions and a barfly asking them.

The man stopped what he was doing and put both hands firmly on the bar.

"Ten years, maybe more."

"You the owner?"

"No."

"Can I speak to him?"

"We're not hiring."

"I already have a job."

The man looked like he didn't believe him.

Beauvoir longed to bring out the ID. Or the gun.

"Look, I know this is strange, but I'm trying to find someone who might've known an artist called No Man."

The man's stance changed. He pushed back from the bar and gave Beauvoir another assessing look.

"Why?"

"Well, I work at a gallery in Montréal and this No Man's art has suddenly gone up in value. But no one seems to know much about him."

Now he had this man's full attention. By dumb luck Beauvoir had said the very thing guaranteed to get both a response and respect. Two things Jean-Guy sorely wanted.

"Really?"

"You seem surprised."

"Well, I never saw any of this No Man's paintings myself, but Luc led me to believe . . ."

"Yes?"

"Well, I guess Van Gogh was a little you-know-what."

"What?"

"Fucking nuts."

"Ahhh." Now there was a description of an artist he could get behind. "And so was No Man?"

For that he got a stern look. "He called himself No Man. What do you think?"

"You have a point. Who's this Luc?"

"He's the owner here. Luc Vachon."

"And he knew No Man?"

"Yeah, well, he lived at that place for a few years."

"What did he say about it?" Beauvoir asked.

"Not much."

"Come on, he lived there for years, he must've said something."

"I asked a few times, but he never really wanted to talk about it."

"Embarrassed, do you think?" asked Beauvoir.

"Maybe."

"Come on, man, you can tell me," said Beauvoir. "Must've been pretty weird."

"I think he got kinda scared there at the end," said the man. "Luc really didn't want to talk about it. I do know he used to ship No Man's paintings to his gallery, or someplace. You guys, I guess. And Luc used to get in the art supplies No Man used."

"They must've been close."

"Couldn't have been that close. Luc said No Man just up and left one day. Took off."

"Where to?"

"Don't know."

"Does Luc know? Is he still in touch with No Man?"

"I never asked. Never cared."

"Was No Man from around here?"

"Don't think so. Never heard of family or anything."

"So he might've gone home?"

"I suppose."

Jean-Guy sipped his ginger beer and thought about that.

"When did Luc open this place?"

"He bought the brasserie after he left the commune."

"Why'd he call it La Muse?"

"Haven't you ever heard of an artist's muse?" the barman asked. "They all seem to either have one or want one. Me, all I want is peace and quiet."

He stared at Beauvoir, but Jean-Guy ignored the hint.

"Does Luc have a muse?"

"Only her."

The barman tapped the menu.

"Is she real?" asked Jean-Guy.

"Wouldn't that be nice?" said the barman. "But no." He leaned across the bar and whispered, as though sharing a confidence, "Muses aren't real."

"*Merci*," said Beauvoir, and once again longed for the heft of his gun in his hand.

"The owner still paints?"

"*Oui*. Goes off a couple weeks of the year. That's where he is now." The man paused. "I don't suppose his paintings will be worth something, since he studied with this No Man?"

It was clear he had a few of those, either by choice or because he had no choice.

"Maybe. But please don't say anything. Let me tell him myself. Can I call him or email?"

"No. He doesn't want to be disturbed. He normally goes off at the end of August, but this year he left early. Guess the weather was good. What's the name of your gallery? Luc'll want to know."

"*Désolé*. I'm trying to be here incognito."

"Ahh," said the man.

"Are there any other members of No Man's art colony still around?"

"Not that I know of."

"Anyone you know have any of No Man's paintings?"

"No. He had Luc mail them all down south, to his gallery." The man paused and thrust out his lower lip. "How can Luc get in touch with you, if you're incognito?"

It sounded pretty silly. And the man himself sounded suspicious. Beauvoir gave him his cell phone number.

"I'm sorry, but I have to ask again," said Beauvoir. "Have you ever heard your boss talk about a muse? His own, maybe, or one that influenced the colony?" He held up the menu.

"*Non.*"

Beauvoir got up and, waving the menu at the barman, he left. Taking the menu with him.

"Find what you were looking for?" one of the backgammon players asked.

Clara was momentarily taken aback, wondering how they knew about Peter. But Myrna remembered.

"We did, and you were right. That picture was painted exactly where you said it was."

And then Clara remembered that she and Myrna had asked these two men for help in finding out where Peter had done the lip painting. And they had helped.

"Strange painting," said one.

"Strange place," said the other.

Clara, Myrna, Chartrand, and Gamache took the table by the edge of the *terrasse* and ordered drinks. While they waited, Gamache excused himself and returned to the two men.

"What did you mean just now when you called it a strange place? You mean the river, where that painting was done?"

"Nah, I mean the one she had in her other hand."

"You knew where that was painted too?" asked Gamache.

"Oh yes. Been there years ago. Helped take down some of the trees."

"In the woods." Gamache waved vaguely in the direction of the forest.

"*Oui.* Recognized it."

"But you didn't say anything?" Gamache asked.

"Wasn't asked. She only asked about the river painting. Funny pictures."

"I liked them," the other man said, studying the backgammon board.

"Do you know anything about the art colony that was built in the woods?" Gamache asked.

"Nothing. I cleared the trees, then left. Saw the guy a few times in the village here. Grew pretty big, I heard. His artist retreat. And then it ended. Everyone left."

"Do you know why?"

"Like all the others, I suppose," said the elderly man. "It'd run its course."

Gamache thought about that. "You called it a strange place. Why?"

The other elderly man looked up from the board and examined Gamache with a clear eye. "I know you. You're that cop. Seen you on TV."

Gamache nodded and smiled. "Not anymore. We're just here trying to find a friend. The man who painted those pictures. His name's Peter Morrow."

They shook their heads.

"Tall," said Gamache. "Middle-aged. Anglo?" But the two men just gave him blank stares. "He was interested in the fellow who ran that art colony. Norman. Or No Man."

"No Man," the elderly man repeated. "I remember now. Strange name."

"Strange man?" asked Gamache.

The backgammon player considered that. "No more than the rest. Perhaps less. Kept to himself. Seemed to want to be left alone."

He laughed.

"What's so funny?"

"So many artists here are desperate for students. They advertise and hold shows and offer all sorts of courses. But this guy builds a small cabin in that clearing, says nothing, and students flock to him."

"You know why?" Gamache asked. "Was he charismatic?"

That brought another laugh. "Anything but. I can tell you one thing, he didn't look like an artist. Most are pretty scruffy. He seemed, well, more like you."

The elderly man eyed him, and Gamache was far from convinced that was a compliment.

"Can you describe him? What did he look like?"

The elderly man considered. "Small guy. Wiry. About my age. My age back then, I mean."

"Were there ever any women?"

"Are you suggesting there were orgies?"

"You made the clearing for orgies, Léon? Wait 'til your wife finds out."

"If there were, I wasn't invited."

"No," said Gamache, pretty sure they were having fun with him. "I'm just asking if it seemed that No Man was married or had a companion."

"Not that I ever saw."

"No muses?" asked Gamache, and watched their response. But there was no response, except that the one elderly man finally made his move and got kinged.

The other man shook his head and clicked his tongue.

"You said the place was strange. What did you mean?" Gamache asked again.

"Where it was, for one thing. Is that where you'd choose to live, if you could've had that?"

He waved at the river.

"Most of the other artist retreats or communities or whatever you call them take advantage of the view. And why not?"

Gamache considered that. "Why not?" he asked.

The elderly man shrugged. "Privacy, I guess."

"Or secrecy," said the other man, his head bowed, studying the board. He looked across at his friend. "For orgies."

They laughed and Gamache returned to the table, and considered what a fine line it was, between privacy and secrecy.

Their drinks had arrived by then.

"What were you talking about?" Myrna nodded toward the backgammon players.

"They knew No Man," said Gamache. "And recognized the place from Peter's painting."

"Did they know Peter?" asked Clara.

"No." He told them what the players had said, then he pulled his notebook and pen from his pocket and set them on the table. "Where're we at?"

He looked for his pen, but Clara had taken it and turned her paper place mat over.

Gamache remembered then who was in charge. And who wasn't.

THIRTY

~

"Did Peter ever talk to you about Scotland?" Clara asked Chartrand.

"Scotland?"

"Dumfries, actually," said Myrna.

"The Garden of Cosmic Speculation," said Gamache.

Chartrand looked momentarily startled, as though his companions had turned into lunatics.

"Or hares," said Clara.

"Hair hair?" Chartrand touched his head. "Or the musical?"

"The rabbit," said Myrna, and could see it wasn't really a clarification.

"What're you talking about?"

"None of this sounds familiar?" asked Gamache.

"No, it doesn't sound familiar," said Chartrand, exasperated. "It doesn't even sound sensible." He turned to Clara. "What did you mean about Scotland?"

"He was there last winter. Visited a garden."

Clara explained what they'd learned about Peter and the Garden of Cosmic Speculation, expecting any moment to hear Chartrand laugh.

But he didn't. He listened and nodded.

"The rabbit turned from flesh to stone, and back again," said Chartrand, as though that was a perfectly reasonable thing for a rabbit to do. "Peter's river turns from sorrow to joy, and back again. He's learned the miracle of transformation. He can turn his pain into paint. And his painting into ecstasy."

"It's what makes a great artist," said Clara.

"Not many get there," said Chartrand. "But I think if Peter's courage holds and he keeps exploring, he'll be like few others. Van Gogh, Picasso, Vermeer, Gagnon. Clara Morrow. Creating a whole new form, one that doesn't distinguish between thought and emotion. Between natural and manufactured. Water, and stone, and living tissue. All one. Peter will be among the greats."

"It took a hare in the Garden of Cosmic Speculation for him to see it," said Myrna.

"It took Peter growing into a brave man," said Gamache. "Brave enough not to explain it away."

"If we find No Man, we find Peter," said Myrna.

"And maybe the tenth muse," said Clara. "I'd like to meet her."

"You already have," said Chartrand. "You might not know who she is, but she's someone in your life."

"Ruth?" Clara mouthed to Myrna, and opened her eyes wide in mock-horror.

"Rosa?" Myrna mouthed back.

Clara chuckled at the thought and looked over the railing, to the woods and the rocks and the river. She wondered if the tenth muse could be a place. Like Charlevoix was for Gagnon. Home.

"I don't understand why the Greeks would erase the tenth muse," Myrna said. "You'd think she'd be more important than the other nine Muses, since the Greeks revered art."

"Maybe that's why," said Gamache.

Across the *terrasse*, the backgammon players stopped rolling the dice and looked at him.

"Power," he said. "Maybe the tenth muse was too powerful. Maybe she was banished because she was a threat. And what could be more threatening than freedom? Isn't that what inspiration is? It can't be locked up, or even channeled. It can't be contained or controlled. And that's what the tenth muse was offering."

He looked from one to the other and rested his eyes on Clara.

"Isn't that what Professor Norman, or No Man, was also offering? Inspiration? Freedom? No more rigid rules, no lockstep, no conformity. He was offering to help the young artists break away. Find their own way. And when their works were rejected by the establishment, he honored them." Gamache held Clara's eyes. "With their own Salon. And for his troubles he was despised, laughed at, marginalized."

"Expelled," said Clara.

"He built a small home here, in a clearing," said Gamache. "But he wasn't alone for long. Other artists were drawn to him. But only the failed ones, the desperate ones. The ones who'd tried everything else. And had nowhere else to turn."

"A Salon des Refusés," said Clara. "He'd created not an artist community, but a home for *des refusés*. Outcasts, misfits, refugees from the conventional art world."

"He was their last hope," said Myrna. Then after a pause she added, "A shame he was crazy."

"I've been called that, lots of times," said Clara. "God help me, even Ruth thinks I'm nuts. What's crazy?"

Armand Gamache pressed on his device, and there, glowing on the table, was the photograph of a portrait of a madman.

No Man.

"That is," he said.

The menu landed on the table the same instant Jean-Guy Beauvoir landed in a chair.

"La Muse," he said. "The owner's name is Luc Vachon and he was a member of No Man's community. He drew that." Beauvoir tapped the menu.

"What did he say about No Man and the colony?" Gamache asked, picking up the menu and looking at the picture.

"Nothing. He wasn't at the brasserie. He takes off painting every year."

"At this time?" asked Myrna. "He runs a brasserie and he leaves at the height of the tourist season?"

"Can you imagine a business owner doing that?" Clara stared at Myrna until the other woman laughed.

"*Touché*, little one," said Myrna, and wondered briefly how her bookstore was doing under the management of Ruth and Rosa.

"When will this Vachon be back?" Clara asked.

"Couple of weeks," said Beauvoir. "And no way to reach him. The fellow I spoke with said Vachon didn't like talking about his time in the colony. He did admit that Vachon and No Man must've been fairly close, since No Man entrusted him with sending his paintings to a gallery down south."

"South like Florida?" asked Myrna.

"No, south like Montréal. No Man apparently had a gallery there, or a representative. He sent art off and got canvases and art supplies in return. The guy didn't know the name of the gallery, but Vachon would probably know."

Gamache had put on his reading glasses and was studying the signature on the drawing.

"I looked," said Beauvoir. "It's signed Vachon. Not No Man."

Gamache nodded and gave the menu to Clara. "It's a nice drawing."

"Pretty," said Clara, her voice neutral.

It wasn't, they all felt, the muse. It was Vachon's idea of a muse. Someone he clearly had not personally met. Yet.

But it was a lone figure, not the classic nine sisters. La Muse. Not Les Muses.

"The community fell apart when No Man suddenly took off. Didn't tell anyone. He just left."

Gamache shifted in his seat, but said nothing. He glanced down at the dancing figure on the menu, but in his mind he was seeing the clearing. The bracken, the wildflowers, the bumps and lumps where homes had once been.

That looked so much like burial mounds.

He looked at his watch. It was past six in the evening.

"I'm afraid we might have to impose on you another night," he said to Chartrand, who smiled.

"I consider you friends now. You're welcome for as long as you'd like."

"*Merci.*"

"What now?" Clara asked. "I think we've spoken to everyone in Baie-Saint-Paul."

"There is one place we could try," said Gamache.

Jean-Guy Beauvoir entered first, and this time he brought out his Sûreté ID.

"Yes, sir. What can I do for you?"

Beauvoir waited for the young agent behind the counter to size him up, and when she didn't he looked at her. She was young. Very young. Fifteen years younger than him. She could almost be . . .

But while a brave man, he wasn't quite brave enough to go there. But he did wonder how, and when, it had happened. That he'd gone from clever, young, whip-smart Jean-Guy Beauvoir, the *enfant terrible* of homicide, to Inspector Beauvoir. Sir.

Not all transformations were miracles or magical. Or improvements.

"We'd like to speak to your station chief."

The young agent looked at him, then behind him to the others who were crammed into the entrance of the small Sûreté detachment.

And then her eyes widened.

Standing at the back, patiently waiting, was a man she recognized.

She stood up, then sat down. Then stood up again.

Jean-Guy Beauvoir suppressed a grin. He was used to this reaction and had been expecting it. Waiting for it.

"Chief Inspector," the agent said, practically bowing.

"Armand Gamache." He stepped forward and, squeezing his arm between Clara and Chartrand, offered his hand.

"Agent Pagé," she said, feeling his grip. "Beatrice Pagé."

She could have cursed. Why'd she give him her first name? *He doesn't care. He's the Chief Inspector of fucking Homicide.* Or was. Until that whole rotten business. Until he retired.

Agent Pagé had joined the Sûreté months before it all blew up. And she knew that while she'd spend most of her career with other superiors, this man would always be, in her mind, the Chief Inspector of homicide.

"I just started," she said, and her eyes widened. *Stop talking, stop talking. He doesn't care. Shut the fuck up.* "My shift, I mean. And in the Sûreté."

Oh, dear God. Take me now.

"This is my first posting."

She stared at him.

"And where are you from?" Gamache asked.

He looked interested.

"Baie-Comeau, up the coast."

Merde, merde, merde, she thought. *He knows where it is. Merde.*

Gamache nodded. "They've cleaned up the bay there. A beautiful place."

He smiled.

"Yes, sir. It is. My family's been working in the mills for a long time."

"Are you the first of your family in the Sûreté?" he asked.

"*Oui.* They didn't want me to join. Said it wasn't respectable."

Maudit tabarnac, she thought, and looked around for a gun to stick in her mouth.

But the large man in front of her, with the scar by his temple, just laughed and lines radiated from his kind brown eyes. "And do they still feel that way?"

"No, sir, they don't." And now all her nerves calmed and she met his gaze. "Not after what you did. Now they're proud of me."

Gamache held her eyes and smiled. "They're proud of you, and they should be. It has nothing to do with me."

By now other agents and inspectors had heard Chief Inspector Gamache was there, and they drifted by. Some said hello. Some just stared and moved on.

"Chief Inspector." A middle-aged woman in uniform came out of an office, her hand outstretched. "Jeanne Nadeau. I'm the station chief."

She led them into her office. It was an even tighter squeeze than the reception area.

"This isn't, of course, official business," he said. "We're trying to find a friend of ours and he was last seen in your area in late spring."

"He's my husband," Clara said, and showed Captain Nadeau a picture of Peter and described him.

"Can we make copies?" Nadeau asked, and when Clara agreed she made the arrangements.

"How can I help?"

"I take it no one matching his description has come to your attention lately?" Gamache asked, and they all recognized the code. Nadeau shook her head and her intelligent eyes went from Gamache to Clara.

"Why was he here?"

Clara explained it, succinctly.

"So you think he was looking for this Professor Norman," Nadeau said. She turned from Clara to Chartrand. "You say he was known as No Man when he lived here?"

"Well, that's what he called himself."

Nadeau barely reacted. It was clear that this was not the first oddity she'd run into in Baie-Saint-Paul. Artists were not, perhaps, best known for conventional behavior.

"Did you know him?" Clara asked.

"No Man?" Nadeau shook her head. "Before my time." She walked over to the wall, where a detailed map of the area was pinned.

"Where was this art colony of his?"

Chartrand showed her and she made a note of it.

"But you say it's long gone?"

"At least ten years, probably more," said Chartrand.

"Any suggestion of criminal activity?" she asked.

"No," said Chartrand. "They seemed to keep to themselves."

Nadeau picked up her phone and spoke into it. A short time later, a bulky older man in uniform came into the office. He smelled of bachelorhood and fried fish.

"*Oui?*"

He looked like he might be in trouble, and his eyes shifted from his station commander to Gamache, who was squeezed into a corner and felt the coat tree digging into his back, as though it was a stickup.

"This is Agent Morriseau," said Nadeau. "He's been here longer than anyone. These people are asking about a man named Norman. He lived here a number of years ago and started an artist retreat, a sort of colony out by the second concession."

"You mean No Man?" Morriseau asked, and suddenly had everyone's attention.

"That's the one," said Clara.

"Got quite popular for a while," said Morriseau. "But then they do, don't they?"

"They?"

"Cults." He looked at their surprised faces. "You must've known. Otherwise, why're you asking?"

"It was a cult?" asked Chartrand.

"Yes."

"What makes you say that?" asked Clara.

"It wasn't just a bunch of artists painting away," said Morriseau. "They were into some sort of weird religion."

"How do you know that?" asked Jean-Guy.

"I made it my business to know," said the agent. "These places can start out pretty normal and then take a nasty turn. I wanted to make sure they stayed on this side of crazy."

There was that word again, thought Gamache.

"Why do you say crazy?"

Morriseau turned in the direction of the talking coat tree.

"And what would you call it, sir?" he asked politely.

Gamache decided not to ask him if he ever prayed his lottery ticket numbers won, or the skidding car stayed on the road.

"And did they?" he asked instead. "Stay on this side of the line?"

"As far as I know they did. Then that No Man disappeared. The spaceship must've come and taken him away."

Morriseau laughed, then stopped, having misjudged his audience. It worked in the bar. It worked in the squad room. But these people just stared, as though he was the one who'd crossed a line.

"Any idea where he went?" Beauvoir asked.

"*Non.* I think people were just happy to see him go."

Driven out of another place, thought Gamache. Or maybe not.

"Is there anyone still living in Baie-Saint-Paul who was a member of the community?" Clara asked.

"Yes. Luc Vachon."

"We already know about him," said Beauvoir. "He's off painting. Anyone else?"

The agent thought about it, then shook his head.

"*Merci,*" said the station chief and Morriseau left. She looked at them expectantly. "Is there anything else I can do?"

There wasn't.

Before they left, Gamache ducked back into Captain Nadeau's office and asked if they had any sniffer dogs.

"For drugs?" she asked.

"For the other," he said.

"You think not everyone left," she said.

"I think there was no spaceship," he said.

She gave one brusque nod. "I'll make arrangements."

He gave her his coordinates, and as he left he saw her walk to the map on the wall.

They returned to the Galerie Gagnon expecting to spend the night there, but Marcel Chartrand surprised them.

"I think I mentioned that this isn't my main home. I stay here on weekends when the gallery's busy. My main home is up the coast a few miles. I need to go back there tonight, but you're welcome to stay here."

"What would you prefer?" Clara asked.

"I'd prefer it if you came with me," he said. And while his eyes swept the group and included them all, they came to rest on Clara.

She didn't shy away from the gaze.

"I think—" Beauvoir began.

"We'd love to come to your home. *Merci*," said Clara.

As they packed, Beauvoir whispered to Gamache, "You should've said something, *patron*. We're better off here than in a house in the middle of nowhere. If we're going to track down Peter, we need to be asking more questions."

"And what questions are those?" Gamache asked.

"Was it really a cult? Did No Man leave voluntarily or was he kicked out of his own community? Where did he go?"

"Good questions, but who would we ask?" Gamache zipped up his case and turned to face Beauvoir.

Jean-Guy considered. They seemed to have hit a dead end.

"Are we so sure No Man really did leave?" Beauvoir asked.

Gamache gave one curt nod. "Captain Nadeau is looking into that. They're bringing in sniffer dogs."

"For corpses?"

Gamache nodded again. He wasn't sure if they'd find anything. And if they did, whether the body would be ten years old, or ten weeks.

Like Beauvoir, he also found it curious that Marcel Chartrand wanted to take them away from Baie-Saint-Paul. They could have stayed above the Galerie for another night. They were already settled in. Surely it was easier, even for Chartrand, to stay.

And yet the gallery owner wanted to move them to a remote home.

Beauvoir was right. There were questions to be asked here. But Gamache suspected most of the answers could be found with Chartrand.

THIRTY-ONE

After stopping for groceries, they drove up the coast highway, the road following the hills and rock cuts and cliffs.

Marcel Chartrand was ahead of them in his van, while Clara drove the others in the car.

Chartrand's turn signal went on after a few miles. Instead of turning left, away from the river, he was signaling right. But there didn't seem to be any "right" to be had. Just a cliff. But they went around a corner and there was a spit of land jutting into the river. And on it a cluster of brightly painted, cheerful homes.

"Once belonged to one family," Marcel explained as he came over to meet them. "All daughters. None married. They built their homes together."

The houses were modest in size, painted bright red and blue and yellow. Lighthouses, it seemed, in the gray landscape. The style of each house was similar, but slightly different, with swooping dormers and fieldstone chimneys and wooden porches. The roofs were sheet metal and looked like silver fish scales. They caught the fading light and turned soft blues and pinks.

"Does it have a name?" Myrna asked.

"The community? No. No name."

"No Name," Myrna repeated.

"Who lives here now?" Clara asked, following Chartrand to the home nearest the river.

"Those places belong to summer people." He pointed to the other two houses. "I'm the only one who lives here year-round."

"Does it ever get lonely?" Myrna asked.

"Sometimes. But what compensation."

His arm swept in an arc, taking in the trees and rocks and cliffs and great dome of sky. And the dark river. Marcel Chartrand was staring as though each was a close friend.

But none had a heartbeat, thought Myrna. It was no doubt glorious, but was it really compensation?

"I bought the place twenty-five years ago. Had been on the market for years, since the last sister died. No one else wanted it. It was derelict by then, of course."

Chartrand swung the door open and they entered.

They found themselves in a low living room, with wooden floors and beams. It would have felt claustrophobic, but Chartrand had used a traditional milk wash to paint the beams and the plaster walls white.

The result was a welcoming, homey feel. Two armchairs and an old sofa were arranged around the large open fireplace. Windows on either side looked out onto the St. Lawrence.

Once settled into their rooms, they poured drinks then gathered in the kitchen to make a meal of pasta, garlic butter baguette and chicory salad.

"You met No Man," Gamache said to Chartrand as he made the salad and Chartrand set the table. "You're the only one here who has—"

"That's not strictly true," said Chartrand. "Clara, you knew him."

"I guess I did," she said. "I keep forgetting. It was so long ago and I didn't take his course. I'd see him in the hallway, but that was all. Barely recognized him from that self-portrait in the yearbook, but I guess that was the fashion at the time. Everyone wanted to look tortured."

"They might have wanted to look it, but Norman actually was," said Myrna.

"But you lectured at the art colony," said Gamache, getting back to Chartrand. "Did it strike you as a cult?"

Chartrand stopped what he was doing and thought. "I don't think so. But what would a cult look like? Would you necessarily know?"

"What's the difference between a commune and a cult?" asked Beauvoir.

"Both have a sort of guiding philosophy," said Myrna. "But a commune is open—members can come and go. A cult is closed. Rigid. Demands conformity and absolute loyalty to the leader and the beliefs. It shuts people off from the greater society."

"Interesting then that No Man invited Marcel in to lecture," said Clara. "That doesn't seem the act of a cult leader."

"No," said Myrna. She looked at Chartrand, then looked away.

Gamache, watching closely, thought he knew what she was thinking.

Maybe Chartrand wasn't invited in. Maybe he was already there.

Gamache had suspected for a while that Marcel Chartrand might've been a member of No Man's community. Not because he knew so much about it, but because he pretended not to.

Chartrand looked up and smiled at Gamache. It was friendly, disarming. A comradely look. And Gamache wanted to believe they were indeed on the same side.

But instead of resolving, his doubts were growing.

"Did they show you any of their works?" Clara asked. She, alone among them, seemed to have no suspicions of Chartrand.

"No, and I didn't ask to see them."

Now Myrna did look up, then over at Clara. Willing her to see what was so odd. Here was an art gallery owner who seemed completely disinterested in any art.

Most gallery owners had a specialty, but were at least curious about art in general. Indeed, most were passionate and quite obnoxious about it.

Clara, who was putting garlic butter on the rounds of sliced baguette, didn't seem to register anything peculiar.

"Did No Man ever show you his works?" Gamache asked.

"No."

"Let me guess," said Beauvoir. "You didn't ask."

Chartrand found that amusing. "When you find what you love, there's no need to look further."

"It's a shame Luc Vachon has taken off," said Clara. "He could've told us more about the colony."

"Yes," said Gamache. "It is."

"You'd think he'd tell someone where he went," said Beauvoir. "The server said 'down the coast,' but that could be anywhere."

His knife that had been cutting tomatoes for the salad paused.

"You know, I asked her where he went, but I'm not sure—"

As he thought, the knife slowly descended until it was resting on the cutting board. He was staring ahead, replaying the conversations in the brasserie.

"*Merde*," he said at last, dropping the knife altogether. "Where's your phone?"

Chartrand pointed into the living room. "Why?"

"I asked the server where Vachon went and she didn't know. Then I asked the guy at the bar when he'd be back and if I could contact him. But I didn't ask him where Vachon goes. The young server didn't know, but he might. *Tabarnac.*"

He reached into his pocket, brought out his notebook, and found the phone number for La Muse.

They could hear him in the living room, punching in the numbers.

Myrna and Gamache were standing together at the sink.

"What're you thinking, Armand?" she asked quietly.

"I'm thinking that No Man disappears, then Peter disappears, and now Luc Vachon, the only member of the art colony still around, disappears."

"And now we've disappeared," Myrna whispered.

"True."

"Come on, Armand, out with it. What're you really thinking?"

"I'm thinking"—Gamache dried his hands on the towel and turned to face her—"that No Man lived here quietly for a number of years, and then word spread that he was a cult leader, and he was driven out."

"That's not thinking," said Myrna. "That's recapping. You can do better than that."

"I'm thinking," said Gamache, giving her a censorious look, "that I need to make a phone call."

"Give Reine-Marie my love," she called after him.

Gamache nodded and, stepping outside, brought out his cell phone.

He didn't tell Myrna that this call wasn't to his wife. It was to someone else in Three Pines.

"What the hell do you want?"

It was Ruth's version of "Hello."

"I want to talk to you about your visit to the art college today."

"Didn't you talk to your wife about that? Why bother me?"

"I wanted to ask you something Reine-Marie couldn't answer."

"What?" came the impatient voice, but he could hear the note of curiosity in it.

"That couplet of yours keeps coming up."

"Which one, Miss Marple? I've written hundreds of poems."

"You know which one, *ma belle*." He could almost hear her cringe. Gamache had long ago learned that if you wanted to endear yourself to Ruth, you gave as good as you got. But if you wanted to terrify her, be kind. *"I just sit where I'm put . . .* That one."

"So?"

"So Reine-Marie said you and Professor Massey quoted it together today. I've never heard you do that before. You must have liked him."

"What's your point?"

"Reine-Marie says he was quite taken with you."

"You sound surprised."

"And you with him." That brought a pause. "And that when she asked you about it you said something. She thought it was in Latin. What was it?"

"None of your business. Is it so laughable that two old people could find each other attractive? Is it so unbelievable?"

Something else that was inexplicable?

Far from being angry, Ruth sounded on the verge of tears. Gamache remembered then, though it was never far from the surface, some of the things he despised about his job.

"What did you say, Ruth, when Reine-Marie asked you about your feelings for Professor Massey?"

"You wouldn't understand."

"Try me."

"I was quoting one of my favorite poets," she said. "And no, it wasn't me."

275

"Who was it?"

"Seamus Heaney."

"A line from one of his poems?" Gamache asked.

"No. It was the last thing he said. Before dying. He said it to his wife. *Noli timere*."

Gamache felt a lump in his throat but pressed forward.

"The poem you and Professor Massey quoted," he said. *"I just sit where I'm put, composed of stone and wishful thinking."*

He waited for her to complete it, as she had with the elderly professor. But she didn't, and Gamache finished it himself.

"That the deity who kills for pleasure will also heal."

"What of it?"

Gamache looked back to the house and saw Clara and Chartrand framed by the panes, their heads bowed together over the meal they were preparing.

Noli timere, he thought.

"Who was that poem written for?" he asked Ruth.

"Does it matter?"

"I think it might."

"I think you already know."

"Peter."

"Yes. How'd you know?"

"A few things," said Gamache. "It occurred to me that in French 'stone' is *'pierre.'* And Pierre is Peter. It's a play on his name, but it's far more than that. You wrote it years ago. You could see it even then?"

"That he was made of stone and wishful thinking? Yes."

"And that there was a deity that killed for pleasure," said Gamache. "But that it could also heal."

"That's what I believe," said Ruth. "Peter didn't. Here was a man who was given everything. Talent, love, a peaceful place to live and create. And all he had to do was appreciate it."

"And if he didn't?"

"He would remain stone. And the deities would turn on him. They do, you know. They're generous, but they demand gratitude. Peter thought all his great good fortune was because of himself."

Unseen by Ruth, Gamache nodded.

"Peter always had a 'best before' date stamped on his forehead," said Ruth. "People who live in their heads do. They start out well enough, but eventually they run out of ideas. And if there's no imagination, no inspiration to fall back on? Then what?"

"What?"

"In the words of Emily Dickinson, you're screwed. What happens when the stone shatters, when even the wishful thinking disappears?"

Gamache felt in his pocket, like a weight, the small book. And the smaller bookmark. Marking a spot beyond which he'd never been.

"Their creations eventually die of neglect, of malnourishment," said Ruth, answering her own question. "And sometimes, when that happens, the artist also dies."

"Driven to it by a deity who kills for pleasure," said Gamache.

"Yes."

"But it also heals? How?"

Gamache found himself keenly interested. And he was honest enough to know it wasn't just for Peter.

"By offering a second chance. One last chance. Don't get me wrong, I believe in using your head. But not in spending too much time in there. Fear lives in the head. And courage lives in the heart. The job is to get from one to the other."

"And between the two is the lump in the throat," said Gamache.

"Yes. Most people can't get over that. Some are born to be brilliant. Peter was. But he just couldn't get there. He got so close he could see it, smell it. He probably even believed he was there."

"Wishful thinking," said Gamache.

"Exactly. He was given a taste of brilliance, of true creativity, and then, like a jest of God, he had it taken away. But the gods weren't finished with him yet. They gave him a wife who was truly gifted. So that he would have to see it every day. Witness it. And then the gods took even that away."

She sounded as though she was telling a ghost story. A horrible, haunting tale, of the thing she herself most feared. Not that a monster would appear, but that what she loved would disappear.

Peter Morrow was living her nightmare. All their nightmares.

"But he was given one last chance?" said Gamache. "To find it again?"

"Not again," said Ruth, her voice sharp. Making sure this ordinary man understood. "For the first time. Peter had to find something he never had."

"And what was that?"

"His heart." She paused before speaking again. "That's what Peter was missing, all his life. He had the talent, the brains. But he was riddled with fear. And so he kept going over the same territory, over and over again. As though Lewis and Clark had gotten to Kansas, then turned back and started over. The same loop. Mistaking movement for progress."

"Peter was doing that?" Gamache asked.

"All his life," said Ruth. "Don't you think? The subject of each painting might be different, but if you'd seen one Peter Morrow, you'd seen them all. Still, not everyone's a Lewis and Clark. Not everyone's an explorer, and not every explorer makes it back alive. That's why it takes so much courage."

"*Noli timere*," said Gamache. "But supposing he found the courage, what next? Did he go to Toronto looking for help, for guidance? To continue your analogy, wouldn't he need a map?"

"What're you on about? Jeez, we're talking about creative inspiration, not geography. Knucklehead," she muttered. "And why'd you bring up something as confusing as Martin and Lewis?"

Gamache sighed. He was losing her. And getting a little lost himself.

"What was Peter looking for in Toronto?" Gamache asked, trying to keep it as clear, as simple as possible.

"He was looking for a map," said Ruth, and Gamache shook his head and breathed in deeply. "And he went to the right place. But—"

"But what?" said Gamache.

"Peter would have to be careful not to fall under the wrong influence. Most people want to be led. But suppose they choose the wrong leader? They end up with the Donner party."

"I think this analogy has run its course," said Gamache.

"What analogy?"

Gamache thought about his friend Peter Morrow. Alone, afraid. Lost. And then at last Peter finds not one road, but two. One would lead him out of the wasteland, the other would lead him in circles. Mistaking movement for progress, as Ruth said. Professor Massey at one road, Professor Norman at another.

Ruth was right. Peter, for all his bluster, was a coward. And cowards almost always took the easy way.

And what could be easier than a magical tenth muse, who'd solve all your problems? Isn't that what cults offered? Shelter from the storm? A clear answer. Unhindered progress.

"Do you believe in the tenth muse, Ruth?"

He braced himself for abuse, but none came. "I believe in inspiration, and I believe it's divine. Whether it's God, the angels, a tree, or a muse doesn't seem to matter."

"Myrna talked about the power of belief," he said.

"She sounds wise. I'd like to meet her one day."

Gamache smiled. This conversation was over.

"*Merci*, you drunken wretch," he said, and heard her laugh. In the background Rosa was yelling, "Fuck, fuck, fuck."

"I'm sorry," she said. "You must have the wrong number."

Ruth hung up and went off to sit with Rosa, her muse, who inspired her not to be a better poet, but to be a better person.

Gamache stood in the dark and looked through the window again. At Clara. And Marcel Chartrand.

Perhaps that was why the gallery owner had invited them here, thought Gamache. Not as part of some sinister plot to get them away from Baie-Saint-Paul. But something far simpler. And far more human.

This was where Marcel Chartrand lived, alone. Clinging to the rocky outcropping. He'd invited Clara into his home.

Noli timere.

Be not afraid.

THIRTY-TWO

⌒

Jean-Guy Beauvoir was on hold. Waiting, waiting.

Gamache could see him through the windows in the living room. Pacing.

The phone in Gamache's hand rang.

"Reine-Marie?"

"*Oui*, Armand. I have news. The registrar at the art college called back."

"So late?"

"Well, she was having difficulty finding Professor Norman's file. I think she'd normally have given up and just gone on vacation, but the fact it was missing was bothering her."

"Did she find it?"

"No."

"I might not hold the presses after all," he said, and heard her laugh.

"There's more. She didn't find it but she did call the temp they had working for them at the end of the semester. She admitted digging out the file for someone else."

"Peter?"

"Peter. And I think I know why he hung around Toronto so long," said Reine-Marie. "He'd asked for the file in the winter, but it took a long time to find it."

"Months?"

"Well, not that long, but all the old files had been put in boxes when repair work was done years ago. What took so long was that she had to make sure the files weren't contaminated with asbestos dust, from the renovations. That fits with the timing that Professor Massey told us about. By the time the temp got the okay that the files were fine, a few weeks had gone by, and it was spring."

"If the temp found the file, why can't the registrar?" Armand asked.

"The temp destroyed it. Before you jump to conclusions"—Reine-Marie had heard his grunt—"you need to know that the temp's job was to enter data, contemporary data, on the students, but since she had Professor Norman's file out for Peter, she simply scanned everything in. And then she destroyed the original. That's why the registrar couldn't find it."

"But that means an electronic version exists," he said.

"Exactly. The registrar is emailing it to me. We will, of course, be long dead by the time it downloads. So I asked her to give me some of the highlights."

"And?"

"Sébastien Norman taught at the art college only one year. As I told you before, it was Massey who recommended him for the job. But what was in the files that was so valuable was a note from Norman asking that his last check be sent to Baie-Saint-Paul. Peter must've seen that and gone there to find him."

"But by then Norman had long since disappeared," said Gamache. "We might have another lead. Norman had a gallery where he sent his works. They might still represent him. Professor Massey met Norman in Toronto when he was starting his career. Maybe the gallery was in Toronto."

"And they'd have his current address," said Reine-Marie. "But there're a lot of galleries in Toronto."

"True, but Professor Massey might know," said Armand.

"Do you want me to call him?"

"It'll be too late to call him," said Armand. "He'd have gone home by now."

"Not necessarily. I think Professor Massey lives at the college, in his studio."

"Really? How strange."

"I suppose he has everything he needs there," said Reine-Marie. "I'll try."

One professor was expelled, thought Gamache as he hung up. One professor never left.

Reine-Marie called back a few minutes later.

"No answer. Maybe he doesn't live there. I'll try him again in the morning."

"Did the registrar say where Professor Norman was from? What part of Québec?"

"I didn't ask, but it might be in the file."

"Can you forward it to me as soon as you get it, *s'il te plaît*?"

They talked for a few more minutes, quiet, private conversation, then Gamache returned to the kitchen to find that Beauvoir had just arrived back as well.

"Anything?" the others asked in unison.

"*Patron?*" Beauvoir gestured for Gamache to go first.

"Reine-Marie's expecting an email from the college with Professor Norman's file. Did you know that it was Professor Massey who put Norman forward for the job?"

Judging by Clara's face, she didn't.

"What would possess him to do that?"

"He admitted to Reine-Marie that he didn't know Norman well. They'd met at a few art shows, and Massey felt Norman needed a bit of help. He didn't know many people and was clearly hard up. So Massey recommended Norman for a part-time job teaching art theory."

"Massey must've felt pretty bad when Norman screwed up," said Beauvoir.

"What did you think of him?" Gamache asked Myrna.

"Massey? I liked him. And I can see why the students adored him. He's magnetic, even now. And he seemed to genuinely care about the students. He reminded me a bit of you, Armand," said Myrna.

"It's true," said Clara. "I knew there was something about the man. His calm, I think, and his desire to help."

"And his rugged good looks," said Gamache, and saw the whites of their eyes. "There was a note in Norman's file telling them to forward his last paycheck here, to Baie-Saint-Paul. Peter saw the file, saw that, and came here. If there's more there we'll find out soon."

The pasta was drained and drizzled with garlic-infused olive oil, fresh basil, and grated Parmesan and the bowl brought to the table.

"Your turn," Clara said to Beauvoir as they sat down. "Any luck with La Muse?"

"None. I waited on hold for a long time, but the manager was too busy to come to the phone." Beauvoir helped himself to the pasta as he spoke.

He didn't say it, but had they stayed in Baie-Saint-Paul he could have gone to La Muse, cornered the man, and gotten the information. Instead, the phone had been hung up with the promise that the manager would call when he had the time.

An hour later, after the dishes had been done and the coffee perked, two phone calls came in at the same time.

"*Excuse-moi*," said Gamache, and again stepped onto the stone terrace with his cell phone. Before closing the door, he heard Chartrand say to Beauvoir, "It's for you."

It was a warm, moonless night, and while Gamache could no longer see the St. Lawrence, it made itself known to all his other senses. He could smell it, and hear it, and even feel it. The lightest of mists on his face.

"Reine-Marie?" As he spoke, he unconsciously turned west and imagined Reine-Marie at home. He imagined he was with her, sitting in their garden. Under these same stars.

"I have the dossier. I've just forwarded it to you."

"Can you give me the broad strokes?"

He listened as she read. And as she read he turned slowly. Away from her. Away from Three Pines. Away from the heart of Québec. To the head of the river. To where the St. Lawrence, and Québec, began.

To where this all began, he now knew. And where it would end.

"*Patron?*"

Beauvoir was silhouetted in the doorway.

"*Ici.*" He'd just hung up from Reine-Marie.

"I know where the owner of La Muse went. Where he goes every year at about this time."

"Let me guess," said Gamache.

The Chief was a disembodied voice, but then, slowly, Beauvoir could see his outline. Dark against the stars in the night sky.

The figure lifted a black arm and pointed.

"Out there," said Gamache.

"*Oui*," said Beauvoir.

"Tabaquen."

"*Oui*." And he too turned and stared into the darkness.

If the world had been flat, Tabaquen would be perched on the precipice.

"There you are," said Myrna, coming out.

"What is it?" Clara asked, joining Myrna and noticing the two men standing so still and silent. Staring to the east.

"We know where the owner of La Muse went," said Beauvoir.

"And we know where No Man went," said Gamache. "And the place where Peter almost certainly is."

"Where?" asked Clara, quickly joining them.

"A village way down there." Beauvoir pointed into the night.

"It's called Tabaquen," said Gamache.

"Do you know it?" Clara asked, and in the darkness she saw the dark head nod.

"It's the sister village of Agneau-de-Dieu," he said. "Side by side, but very different."

Gamache walked past them, toward the house.

"Agneau-de-Dieu," said Myrna, doing the translation. "Lamb of God. But Tabaquen? I don't know how that translates."

"It's a bastardization," said Beauvoir. "It's not really French. It was named by the natives a long, long time ago, before Europeans arrived."

"What does it mean?" asked Clara. "Do you know?"

"It means 'sorcerer,'" said Gamache, as he entered the house.

THIRTY-THREE

⁓

Beauvoir and Clara were up half the night, discussing, considering. Emailing, searching and plotting a course.

Finally, about two in the morning, they had it organized and went to their beds, only to wake up at six when their alarms sounded.

"What time is it?" came Myrna's sleepy voice. "God, Clara, it's just after six. Is the house on fire?"

"We need to leave if we're going to catch the nine o'clock plane."

"What?"

Myrna sat up in bed, completely alert and slightly alarmed.

Down the hall, Gamache was already sitting on the side of the bed. He'd offered to stay up with Clara and Beauvoir, to help them, but had been persuaded that his presence wasn't necessary. At all.

"You were successful?" he said to Jean-Guy, who was looking bleary but eager.

"There's a flight out of La Malbaie in three hours. It'll take us to Tabaquen."

"Really?" said Myrna, when Clara explained it. "Can't we just drive?"

"There're no roads," said Clara, trying to coax the large woman out of the small bed. "It's a fishing village. The only way in is by boat or plane."

"We chose the plane," Beauvoir was explaining to Gamache, who was in the shower. "It stops at all the villages and will take all day, but we'll be there in time for dinner."

They were dressed and out the door by seven.

Chartrand was standing by his van.

"We're taking our car," said Jean-Guy, tossing his bag into the trunk.

"I'm going with you," Chartrand said. "No need to take two vehicles. You can come back for yours when we get back."

The two men stared at each other.

"Get in," said Clara.

She climbed into the van, looked at Jean-Guy and patted the seat next to her.

Beauvoir looked at her, then at Chartrand. And finally at Gamache, who shrugged.

"You heard her, Jean-Guy. Grab your things."

"*Patron*," Jean-Guy started to say, but Gamache put his hand on Beauvoir's arm to stop him.

"Clara's in charge. She knows what she's doing."

"She once ate potpourri thinking it was chips," said Jean-Guy. "She took a bath in soup, thinking it was bath salts. She turned a vacuum cleaner into a sculpture. She has no idea what she's doing."

Gamache smiled. "At least if it all goes south, we have someone else to blame for once."

"You do," mumbled Beauvoir, tossing his bag into the back of the van. "I always blamed you anyway. I'm no further ahead."

Twenty minutes later, Chartrand turned into the tiny airport at La Malbaie and pulled up to the shack.

"Is that it?" asked Myrna, eyeing the small plane on the tarmac.

"I guess so," Gamache said, and tried not to think about it. He was used to taking tiny planes into remote villages and landing on what most pilots would not consider a runway. But it was never fun.

"Dibs on the exit row," said Myrna.

A young man came out of the shack and looked at them, assessing them like cargo. "I'm Marc Brossard, the pilot. You the ones who emailed last night?"

"That's right," said Jean-Guy. "Four to go to Tabaquen."

"Five," Chartrand said.

Beauvoir turned to face him. "You dropped us off. That's far enough. You can't come with us."

"But I can. All I have to do is buy a ticket." He handed over his credit card to the young pilot. "There. Easy. I can fly."

He said it in such a Peter Pan way that Myrna laughed. Beauvoir did not. He scowled at the gallery owner and turned to Gamache.

"Nothing we can do, Jean-Guy."

"Not if we don't try," he said. "Sir."

Gamache leaned in to Beauvoir and said, "We can't stop him. And do we want to?"

But Beauvoir hadn't given up. "Is there even room?"

"Always room for one more, my mother says," said the pilot, returning Chartrand's card to him and looking to the east. "Better hurry."

"Why?" Myrna asked, and wished she hadn't. Sometimes it was best not to know.

"Red sky in the morning." The pilot gestured to the violent red sky. "Sailors take warning."

"Something else your mother says?" asked Beauvoir.

"No. My uncle."

"But you're a pilot, and this isn't a boat," said Clara.

"Same difference. Means bad weather. We'd be better off in a boat." He looked from Myrna to Gamache. "Ballast. Good in a *bateau*. Not so good in the air."

"Maybe he should stay behind." Jean-Guy gestured toward Chartrand.

The gallery owner was staring into the gaudy sunrise, his back to them.

"No," said Clara. "He was kind to us. If he wants to come, he can."

"Are you kidding me?" Beauvoir hissed at Gamache. "She's making decisions based on what's 'nice'?"

"It's worked so far, hasn't it?" Gamache watched Beauvoir's face flush with frustration.

Myrna approached, saw his red face and, taking warning, turned around.

"You coming?" The pilot had loaded their bags and was standing by the door of the plane.

They squeezed in, the pilot directing them where to sit so that the weight was fairly evenly distributed. Even so, the plane waddled into the air, one wing dipping dangerously and almost hitting the runway. Gamache and Clara, on that side, leaned toward the middle. Like mariners, after all, heaving ho.

And then they were airborne, and on their way. The plane circled, and Gamache, his face forced against the window as Jean-Guy's body shifted in the turn, could see what was only visible from above.

The crater. The giant, and perfect, circle where the meteor had struck hundreds of millions of years ago. The cosmic catastrophe that had wiped out all life. And then had created life.

The plane banked again and headed east. Away from there. And into the red sky.

"Have you been flying this route for a while?" Clara shouted above the drone of the engines.

She'd finally stopped praying and felt it was safe to open her mouth without shrieking.

"A few years," he called back. "Started when I was eighteen. Family business."

"Flying?" asked Clara, feeling slightly more confident.

"Fruit."

"Pardon?"

"Oh, for God's sake," Myrna shouted. "Leave well enough alone and let him concentrate on flying."

"*Oui*, fruit. Not much fresh fruit along the coast, and the *bateau* can take too long, so we fly it in. Mostly bananas."

What followed was a monologue on how long various fruit takes to rot. By the time he stopped talking they felt fairly certain they'd all gone bad.

"How often do you get passengers?" Jean-Guy asked, desperate to change the subject.

"A lot lately, but that's unusual. Most people who want to go to the coast take the ship. Takes longer, but it's safer."

No one pursued that, and Clara went back to praying. *Bless, oh Lord, this food to our use . . .*

"Did you fly Luc Vachon recently?" Jean-Guy asked.

"The owner of La Muse? *Oui*. Few days ago. A bit early, but his annual trip to the coast."

"Where'd he go?" Gamache asked.

"Tabaquen. To paint. Like he does every summer. This year I took him all the way there, but most summers I drop him in Sept-Îles, to catch the boat. All the artists prefer the boat. It's—"

"—safer, yes, we know," said Beauvoir.

The pilot laughed. "I was going to say prettier. I think artists like pretty. *Mais, franchement*, it's not really safer. There's no safe way to get to the Lower North Shore. We have turbulence and the ship has the Graves. So it's all a crapshoot."

"Do not open your mouths," hissed Myrna, catching their eyes with a searing look.

The small plane lurched in an air current. Dipping and falling, and climbing again. The pilot quickly turned his attention to flying. In the back, their eyes widened and Clara grabbed Myrna's hand.

Jean-Guy, seeing this, envied the women, and he wondered how the Chief would take it if he held on to his.

The plane pitched again and Beauvoir grabbed, then let go of, Gamache's hand when the plane righted itself.

Gamache looked at him, but said nothing. It was not, they both knew, the first time one had held on to the other, for dear life. And the way things were going it might not be the last.

"Peter," Clara yelled with such force Beauvoir was tempted to look around in case the man had joined them.

Clara leaned forward. "Did you fly my husband? Peter Morrow?"

"*Désolé*, lady," said the pilot, who was perfectly bilingual and seemed to speak in a mixture of both languages. Frenglish. "I don't remember names. Just luggage. And fruit. Now, lemons—"

"He'd have gone to Tabaquen," Clara quickly cut in. "Tall guy. English."

The pilot shook his head. "Means nothing to me."

Myrna pulled out her device and after a few clicks she handed it to Clara, who hesitated for a moment.

"Oh, what the hell," she said. "We're all going to die anyway."

She showed the photo to the pilot, and when he stopped laughing he pointed. "Is that you?"

"That's not important. You recognize the man?"

"Yeah. Tall, old. English."

"Old?" said Clara.

"That might not be the most important thing he's said," said Myrna. "We all look old to him. He's barely begun to rot."

The plane gave a little shudder, as though nudged.

"Oh, Christ, here it comes," said Jean-Guy.

"What's that?" asked Clara.

"What?" demanded Myrna, looking frantically out the window where Clara was pointing.

"That's the supply ship," said the pilot.

"The one the artists take?" Clara asked.

Below them was the river, and on it they saw a ship. From above it looked like a cigar.

"*Oui.*"

"How long does it take for the ship to get to Tabaquen?" she asked.

"From Sept-Îles?" The pilot considered. "About a day, maybe two. Depends on the weather."

"Take us there."

"Where?"

"Sept-Îles."

"Clara?" asked Myrna.

"Clara?" asked Gamache.

"If Peter took the boat, we will too."

"Clara?" asked Jean-Guy.

"But Peter's not still on it," said Myrna.

"I know that. But there's a reason he took it."

"Maybe," said Myrna. "But there's a reason we shouldn't. Wouldn't it be best to get to Tabaquen as fast as we can?"

"Why?" asked Clara.

"To find Peter."

"And suppose he got off the ship?" asked Clara. "Suppose he never made it? No. We need to retrace his steps, as closely as we can."

Beauvoir turned to Gamache. Their noses almost touched, so tight was the squeeze. And there was no mistaking the glare in Beauvoir's eyes. The desperation.

The joke was over. They'd had their fun. They'd let Clara lead them around.

But now it was time to take charge.

"*Patron.*" Beauvoir's voice was filled with warning.

"Clara's in charge, Jean-Guy," said Gamache, his voice barely heard above the wail of the engines.

"We can fly to this village, find out what happened to Peter, and be home before the ship gets halfway there," said Beauvoir. "Don't you want that?"

Gamache looked down at the ship, so small in the huge river. "We gave Clara our word." He turned back to Jean-Guy. "Besides, she might be right. She has been so far."

Beauvoir took in the Chief's deep brown eyes, the lines of his face. The deep scar by his temple. The hair almost completely gray now.

"Are you afraid?" Beauvoir asked.

"Of what?"

"Of being in charge again? Of being responsible?"

There is a balm in Gilead . . . The book in Gamache's pocket dug into his side. A thorn. Not letting him forget. . . . *to cure a sin-sick soul.*

"We're here to support Clara, nothing more," Gamache repeated. "If I have to step in, I will. But not before."

As Jean-Guy turned away, Gamache saw in those familiar eyes something unfamiliar.

Doubt.

The plane didn't so much land as run out of air. It hit the tarmac with a thump and skidded to a stop.

"Phew," said the immortal pilot with a grin. "Almost bruised the bananas."

Myrna laughed, the heady amusement of one spared from certain death.

They climbed out of the tin can and stood on the runway. And looked at the river. The plane had come to a halt within meters of the St. Lawrence.

"*Tabarnac*," said Chartrand, then turned to the women. "Sorry."

"*Merde*," said Myrna, then turned to Chartrand. "Sorry."

"This isn't the airport," said Gamache, looking around.

Their pilot was dumping their bags on the tarmac.

"The airport's big," said Gamache. "It lands jets. This's . . ."

He turned around. River, forest, river.

"This's . . ."

"You're welcome," said the pilot, tossing the last bag onto the pile.

"Seriously," said Gamache. "Where are we?"

The pilot pointed. There, on the horizon, was a dot. And as they watched, it grew. And took shape. Ship shape.

"The *Loup de Mer*. She docks there." He pointed to a pier half a kilometer away. "This's an old cargo runway. Better hurry."

"*Tabarnac*," said Myrna, as she picked up her bag.

"*Merde*," said Chartrand.

They hurried across the rough landing strip, pausing to watch the plane rumble down the runway and lift off. From the ground it looked strangely graceful, as though something awkward was freed.

The plane, and the boy inside, seemed made for the skies and not really of this earth.

The plane bobbed and banked and flew into the sun. And disappeared.

Then they turned their backs on it and walked toward the pier, where the *Loup de Mer* was just arriving.

The Seawolf.

Gamache, who knew the coast well, wondered if Clara had any idea what they were in for.

THIRTY-FOUR

⌒

There were two cabins left. The Admiral's Suite and the Captain's Suite.

It was decided the women would take the Captain's Suite, while the three men would stay together in the Admiral's Suite, since it would be the larger of the cabins.

They showed Peter's photo to the harbormaster, to the ticket agent, to the head steward, to some woman they thought was an employee but turned out to be a fellow passenger.

None of them recognized Peter.

"Maybe he didn't take the boat," said Myrna. "I don't think we specifically asked that pilot if he did."

Clara thought about that, holding her bag in one hand and Peter's now quite worn photo in the other. Myrna had promised not to show the old photograph from the yearbook anymore.

"Still, the pilot recognized him from that," said Myrna. "Though I don't know how. Most of his face is hidden by smoke."

Except, thought Gamache, that one sharp eye. Not an artist's eye, but a cunning, assessing eye. His mother's eye.

Something was bothering Gamache about that whole exchange with the young pilot. And maybe Myrna had hit upon it. It seemed strange that this kid, who admitted to considering his passengers produce, should recognize Peter from that old yearbook photo.

Still, he'd also recognized Clara, so maybe the young man had an eye for faces.

"I think if anyone's going to recognize him"—Clara held up the recent photograph of Peter—"it'll be an employee who saw him wandering the ship every day. Not the captain, and not the harbor-master."

"Good point," said Gamache.

And Clara was right. While the steward who showed the women to the Captain's Suite didn't recognize it, the fellow with the men did.

"He had a single berth," the steward said. "Kept to himself."

"How come you remember him?" Jean-Guy asked as they followed him down the dim, narrow corridor. This was definitely not the *Queen Mary*.

"I watched him."

"Why?" asked Beauvoir.

"Afraid he'd jump."

That stopped them in the middle of the corridor.

"What do you mean?" Gamache asked.

"People do," explained the young steward. He was small, lithe. With a thick Spanish accent. "Especially the quiet ones. He was quiet. Stuck to himself."

They continued on their way along the corridor, and then, to their surprise, down two flights of stairs.

"Most passengers are excited to be under way. They talk to each other. Get to know each other. There isn't a lot to do so they start hanging out together. Your guy didn't. He was different."

"Do you think he was considering jumping?" asked Gamache.

"Naw. He was okay. Just different."

That word, over and over. Peter Morrow, who'd struggled to con-form all his life, was different after all.

"Where did he get off?" Jean-Guy asked.

"Can't remember."

They'd arrived at the Admiral's Suite. The steward opened the door, his hand resting, palm up.

Beauvoir ignored him, but Gamache gave him a twenty.

"Twenty, *patron*? Really?" Beauvoir asked, his voice low.

"Who do you think'll be handing out places in the lifeboat?"

"Oh."

"Oh," said Gamache.

They stepped inside. Almost. The three of them could barely get in standing up, and it wasn't clear how they'd all manage to lie down.

"This's the Admiral's Suite? There must be a mistake," said Chartrand, trying to turn around without getting engaged to either man.

"There must've been a mutiny," said Beauvoir.

Gamache raised his brows. This did look more like the brig. And smelled like a latrine. They were indeed in the bowels of the ship.

The *Loup de Mer* lurched, and left the dock.

"Bon voyage," said the steward as he shut the door.

Out of the slimy porthole the men saw the land recede.

Myrna turned off the taps and swished the water, making sure it was the right temperature. The aroma of lavender, from the bubble bath, filled the mahogany bathroom.

Candles were lit, and their steward had brought two strong cappuccinos and a basket of warm croissants and jams.

Armand had called to tell them that their steward had definitely recognized Peter. Clara was relieved and felt she could finally relax.

She tore the tip off a flaky croissant and sat back on the sofa in their cabin.

They were under way.

Across the suite, in the bathroom, Clara saw Myrna sink deeper into the copper tub, the bubbles forming foaming mountains and valleys over her body.

"I see your ship has finally come in," said Clara, as Myrna hummed "What Shall We Do with a Drunken Sailor?"

"I'm a born mariner," she said.

While Myrna bathed, Clara took a sip of cappuccino and gazed through the large window, watching the thick old forests and bays slip by as the *Loup de Mer* headed east.

Jean-Guy and Armand leaned on the railing of the *Loup de Mer*. The ship was pointed directly into the waves, and both men stared over the side, almost hypnotized by the rhythm. The ship's bow rose and fell, cutting the waves, sending light spray into their faces.

It was both refreshing and lulling.

Had Gamache been humming an old Québécois lullaby, Jean-Guy knew he'd have dropped off to sleep right there and then.

C'est un grand mystère
Depuis trois nuits que le loup, hurle la nouvelle

Just remembering the tune, Jean-Guy felt his eyelids beginning to droop. Then fluttering open. Heavier, heavier. *C'est un grand mystère.* It's a big mystery. The voice of his mother sang to him. About the wilderness. The wolves and foxes. About being afraid. And being saved. Being safe.

His head slowly lowered, then jerked up as he came to.

"Let's get some breakfast," said Gamache. "There must be a cafeteria."

They'd let Marcel Chartrand use the toilet first. When they were paying for the room, the clerk had assured them it was an en suite.

It was not. Unless "en suite" in maritime terms meant sharing a tiny, grimy water closet at the end of the dark corridor.

"If we have the Admiral's cabin, can you imagine how bad the Captain's must be?" said Jean-Guy.

"When I called to tell them about Peter, I asked how they were. They didn't complain."

"Amazing," said Jean-Guy. "I sure would, if I were them."

"If you were them?" Gamache asked.

They found the cafeteria, but it had just closed.

"*Désolé,*" said the steward. "You can get coffee over there."

He pointed to a coin-operated machine.

"I don't have any change," said Gamache, feeling in his pockets. "Do you?"

Beauvoir, increasingly frantic, turned his pockets inside out.

"*Merde.*"

They stared at the machine.

"That was wonderful," said Myrna, leaning back in her chair at their mahogany dining table.

Their breakfast of bacon and eggs, with the unexpected treat of a small fillet of smoked trout, was finished, and now they sipped their coffee and nibbled on the fruit.

"If our cabin's this good," said Clara, getting up to run her own bath, "can you imagine how great the men's must be? The Admiral's Suite. Wow."

Myrna changed from the fluffy bathrobe the ship provided into clean clothes and heard Clara moan as she slid into the tub.

"I'm heading out," said Myrna, pausing in the doorway to the bathroom. "Are you safe in there? You won't fall asleep, will you?"

"Drown and miss the rest of this voyage?" asked Clara. "No way. They're going to have to call the cops to get me off this ship. Where're you going?"

"To see the cops."

Myrna found their cabin down a surprisingly dingy hallway.

Double-checking to make sure the plaque on the door really said Admiral's Suite, she knocked. It was opened by Jean-Guy, and in the background, which wasn't really all that far back, she could see Armand. Going through Chartrand's coat pocket.

"I was looking for change," he stammered, then regaining his composure he squared his shoulders and said with some dignity. "For the coffee machine."

"Of course," said Myrna. She'd have entered the room, had it been possible. Instead she got her head in and looked around.

Chipped and curling wood veneer covered the walls, making a minuscule room seem all the smaller. A single berth sat against a wall, converted into a narrow sofa during the day. The porthole was covered with grime. The place smelled of mothballs and urine.

"We're sorry about taking the better cabin," said Gamache. "Yours must be pretty grim. Would you like to switch?"

Jean-Guy turned and gave him a filthy look.

Myrna assured him that she and Clara were fine where they were. They'd soldier on, somehow. She gave them all the change she had.

Then left.

Their first port of call along the coast was Anticosti Island, in the Gulf of St. Lawrence.

"Says here," said Clara, reading from a guidebook she found in the passenger lounge, "that there've been four hundred shipwrecks off Anticosti."

"Oh really," said Jean-Guy, folding his arms across his chest. "Tell me more."

"Apparently it's known as the cemetery of the Gulf," she said.

"I was being sarcastic," said Beauvoir.

"I know," said Clara. "But at least we now know what that pilot meant when he said the big challenge for the ship was the Graves. We get it behind us early."

"This isn't the Graves," said Gamache. He got up from the arborite table in the lounge and walked to the windows. Through the dirty streaks he could see the island approaching. It was huge and almost completely uninhabited. By humans.

The only settlement was Port-Menier, where fewer than three hundred people lived.

But the waters teemed with huge salmon and trout and seals. And the forests were full of deer and moose and grouse.

Gamache stepped through the door to the deck, followed by Clara, Myrna, Jean-Guy, and Marcel Chartrand. The air was cooler than in Baie-Saint-Paul. Fresher. A mist hung over the forest and crept onto the river, softening the line between land and water and air.

It felt as though they were approaching the past. A primordial forest so lush and green and unspoiled it could not possibly exist in the age of space travel, cell phones, Botox.

The only signs of habitation were the lighthouse and the row of bright wooden homes along the shore.

"What's that?" asked Clara.

"What?" asked Chartrand.

"That." Clara cocked her head to one side and pointed into the air. Applause. Clapping.

She scanned the shore. Perhaps it was a tradition. Perhaps when the supply ship arrived, the residents came out and applauded. She would.

But that wasn't quite right. It wasn't quite human.

"It's the trees," said Chartrand. He guided her gently around until Clara was looking away from the harbor, toward the forest.

"They're happy to see us," he said quietly.

Clara looked into his face, into his eyes. He wasn't watching her. He was taking in the woods. The joyous trees with the leaves that clapped together in the slightest breeze.

Beside her Myrna looked down at the guidebook, and didn't have the heart to tell them that the trees were called quaking aspens. And if they felt anything on seeing the ship approach, it was alarm. She would too, if she was a tree.

"We'll be docking and unloading supplies," the tinny voice over the PA system advised. "You are free to go ashore, but be aware that we will be leaving in four hours."

With or without you was the implication.

"We can jump ship," said Beauvoir. "There must be a plane we can charter."

"No. We stay with the ship," said Clara. "I'm sorry, Jean-Guy, I know this isn't your first choice, but if Peter took this route, then we do too. We don't know where he got off. It might be here."

It did not take four hours to comb Port-Menier.

They split up, with Clara and Chartrand taking one part of town and the others taking the other. An hour after leaving the ship, and speaking to every merchant and villager they could find, Myrna, Jean-Guy, and Gamache arrived at the only restaurant in town.

"You must be starving," Gamache said to Myrna. "I know I am."

"I could eat," she said.

They ordered fish and chips, and Beauvoir ordered a pizza as well. "And one to go," he shouted. "You never know," he told Gamache.

"I honestly don't think we can get the pizza box into the cabin," said Gamache, taking his reading glasses off and putting the menu aside. "And I'm a little worried if we eat the pizza we won't fit in either."

When the food came, they discovered that the fish was cod.

"Caught today," said the young server. "And the potatoes are fresh today too."

He gestured out the window to the huge ship they'd come in on. Clearly "fresh" was a sliding scale.

"You get many people off the ship?" Gamache asked. He cut into the crispy fish.

"Some. Most just want to stretch their legs. Like you."

"Do many stay?" Jean-Guy took up the line of questioning while Gamache ate.

"Here? No," the young man laughed. "Some hunters come for a week or so later in the season. Some fishermen. But no one lives here. Except us."

He didn't seem upset about that. If anything, he seemed relieved.

"We're looking for a friend of ours," said Gamache. It was Beauvoir's turn to eat, and his turn to talk. "He'd have been on the *Loup de Mer* a few months ago. Tall, English."

He showed the waiter the photograph.

"No, sorry," said the waiter, after studying it and handing it back.

By now the restaurant was filling with people who called the young man Cyril. They ordered scallops and cod cheeks and all sorts of things not on the menu.

"Would you like to try some, b'y?"

One of the older women, stout and dressed like a man, came over and offered her basket of cod cheeks to Beauvoir.

He shook his head.

"Ach, come on. I can see you drooling from across the room."

That brought laughter from the rest of the crowd, and now a middle-aged man joined her. "Come along, Mother. Don't be bothering these nice people."

"Oh, it's no bother," said Beauvoir. He'd seen the look of slight hurt in the old woman's face. "Can I have one?"

He took one of the tiny, deep-fried nuggets from her basket, dipped it in sauce, and ate it.

The room grew quiet.

When he reached for another one, they cheered as though the World Cup was theirs.

The elderly woman pretended to bat Jean-Guy's hand away.

"Cod cheeks for the table, Cyril," the man beside her said.

By the time Clara and Marcel arrived an hour later, Myrna and a group of women were dancing in the middle of the room and singing along to the jukebox.

"Man Smart (Woman Smarter)," they sang and danced with their arms waving above their heads, to great cheers.

Jean-Guy was across the diner, chatting with some fishermen.

"Any luck?" Clara asked as she and Marcel slid into the booth beside Gamache.

"No. You?"

Clara shook her head and tried to say something, but the music and laughter drowned her out.

"Let's go outside," Gamache shouted into her ear. He held on to Chartrand's arm, pinning the man in place. "Order the cod cheeks and chips. You won't regret it."

And then he and Clara left.

"What is it?" he asked. He'd noticed the urgency with which she'd tried to make herself heard in the restaurant.

"Marcel and I have been walking around the village and out along the shore," she said. "It gave me time to think."

"*Oui?*"

"That pilot shouldn't have recognized Peter from the old picture."

They'd walked rapidly through the town, and now stood on a small dock. The rowboat tied there knocked gently against the floats.

Gamache stared at her, remembering the image.

"It was too old, too small," said Clara, watching as Gamache's mind raced. "And Peter's face was almost completely hidden behind the smoke."

"My God, it was Massey," said Armand, arriving at the same conclusion as Clara. "The pilot recognized Professor Massey, not Peter."

He pulled out his cell phone. It was only just registering, clinging to one bar of contact with the outside world. He tapped the screen so rapidly and so expertly Clara was surprised. He always seemed the sort who'd be uncomfortable with computers and tablets and devices.

But watching him, she realized this was a tool as powerful as any gun. It gave him information. And no investigator could survive without that.

He tapped it a few more times, turned, walked quickly toward the village, then stopped.

The lone bar was wavering. Appearing, then disappearing. The thread to the outside world fraying and breaking. Then reappearing.

"*Oui, allô,*" he spoke loudly. "Is this Vols Côte Nord?"

Clara watched his strained face. The phone was pressed to his ear as though trying to grip that one bar.

"We took a flight this morning, from La Malbaie to Sept-Îles—"

The person on the other end was obviously speaking, and Gamache's eyes narrowed as he concentrated on the voice that faded in and out.

"That's right. He let us off at Sept-Îles. Is the pilot back yet?"

Gamache listened. Clara waited, trying to read his expression.

"When?"

Gamache listened some more.

"Can you patch me through to the plane?"

Even Clara, a couple feet away, heard the laugh.

"But you must be able to," said Gamache.

Now Clara heard words, in rapid French, that sounded like "idiotic," "impossible," "delusional."

"You can do it, I've done it before. And I insist. My name is Armand Gamache, I'm the Chief Inspector of homicide for Québec. Emeritus." The last word was mumbled at best, and he looked at Clara and grimaced.

While the Emeritus seemed to have been lost on whoever was on the other end of the phone, Gamache's tone of authority was not.

There was another brief pause while Gamache listened and finally said, "*Merci.*"

Clara took a step closer.

"He's connecting us." Gamache stared into the sky, as though that would help. Finally he gave Clara one curt nod.

"*Bonjour.* Is this Marc Brossard? My name is Gamache. You flew us to Sept-Îles today."

Beside him Clara was praying the frayed, fragile connection held. Just a minute more. One minute.

"*Oui, oui,*" said Gamache. "Listen." But the young man continued to talk. "Listen to me," said Gamache sharply.

And the young pilot did.

"We showed you a photograph, on an iPhone. You said you recognized the man. Which man?"

Gamache held Clara's eyes as he spoke. He listened now, with such intensity Clara felt her own heart racing.

"There were two men," said Gamache clearly. Loudly. "An older and a younger."

Clara could hear static. The connection was breaking up, but it hadn't yet broken off. Not yet. Not yet.

"Where did you take him?"

Gamache listened.

"When?"

He listened, and Clara stared into his eyes.

"When?" he repeated, his eyes showing surprise. "Are you sure?"

Clara could feel her heart throbbing in her throat.

"We're in Port-Menier," Gamache was saying. "Can you pick us up?" After a pause he shook his head. "I understand. *Merci.*"

He hung up.

"It was Professor Massey he recognized," Clara confirmed. "Not Peter."

Gamache nodded, grim-faced. "He flew to Tabaquen yesterday."

"Where're you headed?" The old woman slid into the booth beside Beauvoir.

"Up the coast," he waved.

"I figured that. Where?"

"Tabaquen."

"Are you sure?"

He laughed. "Pretty sure."

305

"Here," she said. "You'll need this."

She took the hat from beside her on the torn Naugahyde seat and placed it on his head.

"It's wet and cold out there."

"I'm not heading into the North Atlantic," he assured her, taking it off and smoothing his hair.

"You have no idea where you're headed." She brought something from the pocket of her cardigan and placed it on the table in front of him.

He looked at it.

A rabbit's foot. No, not rabbit. Hare.

"No hares here on the island," she said. "It was given to me years ago, by another visitor. Said it would bring me luck. And it has."

She looked at all her sons. And all her daughters. Not of her loins, but the family of her heart.

"It's yours." She pushed it toward him.

"You need it." Beauvoir pushed it back.

"I've had it. Now it's your turn."

Beauvoir put it in his pocket. And as he did he heard a long, deep horn.

The *Loup de Mer* was calling them.

"Yesterday?" Clara gaped. "I just saw him a few days ago. He didn't say anything about going. What's this about?"

"I don't know," said Gamache. He looked across the calm waters of the sheltered harbor. Then he dropped his eyes. Below the dock he could see fish darting. Flashes of silver in the cold, clear water.

"Professor Norman's in Tabaquen," he spoke to the fish. "And now Professor Massey's gone there. Why?"

"Massey lied to us," said Clara. "He said he didn't know where Norman was."

"And maybe he didn't at the time," said Gamache. "Maybe our questions got him to wondering, and he looked at the file too."

"But why would he go there? It's not just down the street, it's halfway across the continent. You'd have to be pretty desperate."

Yes, thought Gamache. That was the word. And he was feeling increasingly desperate to get there himself.

"I asked the pilot if he could pick us up here but he said the weather had closed in. All along the coast. He wasn't flying in or out of the villages."

"So we couldn't have made it to Tabaquen today anyway?"

"I doubt it," said Gamache. "Red sky in the morning."

The ship's horn sounded, deep and mournful. She looked at her watch. "It's leaving."

She started walking rapidly to the quai.

"Wait, Clara. I have another question. It's about Chartrand."

Clara stopped. And turned. "What about him?"

The ship's horn gave another cry.

"Why do you think he came with us?"

Gamache could see Jean-Guy waving at them from beside the *Loup de Mer.*

"Because he likes our company?" Clara suggested.

"Our company?"

"You think he came because of me?"

"What do you think?"

The ship's horn was now giving off short, insistent blasts.

"You think he's only pretending to like me, as an excuse to get close to us."

Gamache remained silent.

"You think I'm not reason enough for a man to close up shop and join us?"

"I've seen how he looks at you," said Gamache. "How he's drawn to you. And you to him."

"Go on."

"I don't think it's a complete lie."

"Not a complete one. How nice."

But Gamache, while trying to be gentle, wasn't going to be baited. "We need to explore all possibilities."

"Such as?"

"Chartrand knew No Man," said Gamache. "I think it's possible he was a member of his community, or cult, or whatever it was. I think it

307

might even have been Chartrand who told Peter about Tabaquen. And sent him there."

"That's no crime, Armand. You're turning it into something sinister."

"You're right," Gamache admitted. "If Peter asked about No Man and Chartrand told him where to find him, there's absolutely nothing sinister about it. In fact, it was doing Peter a favor. Except—"

"What?"

"If that's what Chartrand did, why not tell us?"

That stopped Clara.

"Why keep it a secret, Clara? What's he trying to hide?"

Clara was quiet for a moment. In the silence they could hear Jean-Guy calling to them.

"You asked why Marcel would join us, but you haven't asked why I agreed."

"I thought—"

"You thought I'd lost my heart to him? The lonely woman, vulnerable to a little attention? Do you really think that's likely?"

"Well, now I don't," he said, and was so clearly embarrassed Clara smiled.

Jean-Guy was waving frantically from the dock and Myrna was standing in the middle of the gangway, refusing to move for the sailors.

"If Marcel knew where Peter went and didn't tell us, it's because he wanted to keep us away from Tabaquen," said Clara. "He might be keeping an eye on us, but I'm watching him too. That's why I wanted him with us."

She turned and started walking rapidly toward the quai, but before she did she looked back and said, "And I am reason enough, Armand, for a man to give up everything."

THIRTY-FIVE

———

"Huh," said Gamache.

The sun was setting and their passage so far had been fairly smooth. The storm predicted by the pilot was ahead of them.

At the sound of Gamache's grunt, Jean-Guy shifted his gaze to the Chief. Beauvoir had been looking at the window. Not through it, but at it. At his own reflection.

"What is it?" Beauvoir asked.

Gamache looked from his device to Beauvoir. It was difficult not to be distracted by the sou'wester. The hat sat at a jaunty angle, manipulated, shifted, arranged over the past half hour to appear as though Jean-Guy had simply grabbed it off a peg and crammed it onto his head as the skipper cried, "Thar she blows."

"Very you, matey."

"Have you ever been to sea, Billy?" Beauvoir leered at Gamache.

"What is it with you and elderly women anyway?" Gamache asked.

Beauvoir took the hat off and placed it on his knee.

"I think they know I don't see them as elderly. Just people."

And Gamache knew it was true.

"Just as I'll never see Annie as old. Even though we will be. One day."

And Gamache hoped that too was true. He looked at Beauvoir, beside him on the bench, and saw him decades from now. Sitting with Annie on the sofa. In what would be their home, their dwelling place, in Three Pines. Reading. Old and gray and by the fire. Annie and Jean-Guy. And their children. And grandchildren.

309

The days of their togetherness.

Just as he and Reine-Marie were having theirs. Until this.

Beauvoir gestured toward the device in Gamache's hand. "What is it?"

"*Pardon?*"

"You were reading a message?" Beauvoir suggested.

"Ah, *oui*. From the Sûreté in Baie-Saint-Paul. The sniffer dogs found something."

Beauvoir shifted on the hard bench so that he was looking directly at the Chief.

"A corpse?"

"No, not yet. It was a metal box, with cardboard rolls inside, like the one that Peter's canvases came in. They were empty. Except for some powder."

"Heroin? Coke?"

"Captain Nadeau's having it tested."

Gamache looked at the windows, wet with spray. It was dark now, and all he could see was the lit bow of the *Loup de Mer*. "Was the commune really a meth lab? Was the art a cover to distribute drugs?"

"We already know that heroin and cocaine come into Québec by boat," said Beauvoir. "It's almost impossible to stop."

Gamache nodded. "Suppose it gets off-loaded in Baie-Saint-Paul, taken to No Man's community in the woods—"

"That would explain why it was in the woods," said Beauvoir. "And not overlooking the river, where the other artists' colonies set up. They didn't want a view, what they wanted was privacy, and warning if anyone approached."

"No Man cuts and packages. Luc Vachon sends them south. Disguised as No Man's paintings. Rolled into those tubes."

The St. Lawrence, while a lifeline, was also a supply line. For all sorts of illegal activity, including hard drugs.

"Maybe it was No Man himself who started the rumors it was a cult," said Beauvoir. "To keep the curious away. But then that cop starts paying attention to them, and No Man closes up shop and moves even further away. To Tabaquen. More remote. More privacy. Less scrutiny."

Gamache shifted, uncomfortable on the hard bench.

He was under no illusion. If that's what No Man was about in Tabaquen, they were in for a world of trouble when they arrived.

His fears, illusions while in Three Pines, were taking form. Taking shape. And coming closer. This was what happened when you ventured into the real world.

A brave man in a brave country. It was easy to be brave, when the country was also brave. But what happened if it wasn't? If it was corrupt, and grotesque, and greedy, and violent?

And what happened if it was waiting for them? Knowing they were coming?

"And Chartrand?" asked Beauvoir. "How does he fit in?"

"A respected gallery owner with connections worldwide? Beyond reproach?" asked Gamache. "Who's better placed to coordinate the operation?"

That explained Chartrand, but what about Professor Massey?

What role did he play in this? He must have some involvement, otherwise he wouldn't have gone all the way to Tabaquen.

"Suppose No Man was involved in drugs back in the days he worked at the college," said Gamache, thinking out loud. "Suppose Massey suspected but couldn't prove anything."

Maybe, like Carlos Casteneda insisting peyote fueled creativity, Professor Norman had been pushing coke. To students eager to blow their minds, and put it on canvas.

"Maybe that was the tenth muse," said Gamache. "Cocaine."

Beside him, Beauvoir fidgeted with the hat. That made more sense to him than some flighty, prancing, embittered goddess.

The one that killed for pleasure.

Now meth. Or heroin. Or coke. The trinity of deadly drugs.

There was something that killed for pleasure.

"Could Massey have gone to Tabaquen to finally confront Norman?" Beauvoir asked. "When he found out Peter might've followed No Man there, he might've gone to protect him. He sounded like that sort of man."

Both Clara and Myrna had said the elderly professor had reminded them of the Chief. And Gamache had gone to hell to bring back Jean-Guy. Maybe Massey was going to Tabaquen, the Sorcerer, to save Peter. To bring him back.

It was all supposition. But it fit.

Gamache's phone rang and he took it.

"*Oui, allô?*"

"Armand, how's the cruise?"

"We're on the lido deck. The conga line just finished." He tried to keep his voice light. "You should see our cabin. Thankfully those interminable baptisms of your ninety-seven nieces and nephews have trained me to sleep standing up. A blessing."

"You're going to hell," she laughed.

He looked at the bow, heaving. And ho-ing. The inky waves had grown. The wind had picked up in the last few minutes, heading straight into their face as though trying to push them back. But the *Loup de Mer* kept chugging, slicing through the water, slicing through the night. Heading deeper into the darkness.

He knew where they were going and she wasn't far wrong.

They chatted for a few minutes about the activities in Three Pines. As they spoke, Armand turned on the bench, until he was facing the stern. Looking back. To the home he'd left behind.

In the night the *Loup de Mer* stopped at a few more outports, depositing food, supplies, people, before moving on.

By morning they were well up the coast. Leaving roads and towns and most of the trees behind. The passengers awoke to a gray sky and a shoreline made of rocks worn smooth by waves.

"Strange place," said Myrna, joining Armand on deck and handing him a strong, sweet tea.

They leaned on the railing. There was a chill in the air that belied the summer season. It was as though they'd left the calendar behind. Time had its own rules here.

Gamache sipped his tea. It was a brew he associated with the Lower North Shore. Where pots sat on woodstoves all day, and arthritic hands added more hot water and dropped more bags in, until it was like stew.

He'd drunk gallons of the stuff as he'd sat in kitchens in the remote fishing villages along this coastline.

"You've been here before, haven't you?" she asked.

"A few times."

"Investigations?"

"Yes. Always difficult in a closed community. These people are proud, self-reliant. They didn't even have running water or electricity until recently. They never asked for help from the government. Not a single person took unemployment, until recently. It would never occur to them to take what they considered a handout. They have their own laws and rules and code of conduct."

"You make it sound like the Wild West."

Gamache smiled. "I suppose it is, a bit. But not so wild really. These are fishermen. They're a different breed. They get enough 'wild' from the sea. When they get home they want peace. There's a deep civility about the people here."

"And yet they still kill."

"Sometimes. They're human." He looked at Myrna. "Do you know what Jacques Cartier called this stretch of coast?"

"Cartier the explorer?"

"Yes, back in the early fifteen hundreds. When he first saw this place he called it 'the land God gave to Cain.'"

Myrna took that in as she watched the shoreline, where the odd, malformed trees lived. But nothing else.

"Cain. The first murderer," said Myrna.

"A coast so forbidding, so hostile it was fit only for the damned," said Gamache. "And yet . . ."

"Yes?"

He gave a small lopsided smile and stared at the far shore. "And yet I find it just about the most beautiful place on earth. I wonder what that says about me."

"Maybe you're drawn to the damned," said Myrna.

"Maybe that's why I've spent my life looking for murderers."

"Have you ever been to Tabaquen?" she asked.

"Once. We arrested an old trapper for murder. He'd never been off the coast before. Never been off his trapline. He died in prison before the trial."

"Poor man," said Myrna. And Gamache nodded agreement.

He stared at the almost unnaturally smooth rocks gliding out of the water in great sheets.

"There're those who seem to turn to the sea, always changing, always adapting. But never settling down. And those who turn to rocks and stones." He waved toward the shoreline. "Solid but stuck."

He looked at Myrna and smiled. "Sorry. I suspect that sounds romantic."

"No, it doesn't."

Perhaps, Myrna thought, in Montréal, or Toronto, or New York, or London it would. But hanging over the rail, looking at the cold gray water, the hard gray stones, the thick gray clouds, it sounded about right.

She watched Armand. Was he of the sea or the stone? Was she?

Clara walked along the narrow corridor, adjusting her step to the growing and unpredictable swell. She was discovering that she was good on boats. As was Myrna.

Chartrand, on the other hand, was not.

He'd stayed in the Admiral's Suite all morning. Clara had taken him some dry toast and tea. It was the first time she'd seen their "suite," and it had shocked her. She'd been a little suspicious of Chartrand's absence, wondering if he was faking it. But seeing the crummy, smelly, uncomfortable cabin, she knew only a man on his deathbed would choose to spend time there.

Chartrand had roused, seen her, and through bleary eyes had thanked her.

"You should go," he said, trying to get up on an elbow. "I don't want you seeing me like this."

"And if I was sick?" she asked.

"I'd want to look after you," he said, and his pale green pallor developed an orangish hue. Had Marcel Chartrand's face been a color wheel, he'd have failed the exam.

They sat on the narrow bed and she'd gotten a cool cloth and a Gravol.

After a few minutes the drug kicked in and Clara could see his eyelids grow heavy, his breathing grow deeper, his skin less waxy.

She let him subside onto the bed and covered him with a blanket.

"Don't go," he whispered. Then shut his eyes.

She lingered for a moment at the door, before leaving.

The report on the substance in the buried container arrived that afternoon.

Gamache and Beauvoir read it with increasing puzzlement.

It wasn't heroin after all. It wasn't cocaine.

"How can this be?" Beauvoir asked, his brows drawn together. "Am I reading it right?"

Gamache had gone over the report two or three times himself. Quickly the first time, scanning the familiar form down to the pertinent line. And there he stopped, as though hitting a wall.

Then he went back and read more carefully. But the conclusion never changed.

The powdery substance in the container wasn't a pharmaceutical. It was natural. But not the prettiest side of nature.

Asbestos.

The two men lifted their eyes from the screen and stared at each other.

"What does it mean?" asked Jean-Guy.

Gamache got to his feet. "See what you can find out about asbestos."

"Right."

Beauvoir excelled at finding facts. Tracking them down, analyzing them, putting them in their place. Not like an automaton, but a skilled and thoughtful investigator.

Gamache left Beauvoir on the laptop in the lounge and went to the communications office of the ship, where they printed out copies of the report. Then he went on deck and found Clara and Myrna on a bench, talking.

"Am I disturbing you?" he asked.

"No, but you look a little disturbed," said Myrna, and patted the seat next to her.

He took it, and told them the latest findings.

"Asbestos?" said Clara. "Could it be natural? I mean, isn't asbestos mined in Québec?"

"*Oui*. There's a whole town called Asbestos," Gamache confirmed.

"Built around mining it. But that's a long way off. This asbestos was found inside mailing tubes, like the one Peter's canvases came in."

"How'd it get there?" Clara asked.

"Where would you even get asbestos these days?" asked Myrna. "I thought it was all removed and destroyed decades ago."

"It was," said Gamache. "There was asbestos removed from the art college the year after you graduated, Clara."

"I remember hearing about it," she said.

"It was happening all over," said Myrna. "I was working in a hospital and they found it in the walls. Used for insulation. No one thought it was dangerous, of course. At the time. And when they found out it was, they had to remove it. Big mess."

"Big mess," said Gamache.

"But how'd it get buried in some field in Charlevoix?" asked Clara.

"In a mailing tube," said Myrna.

The three of them stared at the coastline, and the gulls dipping and floating on the air currents. Their movements growing increasingly erratic as the currents grew increasingly unstable. The gulls themselves seemed surprised, and cried out, as they were tossed about.

Gamache watched this, then looked into the sky. It was dull and gray. Not bright, but neither was it threatening.

"*Excuse-moi,*" he said.

He went inside and called the college. The principal confirmed that work was done, according to Canadian law and code, back in the 1980s.

"Could someone take some of that asbestos?" Gamache asked.

There was a pause. "It was before my time, so I can't say for sure, but I do know they wouldn't have just left piles of it lying around. And even if they did, why would anyone want to take something that would kill you?"

Gamache, the former head of homicide for the Sûreté, knew the answer to that.

It was to kill. That's why someone would take it.

Through the window he watched the gulls bounce and bob, and sometimes they were swept back as though picked up by a strong hand.

This was a harbinger, Gamache knew. The first signs. Something was coming.

THIRTY-SIX

~

"Find anything?" asked Gamache.

He'd returned to the lounge.

Beauvoir nodded, distracted. Lost in reading.

Gamache joined him at the table.

On the screen was the history of the town of Asbestos, Québec, where asbestos had been discovered and mined. It had seemed a godsend to a hardscrabble region. Natural, plentiful. It was both an insulator and a fire retardant. Asbestos would save the region and save lives.

It was magic.

No one seemed to notice the needle-like fibers. That floated in the air when it was disturbed. That lodged in the lungs of those who worked, or played, or lived with it.

Beauvoir scrolled down. They read words like "mesothelioma," that sounded like a geological age, but wasn't. And "friable," that sounded like a cooking term. But wasn't.

They learned a great deal about the mineral that was supposed to be a miracle. But wasn't.

Asbestos turned out to be the thalidomide of building materials. A savior that killed.

Beauvoir leaned away from the screen, as though breathing so close to it would infect him.

"What was it doing in that tube?" he asked. "Where did it come from?"

"And where was it going?" asked Gamache. "And what else was in that tube, and was no longer there?"

They both knew the answer to that.

Canvases. Art. Deadly art.

When they found Myrna and Clara on the deck of the *Loup de Mer*, the women weren't alone. A young woman had joined them.

"This is Julie Foucault." Myrna did the introductions. "She's a new teacher at the school in Blanc-Sablon."

"*Un plaisir*," said Armand, shaking her hand.

Jean-Guy nodded, impatient for this Julie to leave so they could tell Myrna and Clara what they'd found.

"Your first job?" Gamache asked, and sat beside her. She looked no more than twenty, and had bright orange hair down to her shoulders, and ruddy red cheeks. And that newly minted expression. Of excitement and anxiety.

"Yes. I could've flown, but I wanted to see the coast."

"Julie was telling us she'll be teaching everything. You have to, in small schools," said Clara. "But her specialty is science."

"I have a master's," she said. "And am working toward my PhD."

Beauvoir sat down.

"Do you know anything about asbestos?" he asked without preamble.

"I hope that's not a pickup line," she said, and even Gamache laughed. She might look young, she might even be young, but she knew how to take care of herself.

Even Beauvoir smiled. "No. We're looking into a few things, and asbestos has come up."

"As a matter of fact, I do know something about it," she said. "Not a lot. I'm not a specialist, but it was taught at the university. Used as a cautionary tale of science, industry, and government."

"We're not so much interested in the politics of asbestos," said the Chief, "as the properties of the substance."

"Then yes, I can definitely tell you about that. Why?"

"Some was found in a box," said Gamache. "We're trying to figure out why someone would have it, and how dangerous it might be."

"Well, that depends on the form it's in. If it's a hunk, then not so much. Asbestos only really becomes dangerous when it can float in the air. And be inhaled."

"This was like a powder," said Beauvoir.

They all watched the young teacher, waiting for the answer, but they didn't have to wait long. There was no hesitation, no doubt.

"That would be dangerous."

"How does asbestos kill?" asked Gamache. "If someone swallowed it, would it be bad?"

"It wouldn't be good. But with asbestos the real danger is inhaling it. Getting it into the lungs. It works its way into the tissue and causes asbestosis, or mesothelioma. Or lung cancer. Or both. Nasty, nasty stuff. And by the time it's diagnosed, it's too late."

"How long does it take to kill someone?" Clara asked.

"Depends." Now Julie had to pause to think. "One of the reasons it took so long for alarms to go off, besides the desire of the industry and government not to see it—and that was a travesty—"

"Not the politics," Gamache reminded her.

"Sorry. The problem was that it does take a while for the effects to be noticed. The connection between asbestos workers and lung deaths took some time. A miner could be retired for years before showing symptoms."

"And what are the symptoms?" asked Myrna.

"Coughing, of course. Shortness of breath."

"Sounds like a lot of things," said Myrna.

"And that was part of the problem too. Misdiagnosis. But finally the link was found. And asbestos was banned. But by then it was everywhere."

"So," said Beauvoir, thinking his way through this, "you'd have to get pretty close to it, to inhale it?"

"Right. Or it would have to be floating around in the air. Like in a mine. You say yours was a powder in a container?"

"Right."

She shook her head. "That would get into the air pretty easily, I think."

"And would the person necessarily die, if he inhaled it?" Gamache asked, and saw the immediate look of concern on Julie's face. She looked from Gamache to Beauvoir and back again.

"Did one of you?"

"No," Gamache smiled reassuringly. "But if we had, then what? Would we die?"

"You might. It's one of those tricks of fate. Not all asbestos miners developed lung disease. Some people exposed only incidentally did."

"How much would you have to inhale?" asked Beauvoir.

"Again, it depends. Sorry to be so vague, but my memory is that some miners inhaled it all their lives and were fine, other people inhaled it once and died. It just depended on the person, the fibers."

"But theoretically it could be very little," said Beauvoir. "And it could be with only one exposure."

"Could be," said Julie, "but really, that would have to be unbelievably unlucky. But it could happen."

"If asbestos was found in the insulation of an art gallery and was removed, could some of it get onto the canvases?" Gamache asked.

"I'd expect the people removing it would've cleared the place. Asbestos could only be removed by people trained to do it. It wasn't just ripped out."

"Suppose they hadn't taken everything down?" asked Gamache.

Julie studied the large man in front of her.

"If you want clear answers, you'll have to ask clear questions."

Gamache raised his brows slightly and smiled. "Yes, I can see how that would help. The container the asbestos was found in probably held a rolled-up painting. Or a blank canvas. One or the other. Could the asbestos have been on the canvas and fallen off?"

Julie thought about that for a moment. "A canvas would actually be a pretty good vehicle for asbestos. It has a fine weave. Asbestos fibers could cling to it."

"And if it was painted? Would the asbestos stick to oil paint?" Clara asked.

"Not as much. But if it was a blank canvas . . ."

"Yes."

"Well, I'm not an artist—"

"I am," said Clara.

Julie turned to her. "If you got a rolled-up blank canvas, what would you do?"

"I'd unroll and stretch it. Tack it to a wooden frame, so I could paint it."

Julie was nodding. "You'd handle it."

"Of course."

Clara's eyes widened. "And that would dislodge the asbestos. Like dust. It would float in the air."

Julie was nodding. "And because you were handling it, you'd be close enough to breathe it in. But there's another thing."

"The brush strokes," said Clara, seeing where the young teacher was going.

"Exactly. As you brush on the paint, you'd be brushing off the asbestos dust. It would be the perfect way to get it into the air."

"And again," said Gamache, "the artist would be close enough to inhale."

"He'd be less than an arm's length away," Julie confirmed.

They considered that for a moment.

"But suppose the rolled-up canvas was already painted," said Clara. "Could the asbestos be applied then?"

"Not as effectively, as I said. It would slide right off. It needs something to stick onto."

"Like the back of the canvas," said Myrna, and they looked at her. "If the front was painted, the back would still be just raw material, right? Something for the asbestos to"—Myrna turned to Julie—"in your words, 'stick onto.'"

Julie nodded. "It would work. When the painting was unrolled, the asbestos would get into the air."

"But it gets worse," said Clara. "The painting wouldn't just be unrolled. It would have to be tacked onto a frame. I've done it lots of times. Bought a cheap old oil painting at a flea market that wasn't framed. Just rolled up. You have to staple it to a wooden frame."

"And if the back was coated with asbestos dust?" asked Myrna.

"It would get everywhere," said Julie. "On the hands, the clothing. In the air."

"To be inhaled," said Myrna.

Julie was looking at them, her exuberance muted by a dawning suspicion.

"How long would it take someone to get sick?" asked Myrna.

"Depends on the exposure. Like I said, it might never happen," said Julie, guarded now. "But mostly it took years, decades, for asbestos to become lethal."

She looked at their grim faces. "What's all this about? You're not planning to do it, are you?"

"And if we were?" asked Gamache.

"You'd be murderers." She looked pale and Gamache hurried to reassure her.

They weren't planning murder. Just the opposite.

"You're trying to stop a murder?" she asked, incredulous. Looking from face to face and back to Gamache. "But if it's asbestos, you're probably too late. The person would've already been murdered. They just haven't died yet."

She left then.

Armand watched as she walked away, steadying herself in the increasing roll and pitch of the ship. She looked like a gull in trouble.

And Gamache knew that while she'd helped them, they had not helped her.

Julie wasn't as cheery, not as bright as before she'd joined them. They'd tarnished her.

Now the four friends walked around the deck, mulling the young teacher's information. As they circumnavigated the ship, the *Loup de Mer* made its way up the coast. Every now and then they needed to steady themselves as the ship plowed up and through and down a wave. The wind was stronger now, and the waves higher, splashing over the sides and turning the deck slick.

"Those tubes almost certainly contained paintings," said Gamache. "No Man's paintings."

"But why would there be asbestos on them?" asked Clara. "Who put it there?"

"And why?" asked Myrna.

They walked in silence, each trying to work it out.

"Asbestos is deadly," said Gamache. "There was no guarantee, but there was a pretty good chance that whoever handled his asbestos-infected paintings would inhale it and eventually die."

"Was he like those maniacs who sent anthrax through the mail?" asked Beauvoir. "Are we dealing with a serial killer?"

"Do you think he sent those paintings to galleries all over Canada?" asked Clara.

Myrna, Clara, Beauvoir, and Gamache walked, and thought, and remembered the only picture they had of Professor Norman. A self-portrait. Of a madman.

A sin-sick soul, thought Gamache. Who smeared asbestos onto his own paintings. And shipped them off. Knowing whoever opened the container, unrolled the canvases, held them, admired them, was sealing their own fate.

The asbestos would be dislodged, would float into the air and hang there, little crystals, tiny fibers. To be inhaled, to nest in the person's lungs. And from there to burrow. And burrow. Digging deep tunnels.

While outside, the lover of art would carry on with his or her life. Unaware they'd just inhaled the scent of Samarra. Their own death.

The deck was too difficult now, and they'd retreated to the shelter of the lounge when Gamache's phone rang.

It was the principal of the art college.

"I got worried after our conversation, Monsieur Gamache," he said. "So I asked the health and safety person to check out some spots in the college for asbestos. She won't have the definitive results for a few days, but it looks like we're clear, with one exception. There's a suspicious spot in Professor Massey's studio."

"What does it mean?" Myrna asked.

"I think it's pretty clear what it means," said Clara. They'd used the last of their change to get scalding hot chocolates out of the vending machine, and now they took a table by one of the water-slashed windows.

The bow of the *Loup de Mer* was rising and falling, rising and falling. Every now and then it rose higher, higher, paused there, then crashed down. A gale was building, coming straight at them. And they were heading straight for it.

They held on to their hot chocolates, but still some slopped over the sides. Clara spared a thought for Marcel Chartrand, downstairs, in the bowels.

"It means we know who Norman sent his asbestos-infected paintings to," said Clara.

"Professor Massey," said Beauvoir.

"But why?" asked Myrna. "Massey got him fired. Why would he trust him with his works?"

"He wasn't trying to trust him, he was trying to kill him," said Gamache.

He turned, by habit, to Jean-Guy Beauvoir.

This was familiar territory now, to both men. How often had they sat just like this, facing each other across arborite tables, at hacked wooden tables, at desks and in muddy fields, in cars, and planes, and trains. In the bright sunshine, and in winter blizzards.

The two of them.

Trying not to see their way clear, but to see their way into a dark heart. Trying to solve the first, the oldest, crime. Cain's crime. Murder.

Beauvoir thought about it. "But if No Man infected his paintings and sent them off to Massey, wasn't there a chance Massey would sell them on? Find buyers?"

That had been troubling Gamache too. Once out of No Man's hands anything could happen to the canvases. He had no way of knowing if they'd kill Massey, or a student, or some poor anonymous art collector.

Maybe No Man didn't really care who else he killed, as long as Professor Massey was one of them. Or maybe . . .

"Maybe they weren't very good," said Gamache. "Maybe he deliberately sent paintings he knew Massey wouldn't show to anyone else."

"It still doesn't make sense," said Myrna. "Professor Massey hated Sébastien Norman. He got Norman the job, and then Norman took complete advantage of the situation to lecture on his own pet theory of the tenth muse. Then he held the show for the rejected artwork. Professor Norman did everything but burn down the college. Why would Massey help him?"

"Would you?"

The question came from Beauvoir, and it was directed at Gamache.

"Clara and Myrna here both thought Professor Massey reminded them of you, *patron*. I've seen you do some pretty weird things for people everyone else had given up on. Including me. Do you think Massey might still try to help Norman?"

Gamache considered that. "He might. Maybe he didn't hate Norman," Gamache said to Myrna, "but felt sorry for him. Maybe he even felt responsible. For putting both Norman and the school in that position."

Myrna looked at Armand. And Armand looked at Myrna.

"Yes," she said, remembering their private therapy sessions. "It's possible."

"I think Massey was the agent that Luc Vachon was sending the canvases to," said Gamache.

"Asbestos-infected canvases," said Beauvoir. "Massey might not have hated Norman, but Norman hated Massey. For getting him fired."

"How many embittered employees go into their workplaces with a gun?" said Myrna. "The paintings were Norman's gun."

"But where did he get the asbestos? And where're the paintings now?" asked Clara. "Where did Professor Massey put them? We didn't see any on the walls."

"They might be in a storage room," said Gamache. "Maybe that was the hot spot they found. I'll call the principal back."

"Fortunately it looks like No Man's plan didn't work," said Myrna, as Gamache placed the call.

"What do you mean?" asked Beauvoir.

"I keep forgetting that you didn't see Professor Massey. A more healthy eighty-five-year-old would be hard to find. If those paintings began arriving decades ago, and the asbestos had done its job, he'd be either dead or dying."

"What was it Julie called it?" said Clara. "A twist of fate."

"Sometimes the magic works . . ." said Beauvoir. "But why would Massey suddenly go to Tabaquen now?"

Gamache hung up, having left a message on the principal's voice mail with both his and Beauvoir's numbers.

"Why would Peter go all the way to Tabaquen?" asked Clara.

"To find the tenth muse," Myrna reminded her. "To become a better painter. He didn't know any of this stuff. All he knows is that he's desperate and lost and Professor Norman was offering an easy way to get from his head to his heart. The quick fix. A muse for the modern man."

The ship shuddered as it hit a particularly massive wave. The river leapt up and beat against the windows.

But while slowed for a moment, the *Loup de Mer* plowed ahead. Getting closer and closer to its destination. The Sorcerer. The source.

THIRTY-SEVEN

⁓

They spent the afternoon apart. Each trying to just ride out the storm.

Armand Gamache came upon Clara in the men's cabin, the so-called Admiral's Suite. She'd brought soup and bread down to Chartrand, who was still asleep on the narrow bunk. There wasn't much soup left in the bowl, most of it having slopped out as Clara tried to carry it.

The gale was upon them now. Battering the ship. Pushing it and pulling it, so that the people inside were tossed this way and that, without warning.

"I was just coming to check on him myself. Is he okay?" Gamache whispered as he clung on to the door frame.

"Yes. Just really seasick."

Clara put the bread on the bedside table, but held on to the soup. No use leaving the bowl, it would just end up on the floor. Or on Chartrand.

She got up, but not before feeling Chartrand's forehead. It felt like a cod and looked like underwear. An improvement. She rested her large hand on his chest. Just for a moment.

They left him and fought their way back to the observation deck. The river was froth and foam. The deck was awash.

Clara had chosen a bench next to the window and Gamache sat beside her, as they had each morning in Three Pines. Like strangers waiting for a bus.

Clara had her sketchbook and pencil case on her lap, but kept them unopened.

"Were you planning to do a drawing?" Gamache asked.

"No. I just feel safe, holding them."

She brushed the metal pencil holder with her finger, like a rosary. And held on to her sketch pad like a bible.

A wave battered the window and they pulled back. But the Plexiglas held. They sat in silence then. The sort of strained silence mariners for centuries would recognize, as they rode out a storm.

Gamache looked at Clara, in profile, as she watched the waves batter the shore. Leaping onto the rocks. Wearing them down. Wearing them smooth.

Her eyes were both calm and concentrated. Taking in every detail. Of the physical and the metaphysical world.

"It was particularly cruel, wasn't it?" she said, still staring at the shore. "Using art to kill."

"I've seen worse," he said.

Now it was Clara's turn to look at his face in profile. She believed him.

"I mean, to use something you love against you," she said.

"I knew what you meant," he said.

The *Loup de Mer* lurched and shuddered, and both were tossed forward, just managing to stop themselves from falling off the bench completely.

"Coward," said Clara.

"Pardon?"

"Norman. He's a coward. He didn't have to see it. Didn't have to face what he'd done. He could just smear the asbestos in, mail it off, and get on with his own life. Cowardly."

"Most murder is," said Gamache. "It's done by weak people, or strong people in a moment of weakness. But it's almost never a courageous thing to do."

"Almost never?"

Gamache remained silent.

She brought a cough lozenge out of her pocket and put it on the bench between them.

"Is there anyone you'd kill, if you didn't have to see it?" she asked. "If you could just press down on this"—she pointed to the cough drop—"and they'd die. Would you?"

Gamache stared at the small white square.

"Would you?" he asked, looking up again.

"Oh, all sorts of people, every day. Myrna this morning, when she took too long in the bathtub—"

"You have a bathtub?"

"It's a metaphor," Clara said, and hurried on, leaving a slightly perplexed Gamache to ponder bathtubs. "Ruth. Art critics. Olivier when he gives me too small a croissant. Ruth. Gallery owners who pay more attention to another artist."

"Ruth."

"Her too," said Clara.

"Would you have been tempted to press the lozenge on Peter?"

"Kill him? There were times I wanted him to be gone," she said. "Not just away from Three Pines, but gone completely. So that I could stop thinking about him. Stop hoping, and maybe even stop hating him. Or loving him. If he was gone, I could. Maybe."

"You didn't really want him dead," said Gamache. "You wanted the pain to stop."

She looked down at the pastille on the bench.

"There've been times I've wished him dead. I've wanted it, and dreaded it. It would be a terrible end to our life together. But it would at least be an end."

She looked around at the deck, slick with water from the river. At the metal hull of the ship. At the heaving waves and the desolate shore beyond.

So different from the solid, gentle village. From their home. And their studios and their garden, with the two chairs, and the rings, intertwined.

She'd fought to think of it as "her" home now. To call it "my" home, in conversation. But it wasn't. It was their home. Infused with them.

She missed him so much she thought her insides would cave in.

And she had to know. How he felt.

She was pretty sure she already had the answer. His silence said it

329

all. Surely his absence should be enough. But it wasn't. She needed to hear it from his own mouth.

Had he stopped loving her? Had he left her, and Three Pines, and made a home somewhere else?

The fucker wasn't going to get off that easy. He had to face her.

Dear, beloved Peter. They had to face each other. And tell each other the truth. And then, she could go home.

Gamache got up and walked carefully to the window. He stood looking out for a long while, gripping the frames for support against the lunges and heaves of the ship.

"Can you join me?"

"I'm not sure I can," she said, and timed her jump between waves.

He held her steady, his large hand on her back, practically pinning her to the window.

"See that cove?"

"Yes."

"Those are the Graves."

She braced herself and looked across to a bay that should have been sheltered, but was in fact a churning mess of eddies, of whirlpools. It was a different movement altogether from the relentless waves. They came straight at them. But the movement in the cove was as though some creature was writhing and swirling just below the surface.

"Rocks under the water," Gamache explained, though she hadn't asked. "They create that effect. Any vessel caught in them hasn't a chance."

Clara felt her skin grow cold, from the inside out. Felt it crawl. Felt it try to crawl away. From the killing eddies, from the bleak shore.

"Is that what sank the *Empress of Ireland*?" she asked.

Clara had read about it in school and knew they must be close to where it happened.

"No, that was another phenomenon. The fog around here is apparently like no other. The two ships got lost in it."

He didn't need to finish. They both knew what happened next.

In 1914 the passenger liner *Empress of Ireland* went down, rammed by another ship. In the dark. In the fog. In these waters. In fifteen minutes. With a loss of more than a thousand lives. Men, women and children.

Clara looked into the roiling waters. The river beneath them teemed with life, and with death. Those lost beneath the waves. Souls not saved.

"My grandmother raised me on tales of *voyageurs* condemned forever to paddle their canoe through the skies," said Gamache. "They'd swoop down and pick up naughty children and bring them here."

"To the Graves?" she asked.

"No. Further along the coast. To the Île aux demons."

"Demon Island," said Clara. "This place is just one big fun park."

Gamache smiled. "I didn't believe her, of course. Until I came here myself."

He looked across, at the shoreline. Barren. Without a sign of life.

But he knew that wasn't true. Lots of things lived here. Unseen.

"I'd love to draw it," she said. "If this ever calms."

"I envy you your art," he said. "It must be therapeutic."

They lurched back to the bench.

"You think I need therapy?"

"I think everyone on this boat probably does."

She laughed. "The Voyage of the Demented."

Clara watched as Gamache reached into the innermost pocket of his coat. And brought out *The Balm in Gilead*.

"I found this by my father's bedside," he said, looking down at it. "When I was nine years old. The night my parents died. I was inconsolable. I didn't know what to do, so I did what I always did when I was frightened. I went into their bedroom. And I crawled into bed. And I waited for the nightmare to be over. To wake up, and there they'd be. On either side of me. Protecting me. But of course, there was no sleep and there was no waking."

He paused, to gather himself. Wave after wave pounded the windows in front of them, as though the river was throwing itself against it on purpose. Trying to get in. Trying to get at them. Trying, perhaps, to shelter from its own storm.

"They'd been killed in a car accident. But not just an accident though, I learned later. When I first joined the Sûreté I looked up their file. I don't know why."

"You needed to know," said Clara. "It's natural."

"A lot of things are natural, but not good. Like asbestos. This was like asbestos. It burrowed into me. I wish now I hadn't looked. My grandmother hadn't told me that my parents had been killed by a drunk driver. He survived, of course."

Clara looked at Gamache. Over the years she'd heard many things in his voice. Tenderness, wonder, rage, disappointment. Warning. But never bitterness. Until now.

"Anyway," he said, as though what he'd just told her was trivial, "I found this book on my father's bedside table. The bookmark exactly where he left it. I took it and put it in a box with other things."

Treasures from childhood. Old keys to old homes he no longer lived in. Pennants from races won. A particularly fine chestnut. A piece of wood someone assured him was from Jean Béliveau's hockey stick. Relics from the saints of childhood. Talismans.

He'd been given the crucifix his father always wore, and had been wearing when he died. They'd wanted to bury him with it, but his grandmother had retrieved it, Armand didn't know how and never asked.

She'd given it to him when his first child, Daniel, had been born.

He'd cherished it. And given it, in turn, to Daniel when Florence was born.

But this book he'd kept. Just for himself. Safe in the box. Sealed in the box.

Always there but never touched. The box was brought out and looked at sometimes, but never opened.

Until he and Reine-Marie had moved to Three Pines.

Until he'd stopped hunting killers. He'd done his duty by the souls of the dead and the souls of the damned. And he could, at long last, rest in peace in the little village in the valley.

Only then was it safe to open the box.

Or so he'd thought.

Out of it came the scent of the book, and the scent of his father. Musky, masculine. Embedded in the pages of the book. Like a ghost.

"*There is a balm in Gilead,*" he'd read that first morning, in their garden. "*To make the wounded whole.*"

He'd been overwhelmed then. With relief. That maybe now he could put down the burden.

Armand Gamache had long suspected that far from being one of the passengers on the bewitched canoe, he was one of the *voyageurs*. Forever paddling, never stopping. Taking the souls of the wicked away. Endlessly.

"*There's power enough in Heaven*," he'd read. "*To cure a sin-sick soul*."

The words he needed to hear. It was as though his father had spoken to him. Taken him in his strong arms, and held him, and told him it would be all right.

He could stop.

Every morning after that he sat on the bench overlooking the village, and he had a small, private visit with his father.

"But you never read beyond the bookmark," said Clara. "Why not?"

"Because I don't want to go beyond it. I don't want to leave him behind."

He inhaled the maritime air. And closing his eyes, he tilted his head slightly back.

Something else had come out of that sealed box. Something so unexpected it had taken Gamache a long time to even recognize it. And admit it.

Gamache shifted his gaze to the pastille now wedged between two slats by the rolling of the ship.

"I read the report on my parents' death." He spoke to the white lozenge. "And the boy who'd survived. He was a minor. His name had been expunged."

Clara couldn't think of anything to say, so she said nothing.

"He only had his learner's permit. Driving illegally. Drunk. He was less than ten years older than me. He'd be in his mid-sixties now. Probably still alive."

Gamache put out his finger. It hovered over the cough drop until the slightest heave of the boat would have driven the pastille into his finger.

But the boat didn't heave. It didn't ho. The waves seemed to calm for a moment.

Gamache looked over the side. To the shore.

They'd cleared the Graves and were plowing through the waters, ever closer to the end of the journey.

He brought his hand back, to the book. And there it rested.

"*Patron.*"

Beauvoir wove across the unsteady floor like a cowboy just off a long trail ride. Myrna was behind him, lurching from bench to bench.

Gamache put the book back in his jacket just as Beauvoir arrived.

"The principal got back to us. He tried calling you, but you didn't pick up."

"The phone's in my pocket," said Gamache. "I didn't hear it."

"You asked where the asbestos in Massey's studio was all found."

"Yes. And?"

"They've sealed the room and are doing more tests but so far the asbestos seems concentrated in only one place."

"The storeroom?" asked Gamache. "Where Massey probably kept No Man's paintings."

"No. It was at the back of the studio, on one of the paintings."

Clara drew her brows together in concentration and some confusion. "But there was only one painting back there." She paled. "I didn't see it, but you did," she said to Myrna.

Gamache felt his heart take a sudden leap, as though hit from behind. Reine-Marie had also seen that painting. Had stood close enough to appreciate it. To breathe it in.

"And it was covered in asbestos?" he demanded.

"Not covered. There were traces." Beauvoir immediately understood the concern. "Only at the back. That science teacher was right. No Man put the asbestos where Massey would dislodge it when he handled the painting. But it wouldn't be a danger to anyone else. It wasn't in the air anymore. You couldn't breathe it in."

Gamache's heart calmed while his mind picked up speed.

"That painting"—he turned to Clara—"it was the really good one, right?"

"I didn't actually see it, but Myrna did."

"It was wonderful," Myrna confirmed. "Far better than the rest."

"But it was painted by Professor Massey," said Clara. "Not No Man. So how could it be infected?"

Gamache sat back on the bench, perplexed. It all fitted so well. Almost. If he just ignored that one question.

If Massey had painted that picture, how could No Man have put asbestos on it?

How had No Man gained access to it? And to asbestos, for that matter.

"We're missing something," said Gamache. "We've gone wrong somewhere."

It was dinnertime, but the cooks didn't dare put the ovens and stoves on, so they had sandwiches. And held on tight as the waves deepened and broadened. And as even the seasoned sailors' faces grew strained.

The friends took their minds off the pitching ship by going over and over what they did know. The facts.

Peter's trek across Europe. The Garden of Cosmic Speculation. The stone hare.

Beauvoir reached in his pocket and felt the rabbit's foot, still there.

Peter's trip to Toronto, and the art college. His meeting with Professor Massey.

And then taking off for Charlevoix. Baie-Saint-Paul. In search, it seemed, of the muse. The tenth muse. The untamed muse, who could both heal and kill. And her champion. No Man.

This the four of them went over and over. And over.

But it still wasn't clear what they'd missed, if anything.

"Well," said Clara. "We'll have our answer tomorrow. The ship gets in to Tabaquen in the morning."

She held out her hand, and from it dangled a large key.

"What's that?" asked Beauvoir.

"The key to our cabin," said Myrna.

"Is this a proposal?" he asked.

"We haven't been at sea that long," said Myrna, and heard a grunt of laughter from Gamache. "It's an invitation. Our sofa turns into a bed."

"But you'll be using it," Beauvoir pointed out.

"No, we'll be in the bedroom."

"Bedroom?"

"I believe they call it a stateroom," said Myrna. "Feel free to use our shower, or the tub."

"For a metaphoric bath?" Gamache asked Clara, who reddened.

335

Beauvoir's eyes narrowed and he grabbed the key from her hand.

"And help yourself to what's in the fridge," said Myrna as they left, zigzagging back across the observation deck.

Beauvoir put the key in his pocket, next to the hare's foot.

They talked a little longer, going back over some of the details. But still couldn't see their way clear.

Gamache stood up. "I'm tired, and Clara's right. We'll arrive at the answer tomorrow."

The two men got to the Captain's Suite, having stopped at the Admiral's to check on Chartrand and get their toiletries and clean clothing.

On opening the door to the Captain's Suite, Beauvoir stopped.

"What is it?" Gamache asked. "Can you fit in?"

"The fleet could fit in," said Beauvoir, and stepped aside so that the Chief could see.

The kitchen. The polished dining table. The picture windows. The armchairs. The closed mahogany door leading, presumably, to the stateroom where Clara and Myrna slept.

And then there was the sofa, opened to a large bed and made up with clean, crisp linens and pillows and a duvet.

"It's the most beautiful thing I've ever seen," whispered Beauvoir. "I'd like to marry this room."

"Not while I'm in it," said Gamache, brushing past him.

They took turns taking hot, sloshing baths, not trusting themselves to keep their footing in the shower. When Beauvoir emerged, wearing one of the fluffy bathrobes, he found Gamache gripping the edge of the dining table, examining one of Peter's paintings.

"The lips," said Beauvoir, joining him. They frowned up at the men and the men frowned down at them.

After traveling on this same waterway for two days, Beauvoir could appreciate even more what Peter had been trying to capture.

Peter had seen and felt and tried to paint the ever-changing face and fortunes of the river.

"We're still at sea," said Jean-Guy.

"But perhaps a little closer to the shore."

"Yeah, well, the shore isn't always such a great place to be," said Beauvoir, stumbling over to the bed.

"True, *mon vieux*," said Gamache. "I'm going to take a bath."

Outside the picture window the darkness was complete, but every thirty seconds or so a fist of water hit it.

Half an hour later Gamache turned off the lights and got into bed.

"We'll be there tomorrow," said Beauvoir, already half asleep. "Do you think we'll find Peter?"

"I do."

Gamache drifted closer to sleep, thinking of what awaited them.

Isolation and the company of a madman could twist even the most stable person, never mind someone already foundering. As Peter was.

They would almost certainly find Peter Morrow the next day, but Gamache was far from sure if he'd be a Peter they'd want to find.

Jean-Guy woke up to pale pink light coming into the cabin and the smell of coffee. It was early. The women weren't yet stirring.

But Gamache was up and at the dining table. Staring at Peter's paintings and humming to himself.

"Okay, *patron*?" Jean-Guy asked, sitting up in bed. Something seemed off. Wrong.

And then he realized what it was. For the first time in days the *Loup de Mer* wasn't lurching and twisting and heaving.

"*Oui*." But Gamache's voice and mind were far away.

"Are we still moving?" Beauvoir looked out the window.

The storm had gone, moving off down the river. Toward Anticosti, and Sept-Îles, Quebec City and finally Montréal.

On his way to the bathroom, Beauvoir paused at the table long enough to see that Peter's painting had been turned around. So that the overwhelming sorrow was now giddy joy.

And yet the expression on the Chief's face was grim.

"What is it?" Jean-Guy asked when he returned and set mugs of strong coffee on the table.

"*Merci*," said Gamache, still distracted.

And then he told Jean-Guy what he'd found hiding in that painting.

There, among the lips, the waves, the sadness and hope, he'd found a sin-sick soul.

Myrna and Clara woke up to shafts of sunlight through the picture window.

The *Loup de Mer* seemed not to be moving at all. If it wasn't for the now-comforting thrum of the engines, they'd have thought the ship was dead in the water. But out the window, Clara and Myrna could see the shoreline gliding past.

The sky had cleared and the river was glass. The *Loup de Mer* sailed into a gleaming, pastel day.

The shore rose smoothly out of the water, as though the river itself had simply turned to stone.

The main cabin was empty. The men had gone.

The women poured coffee and took turns in the bathroom. Then, dressed, they went up on deck, where they found Gamache, Beauvoir, and Chartrand leaning against the railing.

"Feeling better?" Clara asked, standing beside the gallery owner. He looked pale, but no longer green.

"Much. I'm sorry, I haven't been much help, or good company."

Clara smiled, but saw Myrna and Gamache watching Chartrand. And Clara could guess what they were thinking. Exactly what she was thinking.

It was a miraculous, and timely, recovery on the part of Marcel Chartrand. So sick for so long. But resurrected just in time to arrive in Tabaquen.

Clara knew he'd been genuinely seasick. But perhaps not quite as sick as he seemed.

And now all five leaned against the railing as the *Loup de Mer* sailed down the coast, almost eerie now in the extreme calm.

Myrna switched her gaze to Armand. Where the others watched the shore, Gamache was facing forward. Not looking at where they were, or had been, but where they were going.

Here was a mariner. A man before the mast. But he also, this bright morning, looked like what he was by nature. A homicide detective. In the land God gave to Cain.

And Myrna knew then that this day might begin with startling calm, but it would almost certainly end in death.

THIRTY-EIGHT

~

"That's Agneau-de-Dieu," said Jean-Guy.

Clara hadn't spoken in half an hour. No one had spoken in fifteen minutes.

In silence they'd watched the coastline and listened to the familiar sound of the hull through the tranquil water.

The sun was up, revealing a land almost unspeakably beautiful. Simple. And clear. Rocks, lichen, shrubs. Some determined trees.

And then the small harbor and the homes built on stone.

Agneau-de-Dieu. A few children stood on the shore and waved. Greeting the ship that didn't pause.

Clara forced herself to wave back and noticed that Chartrand did too.

Did he know them? Is that why he waved?

But her mind couldn't rest on that thought. It went back to the only thing it could contain.

Peter. Peter was here, somewhere.

Then Agneau-de-Dieu was behind them, out of sight, and they couldn't yet see Tabaquen. A jagged fist of rock jutting into the river separated the two.

Clara's breathing came in quick shallow gasps, as though she'd run a great distance. She felt her hands grow cold. Was she turning to stone, she wondered. Like the hares.

They rounded the outcropping and Clara squared her shoulders and finally took a deep breath, preparing herself. Steeling herself.

And then she caught her first sight of Tabaquen.

The harbor was a natural shelter, the rocks reaching into the river on both sides, like stone arms. Here, unexpectedly, there were trees. Dwarfed, clinging to the ground. But determined to live. It looked like stubble on a worn face.

The harbor formed a sun trap, a rocky bowl. So that things lived here that would perish elsewhere. It was an oddity of nature and geology and geography.

As the ship glided to the long quai, the harbor felt like a sort of a haven.

Was that how a sorcerer lured his victims?

Was that how a muse might do it? Lull you in, lure you in. From the storm. With the promise of eternal safety. Eternal peace.

Was this what death felt like?

Clara took a step back from the railing, but Myrna stopped her. Held her firm.

"It's all right," she whispered.

And Clara, her heart pounding, stopped. And stepped forward again.

They grabbed their cases and waited for the gangway.

Gamache was first in line, but Clara, wordlessly, stepped in front of him. And he, wordlessly, stepped back.

When the bridge from ship to shore appeared, Clara was the first to take it.

Down, down, down. She led them, until she was standing on the dock. Her friends behind her.

"With your permission," Gamache said, and Clara could see that something had shifted. He was asking, to be courteous. But that was all.

Clara nodded and Armand Gamache did not hesitate.

He walked briskly to the first person he saw, an elderly man with a large oiled hat, watching the *Loup de Mer* unload.

"We're looking for a fellow named Norman," he said. "He might go by the name No Man."

The man looked away, out to the open river.

"Get back on the boat. There's nothing here for you."

"We need to see No Man," Gamache repeated, his voice friendly but firm.

"You should leave."

"Armand?" Myrna asked.

She and Clara were standing a distance away, scanning the harbor and the village for Peter. But there was no one about. No man, no woman, no child. The place felt more abandoned than deserted. As though everyone had fled. One step ahead of a disaster.

Myrna could feel her resolve slipping away. Flowing and flooding away. Pouring through the cracks in her courage. Behind them was the ship. With the croissants and the bathtub and the soft, rhythmic rocking.

It would take them home. To her croissants and her bathtub, and the solid ground of Three Pines.

Gamache and Beauvoir walked over to them.

"Jean-Guy and I need to find Norman. And you need to stay here."

"But—" Clara was silenced by the slightest movement of his hand, and the determination in his face.

Whether he held the rank of Chief Inspector or not, this man would always lead, and would always be followed. Even if following sometimes meant staying behind.

"We've come this far," said Clara.

"And this is far enough," said Gamache. His look was so kindly she felt herself calming down.

"I need to find Peter," she insisted.

"You will," said Gamache. "But we need to find Norman first. The fisherman says he's up there."

Gamache pointed. Toward a rise, a hill. Where there were no dwellings, no buildings at all. It was just rock and scrub.

"There's a diner." Beauvoir waved at a weathered clapboard building. "You can wait for us there."

Clara had forgotten that they'd been here before.

"I should go with you," said Chartrand.

"You should stay here," said Gamache. Then he turned to Clara. "You've brought us this far. Now you need to wait here. If we find Peter we'll bring him to you. I promise."

He gave a brief nod of thanks to the elderly man, who'd turned away and was again staring out at the harbor, and the river beyond.

And in that instant Gamache had the sense the elderly man hadn't so much been watching for the ship, as waiting.

A mariner on dry land. But always a boatman. Perhaps even a *voyageur.*

Clara stopped at the door to the diner and watched as Armand and Jean-Guy walked out of town. And on the top of the hill, they paused.

Two figures, a few feet apart, against the morning sky.

Clara tilted her head slightly and narrowed her eyes. Then she felt her heart squeeze. They looked like the ears of a hare. Like in Peter's painting.

In the diner she unrolled one of his canvases. Marcel Chartrand brought over a plate of lemon meringue pie and put it on one of the corners, to keep it from curling up.

Then Clara sat down and stared into the painting, the closest she could come, for now, to being in Peter's company.

Ahead of them, in the distance, Gamache and Beauvoir could see the village of Agneau-de-Dieu. And at their backs was Tabaquen.

And in between was a stretch of terrain. Desolate. Empty.

No Man's land.

Except for one neat little house.

No Man's home.

As they watched, a figure slowly unfolded from a chair. Lanky, gangly, like a puppet or scarecrow. He stood, framed in the dark rectangle of the door. Then he took a step toward them. Then another.

And then he stopped. Paralyzed.

The man stood up when he saw them on the hill. He stood, and he stared. And then he reached out to grasp the weather-beaten post holding up the porch. He gripped it tight, clinging to it, and to his reason. Knowing what he saw could not possibly be real.

It was a mirage, a jest, a trick. Conjured from exhaustion and shock.

He leaned against the rough post and stared at the men.

It could not be.

Gamache and Beauvoir stared at the man on the porch.

And then they broke into a rapid walk that verged on a run.

The man on the porch saw this and backed up. He looked behind him, into the cave of the small house.

Then he looked at the specters, making their way toward him. Swarming toward him, down the hill. From Tabaquen.

"Peter?" Jean-Guy called.

Peter Morrow, frozen in place, stared.

"My God, it is you," he said.

Peter was disheveled, his hair unruly, unkempt. The normally well-groomed man had two days' stubble on his face, and purple under his eyes.

He hugged the post and looked like he'd buckle to the ground if he let go. When Gamache was within reach, Peter let go of the post and gripped Armand.

"You came," Peter whispered, afraid to blink in case they disappeared. "Armand, thank God. It's you."

He squeezed Gamache's arms to make sure this wasn't some illusion.

Armand Gamache stared into Peter Morrow's blue, bloodshot eyes. And saw exhaustion and desperation. And perhaps, just there, the tiniest glint of hope.

He took Peter by the shoulders and sat him in a chair on the porch.

"Is he inside?" Gamache asked, and Peter nodded.

"Stay here," said Beauvoir, though it was clear that Peter Morrow had absolutely no intention of going anywhere.

Inside the one-room cabin, Armand Gamache and Jean-Guy Beauvoir stared down at the bed.

A pillow lay over the head of the body. And from underneath it the blood had poured, flooding out, turning the white sheets a brilliant red.

But that had stopped hours ago, the investigators could tell. When the heart had stopped. Hours ago.

Gamache felt for the man's pulse. There was none. He was cold as marble.

"Did you put the pillow over his face?" Gamache called out the door.

"God, no," came the reply.

Gamache and Beauvoir exchanged glances. Then, steeling himself, Armand Gamache lifted the pillow, as Jean-Guy recorded the events.

And then Gamache sighed. A long, long, slow exhale.

"When did Professor Massey arrive?" the Chief asked, staring down at the bed. The dead man's mouth was slightly open, as though a thought had occurred to him in the instant before he died.

What would he have said? Don't do it? Please, please, for God's sake. Would he have begged for his life? Would he have screamed recriminations? Empty threats?

Gamache doubted it. Rarely had he seen a man so apparently at peace with being murdered. With being driven to Samarra and dumped in front of Death.

But perhaps, Gamache thought as he looked at those calm eyes, this appointment was fated.

Two men whose lives had crossed decades before, walking to this terrible moment in this desolate place.

"He arrived a couple days ago, I think." The voice drifted in through the open door as though the wider world was speaking to them. "I've lost track of time."

"When did this happen?" Beauvoir asked. "Not a couple of days ago. He died fairly recently."

"Last night. Early this morning maybe. I found him like that this morning."

There was a pause and Gamache walked to the door. Peter was sitting, collapsed in the chair, stunned.

"Look at me," said Gamache, his voice calm, reasonable. Trying to bring Peter back to reality. He could see Peter detaching, drifting away. From the cabin, from the coast, from the horrific discovery.

From the blood-sodden bed, and the stone man with the slit throat.

Like a grotesque sculpture. Gamache couldn't decide if the look of extreme peace made it better or worse.

"What happened?"

"I don't know, I wasn't here. Professor Norman sent me away, asked me to leave the two of them alone and come back in the morning. This morning. When I did, I found—" He waved toward the cabin door.

Gamache could hear Beauvoir taking pictures and dictating into his device.

"White male. Cause of death, a wound to the throat made with a large knife, cutting from the carotid artery to the jugular. No sign of struggle. No sign of the weapon."

"Did you touch anything?" Gamache asked.

"No, nothing." And Peter sounded so revolted that Gamache believed him.

"Has anyone else been here since you arrived this morning?"

"Only Luc. He comes by every morning. I sent him away to call for help."

Now Peter really focused on Gamache.

"Isn't that why you're here, Armand?" Then Peter became confused, flustered. "But what time is it?" He looked around. "It can't be that late. How'd you get here so fast?"

"By Luc you mean Luc Vachon?" said Gamache, sidestepping the question for the moment. Peter nodded.

"A follower of No Man?" asked Beauvoir from inside the cabin.

"I suppose. A student, really."

"Did Vachon get close to the body?" Gamache asked.

"Close enough to know what had happened," said Peter. His own eyes widened, remembering the sight.

"Close enough to take something?" asked Beauvoir. "Like the knife?"

He'd come out onto the porch and was staring at Peter. So like the Peter they'd known for years, but so unlike him too. This Peter was vague, unsteady. At sea. His hair was long and windswept and his clothing, while clean, was disheveled. It was as though he'd been turned upside down and shaken.

"I don't know," said Peter, "he might have gotten close enough."

"Think," said Gamache, his voice firm, not bullying, but commanding.

Peter seemed to steady himself. "It was all so chaotic. We were yelling at each other. Demanding to know what had happened. He wanted to move the pillow, but I stopped him. I knew enough to know nothing should be touched."

"But was Vachon close enough to take the knife?" Beauvoir asked.

"Yes, I guess so." Peter was getting upset now, belligerent, feeling badgered. "But I didn't see a knife and I didn't see him take one. He seemed as shocked and upset as me. You don't think Luc did it?"

Gamache looked at his watch. "It's almost noon."

But that meant nothing to Peter.

"When did you send Vachon to call?" asked Beauvoir.

"I got here about seven, as usual. Luc came a few minutes later."

"Five hours." Beauvoir looked at Gamache.

"Where would Vachon have gone to call?" Gamache asked. "Tabaquen?"

"Probably. Phone service is sketchy here, but the harbormaster generally has a good line. Needs it in case there's an emergency on the water."

"As far as we know, Luc Vachon never made that call," said Gamache. "Either because he didn't want to, or because he couldn't."

"If Luc did it, why'd he come back?" Peter demanded, his brain kicking in.

"Maybe he left the knife behind," Gamache suggested. "Maybe he needed to make sure the professor was really dead. Maybe whoever did it sent him back, to retrieve the knife or other evidence."

"'Whoever did it'?" Peter asked. "Who do you mean?"

Gamache was looking at him. Not with the eyes of Armand, his friend. But the sharp, assessing, unrelenting gaze of the head of homicide.

"Me? You think I killed him? But why?"

"Maybe the Muse told you to do it," Gamache suggested.

"The Muse? What're you talking about?"

Gamache was still staring at him and Peter's eyes widened.

"You think I've gone mad, don't you? That this place has driven me insane."

"Not just the place," said Gamache. "But the company. Professor Norman lectured on the tenth muse. Isn't that why you came here? To find him. And her?"

Peter flushed, either with rage or embarrassment at being caught out.

"Maybe it was all too much for you, Peter. You were lost, desperate to find a direction. Maybe the combination of Norman's beliefs and this place was too much." Gamache looked out at the vast, open, empty terrain. Sky and rock and water. "It would be easy to lose touch with reality."

"And commit murder? I'm not the one who's lost touch with reality, Armand. Yes, I can see how it might appear that I could've done it. And yes, Luc might've done it. But aren't you forgetting something, or some-one?"

"No," said Gamache.

He wasn't forgetting that someone was missing, besides Luc Vachon.

"Was Professor Norman surprised when Massey arrived?" Beauvoir asked.

"I think Professor Norman was beyond being surprised by any-thing," said Peter. "He actually seemed pleased to see him."

"And you left the two of them here, alone, last night," said Beauvoir.

Peter nodded. Gamache and Beauvoir walked back into the cabin, and over to the bed.

Two young professors had met decades ago. Met and clashed. And then met again as old men. In the land God gave to Cain. They'd sat here. One on the chair. One on the bed.

And in the morning, one was dead. And one was missing.

Gamache looked down at the peaceful, almost joyous, face. And at the long, deep cut, from artery to vein.

Whoever did this had left nothing to chance.

He wanted to make sure Professor Norman, No Man, was dead.

And he was.

THIRTY-NINE

～

Armand Gamache didn't know who had drawn the knife across Norman's neck.

Professor Massey? Luc Vachon? Or Peter Morrow.

One of them had.

Gamache was sure of only one thing. He'd been wrong. Way off.

It wasn't until that very morning, on the ship, in the pastel light of the new day, that he began to see the truth.

At about the same time Peter Morrow was staring down at this bed, he was staring down at Peter's lip painting.

And once more Gamache had turned it around.

Changed the way he was looking at it.

That was what he'd needed to do with this case. Turn it around. They'd presumed so many things. Made so many conclusions fit the facts.

But they actually had it upside down.

If Professor Massey had painted that wonderful picture at the back of his studio, how had Norman, so far away, infected it with asbestos?

How? How?

The answer was, he couldn't have.

The answer had to be that Professor Massey hadn't painted that picture.

Norman had.

Norman hadn't put the asbestos on. Massey had.

Gamache realized he had everything backward.

No Man wasn't trying to kill Professor Massey.

Massey was trying to kill No Man.

And he'd succeeded.

Professor Norman's throat might have been cut that morning, but this murder had actually been committed decades ago. With a sprinkle of asbestos on blank canvases. Shipped to the disgraced and dismissed Professor Norman. As a favor.

Norman had eagerly opened the containers of art supplies, like a child at Christmas. Inhaling the asbestos liberated into the air. Then he'd happily, gratefully, unrolled the blank canvases, further disturbing the deadly fibers. As though that wasn't enough, Norman would then have stretched them onto a frame. And finally he'd have painted them.

All the while believing kindly Professor Massey was his friend.

If Reine-Marie's and Myrna's opinions were to be believed, Sébastien Norman had been a gifted, perhaps even masterful, painter. But each stroke of the brush had brought him closer to death. The very act of creation had killed him.

As Massey knew it would.

Gamache felt a fool. He should have seen this sooner, much sooner. Who had access to the asbestos? Not Norman. He was way far away in Baie-Saint-Paul by the time it was taken out of the walls of the art college.

No. Professor Massey had access to it.

"But why would Massey want to kill Norman?" Beauvoir asked. "Shouldn't it be the other way around? Massey got Norman fired. Why would he then send Norman infected canvases for years?"

Instead of answering, Gamache turned to Peter, who was now standing in the doorway. His eyes averted from the bloody bed.

"We found your paintings. The ones you gave to Bean."

"Oh." Peter looked as though Gamache had just pulled down his pants. "Did Clara see them?"

"Would it matter?"

Peter thought about that, and shook his head. "It would have, a year ago. Even a few months ago. But now?" He searched his feelings and almost smiled. "It's okay." He looked at them with wonder. "It's okay. They're a mess, but they'll get better. What did Clara think of them?"

This was all that really mattered to him. Not their opinion, only Clara's.

"Do you want to know?"

He nodded.

"She thought they were a dog's breakfast." Gamache studied Peter as he said it. The old Peter would have gotten huffy, taken offense. Been deeply insulted that anything he did could be greeted with anything short of wild applause.

But this Peter just shook his head and smiled. "She's right."

"It's a compliment, you know," said Gamache. "She said her first efforts were the same. A lump in the throat."

"Oh, God, I miss her so much." The little energy Peter had summoned disappeared and he seemed to deflate.

His lower lip trembled and tears welled up. Saltwater. A sea of emotion, withheld. He looked desperate to say all the things unsaid, for decades. But all that came out was ragged breath.

"I want to sit in our garden and hear about her year, and tell her about mine," he finally said. "I want to hear all about her art. And how she paints and how she feels. Oh, God, what've I done?"

Clara grabbed Peter's rolled-up paintings. "I can't wait any longer."

"Sit down," Myrna commanded. "Sit."

"Could we at least call them?" Clara pulled out her device.

"Give me that," said Myrna, holding out her hand. "Give it."

"But—"

"Now. Lives might be at stake. We don't know what's happening and we can't interrupt. Armand said to wait for him."

"I can't."

"You have to. This is what he does. What they both do. Leave them."

Their coffees were cold and the lemon meringue pie sat untouched in the middle of the table.

"Do you think they've found Peter?" Clara asked.

"I hope so." Myrna looked out the window and couldn't imagine what might be beyond this place. Where else could they look? Where else could he hide?

"Does the Muse live here?" Clara asked. Of Chartrand.

"Why do you ask me?"

"Because you've been here before."

"No, I haven't."

"Are you sure?" Clara's eyes held his, and wouldn't let them drop.

"I've never been here in my life," said Chartrand. "But I'm glad I'm here now."

"Why?" asked Clara.

He smiled weakly, got up, and left. They could see him through the window of the diner, his hands shoved into his pockets, his collar turned up against the wind. He stood hunched, staring out at the water.

Clara clasped one hand tightly in the other under the table. How long would she have to wait? How long could she wait? She looked at the Bakelite clock on the diner wall. But while it told time, it wasn't helpful. Clocks were meaningless here.

Time seemed measured in other terms. Here.

The clock said they'd been in the diner for three quarters of an hour, but Clara knew it was really an eternity.

"Why did you come here?" Gamache asked.

"To find the tenth muse?" asked Beauvoir.

"You know about that?" asked Peter, and when they said nothing he went on. "No. I came to tell Norman what a shit he was. When I visited Professor Massey at the art college, it all came back to me. I'd always regretted not telling Norman about the damage he'd done."

"With the Salon des Refusés," said Gamache.

"Yes. He'd hurt Clara, and I'd said nothing at the time. When I left Three Pines, I had no idea how she would feel about me when I returned. I suspected she'd want to end our marriage for good, and I couldn't blame her. But I wanted to take her one special thing. A gift. I thought and thought about it, and realized what a coward I'd been all our lives. Never defending her or her art. Letting everyone criticize and belittle. And finally even doing it myself when I realized how brilliant she really was. I tried to ruin her art, Armand."

He looked down at his hands, as though he had blood all over them. The hollow gaze of a sin-sick soul.

"When Professor Massey mentioned Norman, I remembered the Salon des Refusés and knew what I could give her," said Peter, raising his eyes again. "My apology. But not just words. A deed. Even if I had to go to hell and back, I'd find Professor Norman, and confront him. Only then could I go home. And face her."

"You'd bring her the head of Professor Norman," said Gamache.

"In a manner of speaking, yes."

When Gamache continued to stare at him, Peter blanched.

"You don't still think—" He waved toward the bed.

"Go on," said Gamache, not taking his eyes off Peter.

"I went to Baie-Saint-Paul, where the files said Norman's last check had been mailed, years ago. He wasn't there, but it was so beautiful, and peaceful, and I'd been on the road for so long. So I rented a room and caught my breath. It was only then I remembered the paintings from my mother's house. The ones I'd stared at for hours. Wishing myself into them. The Clarence Gagnons. They were done in Baie-Saint-Paul. So I found the Galerie Gagnon, and when I wasn't painting I spent hours staring at them."

"Why?" asked Beauvoir.

"Have you seen them?" Peter asked. Beauvoir nodded. "How did they make you feel?"

Jean-Guy answered without hesitation, "Homesick."

Peter nodded. "They became like a window for me, back to Three Pines. Back to Clara and what I had. And what I'd lost. At first they made me indescribably sad. But then, the more I looked, the calmer I became. They gave me a sort of settled happiness. A hope."

"The lips," said Gamache.

Peter turned to him and smiled. "Yes. That's when I painted the lips."

"How'd you know No Man was here?" asked Beauvoir.

"Luc Vachon told me. He was still in contact with Professor Norman."

"He'd belonged to the art colony Professor Norman created," said Beauvoir.

355

Peter nodded. "But 'create' is probably the wrong word. It sorta grew up around him. People were drawn to him. Because he seemed to know."

"Know what?" asked Beauvoir.

"That there was a tenth muse. And he knew how to find it," said Peter. Then, unexpectedly, he laughed. A derisive, unpleasant sound.

"You think it's bullshit," said Beauvoir.

"I think I didn't have to come all the way to the end of the earth to find it," said Peter. "It was there all along. Beside me in bed. Sitting in the garden. It was in the studio next to mine. In the chair next to mine. I came here to find what I already had."

"You came here to confront Professor Norman," Gamache reminded him.

"True. When I arrived it was clear Norman was very sick. This was a couple of months ago. He was dying and alone."

Now Peter took a step forward, crossing the threshold.

"Did you confront him?" asked Beauvoir.

"No. The place was a mess. So I thought I'd clean it up first. After that, I'd let him have it. But then I realized he hadn't eaten in a while, so I bought some food and cooked it. I'm not much of a cook, but I made scrambled eggs and toast. Something nutritious and light."

"Did you tell him after that?" asked Beauvoir.

"No. His clothes and bedding were filthy. So I took them to the Laundromat in Tabaquen and washed them."

Beauvoir had stopped asking, and was now just listening.

"His clothes and linen were clean then," said Peter. "But he hadn't had a bath in days. He was too weak." Peter took a deep breath. "So I bathed him. I poured a bath and put in rosewater and lavender and a little essence of lily. Anything I could find." Peter smiled. "I might've overdone it." He looked down at the man in the bed. "I picked him up and put him in the bath. And washed him. It smelled like our garden in Three Pines."

By now he'd come all the way into the room and was looking at the dead man with such tenderness. Seeing past the blood and the gaping wound. To the man.

"I stayed on, to look after him."

Beauvoir's voice broke the spell. "Did you know what was wrong with him? Did he?"

"If he did, he didn't tell me. It was something to do with his lungs. I wanted him to go to the hospital in Sept-Îles, but he didn't want to leave. I could understand that. He wanted to die at home."

Peter looked at Beauvoir, then over to Gamache.

"Do you know what was wrong with him?" Peter asked.

"Do you know why Professor Massey came here?" Gamache countered.

"No." Peter looked at Gamache closely. "But I get the feeling you do."

"I think it might have been to confess," said Gamache.

"Confess? To what?"

"You were right," said Gamache. "Professor Norman was dying. Had been dying for a long time. Well before he realized it. Massey had killed him."

"Massey? But that's ridiculous. Why? How? Voodoo?"

"No. Asbestos."

That stopped Peter.

"I think when Massey heard we were looking for you," Gamache continued, "and that you were looking for Professor Norman, he realized we'd almost certainly find both of you. And learn everything."

"But what's there to learn?" Peter asked, lost.

"That Professor Massey had been sending him asbestos-infected canvases, for years."

"Why?" Peter asked, astonished.

"Because Norman was a threat," said Gamache. "Just like Clara was a threat to you. You loved Clara, but that didn't stop you from trying to destroy her art, and actually destroying your marriage."

Peter looked as though he'd been kicked in the gut. But Gamache didn't let him off. He stood firm, staring at Peter until Peter nodded agreement.

"You loved her, and still you did that," said Gamache. Drilling it home again. "Imagine what you might have done had the love not been there? Had there been hate instead? Love of Clara gave you some brakes, at least. A line beyond which you wouldn't cross. But Massey had none.

357

He felt he had everything to lose. And that Norman was about to take it away."

"But he got Professor Norman fired," said Peter. "Wasn't that enough?"

"This wasn't about revenge or vindictiveness," said Gamache. "For Massey it was about survival. The art college was everything to him. It was his home, physically, emotionally, creatively. And the students were his children. He was the respected, revered professor. The brilliant one. The one they idolized and adored. But suppose a better painter, a more courageous artist, a truly avant-garde teacher appeared?"

Peter's face had gone slack. And finally he conceded. He knew how that felt. To be usurped. Left behind. To see it all slipping away.

Massey was fighting for his survival. And getting Norman fired wasn't enough. If Norman's paintings started appearing in shows, then questions would be asked of the man who'd gotten rid of him.

Massey could not let that happen.

"When the asbestos was taken out of the walls of the college, he kept some, and sent asbestos-infected canvases to Norman," said Beauvoir. "As a gift. One artist to another."

"But how'd he do that, just logistically?" asked Peter. "Professor Norman lived in the middle of the woods, in Charlevoix."

"He had help," said Beauvoir. "Luc Vachon."

Peter opened his mouth to protest, but paused, then closed it. And thought. And rethought all he knew.

"But if Professor Massey came to confess, then where is he?" Peter looked around. "And if he confessed, there'd be no need to kill Norman, would there? So who did that?"

He pointed to the bed.

Gamache turned to Jean-Guy. "Can you find Luc Vachon?"

"*Oui, patron.*"

"Arrest him. But be careful. He might still have the hunting knife."

"*Oui.* And I'll keep an eye out for Professor Massey."

"I wouldn't worry about that right now, Jean-Guy."

"True."

Beauvoir left, and Peter turned to Gamache.

"What was that about? Why shouldn't he worry about Professor Massey?"

"Because he's almost certainly dead," said Gamache. "We'll start a search once we've arrested Vachon."

"Dead? How do you know?"

"I don't know, for sure. But you were right—if he came here to confess, he'd have no reason to kill Professor Norman. And he allowed you to see him, so he didn't try to hide his presence. No, I think Professor Massey might have regretted what he did. What seems acceptable, even reasonable, in youth can look very different in old age. I think he came here to confess to Norman, perhaps even ask for forgiveness. And then he was going to turn himself in. But Luc Vachon couldn't allow that."

"Holy shit," Peter said, and sat down. Then he looked around again.

"But why isn't Professor Massey here too? Why not kill them together?"

"We'll have to wait until Jean-Guy arrests Vachon, but I think Vachon needed a scapegoat. I suspect his plan was to make it look like a murder-suicide. So that we'd think Massey killed Professor Norman and then killed himself. It wouldn't be hard for Vachon to knock him out and hold him underwater."

One more soul for the St. Lawrence, thought Gamache, and knew if that was the case they would almost certainly never find Professor Massey.

But they would find Vachon. If not here, then somewhere. Eventually. They would track him down and try him.

"Why would Vachon do it?" asked Peter.

"I've just explained," said Gamache. "Though I might be wrong."

"No, I mean why would he agree to help Professor Massey in the first place?"

"Why would anyone?" asked Gamache. "Money, almost certainly. Enough to start his own bar. To keep it running. To paint and travel. And all he had to do was deliver art supplies once or twice a year. And take the finished paintings back to Toronto."

"And he could pretend he didn't even know they were infected," said Peter. "What did Massey do with the finished paintings?"

"He must have destroyed them," said Gamache. "All except one. Myrna and Reine-Marie saw it, in Massey's studio. Massey claimed it for his own, and they didn't question it, but they did say it was far, far better than the rest."

"Why'd he keep it?" Peter asked.

"I've been wondering that myself," said Gamache. "Why would Massey keep one of Norman's small masterpieces? As a trophy? Killers sometimes do."

"I think it might be simpler than that," said Peter. "For all his faults, Professor Massey loved art. Knew art. I think that painting by Professor Norman must've been so great even he couldn't destroy it."

Peter sighed, a deep exhale. And Gamache knew what he was thinking about. The masterpiece in his own life. The one he'd destroyed. Not Clara's painting, but her love.

"I've come too far, and waited too long." Clara got to her feet. "I'm going."

Myrna stood in front of her in the diner, blocking her route out.

Clara stared at her.

"I have to know," Clara whispered, so that only Myrna could hear. "Please. Let me go."

Myrna stepped toward Clara, who stood her ground.

And then she stepped aside.

And let her go.

"Clara waited for you," said Gamache quietly. "That night of your anniversary."

Peter opened his mouth but the words were stuck at the lump in his throat.

"I wrote," he said at last. "To say I wasn't going to make it, but that I'd be home as soon as I could. I gave it to that young pilot."

"She never got the letter."

"Oh, my God. That shithead must've lost it. She must think I don't care. Oh no. Oh, Christ. She must hate me."

Peter stood up and started for the door. "I have to go. I have to get home. I have to speak to her, to tell her. The plane'll be here soon. I have to be on it."

Gamache put out his hand and gripped Peter's arm.

Peter tried to jerk free. "Let me go. I have to go."

"She's here," said Gamache. "She came to find you."

FORTY

—

"Clara's here?" Peter demanded. "Where?"

"She's with Myrna at the diner," said Gamache.

"I'm going," he said.

"No, you need to stay here until Beauvoir returns and we know where we stand. I'm sorry, Peter, but the priority has to be to arrest Vachon for murder. Time enough to see Clara after that."

Gamache walked to the door and stepped onto the porch, scanning the horizon in case Beauvoir was returning with Vachon. But there was no one, and nothing, there.

He turned back to the cabin and saw Peter approach the bed. Then Peter reached out and did what he knew he shouldn't. He broke the rules, and brushed Norman's hand with one finger. The lightest of strokes.

Gamache gave him that private moment. He stepped off the rickety porch and looked around, turning full circle in the bright sunshine.

There was no movement. There was no sound.

Nothing.

How bleak it must have been for No Man.

For Peter.

When the only sound was the hacking, rattling cough of a dying man.

When the only activity was shopping, cooking, cleaning. Bathing a dying man.

How tempting it must have been, to leave.

But Peter Morrow had stayed. Right to the end.

"I'll pray that you grow up a brave man in a brave country," said Gamache.

"Pardon?"

Peter had come onto the porch and was watching Gamache.

Armand turned and said to Peter, "I will pray you find a way to be useful."

Peter stood, as silent and solid as the world around them.

"*Gilead*," said Gamache. "The tenth muse is not, I think, about becoming a better artist, but becoming a better person."

Gamache stepped onto the porch. "You found a way to be useful."

Maybe this wasn't Samarra after all, thought Gamache. Maybe it was Gilead.

Peter seemed to relax. Some tension, held all his life, escaped.

He followed Gamache inside.

Armand stared down at the body in the bed. Thinking, thinking.

Peter had been here alone this morning. Standing sentinel. Guarding the body until help arrived. But there had been one visitor.

Luc Vachon. Who'd helped Massey kill Norman. Who'd delivered the asbestos-infected supplies.

But, but . . . what had Beauvoir said? What had Peter said, when told?

That the beauty of the plan, for Vachon, was that he could delude himself into believing he wasn't doing anything wrong. But suppose. Suppose. It wasn't a delusion?

Gamache held his hand to his mouth and rubbed as he looked down at Sébastien Norman.

He brought out his device and hit it rapidly with his finger until that painting appeared again. The distorted, demented face glared at him. Dared him.

Peter looked at it. "I remember that. From the yearbook. Professor Norman painted it. We'd assumed it was a self-portrait."

Peter was caught between revulsion and awe. He looked over at the body on the bed.

"But it's not him."

"No," said Gamache. "It's Massey. Professor Norman had seen it even then. That there was some other Massey, beneath the veneer."

Gamache looked closely. His eyes sharp. Studying the contours of the face, the eyes, the strong chin and cheekbones. Looking beyond the expression, to the man.

"Oh," he said, the word coming out as a sigh. "Oh no."

Gamache knew that face. Not the same expression, but the man.

He'd seen it on the dock, when they got off the ship. The elderly, grizzled fisherman in the wide-brimmed hat and thick, battered coat.

Not watching for the boat. But waiting for it.

The man who'd warned him to leave.

Had Clara and Myrna turned around, had they come closer, they might have recognized him. But they didn't.

Vachon wasn't setting it up to look like a murder-suicide. Massey was. If there was another body to be found, it would be Luc Vachon's.

And Massey would be long gone. Presumed drowned. Another victim of Vachon. But actually safely on the ship.

"Damn." Gamache shoved the device back into his pocket. He looked at his watch. He hadn't heard the cry of the *Loup de Mer*'s horn. It was possible it hadn't left port.

"Peter—"

Gamache turned to Peter, about to ask him to stay there while he ran back to Tabaquen to stop the boat. To find the fisherman. To tell Beauvoir to stop looking for Vachon, and start looking for Professor Massey.

But the words died when he saw Peter's face, and followed his eyes.

To the door.

Clara Morrow was standing there. A knife to her throat.

Behind her was Massey, out of breath.

He held Clara to his chest. In his hand was a huge knife. A hunting knife. Used, Gamache knew, for gutting deer. Sharp enough to cut through sinew and bone. To cut a throat. As it had last night.

Armand Gamache put his hands up where Massey could see them, and Peter immediately did the same. Peter had gone pale, and Gamache thought he might pass out.

"Clara," said Peter, but Clara couldn't talk. The knife was against her skin, up under her jaw. Ready to slit.

Peter's eyes went to Massey. "Professor. Please. You can't."

But Massey only had eyes for Gamache.

"I'm sorry you're here," Massey said, catching his breath. "I saw your assistant in Tabaquen. Asking about Luc. Trying to find him. I presumed you'd also be out looking. He even asked if I'd seen him. I had, of course."

"Vachon didn't know what you were doing, did he?" said Gamache.

He moved slightly to his right, so that he cleared the bed and had a direct path to Massey.

But Gamache knew he could never cover that short distance before Clara was dead, or dying. He hoped Peter knew the same thing. Massey was an elderly man, but still vigorous. And it didn't take much for a sharp knife to go through flesh.

"Of course not. Why would I tell him that the canvases he was taking back and forth were riddled with asbestos? Do you think he'd have done it?" Massey glanced quickly over to the bed. "He served his purpose. But he had one last thing to do for me."

"Take the blame," said Gamache.

In his peripheral vision he could see Peter. Petrified.

Turned to stone. And wishful thinking.

Clara stared ahead. At Peter.

And Peter stared at her.

Massey, on the other hand, was staring at Gamache.

"Yes. And it almost worked. I came here to confess to something that was now obvious. I'd put asbestos on the canvases. In my dotage, and as I prepared to meet my own maker, I was consumed with guilt and regret. So I came here to beg Sébastien for forgiveness. And then turn myself in. But my accomplice, Vachon, couldn't allow it. He'd be implicated. So he killed Sébastien, then me. And it worked. Your man was looking for Vachon, to arrest him. For murder."

"*Oui*. That's what I thought," Gamache admitted.

"What changed your mind?" asked Massey.

"The picture."

"What picture?" Massey was getting agitated.

"The portrait from the yearbook. Everyone assumed it was a self-portrait, by Norman. But it wasn't, was it? It was you. He recognized the rage, the fear in you. And you hated him all the more for it."

"You recognized me from the dock just now. I thought maybe you had. I actually thought Clara would. And when she left the diner in such haste, I was sure she was coming here. Looking for you. To tell you."

"So you followed her."

"I'm sorry, Clara." The professor held her tighter and breathed into her ear. "You moved faster than I expected. I couldn't get to you before you got here."

His breathing had settled down. He seemed to expect Gamache to say something, but instead he remained silent.

"I was going to get on the plane," Massey explained. "But the storm delayed it. So I had to wait for the boat. Otherwise I'd be long gone. Bad luck, all around. And then when the ship arrived, what did you do? You came straight for me."

"That must have been a bad moment for you," said Gamache, as though this was a cocktail party, and a man with a knife was perfectly normal.

He needed to get Massey calm. To have him see the reality of the situation.

The man was clearly terrified. Terrified animals ran off cliffs.

And Massey looked headed for a cliff.

"It was. But then you headed away and I thought I was free. But then I got to thinking about Clara. And your portraits. And how closely you must look at faces." He spoke to the woman clutched to his chest, but he watched Gamache. "I knew if anyone would recognize me, you would, Clara. It might take some time, but you'd get there eventually. And then when you ran out of the diner, I knew you knew."

"But she didn't," said Gamache. "She came here to see Peter."

He watched as the reality dawned. Had Professor Massey stayed where he was. Had his nerves not failed him, he might have gotten away. But now here he stood, a knife to Clara Morrow's throat.

"It's too late," said Gamache. "Let her go."

"I haven't painted in years, you know," said Massey, as though Gamache hadn't spoken. "Nothing. Empty."

He looked at Gamache, and the former head of homicide's heart froze. There was the face from the portrait. Filled with hate, for those who had what he did not. Not a canvas filled with paint, but a home, and friends and people who cared about the man more than the work.

Gamache edged a little closer. Massey's knife didn't waver. Didn't lower.

Massey glanced quickly over to the bed.

Gamache shot a look at Peter. To warn him to stay still. As long as Massey was talking, they had a chance.

Behind Clara, behind Massey, Gamache saw movement.

Someone was coming. Still a distance away, but approaching.

Gamache knew the gait, recognized the shape.

It was Beauvoir.

Peter saw none of this. He only saw Clara.

"I love you, Clara," he said, softly.

"Be quiet, Peter," Gamache warned. He didn't know what would set Massey off, but he knew it wouldn't take much now.

"I'm sorry," said Peter. To Gamache. Or to Clara.

Massey's grip on Clara tightened. He was a man with nothing, and nothing to lose.

He was Death. And this was Samarra. After all.

Gamache knew it then.

His eyes darted over Massey's shoulder, and he gave the faintest of nods. But it was enough.

Seeing this, Massey turned his head slightly. It was all Gamache needed. He sprung forward just as Clara ducked down and twisted away from the knife. But Massey still grasped her clothing.

Clara strained to get away, but without hope.

The knife moved swiftly forward, and struck.

Not Clara. Not Gamache.

Peter took the blow in the chest as he pulled Clara clear.

Gamache pinned Massey, kicking the knife away and hitting him so hard the man passed out.

Armand swung around. Clara was on her knees, beside Peter. Holding her hands to his chest. Gamache stripped off his jacket and, balling it up, he pressed it into the wound.

Beauvoir had sprinted the last few yards. He looked, then wordlessly turned and ran back up the hill, where he could call for help.

"Peter, Peter," Clara shouted.

Her bloody hands found his, and held them, while Gamache tried to stanch the wound.

Peter's eyes were wide and filled with panic. His lips were turning pale. Paler. As was his face.

"Peter," Clara whispered, staring into his eyes.

"Clara," he sighed. "I'm so sorry . . ."

"Shhhh. Shhhh. Help is coming."

"I wanted to come home," he said, gripping her hands. "I wrote . . ."

"Shhh," she said, and saw his eyes flicker.

She bent low, until she was down beside him, whispering in his ear, looking into his eyes. "You're at the top of the hill in Three Pines," she spoke softly. "Can you see the village green? Can you smell the forest? The grass?"

He nodded slightly, his eyes softening.

"You're walking down the hill now. There's Ruth. And Rosa."

"Rosa," Peter whispered. "She came home?"

"She came home, to Ruth. Like you've come home. To me. There's Olivier and Gabri, waving to you from the bistro. But don't go in yet, Peter. You see our home?"

Peter's eyes had a faraway look, the panic gone.

"Come up the walkway, Peter. Come into the garden. Sit beside me in our chairs. I've poured you a beer. I'm holding your hand. You can smell the roses. And the lilies."

"Clara?" said Gamache gently.

"You can see the woods, and hear the Rivière Bella Bella," said Clara, her voice faltering.

Her warm face was touching his cold cheek, as she whispered, "You're home."

FORTY-ONE

⁓

They held Peter Morrow's funeral in Three Pines. Friends and family gathered in St. Thomas's chapel and sang, and sobbed, and grieved and celebrated.

Clara tried to give the eulogy, but couldn't speak. Her words stuck at the lump in her throat. And so Myrna took over, holding her hand while Clara stood beside her.

And then they sang some more. And finally they took Peter's ashes around the village, sprinkling a bit here. A bit there. Some in the river, some by the bistro, some beneath the three great pines.

The rest were spread in Peter and Clara's garden. So that Peter would bloom each spring, in the roses and lilies and lavender. And the gnarled old lilac.

Marcel Chartrand had come to the funeral. And stood at the back. But had left before the reception.

"It's a long way home," he explained to Gamache, when asked why he was leaving so soon.

"Perhaps not," said Armand. He was standing with Jean-Guy and Henri, while Reine-Marie and Annie were across the hall, with Clara.

"Come back again, in a year or so," Gamache suggested. "It would be nice to see you."

Chartrand shook his head. "I don't think so. I'm a bad memory."

"Clara will never forget," said Gamache. "That's for sure. But the cure for lost love is more love." He looked down at Henri.

Chartrand scratched the shepherd's ears and smiled a little. "You're a romantic, monsieur."

"I'm a realist. Clara Morrow will not spend the rest of her life in that one horrific event."

After Marcel left, Armand walked over to Ruth, who was holding Rosa and looking at the punch bowl.

"I don't dare have any," she said. "It might not be spiked."

"*Noli timere*," said Gamache, and when she smiled, he said, "You knew?"

"About Professor Massey? No. If I had, I'd have said something."

"But you were afraid of him," said Gamache. "You saw something in him that scared you. That's why you were so nice to him. Jean-Guy caught on. We all assumed you were nice because you liked him, but Jean-Guy said you probably hated him."

"I didn't hate him," said Ruth. "And how can you trust the opinion of someone who's sober?"

"But Jean-Guy was right, wasn't he? You might not have hated him, but there was fear there. Otherwise why say, *noli timere*? Be not afraid."

"That blank canvas on his easel was one of the saddest things I've seen," said Ruth. "An artist who's lost his way. It builds up. Eats away at you. Beauvoir over there"—she gestured with the duck across the room, where Jean-Guy and Annie were talking with Myrna—"he's a numbskull. And you?" She gave Gamache a sharp assessing look. "You're a fool. Those two?" She turned to Olivier and Gabri, putting food onto the long table. "Are just plain ridiculous."

She turned back to Gamache.

"But you're all something. Professor Massey was nothing. Empty. Like the canvas. I found that terrifying." She paused, remembering. "What happened to that painting? The only one of Professor Norman's that survived?"

"The one at the back of Massey's studio? The good one?"

"The great one," said Ruth. "It was poetry."

"The asbestos would never come out. It was destroyed."

Ruth lowered her head, then raised it again. Her chin high, her eyes hard. She gave a curt nod and limped away, to stand beside Clara.

Noli timere, thought Gamache as he watched the two women. And Rosa.

The next morning Armand sat on the bench overlooking the village. Olivier and Gabri waved to him from the bistro. And he waved back.

He saw the pines sway in the slight breeze and smelled the musky forest and the roses and the lilies and the strong coffee in the mug beside him.

He tilted his head back and felt the warm sun on his face.

Beside him Henri slept, the ball in his mouth and his tongue lolling. Snoring slightly.

And in Armand's hands was the book, closed on his lap.

Clara joined him on the bench. They sat in silence, side by side. Then Clara leaned back, her body touching the words someone had freshly carved into the wood. Above *Surprised by Joy*.

A Brave Man in a Brave Country

She looked out, across to the mountains and the world beyond. And then her eyes returned, as they always would, to the calm little village in the valley.

Beside her on the bench Armand opened *The Balm in Gilead* to the bookmark, took a deep breath, and started forward.

Clara held the letter in her hand. From Peter. That had finally found its way to Three Pines.

And she opened it.